SARA'S BOUNTY

Deke hit the door of the bathhouse with his elbow and bellowed, "Will you hurry it up, Sara? And hold it down in there? You're going to have cats caterwauling out here any minute now."

The splashing and the singing ceased after he called out. Deke relaxed—that had been easy. Then the splashing and singing began again with renewed vigor. But this time the song was a decidedly bawdy one that startled Deke into an upright position and stopped traffic on the dusty street in front of the bathhouse. Jerking open the door he practically catapulted himself inside.

The scene in front of him made him forget he was angry, made him even forget he had a name. Sara was standing in the low tub, all clean and pink in places, brown in others, and steaming water and suds down every exposed female curve.

"Get out! I told you I wanted my own bath! You'll just have to wait, Mr. Bonner."

"I'm through waiting, Sara."

Waving her hand in his general direction, Sara asked, "What are you doing?"

His hands stopped. "I'm making damned certain every lowlife son-of-a-bitch in this godforsaken hellhole knows that you're my woman. That's what I'm doing."

Other *Leisure Books* by Cheryl Anne Porter:
KANSAS WILDFIRE
JESSIE'S OUTLAW

Sara's Bounty

CHERYL ANNE PORTER

LEISURE BOOKS NEW YORK CITY

A LEISURE BOOK®

May 1995

Published by

Dorchester Publishing Co., Inc.
276 Fifth Avenue
New York, NY 10001

The name "Leisure Books" and the stylized "L" with design are trademarks of Dorchester Publishing Co., Inc.

Printed in the United States of America.

To Paul—always my inspiration.

To my father, Jimmie H. Deal Sr., my idea man. Thanks, Daddy, for the story idea for *Sara's Bounty,* and for passing on to me, in some small measure, your wonderful storytelling talent—not to mention your tall tales, including craters on the moon and roosters pulling boxcars.

To my sister, Paula Diane Clark, for her research efforts on my behalf and for her tireless listening to my "talking out" of my plots. I can't thank you enough.

To my friend and neighbor, D.L. Colburn, a charming talker who inspired a character.

My love and thanks to you all.

Chapter One

"My brother and cousins just might kill you before you kill them, you know. Have you thought about that?" Sara Dalton challenged, pulling a long wisp of windblown silver-blond hair out of her face and tucking it behind one ear.

The large man to her left, Deke Bonner, bounty hunter, rode his buckskin stallion as if he were part of it. After a moment or two of silence, he drawled, "Yeah. I've thought about that."

Cold, that's what he was, she thought, daring a quick look at him, glad he still had his gaze fixed on the flat expanse of the horizon. She certainly didn't want him to catch her staring at him—a mean, level look from him even scared her horse. She let her gaze slide to her pommel. He never talked, just answered questions—if he felt like it. Sara bit at her lower lip and gathered her courage, willing him to talk to her. "Well, have you thought that I just might kill you before we ever get to their hideout?"

He turned his head slowly to look at her, deliberately holding her gaze. His eyes were as black as the Stetson he wore low on his forehead. Sara looked away first and swallowed hard; sweat that had nothing to do with the heat trickled down her spine.

"You won't," he stated simply, having drawn her measure.

Sara bit hard on her bottom lip and refused to name the emotion that knotted her stomach. After a moment, she tried again. "They weren't always outlaws. They were little boys at one time, just like—"

She was going to say "just like you," but found she had trouble picturing him as a boy, someone who'd known a family's love. If he had, how could he do what he did for a living? No, she was sure he'd always been this big, this distant, this cold. "It was the war," she went on, not that he'd given her any encouragement or the least sign that he even heard her. "The War Between the States did this to them . . . so much killing."

Sara squeezed her eyes shut, willing from her mind's eye the dead look in her brother's and cousins' eyes when they'd come home to Plains, Kansas, after the war. Opening her eyes, but keeping her gaze downcast, she said, "Travis—my cousin—has a wife and a son, Robert. He's only two."

Nothing. Not a word. Not a flicker. Sara looked over at him, pressed her lips together, and fiddled with her reins. She couldn't give up; she absolutely had to make him see her brother and cousins as people. If she succeeded, then he might not be so quick to kill them. "And Cody's not more than a boy himself. He just does what Travis says."

There! His head bobbed once. Sara couldn't tell if it was deliberate, because he was listening, or if he was merely adjusting to his horse's gait. On the off chance that he was listening, that she was getting through to him, she began to talk about her brother. "Jim's wife was killed by some deserting Yankees while he was off fighting for the Confederacy."

She didn't think he was going to say anything at first, but

then he added, "My mother and sister were killed by Rebs . . . after the war . . . before I got home from fighting for the Union."

Chills replaced the sweat running down her spine; his voice, as well as his words, froze her. Southerners had done that? But that was Yankee behavior. Still, Sara despaired of ever enlisting his sympathy for her family. He had as much reason to hate Rebels as she did Yankees—providing he was telling the truth. But she didn't doubt that he was; she'd seen the same look on her brother Jim's face that was now on this man's. So, despite her fear of the bounty hunter, her enemy, she gave in to her sympathetic instinct, saying simply, "I'm sorry for your loss."

After a pause, with only the sound of creaking leather and plodding hooves to be heard, he said, "Yeah. So am I."

For his loss or her brother's? She didn't dare ask. Besides, she had another question she wanted to risk. "Is that why . . . why you do . . . this?"

He shifted his weight in his saddle and tipped the wide brim of his black hat up a notch with his thumb. Sara half-expected him to shoot her for her brazen questioning, but instead he remarked, "Partly."

"Didn't you get enough of killing in the war?" She heard the sharp edge in her voice, but suddenly enough was enough—of death, of her fear, of this man, this—this Deke Bonner, bounty hunter. He deserved her anger and her scorn, she told herself. After all, bounty hunters were scum, bounded by no laws.

"I could ask the same about your kin, Miss Dalton."

"They killed the men who shot my father and my oldest brother. But I expect you know that." Angry tears pricked her eyes, just as his words pricked her conscience. Her family was different, couldn't he see that? They weren't common outlaws. They weren't. They'd never set out to kill anyone once the war was over two years ago. But they'd sure done it when they got home and learned that the Cooper boys, neighbors and Union sympathizers, had cold-bloodedly killed her father and brother, Jude, home from the war due to a crippling injury dealt him by a Yankee cannon. Sara still couldn't forgive herself for having been in town that day with her mother. Maybe she could have done something to stop the Coopers.

She raised her chin a notch, blinked back her tears, and tried another tack. If he couldn't feel anything for the Dalton boys, maybe he could for their families. "My mother's dying of consumption. We just found out."

He rode on in silence for a moment or so. "I know."

His offhanded response, with no offer of sympathy, provoked in Sara a certainty that under dire circumstances, she just might be able to shoot Deke Bonner. Still, she had to try again. "My mother's last wish is to see Jim and Cody and Travis before she dies."

"I know."

Sara swallowed a scream of frustration. Did he care about no one or nothing? What she yearned for was an agitated, even bellowing response out of him just so she could yell all her anger and fear right back at him, the low-life snake-belly. "So I suppose you'll let her see them—but draped dead over their horses?"

Only his stallion reacted at first; he flicked an ear back and forth and snorted. Sara's gaze went from the horse to the man when he said, "That depends on them."

She closed her eyes, feeling the fatedness, the sheer inevitability of her brother's and cousins' deaths, coil in her stomach. Fighting the resulting weakness in her limbs, she grabbed for her pommel and tightened her legs around her horse to steady herself. When she opened her eyes, she was looking at her hands. They were shaking.

Even if it meant the lives of her whole family, she couldn't talk to him anymore—not now. She supposed she would have to before this nightmarish trip was over. But not right now. As if her mother being ill and this man hunting her brother and cousins weren't enough, she had to weigh in the fact that she was the one leading Deke Bonner, a relentless bounty hunter whose name struck fear in the hearts of outlaws and fearsome awe in the hearts of law-abiding folks, to Jim and Cody and Travis. A Judas goat, that's what she was. But it couldn't be helped.

She'd begged her mother, when the doctor diagnosed consumption and gave her at most six months to live, to let her go find the boys and bring them home. Sara hoped the pitiful sight of Emma Dalton dying would bring them around and make them turn themselves in. There was still a chance, if they didn't kill anyone else, that the law might be lenient with them. God knew they were needed at home.

She looked over at the bounty hunter who had shown up in the dusty western Kansas town of Plains about a week ago, asking questions, watching her house, following her. She was used to that; the law came snooping often enough because the boys showed up periodically at the farm. But this one was different. He had no badge, just a bounty warrant and the desire to turn in his prey—dead or alive—for the reward money. Sara swallowed the bitterness in her mouth.

This morning she had left her mother with Aunt Jean—Travis and Cody's mother. When she'd ridden out of town, Deke had been waiting for her. He'd simply walked his huge buckskin stallion right out of the shadows and assumed his present place alongside her, much as if he'd been invited. She'd let him know right off that he was not going to ride with her, but here he was. After all, what could she do? Beat him up? She looked over at him. Hardly. Outride him? Her little mare against that stallion? Not likely. Shoot him? He'd have her dead and buried before she could get her rifle out of its boot. And it was a free country; she couldn't stop him from traveling the same route she was just because she willed it. She didn't even have the luxury, given her mother's condition, of setting a meandering course to delay and tire him. And he knew that, too.

She assessed him again from out of the corner of her eye. He certainly didn't look like a bounty hunter—not any that she'd ever seen. When his features were relaxed, as they were now, and he wasn't scowling, he was actually handsome. Hadn't her heart flip-flopped when he'd first ridden up to the house? But that was before she knew who he was and why he was there. Sara decided that with his black hair and black eyes, he could even be related to the Daltons—to any of them except her, that was. She was the only Dalton who'd inherited their great-grandmother's legacy of thick, wavy, silver-blond hair. The bounty hunter wore his hair longish— just like Jim, her older brother. There wasn't much opportunity for a haircut when you're on the run—or on a runner's trail. But the similarities ended there. This Bonner was bigger than any Dalton, but not a brawny big—more of a well-muscled leanness. Still, he looked as if he could tear a man in two with his hands. He probably rarely needed to use that gun he had holstered so low on his hip.

Sizing him up, Sara took a small measure of comfort in there being three Daltons to one Bonner at the end of this long trip. Make that four Daltons; she fingered the rifle that slapped against her leg. Everyone knew how to use a gun; the South had fallen barely two years ago. Not that she'd ever had to kill anyone before, but she'd come close enough with the Coopers to know that if it was her life or Deke Bonner's, he'd just better have a care for himself. He might be as big as a tree, and there was no way she could best him physically, but a gun in her hands had a way of equalizing things.

"Can you use that rifle if you have to?"

Totally unprepared for the sound of his voice, but startled by his question, which reflected her own thoughts, Sara jerked, sawing back on her reins. Her mare responded by coming to a sudden, stiff-legged halt, thrusting Sara forward over the pommel and nearly unseating her. As she struggled to right herself and maintain her hat and her dignity, she looked over at Deke Bonner. He offered no help, no outstretched hand, nothing. He just sat his horse, eyeing her speculatively.

Sara returned him look for look, wishing her black eyes could match his even blacker ones for intensity and fierceness. ''Why do you want to know?''

He shrugged a shoulder. ''Where you're taking us, you're going to need it.''

How'd he know where she was going? Sudden fear began to ooze from every pore in her body; she flicked her tongue over her lips. But she couldn't look away. He was like a snake—if you looked him in the eyes, you were lost, mesmerized, mindless of the danger. ''How'd you—I mean, just where exactly do you think I'm taking us?''

He smiled, but the smile wasn't the least bit friendly; it was cunning, like a cat's watching a canary. ''Don't ever play poker, Miss Dalton. We're going to Robber's Cave in the southeast part of Indian Territory, aren't we?''

Sara said nothing, seeing no need to confirm what he already knew. Still, she felt as if her heart and stomach had just hit the ground. As the silence stretched out, along with Sara's nerves, she felt the need to take him on, to face him down. He scared her so much that she needed to strike back. With a lot more bravado than she felt, she asked, ''So why are you riding with me if you know where they are? I'm sure I'm slowing you down.''

That smile again. ''You're my insurance, Miss Dalton.''

''You mean Judas goat, don't you?''

''What innocent lambs are you leading to the slaughterhouse? No one is innocent.''

''I am! You're counting on them not killing you—at least not right off—if I'm with you, aren't you? You'd be close enough to get a good shot at them before they ever knew you were a—a—''

''A bounty hunter,'' he finished for her. He nodded his head to indicate her rifle. ''I asked you if you can use that fancy Spencer repeater.''

''Why? Having second thoughts about me shooting you?''

''No. You had a week's worth of opportunities back in Plains to do that.'' Then, after a slight hesitation, he added,

"You have to know that your kin aren't the only outlaws where we're going. And most of the trip is through the Indian nations."

Sara weighed his words. He was telling her she had to look out for herself and not rely on him to defend her. She sat up straighter in her saddle. "Look, Mr. Bonner, I didn't invite you along with me. But it appears I have no choice in the matter. I intended to make this trip alone. Would I have set out by myself if I couldn't take care of myself? And taking care of myself, as well as my family's farm, is what I've been doing almost single-handedly for years."

It was his turn to assess her. She firmed her jaw as his gaze swept over her. For once she was glad that she was not a diminutive woman; she might be fine-boned, but she was also tall and fit. Not too many tender little misses lasted out on the Kansas plains. But suddenly she didn't like the way he was looking at her; his gaze had stopped level with her chest. She instantly relaxed her posture and shifted her horse slightly away from his intense stare. Oh, God, what if on this long trip, he thought he could—

"I guess you'll do."

Sara blinked. Had a corner of his mouth quirked up? "Imagine how happy I am that you think so." This wasn't the first snake she'd played with in her life.

This time he did grin. There was no doubt about it—he grinned; and his black eyes lit up for an instant. He looked almost human. With a deep chuckle, he put his heels to his stallion, and they were off again, heading southeast through Indian Territory, loosely following the meandering course of the South Canadian River. But they weren't even out of Kansas yet. Sara huffed a deep sigh; she wondered if they'd both reach their common destination, about six weeks away, or if one of them would kill the other first. She was more worried about that possibility than she was of the coming showdown with her kin, the Indians, desperadoes, or this blistering late-August heat.

Her worries drying her mouth, she reached for her canteen.

Every drop of water was precious, so she took just enough to allow her to swish the water around in her mouth before swallowing. Holding the welcome wetness in her mouth for a moment, she closed the lid and looped the canteen's straps over her pommel.

"Miss Dalton?"

Sara looked over at him, her cheeks full of the water.

"Have you thought about this—your brother and cousins just might kill you, too, for showing me to the door of their hideout."

Chapter Two

Sara swallowed the water directly into her windpipe.

If the bounty hunter hadn't acted fast, faster than Sara would ever have believed possible, she might have died right there, not more than a few miles from home. She couldn't get air in or out. She made great gasping and heaving sounds while she clutched her throat.

He was off his huge horse and reaching for her almost before she knew it. When his hands grabbed her waist, she pitched forward in mortal desperation, coming off her horse and hitting the bounty hunter's broad, rock-hard shoulder squarely with her ribs and stomach. The contact spurted the water out her mouth; the arid ground behind Deke Bonner absorbed the moisture in a flash. She went limp with fear and relief, lying over his shoulder like a sack of flour and just as helpless.

Tears in her eyes, her hat on the ground, her hair over her face, her riding skirt twisted and her shirt pulled loose at the waist, she found herself set down—gently—to stand in front

18

of her savior. With one hand, he gripped her upper arm to steady her; his other hand brushed her hair out of her face.

"Better?" he asked, reaching to a back pocket and coming up with a red bandanna, which he offered her. Sara's gaze went to his hand on her arm and then up to his midnight-black eyes and wide mouth.

She managed to nod that she was better; when he let go of her, she took his clean bandanna and covered her mouth with it while she coughed out the remaining water. She was shaking from choking, but also from the feel of his hand on her arm; it had been warm. She realized that she had expected his touch to be as cold as the snake she kept telling herself he was.

She tried three times to thank him, but her voice was not ready yet. All she could do was gesture her appreciation helplessly and breathe in the disconcerting scents of him through his bandanna—warm male, some trail dust, and saddle leather. Not at all unpleasant.

He nodded and simply said, "Let's go." Then, turning away abruptly, he left her where she stood and remounted his buckskin. Once he was astride and settled, he looked at her still standing there. "Well?"

Well? Well! Was she allowed no time to recover from the shock of nearly dying before she was to be hustled back onto the trail of her kinfolk so he could kill them?

"*Well,*"—she stressed the word sarcastically—"where's Cinnamon?" *You ass,* she added to herself, bending over to retrieve her hat and not the least bit surprised when he didn't answer her. She crammed the old felt hat on her head, then tucked her plain cotton shirt into the waistband of her split riding skirt. She put his bandanna in her pocket, not even slightly embarrassed to be arranging her clothing in front of a man; she was used to her male relatives intruding on her privacy.

"Well?" she asked, again echoing his terse word. "Cinnamon? My horse?" She put her hands on her waist and glared at him, trying to forget that he'd just saved her life.

When he continued to just stare at her without comment, Sara, willing her fear of him into exasperated anger, mentally measured the distance between them. Only four or five yards. She looked around her on the ground for a large rock. She was pretty accurate from this range.

That was her last thought before she let out a gawking gasp as she was snatched up off the ground by a steely arm around her waist and plopped down sideways in front of the bounty hunter. Her shoulder met the wall of his chest. His pommel pushed into her buttock. She'd never even heard his horse move! Sara was sure the air was knocked out of her again; why couldn't she breathe? She grabbed a handful of coarse black mane on the buckskin's powerful neck to steady herself. But it wasn't necessary; she was held so tightly against him that she might as well have been glued to him. Scared again, not knowing what he intended, she squirmed around desperately on his lap.

"Don't do that," came the warning, his warm breath fanning her hair and sending goosebumps down her neck. His hold on her tightened reflexively with his words.

Sara stilled instantly—just because he told her to. When she turned her face to look up at him, he pulled back to allow for her hat.

"What do you think you're doing?" To her dismay, her voice sounded nowhere near as challenging as her words. As she waited for his reply, if he deigned to give one, she gained impressions of a smooth, determined jaw, a wide mouth set in its usual grim line, high cheekbones, and a straight nose. His eyes were shaded by the brim of his hat.

"I think I'm taking you to your horse. At least it spooked in the right direction—on down the trail."

Sara tried to move around again, twisting this way and that to see Cinnamon somewhere down the trail, but his grip tightened again threateningly.

"Just . . . sit still," he rasped out.

Finally, some note in his voice told her in plain enough language what effect her squirming around in his lap was having on him. Hadn't she tagged after her brothers and male cousins and heard and seen all their crude, boyish allusions and gestures for years? She hadn't understood most of them at the time, but she was now twenty-four, a woman; a virgin, yes, but a farmer's daughter. Feeling a scorching heat on her cheeks that had nothing to do with the sun, she offered, "I'm sorry. I didn't—"

"Think nothing of it."

And she didn't. She didn't dare. He turned his powerful mount around, using only one hand for the reins since he had his other arm around her, and nudged it with his knees into a walk. Sara remained stock-still, except for her head.

Forgetting to allow for her own wide-brimmed hat, she turned her head slightly toward him again and was instantly sorry. Her hat went askew when her nose rubbed against the tanned, muscled column of his neck. Grabbing for her hat, she pulled away sharply and was startled to see goosebumps form on his bare forearm. In this heat? A quick turn of her head brought the sight of black and crisply curling hair, which began just below the pulse beat in his throat. She gulped and didn't allow herself to even think she was thinking anything. Where else was she supposed to look, jerked up against this huge man like this?

"Where is my horse—in Texas?" she asked, more anxious to get away from this enforced contact with him, her enemy, than she was angry.

No sooner were the words out of her mouth than she felt herself being lifted up and off him. Her first crazy thought was that he was going to dump her onto the ground. She cried out and grasped at his forearm. Her legs swung awkwardly in the air; she feared her boots would come off. Then she felt her bottom hit something hard, but it was too high to be the ground. Her teeth rattled when she made bone-jarring contact with what she realized was her saddle. She clutched at the pommel and Cinnamon's mane; the reins trailed loosely on the ground.

She watched wordlessly as The Bounty Hunter, as she'd

come to think of him, urged his horse forward until he could grab her reins and hand them to her, threading them over the now-docile mare's head.

"Here's your horse," he said. An eyebrow and a corner of his mouth quirked up at the same time.

"So I see," Sara drawled, determined to have the last word. She fairly snatched the reins away from him, inadvertently slapping the mare's neck with them. Cinnamon reared her head again.

"Whoa there, whoa," Deke crooned, taking hold of Cinnamon's bridle. He turned angry eyes on Sara. "Unless you want to chase this damned animal all the way to Texas, like you said, you'd better take it easy."

Fifty sarcastic, hateful retorts came into her head, but never made it past her lips. That was because she was holding her jaw closed so tightly that her back teeth hurt. She could think them, though.

He let go of the bridle and turned his buckskin away, taking up the trail again. Sara had no recourse but to follow, feeling embarrassed and much like a chastised child. She also felt badly for her rough treatment of Cinnamon; the poor mare had done nothing wrong—only reacted out of fear. Sara could certainly understand that. She reached out to pat Cinnamon's neck soothingly and spoke to her in a low voice. Her mare twitched an ear backwards as if she were listening. Sara smiled, making a mental note to give Cinnamon one of the precious sugar lumps tonight.

Feeling better now, she prodded Cinnamon into a trot so she could catch up with Bonner. Not that she wanted to ride alongside him. She had to. Despite her earlier bravado, she really had nothing more to guide her than her innate sense of direction and a crude map given her by her brother Jim on his last surreptitious visit home. The map showed the way to the area known as Robber's Cave, which was situated right smack in the Choctaw Nation in the southeast corner of Indian Territory. Jim had given her the map and instructions to use it only under the direst of circumstances—and he'd also admonished her not to make the trip alone. She looked over at Bonner. Well, she certainly wasn't alone; and if this wasn't a dire circumstance, she didn't know one.

But Bonner obviously knew the way, for he certainly hadn't consulted any map, as she'd had to do already under his curious gaze. No doubt, Sara mused, his work took him into the lawless territory often. She kept her eyes on his broad back as she approached him, mentally picturing herself putting a bullet in that same back. She was ashamed of her thoughts, but still felt they were justified. Though they would arrive at the cave together—barring one of their deaths at the other's hand—she fully intended to get to her kin first. Somehow. She sighed, a sound as vague as her plan or her map.

But one specific the map did contain, which explained Bonner's need to ride with her, was the location of the exact cave in the rabbit warren that was Robber's Cave, being used by the Daltons—a detail that any bounty hunter would probably kill to know. Therefore, she had to keep that map from him at all costs. Even if he tortured her. Her breath caught in her chest. Would he? Sara eyed his physique critically and decided she wouldn't put it past him. She definitely needed a plan, but six weeks was a long time. Anything could happen. And probably would.

One day at a time, she reminded herself as she drew up next to him. She had too many other things to worry about before she ever got to Robber's Cave. And her biggest worry, then and now, was the man riding next to her.

Chapter Three

On that first night on the trail, Deke stretched forward to pour himself another cup of coffee. Dinner had been plain but filling. They'd each gotten their own fixings from their respective bags, in an awkward silence tacitly agreeing they would not be sharing each other's supplies. Well, not completely. Deke had wanted his food hot, so he'd built a campfire, even though it was not necessary for warmth in August, even at night. Seeing it, she had made coffee. He'd said nothing; in turn, she'd said nothing when he helped himself to the strong black brew. His mug full, he leaned back to rest against his saddle, which lay on the hard ground. He stretched out his cramped legs and crossed them at the ankles. Satisfied now and at relative ease, he couldn't resist any longer. Something had been bothering him all day. ''Why'd you name your horse?''

The Dalton woman turned from giving her horse a sugar cube. She always looked surprised or spooked when he said something. "Doesn't everyone?" she asked. She was actually serious.

"Hell, no."

He didn't appreciate her look—as if he were the strange one. He watched as she perched on her knees across the fire from him. She was bouncing another cube in her hand. "You mean your horse doesn't have a name?"

"No." Deke was sorry he'd started this conversation.

He watched her looking at the cube in her hand; she turned it over and over, as if she were pondering something. Deke wished she'd hurry up and say it, so he'd have something else to think about other than the way the firelight played on her waving riot of silver hair, or how it outlined her trim but definitely womanly figure.

"Well, if he doesn't have a name, how do you get him to come to you? What do you say?"

"Say? I don't say anything. I whistle."

"You don't say 'Here, boy,' or anything like that?"

Deke ran a hand over his mouth and chin to stifle a chuckle. "No."

"Oh." She frowned at him slightly. "Well, do you mind if I give him this sugar?"

Deke looked at her and then at the sugar cube in her hand. He was definitely sorry he'd started this conversation. The last thing he needed was to get comfortable with this woman, of all women. Still, he couldn't say no to that face. He signaled his assent with a vague gesture toward his horse.

He waited until she was up and offering the cube to the buckskin stallion before saying, "I guess he won't bite."

She snatched her hand back, cube and all, and turned to glare at him. He held her gaze, challenging her, waiting to see if she had enough guts to stick her hand out there again. He couldn't have said right then why he kept prodding her, except that he needed to try his damnedest not to like her. It was a hard task he'd set for himself—he already admired and respected her. He hadn't spent a week in Plains watching her and hearing about her without finding out what she was like.

Good girl, he thought, when she narrowed her eyes at him and resolutely stuck her hand out, palm flat with the cube in the middle of it, to the huge stallion. Her arm didn't even shake when the horse stretched his neck forward and nuzzled the treat. Finally, he very delicately took it with his big teeth; she even dared to pat his soft nose. The buckskin jerked back at that familiarity. Deke allowed himself a low chuckle when she backed off just as quickly as his mount did.

He silently watched her settle herself across the fire from him, acting as if she hadn't just fled from his horse. He could tell she was seething, but she didn't say a word. She just poured herself some coffee and struggled to keep her thoughts off her face. Deke figured he was suffering terribly in her mind. Finally, she looked at him; the fire couldn't hope to match the sparks that leapt from her gaze.

Deke sipped his coffee and waited. He wasn't given much to words, but she was. And this was one time he was glad for a talkative woman. He knew from a whole day with her on the trail that she'd get over her anger and think of something to say. All he had to do was wait. He ignored the sudden stab of guilt over his motive in letting her chat on: She might reveal a detail or two that would be of use to him later on. Just listening to people chatter revealed a hell of a lot more than all the questioning in the world.

"Earlier today," she began, stopping to blow on her coffee; she held the hot tin mug gingerly. "You said something that's not true."

She stopped again. Deke said nothing, knowing she was waiting for him to deny it.

She frowned. "You said my brother and cousins might kill me for showing you where they are. Do you really believe that they could kill their own family?"

Deke heard the challenging note in her voice. For someone who'd survived the War Between the States and run a farm with little help, she was sure naive about the ways of the world—and of desperate men. ''Do you?'' he threw back at her.

''I most certainly do not.'' Her chin came up a notch.

''Why'd you choke on your water when I asked you?''

He couldn't be sure, because the fire reflected red on her face, but he thought her color deepened. Indeed, her next words were sharp enough to justify heightened color. ''I choked because your question was so asinine.''

Deke smiled, letting her have the last word. It didn't matter. He'd given her something to think about. And that was only fair, he figured. All he could think about was the soft feel of her in his arms earlier today. He could bluff all he wanted with his quiet, withdrawn manner, but his body's damned honest reactions told their own story. He had to remember to keep his distance from her—physically now, as well as emotionally.

Try as he might, Deke couldn't help but feel sorry for her; she was in a mighty tough position. She carried a heavy load, and his presence was the heaviest part. But he couldn't waiver in his intent. When he found the Daltons, he fully intended to kill them—after he told them who he was. No mercy had been shown his mother and sister before they'd been shot to death by the Daltons in a botched bank robbery over in Missouri less than two years ago. Earlier today, he mused, Sara Dalton had told him she was sorry for his loss. Did she know it was her kin who'd killed his mother and sister? If she did, she hadn't said as much. And if she knew, how could she continue to defend them to him? But if she didn't? Well, she'd find out soon enough.

He forced his mind away from the old wound of his family's brutal deaths. He preferred to think about what he could do, instead of what he hadn't been there to prevent. Bringing in the Daltons served a twofold purpose in his mind. Besides the revenge factor, the ten thousand dollars on the Dalton boys' heads would give him a tremendous start on a new life. God knew he needed one. Spying for the Union Army during the war and now bounty hunting—easy money, for one with his expertise—had changed him, made him hard, an outcast. He couldn't remember the last time he'd relaxed and let himself go. To do so could mean death.

So could developing a conscience. Damn, he wished Sara Dalton wasn't so crotch-tightening, gut-wrenching beautiful. And her talk about her family was definitely not the type of information he wanted to hear. The last thing he needed was to see the Dalton boys—now she had him calling them boys—as living, breathing people. Yeah—living, breathing people who'd be doing their damnedest to see he stopped doing both of those things once he caught up to them. If Deke had any saving grace left for himself in his own heart, it was that he always tried to bring his man in alive. But these three? No. There'd be gunplay, and there'd be deaths—maybe even his own. Probably even his own since there'd be four guns against him, counting Sara's. Could he kill her? He looked at her and tried to see himself shooting her.

A repugnant wave swept over him, telling him he couldn't. And that could be fatal to him. He covered a shiver by clearing his throat and shifting his position on the hard ground. He saw her look questioningly at him.

So maybe he wasn't as far gone, as hardened, as he'd thought. After all, here he was, this minute, saying he couldn't—wouldn't—kill her and wishing he didn't have to kill anyone related to the fine young woman sitting across from him. If nothing else, she had his thanks for that insight into himself. He sipped his coffee and eyed her over the rim of his mug. Maybe he'd better keep that thanks to himself.

"Why are you looking at me like that?" There was no alarm in her voice, but it was a little high.

Deke looked away, forcing his features to relax. Still staring out into the night, he asked, "Like what?"

"Like I'm . . . food . . . or something."

He swung his gaze back to her. Her face reflected her fear of him. Good; she'd keep her distance. "Food? Do I look like a vulture?" Instantly, Deke thought of several comparisons—all of them valid—that she could make between him, a bounty hunter, and a vulture. He steeled himself to hear several of them fall from her lips. What an opening he'd given her.

"No. No, you don't." Her voice was soft and shy.

Warning bells went off in his head. She needed that fearful look back on her face. He hated to do this to her, but it was for her own good. "Make no mistake, Miss Dalton. I can be like a vulture, but I'm not usually patient enough to wait for my . . . prey to die before I devour it."

She gasped and jumped up, then stood staring at him, her eyes as round as her open mouth. Heavy, silent seconds crawled by before she moved a muscle. Still keeping a wary eye on him, she backed away, almost stumbling on the uneven ground behind her. She spun around then and stalked off to her saddle, which was lying on the ground near her horse.

Deke watched as, with jerky motions, she untied her bedroll and spread it on the ground right there, as far away from him on the other side of the campfire as she dared get in the dark night. He was amused to see that she'd brought along a pillow.

She lay down on her bedroll and pillow, presenting her back to him. Deke had barely a moment to let the gentle rise of her hip form an impression on his male psyche before she jumped up again. Kneeling by her saddle, she pulled her Spencer rifle out of its boot and took it to bed with her, her back once again to her campmate.

Deke stifled a rare urge to laugh out loud. What a woman. That sobered him. She could never know that he was not totally immune to her femininity; that knowledge could be his undoing if she decided to use it to save her brother and cousins. Other women had tried that very thing, but Deke had never succumbed to such obvious wiles. But looking at the enticing figure across the fire from him, he experienced a gut feeling that this time and this woman could both be different.

No, there'd be no laughter, no easy banter between them. It was much better for them both that she cling to her rifle, her anger, and her fear of him and his reputation. They just might be the only things that kept her safe from him.

Chapter Four

The days, nights, miles wore on, as relentless in their monotony as the prairie, burned brown by the full heat of the August sun. Sara's aloneness with Deke Bonner wore on. There were no towns to pass through, no other people to speak to, no sign that they weren't the only two people left on the planet. And conversation between them was as scarce as water.

They'd left west Kansas and were now in the eastern part of No Man's Land, a narrow, rectangular strip just west of Indian Territory peopled by outlaws seeking refuge from the law and from men like Deke Bonner. Jim, Travis, and Cody Dalton had hidden out here for a while after killing the Coopers, but it'd proved too close to home and too obvious a refuge for anyone with a notion to pursue them. After Travis's son, Robert, was born, the boys had been forced to push farther south. Travis had seen his son only once since then.

Since that first night on the trail when Deke Bonner had surprised her by asking her about her horse's name, he'd hardly talked to her, or touched her—not that she wanted him to—or made the least overture toward her in any way. She supposed it was for the best, given their destination and the coming confrontation; but still, in her whole life she'd never felt so alone while still being with someone. Right now, she'd welcome an Indian sighting, a stampeding buffalo herd, an onslaught of outlaws, even the sky falling—anything but this entombing silence that had settled over them. Even the horses' hooves fell to a muffled tattoo on the dry, sandy ground. It was as if Earth was holding her breath, waiting to see what would happen next.

Sara got her wish. And too late remembered the old saying: Be careful what you wish for, you just might get it.

The ground began to shake. It rumbled and thundered under their horses' feet. Dust blew up in an unnatural wind. Deke's buckskin stallion whinnied and pranced in tight circles. Cinnamon sidestepped and fought her bit. Sara's full attention was riveted on trying to control her normally sweet-tempered mare. But she wasn't immune to what was happening around her. In fact, she was terrified by it.

"Son of a bitch," Deke whispered, a look of fearful awe on his face as he stood in his stirrups and peered in the distance behind Sara's shoulder. She did not want to turn to see what it was, not if it could put that look on the face of someone as fearsome, in his own right, as Deke Bonner. But look she did, with the same reckless curiosity that had killed countless cats.

"Son of a bitch," Sara echoed. It came out as a near-reverent intonation, considering what was heading their way. She looked at Deke; his expression was as serious as a lynch mob. Their gazes locked for the briefest of moments.

The low, hilly rises of the prairie seemed now to be rippling in earnest, like the waves of an incoming tide. The tall grass waved, warning the two humans out of the way—out of the way of the mile-wide sea of stampeding, thundering, trampling, death-bringing buffalo. There were only two things that could stampede buffalo in this heat—water and hunters. And the only hunters out here were unfriendly Indians and even unfriendlier desperadoes.

But hunters of any variety were not the immediate concern—getting out of the way was. The problems were as numerous as they were obvious. They could never hope to outrun the herd by racing across their path—the animals were spread as far as Deke and Sara could see. Obviously they couldn't run into them; to do so was sheer folly and certain death. There was no hope of turning the buffalo. That left only one route—run ahead of them until they stopped and pray hard the buffalo gave out before their horses did. And pray the shaggy beasts were running to water and not away from hunters.

Almost as one, as if the same solution came into their heads at the same time, Deke and Sara turned their mounts and urged them into a dead run, which was exactly what it was. But the buckskin and the roan mare didn't need much prodding. Their own self-preservation instincts were completely intact.

Ahead of the rumbling, pounding herd, the steeds raced, their riders crouching low over their mounts' necks. The riders' vision blurred, wind whistled through their ears, palms sweated into tightly held leather reins, shirt and skirt alike billowed, and hearts pounded. They prayed while murmuring encouragement to their straining mounts.

At first leap, the mighty buckskin left Cinnamon in the dust. His powerful haunches acted as a beacon for Sara to center on and to follow. But not for long, because the stallion slowed, swung out to the right, and dropped back until he was even with the lathered mare. After a few more ground-covering strides, the mare pulled ahead, and finally the stallion was behind her. Sara's mind screamed—something was wrong with Deke's horse! She tried to turn her head to see what was happening, but her flying silver hair whipped full across her face, blinding her. She tossed her head to clear her hair away, which worked only if she looked straight ahead. Tears of frustration and fear flowed straight back from the corners of her eyes into the hair at her temples.

And then Deke appeared at her side, his muscles straining as mightily as his horse's. She heard him yelling something. What was it, dear God? She couldn't make out the words. Deke made a desperate face and did a most dangerous thing. He urged his stallion in close to Cinnamon, as close as he dared without letting the two touch, and then he reached out and yanked on the reins Sara held wrapped around her hands. She couldn't look over at him; she was too scared. Then, miraculously, she heard him. "Let them out. Give Cinnamon her head. Dammit, Sara, do it!" he thundered.

Sara instantly, unquestioningly, unwound the reins. Cinnamon leapt forward, leaving the mighty buckskin in her wake. But what was wrong with Deke? Why couldn't he overtake her? There was no doubt that his buckskin could easily run circles around Cinnamon, even with her at a full gallop. Then it hit her—there was nothing wrong with the buckskin. Deke was purposely keeping himself behind her, between her and the buffalo. Deke Bonner was protecting her. He was putting himself in harm's way—for her.

Sara wanted to cry and found, indeed, that she was. She couldn't have said if her tears were from emotion or from the wind whipped up by the flat-out, pounding gait set by Cinnamon. All she knew was that she tasted wet, salty tears in her mouth, opened so she could drag in great gulps of air, as if she were aiding Cinnamon in breathing. She didn't know how much longer she and her mare could last. She expected Cinnamon's lungs or heart to burst at any moment—or her own. All she could hear behind her were pounding hooves; she prayed they were the buckskin's and not the buffaloes's.

And then it was over as quickly as it had begun. Coming over a rise higher than the rest, there was the water. Sara let out a strangled cry of relief, but didn't dare let up—not yet. The ground was shaking even now under Cinnamon's flying hooves. The buckskin pulled level with her roan mare. Sara looked over. Deke was stabbing the air with his finger, pointing out the way to her. She nodded that she understood and followed his lead when the buckskin shot ahead of her.

Deke took his stallion right into the water with a huge splash. Sara did likewise. Almost together, they forded the lazy, meandering river. The water was cool and not very deep, reaching only Sara's lower calves as she sat on Cinnamon. They were in the water, fording it, and then out of it on the far bank in a matter of seconds, only moments before the buffalo herd reached it. But the two riders didn't stop on the bank; they urged the buckskin and the roan up the grass-and-gravel slope to dry land. With great groaning effort, the horses struggled to safety.

Numb, Sara and Deke sat on their winded mounts and wordlessly watched as the herd, now docile, drank their fill. Sara couldn't put two thoughts together as she watched the now-tame animals and listened to their deep grunts and huffs as they jockeyed for position all up and down the opposite bank. Some even crossed over to drink, ignoring the horses and riders on the grassy knoll above them. The herd appeared no more threatening now than a litter of puppies—a huge litter of huge puppies.

All Sara was capable of was registering sensations. The air was hot and still, but smelled of water and damp earth. Her hair was tangled and limp. Her hat was gone. Her clothes were covered in sweat, grime, mud, and water. Her palms felt raw from the reins, which she now let go slack so Cinnamon could droop her head. Her muscles ached with tension and tiredness. Her heart pounded, and her lungs heaved. She looked over at Deke. He didn't look any better. They could have been killed.

With that thought, to her shame and horror, Sara felt her chin begin to tremble. And no amount of pride or forbearance could stop it. She hung her head forward, let the reins slide to the ground, put her hands over her face, and began to cry. Her shoulders shook and wrenching sobs escaped her.

Then, hands were reaching for her—big, strong, warm hands. She felt herself being lifted off a heaving and blowing

Cinnamon. She could not have stood, had it not been for the damp, warm chest she was leaning against. Her nostrils were assailed by the pungent but not unpleasant scents of sweat, dirt, and man. Arms went around her; a hand gently rubbed up and down her back; another hand caressed the back of her head. Her own hands were fisted balls that clutched the heavy fabric against which she rested. She felt kisses being planted on her head and heard soothing words, but she couldn't make them out. She didn't care. They were being said and that was enough.

Slowly, slowly, her sobs lessened and then quietened. Her breathing returned to normal, but only until she tried to take a deep breath. Then watery, jerky sounds came out on heart-rending sighs. Even though she was feeling stronger, she felt no urge to pull away. Neither was she pushed away. She sighed into her cocoon of quiet strength, relaxing enough to put her arms around the warm wall she was clinging to. A heavy drowsiness came over her, forcing her eyes shut.

Chapter Five

She heard a gurgling, chuckling sound of gently flowing water; a warm, light wind passed over her, lifting her hair and cooling her limbs. The soft nicker of a horse responded to someone's low, deep and soothing voice, and a bird called sweetly somewhere overhead. Sara smiled and turned over on her side, supporting her head with her outstretched arm. Something tickled her nose; she wiped at it furiously with the back of her hand and settled her head once more. Something tickled her nose again. Frowning, she opened her eyes sleepily.

Grass. Lots of grass. That's what was tickling her nose. She rubbed at it again. Why was she lying in the grass? Where was she? A feeling of disoriented panic swept over her, and she sat up abruptly, looking around her. She was alone. Something awful, something . . . then she remembered the buffalo stampede. A nervous thrill ran through her; she hugged her knees to her chest. No, it was all right now. It was over; she was unharmed. She looked down at herself. She was also nearly naked.

She drew in a sharp breath and looked up again, but the scene before her didn't register, even as she searched her mind for the memory of undressing herself and lying down here. It wouldn't come. She stretched her legs, bare now except for her short summer drawers, out in front of her. Playing with a strand of her hair, she focused on her legs as if they belonged to someone else, while her mind churned out a score of "what ifs." Chief among her what-ifs, even though a tentative search of her head revealed no painful bumps or lumps, was what if Deke Bonner had knocked her out, taken her clothes and her horse, and left her here to die? What if he now had the map?

That brought her to her feet. Muttering dire epithets while she turned this way and that, trying to catch a glimpse of his departing figure, she ignored her pounding heart that told her he was long gone. The low-down, rotten, horse-thieving son of a mule-headed jackass ... The list went on without a pause as she turned round and round, looking, scanning.

A horse nickered. She froze. There, it sounded again. She spun around, her body going tense and alert. A voice. The same voice, low and soothing, that she'd heard when she was waking up, she realized. Where was he? Who was he? It didn't have to be Bonner. A throat-closing thought. Sara very quietly backed up to the scrub oak she'd been lying under and braced herself against it. Her gaze remained riveted to her left, the direction of the sounds. Every sense heightened in instinctive self-preservation as Sara listened.

She then realized why she couldn't see. Whoever it was, he was down at the river at the bottom of the bluff. Even more important to her, he couldn't see her because she was at the top of the steep rise and back a good number of yards from its rim. She kept telling herself that it had to be Bonner, it just had to be. Because if it weren't, she was a dead man ... woman. But the evidence was to the contrary. Not one single, solitary thing of hers or his was up here. Not a saddle, a blanket, a gun, an article of clothing, a bite of food. Sara forced herself to stop before she panicked and did something foolish. Like give herself away.

Taking her first deep breath since she'd awakened, she
steeled herself for what she had to do. A resolute lift to her
chin, she stepped away from the tree and edged her way
toward the rim of the bluff. The closer she got, the more she
slouched until she was down on all fours. She didn't worry
about making a noise and giving herself away—she was
barefooted. The bounty hunter had even taken her boots. Lying on her belly now, and feeling every rock and blade of
grass through her thin cotton camisole and drawers, she
inched forward until she could peek over the rim, all the time
praying that whoever was down there wasn't looking up
here.

He wasn't. Bonner had his back to her. He was watering
the horses. Nearly crying out her relief, she touched her forehead to the sandy dirt and said a silent prayer of thanks.
Never in all her born days had she ever thought she'd be so
relieved and thankful to see a bounty hunter. Looking back
up and brushing away the sand from her forehead, Sara intended to call out to him, but the words died on a caught
breath. For right before her eyes, there was a magnificent,
magical scene being played out against the backdrop of the
sun's sparkling glint off the flowing waters of the Cimarron
River. Caught up, Sara lowered her head to rest her chin on
top of her hands.

Bonner stood at the water's edge, one knee bent, which
pulled his pants tightly around his buttocks and thighs. His
gunbelt only added to his aura of masculine power and authority. Barefooted, he was standing casually between the
two horses; while they drank, he held their reins loosely in
one hand. He must have just bathed, because he was shirtless
and the sun glinted off his damp, deeply tanned back and
sparkled in his black, curling hair whenever he moved. He
was every bit as finely muscled and powerful as the two
horses he controlled.

As Sara watched, spellbound, he reached over to run his
hand down Cinnamon's shoulder. The mare's muscles

twitched and rippled in response; so did Sara's. Her gaze and her breath were caught by the glimpse of paler flesh just below the waist of his pants, revealed when he stretched.

Sara's mouth went dry as she continued to watch him for another few minutes, trying to name the strange new tingling heaviness below her waist. The pressure of the ground against it didn't help, either. In fact, it made it worse if she moved at all. This was so confusing. She'd certainly seen her share of men—young, tan, muscled men, just like this one—in her life. Well, men without their shirts, anyway, men in their underwear even. And they hadn't all been her brothers and cousins. Of course, she'd had a passing curiosity and had stolen looks at them, but she'd never, ever had her breath taken away like this or had this feeling . . . down there.

A shudder seized her. She couldn't keep watching the bounty hunter like this. It was wrong. But she wasn't eager to face him, either, dressed—undressed—as she was. Well, danged if that wasn't his fault. Remembering to be angry at him for undressing her helped Sara push down the unaccustomed feelings in the pit of her belly. She'd just as soon not have those for him, thank you very much.

She sat up abruptly, feeling only appropriate things and thinking only appropriate thoughts again, and looked around her for a rock. Leaning over slightly, she picked one up. This would serve him right, she thought devilishly, all the while hefting the rock in her palm, getting its feel. When she judged the moment to be right, she chunked it in his direction, intending for it to splash in the water in front of the horses and just surprise them. Her aim was better—or worse—than she thought. The rock hit the bounty hunter square in the middle of his back.

Before she could blink, he was facing her, his eyes riveted on her, his six-shooter pointed directly at her heart. His sudden movement brought the two horses' heads up, water dripping from their muzzles. They stared at Sara, too, but their looks were a heck of a lot more benevolent than the bounty hunter's.

Mindless of her state of undress, Sara jumped up, perhaps foolishly, for she could have been shot before he realized who she was. She had her hands out in front of her as if to ward off a bullet. An apology was on her lips.

"Dammit, Sara, I could have killed you," he called up to her. "What the hell do you think you're doing? Were you trying to spook the horses again?" He pulled the gun up to a neutral position, uncocked it, heaved a sigh, and reholstered it, shaking his head. Then he just looked at her—really looked at her.

"I'm sorry," she called back to him, stifling the urge to squirm under such close inspection. "I didn't mean to hit you. I was just . . ." Trying to hit the water and spook the horses again, she finished in her head. He was right. Not comfortable with her own guilt, she called out, "Where are my clothes?"

"Over there." He pointed to a place out of Sara's line of vision. "Drying out."

She nodded. "Who undressed me?"

His look told her what she already knew. If she hadn't undressed herself, then that left—

"I did, Sara. I thought you'd want me to."

When had he started calling her Sara? "What made you think that I'd want you to?"

She didn't like having to yell at him over the distance, but she had no other choice, since he hadn't moved. She certainly wasn't going to go to him while all she had on was her underwear. She put her hands to her waist, waiting. He seemed to be more interested in staring at her than he was in answering her. "Well?"

A slow grin came over his face; Sara caught her breath. That grin, combined with those black eyes, tanned face, and black curling hair, advanced on her nerves like shock waves. She willed herself not to step back when, the horses trailing him since he still held onto their reins, he took long-legged strides until he stopped at the foot of the bluff just below her. His upturned face was at the level of her ankles. "What made me think you'd want me to take your clothes off you? Well, the ton of dirt and water on them, which makes mud, Miss Dalton. And with you practically passing out on me, I had to do what I thought best. Was I wrong?''

Sara swallowed. He was looking at her feet. She wiggled her toes self-consciously. She answered him, but not really. "How long was I out?"

"Long enough," he grinned, letting his gaze slowly rake back up her length until he was once again looking into her eyes.

"Long enough for what?" Her voice came out thin and thready.

"Long enough for me to wash your clothes and mine, and unsaddle and cool the horses. Long enough for me to bathe."

Sara would have sworn she was going to be relieved by his words, and she was until he said those last ones. She blinked rapidly, trying not to feel his eyes burning into hers, trying not to picture him bathing. God, she wished he'd quit—what? He wasn't doing anything. Still, Sara felt the insane urge to step back, as if he were too close.

"Where are the buffalo?" she asked, desperate for anything to say. She did finally take one step back.

He chuckled, running a hand through his damp hair. Crystal droplets of water ran through his long fingers. "Where are the buffalo, Miss Dalton? You say that like you're asking where are the children. Do you really want them to come back? The buffalo, I mean."

"No," she said, looking down at his upturned face. She noticed that he hadn't called her Sara again.

"Come here," he said, holding his hands up to her as if she were a child he needed to help down. He still held the horses' reins threaded through his fingers, but he looked as if he'd have no trouble controlling two horses and one woman.

But Sara couldn't oblige him. She felt she was on shaky ground. "I can manage by myself, Mr. Bonner."

An eyebrow came up; his hands went down. He stepped

back. "As you say, Miss Dalton."

Sara looked at him, taking his words as a challenge. Didn't he think she could shimmy down a sloping bank? Her bravado disappeared with her next thought: No clothes, and therefore no protection for her backside. Good God, her bare skin! She'd been standing here carrying on a conversation with a man while she wore nothing but her underwear! Thinking to berate him for having no shame and for staring at her so openly, Sara took one big step forward.

And went careening down the slope, pitching forward with arms and legs waving wildly, and yelling just as wildly. In the same second, she saw Deke drop the reins and rush forward to grab at her. She also saw the horses bolt and run off toward a bend in the river. With a *whumfph,* Sara landed in Deke's arms; she felt her shoulder hit something soft, which crunched slightly. Completely off balance, they fell together onto the sandy ground and rolled crazily two or three times.

When the world righted itself, and the only sounds to be heard were grunts and groans, Sara was on top of Deke, but couldn't get up because her arm was under him and her legs were tangled with his. She pulled back slightly and stared into his face, only inches away. His eyes were closed—no, squeezed shut in pain. She knew it was pain, because his nose was bleeding. Knowing instantly what her shoulder had hit, Sara confessed, "Your nose is bleeding."

His string of epithets, which by all rights should have dried up the river, told her that he was aware of that fact.

Pinned as she was by him, she couldn't get up. But he had no trouble sitting up with her weight on top of him. Wordlessly he drew her off him, leaving her sitting in the sand, and wobbled his way to the water's edge. As Sara looked on, feeling wretched and biting at her bottom lip, he knelt down on one knee, resting an arm on his thigh, and dipped his other hand into the cool river water. He brought handful after handful of clear water up to his face; handful after handful of blood-tinged smear rinsed away.

Sara was becoming alarmed. Was he going to bleed to

death? Much as a child would scoot up out of sand, Sara got up in one scrabbling movement and went to him. She brushed the sand off her as she walked. She noticed that his back and the back of his head now had sand mixed in their dampness. She didn't feel any better to see a few scrapes and scratches on his back—fresh ones. Well, she certainly had her share, too, she rationalized, willing away her guilt.

His skin felt warm and sandy and firm when she placed her hand on his bare shoulder, which tensed at her touch. This was the first time she'd ever touched him voluntarily, so she couldn't help but register some sensations, some observations. Like his hair curling along the nape of his neck, the curve of his ear, the small jagged scar on the crest of his cheek, and the powerful muscles that corded his neck. Leaning over him, she asked, "I really am sorry, you know. Is it broken?"

Without looking at her, he very gingerly probed his nose. At least the bleeding had stopped. "No."

She straightened up, taking her hand off him, knowing that was all he would say. Well, she certainly hadn't expected cheerfulness, but forgiveness would have been nice.

He stood up just inches from her and pierced her with his dark eyes. Sara knew him to be wet, in pain, scratched up, scraped, covered in sand, bloody, tired, probably hungry, and about fifty other things she could name. But the look on his face held an emotion she couldn't name. He was so big that he blocked out the lowering sun behind him. Sara's gaze was riveted to his face. He looked like a god standing there with his arms hanging loosely at his sides.

Finally able to tear her gaze away from his, Sara lowered her eyes until she was looking straight ahead. His chest became her visible world. A physical ache, which she was barely able to resist and could in no way name, urged her to reach out and gently rake her nails down the rippling muscles of his abdomen. She wanted, for the first time in her life, to allow her fingers to trace the thin line of black curling hair that vertically halved his torso and dipped down into his pants. She wet her lips and looked up, past the crisp, curling hair of his chest, to stare openly, perhaps hungrily, into the intense depths of his eyes.

A slow grin that looked so knowing, so capable of naming what she hungered for, softened his features. He reached out to rub the backs of his fingers on her upper arm. "Sara, can you . . . ?"

"Yes?" she breathed, still trapped in his aura.

"Can you swim?" He began unbuckling his gunbelt.

She blinked. "What?"

"Can you swim?" His chuckle had a teasing note to it, but she couldn't be sure; this was only the third time she'd ever heard it. He tossed his gunbelt onto the ground.

Sara pulled herself up. "Of course I can. Why?"

"Good. I think you need a good dunking. I know I sure as hell do." With that, he picked her up in his arms and waded right into the dappled water at the river's edge. As he splashed in, he let go of her, dumping her unceremoniously into water just deep enough for buoyancy.

Sara started to cry out, but wisely closed her mouth before it was filled with water only recently churned up by milling buffalo. Still, her head went under, and she came up gasping and sputtering. He was right in front of her and smoothing his hands up and over his face, continuing right up over his hair and then down to his nape. Sara's first sight when she cleared the water out of her own eyes was of the whiter skin of his forehead which was usually covered with hair or his hat, and the sight of his raised arms, revealing bunching of muscles and black underarm hair. She held her breath and went under again, this time staying under until her lungs burned.

When she surfaced, he was gone. Sara bobbed and treaded against the undertow in what to her was chest-deep water. Goosebumps suddenly shivered her whole body; the water was not very cold, but she was sure he was somewhere under the water and was going to grab her legs and pull her under, just the way her brother Jim used to do. Somehow, she couldn't picture him doing something that playful. Still, he *had* thrown her in the water.

Clearing the water out of her eyes, she saw him wading towards shore, making slow and awkward progress against the sand and the drag of his wet, heavy denims. He was heading around the same bend where she'd seen the horses flee only moments ago. Silently she watched him, her thoughts in a jumble, her arms gently treading against the sluggish current. Why in the world was she feeling disappointment that he was no longer in the water with her? She should be relieved, glad even. But she wasn't, and she didn't try to deny it to herself or to shrug it away. But if she were glad of anything, it was that he had disappeared from view. To have him see her face, which she suspected was soft with yearning for him, would have been too much to bear.

Enough, her sensible side told her. Heeding the voice in her head, she exhaled sharply, deciding to go help The Bounty Hunter, her enemy, find their mounts. But not before she put on her dry clothes; all she had to do was look down at herself to know that her underclothes were completely transparent when wet. Well, there it was—another good reason to be glad he was nowhere near her. But, as if he were standing right in front of her still, Sara crossed her arms over her breasts and shivered.

Suddenly—finally—put out with herself and berating her girlish fantasies of the man who was most likely going to kill her brother and cousins, she told herself she couldn't stay in the water the rest of her life. She needed to find her clothes and get dressed. Putting one foot in front of the other, Sara began the slogging journey up the sloping riverbed, fighting the gentle, loverlike tug of the current that seemed reluctant to free her from its embrace.

Dripping and slightly chilled once on the shore, Sara stepped over Bonner's gunbelt without giving it more than a cursory glance. She was more concerned with locating her dry clothes and getting into them before he came back. She looked in the direction in which Deke—The Bounty Hunter, she quickly corrected herself—had indicated she could find her clothes. And sure enough, there were her plain white cotton shirt, tan split skirt, and hose draped over a scrubby bush, along with his faded blue shirt. For some reason, the sight of his shirt hanging so intimately, yet so innocently, with her clothes stopped her in her tracks. There was really nothing wrong with the sight—or right with it, either.

Then she spied her boots on the ground next to his black Stetson, and right now she wanted her boots more than her clothes; the gravel-and-rock-strewn river bottom, up a ways from the sandy shore, was making mincemeat of her soles. Forcing herself onward, Sara oohed and ouched her stumbling way off the rocks and onto the dry, grassy ground closer to the bluff.

Afraid Deke—Mr. Bonner—would round the bend at any moment, she quickly tugged her shirt free of the bush and dragged it over her skin to dry herself. There was no help for it—she'd have to put her dry clothes on over her wet underwear. Slipping into her now-damp shirt first, she leaned forward from the waist to bring her wet and streaming hair forward over her head. After wringing out the sodden mass as best she could, she ran her fingers through it, trying to untangle it a bit. She thought to get her brush out of her saddlebag, but decided against wasting any more time brushing her hair when Mr. Bonner might need her help. So she just straightened up and tossed her head, much as a horse would, sending her silvery mane flying. She made a face when the damp, heavy hair slapped against her back, instantly wetting the back of her shirt.

She next reached for her skirt, hose, and boots, all the while keeping her gaze on the curving bend of the bank as she dressed. There was a certain fierceness in her movements, born of a desire not to deal with the bounty hunter ever again while in her underwear. Dressed now and feeling as if her clothes added protection against Deke Bonner's black-eyed gaze, she took off at a trot to see what was keeping him. Just how far had the horses spooked?

Sara's turning the bend of the river was met by the sharp crack of gunfire. Responding instinctively to the echoing report of a rifle, she jerked back around, diving for the cover of the hard-packed embankment. Frozen with fear, she half-sat, half-crouched, keeping her back against the rock-hard earth of the overhanging embankment, her knees drawn up against her chest. Holding her breath, her gaze darting this way and that, she strained to hear any noise, any movement. As she tried to think at what or at whom Deke could possibly be shooting, she remembered that his gunbelt was still lying on the ground about a hundred yards downriver. Her heart nearly stopped. Deke wasn't shooting at anything or anybody. Someone was shooting at him.

Chapter Six

For several hour-long seconds, Sara was too terrified to move. But when no more shots were fired, she gathered her courage, unlocked her frozen muscles, and turned enough to look over her left shoulder and around the jutting embankment that was her protection. She sucked in a great gulp of air. Deke was lying facedown on the ground—and he wasn't moving at all. Oh, dear God. She put a trembling hand to her mouth to stifle the scream that threatened to rip out of her lungs. A convulsive swallow sent the bile back down her throat.

Deke's gun. She had to get it; it was closer than her rifle, which was with her saddle. If he was dead, there was nothing she could do to help him. But she would need his gun to defend herself. And if he wasn't dead but was only wounded, then she would need his gun to kill whoever'd shot him so she could get to him quickly to help him.

She closed her eyes and lifted her chin, taking in a deep and fearful breath. She'd have to make a run for it and pray that she made it to the gunbelt before a bullet found her back. Which would be a blessing in her situation, for she'd much rather have a bullet end her life quickly and painlessly than face whatever form of sadistic pleasure she knew would be her fate if she fell into the wrong hands out here alone. And here she'd thought her plight with Deke Bonner was the epitome of being in the wrong hands.

Opening her eyes again, she chanced one last look around the bend. Sara was unnerved at not seeing a single living, moving thing, except for Cinnamon and Deke's buckskin. There was no one along this bank or the opposite one who could have done the shooting. Sara took a shuddering breath and her life into her own hands by jumping up and dashing back downriver to where Deke's gunbelt lay so innocently by the gurgling water. She prayed that the long shadows cast by the setting sun might afford her some natural cover as she raced along at a crouch. All her senses keyed on that six-shooter.

With a gasp of sheer relief, she wrenched to a stop, dropped to her knees, and yanked the huge, long-barreled six-shooter out of its holster. Feeling better with it in her hand, she jerked around, heading back to the turn in the bend—and to Deke. She'd run only a few feet when, from around the curving bend, out stepped the shooter.

Sara cried out, stopping so quickly that she stumbled over her own feet. Righting herself, she brought Deke's gun up with both hands and aimed it at the man. But she didn't shoot; she couldn't. Her muscles were locked. While her panicked mind screamed orders to her fingers to pull the trigger, the man began to advance on her. Sara sobbed, and her arms began to tremble. Then her mind began to register impressions. A lone man; a lone, old man. An unarmed, lone, old man with his hands up. An unarmed, lone, old man with his hands up and a terrified look on his face.

Sara's breathing and her posture began to relax. But then she tensed right back up into a shooting stance, stiff-legged, arms extended. She had no way of knowing if the stranger was alone; this could be a trick. And even if it weren't, old man or no, he had shot Deke, an unarmed man himself, for no reason. But where was the man's weapon? Emboldened by the realization that the gun in her hand gave her the advantage, Sara called out, "Stop right there if you value your life, mister! Who are you? And why'd you shoot Deke?"

"My name's Coburn," the old man called out, keeping his empty hands raised as high as he could. "And I didn't shoot nobody."

"Liar!" Sara screamed, a sobbing catch in her voice. "I saw him with my own eyes—lying back around that bend, facedown."

The old man's look of terror did not lessen as he stared wide-eyed at the gun in Sara's hand, which she kept aimed at his heart. "I tell you, I didn't shoot no one. I was shooting at my supper—a prairie chicken."

"You'll have to do better than that, mister. Can't no one confuse Deke Bonner with a prairie chicken."

"Dang it, girl, if you'll just lower that gun a little, I can explain myself." He took a tentative step toward her.

Sara didn't lower Deke's gun. "Just explain yourself from right there."

He stopped as suddenly as if he'd met a solid obstacle. "Yes, ma'am. I didn't shoot your man—"

"He's not my man!"

"Yes, ma'am. I didn't shoot no man. I swear to you I didn't. I'd just crossed the river back there and shot at a prairie chicken—"

"So you said. Get on with it."

"—and I suppose your—the man just thought I was shootin' at him, and he dropped down to play dead. In case I *was* shooting at him."

He quit talking, and the silence stretched out between the two. Sara bit at her bottom lip nervously while her mind worked past her terror to try to sort out what he was saying. "Then, if you didn't shoot him, where is he now?"

"Can I put my hands down, ma'am?"

"Just answer the question!" Sara screamed.

The old man did not put his hands down. "He's just around the other side of this here bend." He nodded his head in the direction from which he'd just come.

"Well . . . why won't he come back around here so I can see him?" *And so he can help me,* she thought.

"I can tell you that one, ma'am. He sent me around first, saying if he knew you, you'd be shootin' the first man to round that there bend. And danged if he wasn't right."

"He *what*? I don't believe you!" Still trembling with gut-churning fear, Sara couldn't at first assimilate this new piece of information. Then it struck her. To think that Deke Bonner felt he knew her well enough to know how she would react in a given situation galled her somewhat, but not half as much as the thought that he was alive and well and around that bend smirking at her dilemma. Well, he'd said early on that she would have to take care of herself. Did the son of a swaybacked mule think this was a test of her mettle? Was he teaching her a lesson, waiting to see how she got herself out of this one? Waiting to see if she would believe this old man—or shoot him? Truth to tell, and well she knew it, her very life could depend on her decision whether or not to believe the man in front of her.

Thinking that, she looked at the old man. Coburn, he'd said his name was. He really did look harmless enough— and he was unarmed. Making her decision, Sara said, "You can put your hands down now."

He did. "Thank you, ma'am. I'm mighty grateful for that—and for your not shootin' me." Then he turned his head slightly to look over his shoulder and called out, "You can come on out now, mister. She ain't going to shoot no one."

"I wouldn't be so sure about that, if I were you," Sara said under her breath, narrowing her eyes. If that sorry bounty hunter stepped around that bend, not wounded and smirking, one of his own bullets would have his name on it.

The sorry bounty hunter stepped around the bend, not

wounded but not smirking either. His sober expression was probably the only thing that saved his life.

"You can put the gun down now, Sara," he called out. He sounded confident enough, but he didn't come any closer than to stand alongside Coburn. When Sara didn't lower his six-shooter but instead swung it ever so slightly to aim at his heart, she saw the look in his dark eyes and recognized it for what it was—acknowledgement that this was what it could come down to at any moment on their long journey, one of them facing the other one with a gun.

Sara licked at her lips and steadied her stance; for the life of her, she couldn't put the gun down.

Coburn looked from her to Deke and back again. "Now, hold on, ma'am. I don't know what's between you and this here man. But I ain't got nothin' to do with it. I'll be more than glad to just go back the way I came and get my chicken and my horse and get on out of you folks' hair. You just say the word, and I'm gone."

"What's it going to be Sara?" Deke Bonner challenged.

Pretty brave dare for a bare-chested, empty-handed man to be making to a woman with a gun in her hands and a damned good reason to want him dead. But did she want him dead? No, she realized—not by her hand. Not like this, anyway. With a defeated but relieved slump, she was finally able to relax her stance, uncock the gun, and lower it to her side. "I'm not going to shoot you," she said needlessly.

"I thank you again for that, ma'am," Coburn crowed, a relieved smile lighting his ruddy face. He pulled at his grimy suspenders and righted his beat-up hat on his head.

Sara let him think she'd aimed her remark at him. When Deke approached her and held out his hand for his gun, she looked up into his black, glittering eyes. Grim and silent, he took the gun from her nerveless fingers and brushed by her. The moment gone, the tension drained, Sara found she didn't know what to do with herself. She looked around helplessly, twisting to see Deke retrieve his Stetson, settle it on his head, and then bend over to pick up his gunbelt, which he put on with angry, practiced motions. She swung back to face the old man; he was still standing in the same spot where Sara'd halted him a few minutes ago. He offered a tentative smile. Sara found she couldn't match it; she closed her eyes tightly, willing away the impending flood of tears she felt pricking her eyelids.

"I'd be happy to share my supper with you folks, if you like."

Sara opened her eyes and stared at the old man.

"It gets a might lonesome out here in these parts. And my horse ain't much of a one for conversation."

"That would be fine," Deke answered for them, brushing by Sara, apparently on his way to get the horses. His voice, so close by, startled a jump out of her; she turned to look at him, but all she saw was a glimpse of his broad back as he shrugged into his shirt and began buttoning it.

When he was even with the old man, Deke motioned for him to come with him. Coburn quickly followed; he glanced back at Sara once or twice before they disappeared around the bend.

Shaken, angry, and feeling somehow empty, Sara turned on her heel and immediately busied herself setting up a camp for the evening. Doing something physical forestalled thinking, she knew from long experience on the farm. Doing for herself and her family for all the years of the war had taught her that. It was no different out here. Only more dangerous, more desolate. Sara was glad for the setting sun; it hid the flatness, the openness, the stark and primitive lay of No Man's Land. What had made her think she could make this trip all by herself? Admitting that she needed Deke Bonner— at least his intimidating presence and his gun—did nothing to improve her mood.

About an hour later, Coburn proved to be a man of his word. He had indeed been shooting at a prairie chicken. In fact, it proved to be the main course for a delicious late supper. Just as Coburn himself proved to be the main and only source of distraction for an edgy Sara and a wary Deke.

Those two sat on opposite sides of the small campfire facing the water, with Coburn between them.

"That's a mighty fine piece of horseflesh you got there, mister. How's he called?"

Sara flashed Bonner a look; he refused to acknowledge her. "He doesn't have a name," he answered testily, notching his hat up with his thumb.

"He gets him to come by whistling," Sara felt compelled by minor demons to add. She smirked when The Bounty Hunter narrowed his eyes at her.

Coburn cut his eyes from one to the other of them and wiped his hands on his shirt. Lifting his plate off his knees and setting it on the ground, he tried again. "Well, that's one way. As for me, I get kinda lonely-like out here, and so it helps to have a name for my horse. So's I can feel like I'm talkin' to someone, not something." When no one commented, he went on gamely. "I call my mount Jezebel."

Sara smiled in spite of herself. She opened her mouth to tell Coburn her horse's name, but before she could say a word, Deke asked abruptly, "What are you doing out here?"

Sara frowned at Deke's questioning of the old man. He sounded as if he didn't trust Coburn. In fact, he'd even warned her against telling Coburn their last names. She had to admit that Bonner was right there. Both their names were widely known, for very different reasons, in these parts. No sense alerting anyone to their presence, he'd said.

But apparently Coburn didn't think anything about Deke's challenging tone, because he answered amiably enough, "Oh, various and sundry things. Just gettin' by mostly. I trade some with the Cherokee, the Cheyenne, other tribes. Been all across this Indian Territory, me and Jezebel."

"Where's home?" Sara asked, warming to this white-haired, ruddy-faced older man, whose eyes sparked warmth and humor.

He smiled and rubbed his hand over his stubbled chin. "Well, ma'am, right now home is here with you folks."

Sara frowned; what an odd answer. She started to ask him

what he meant by that, but a sudden clearing of Deke's throat and an abrupt but small movement by him caught her attention. When he gained her eye, he shook his head no. Then it hit Sara; they were in No Man's Land, a place where desperadoes, outlaws, and misfits lived. A person's past was his own business, because knowing a man's secrets could get you killed. And didn't Sara and Deke have problems of their own that were best not discussed with anyone else, much less between the two of them? Embarrassed at her breach of the silent code of anonymity, Sara immediately lowered her eyes and then covered the moment's awkwardness by rising to gather and take the tin plates to the sandy shore to wash them.

Squatting down on the shore, intent on her chore and her roiling thoughts, Sara jumped, dropped a plate, and almost fell into the river when a hand clamped on her shoulder. Her gasp brought another hand to her other arm; steadied now, she twisted and looked up into Deke Bonner's face. He pulled her to her feet, turned her around, and let go of her as if she were hot.

"You nearly scared"—She instantly lowered her voice when Deke shushed her—"the life out of me. What's wrong?"

"Nothing. Probably." When Deke cut his eyes up the rise of the shore to the campfire and Coburn, who was reaching for the coffeepot, Sara's gaze followed his. When he looked back at her, his black eyes were glittering as brightly as the moonlight on the water. Despite her most fervent intention not to respond in any womanly way to Deke, Sara's knees went weak. His next words banished that weakness. "But you better sleep close by me tonight."

"What?" Sara said aloud, stiffening. Then in a whisper when he shushed her, she repeated, "What? If you think that you—"

"Dammit, Sara Dalton. You flatter yourself. Look around you. Look where you are. At least you know I won't kill you in your sleep. Can you say the same thing about *him*?"

He jerked his thumb toward Coburn.

Sara followed the motion of his thumb and then brought her gaze back to The Bounty Hunter. She was having more and more trouble thinking of him in those terms, but less and less trouble thinking of him as Deke. Still . . . "You're right, I suppose. But he does seem harmless enough. I mean, he did share his chicken with us, even after I nearly killed him."

"You mean after he nearly killed me. That bullet whizzed by my head close enough for me to feel it. He's damned lucky there was a dead bird on the ground when I made him go back around the bend with me. Had there not been, we'd've been burying that old man's bones instead of picking that chicken's bones clean."

Deke's almost casual attitude toward violence still had the power to surprise Sara. "Oh, surely you don't think—"

"I think I know that an Indian trader would need at least to have some goods in his possession, as well as a pack animal to carry them. Which he doesn't. And no provisions, except for a bedroll and saddle bags. Think about it, Sara. All he has is himself and that mangy nag he calls Jezebel."

A thrill of fright raced through Sara. Deke was right. She turned her head slightly to eye Coburn. If she'd been alone and had made it this far safely, tonight very well could have been her last if she'd been lulled into trusting such a kind-looking old man as Coburn. It was yet another reminder that she was ill-equipped to make this trip alone and that she needed Deke Bonner. Her exhalation slumped her shoulders. She looked up and caught Deke moving his eyes slowly over her face, which he abruptly stopped doing when she met his gaze. Surprised and mysteriously warmed by his inventory of her features, Sara forgot what she'd been about to say.

She watched silently as Deke seemed to come to himself; he drew himself up to his considerable height, casting a now-critical eye over her face and hair. "And do something about covering all that silver hair of yours. It's as bright as the moon, and there's enough of it to light up the countryside

for miles. You'll have every depraved outlaw for twenty
miles sniffing after us. Put a hat on or something. And don't
even think about hiding behind a bush and undressing and
wearing that damned gown-thing to bed with a stranger in
camp. You're out on the prairie, for God's sake; you don't
wear a bed-gown on the prairie.''

Turning on his heel, he stalked off, leaving a stunned Sara
on the shore. Her hand went to her hair, now dried into the
untamed riot of curls that had always defied combs, hats, or
a ribbon. How dare he compare her to a bitch in heat that
could attract sniffing dogs from miles around! That was absolutely disgusting and insulting and it was a good thing for
him he was out of reach of her booted foot or he'd feel one
of them in the seat of his pants right now. She relished that
image for a moment, but then called herself a coward, knowing she might think it, but she'd never risk it.

And he knew darned well she'd lost her only hat during
the buffalo stampede. How he'd managed to keep his own
on through all that, she'd never know. She snatched up the
dripping dishes. And what was he doing looking at her hair?
She stalked back up the shore to the camp. He'd never mentioned her hair or her choice of bed clothes before now. Why
couldn't a body be comfortable out on the prairie? Was there
a law against that? Just what else about her bothered him?
Damned bounty hunter. And telling her she'd better sleep
close to him tonight!

Sara grabbed the rag she used as a pot holder, jerked the
coffeepot off the banked fire—shocking Coburn, who'd been
about to reach for it again—and went back to the stream to
rinse it out and prepare it for tomorrow morning. Fuming
and mumbling under her breath, Sara vowed that they'd see
just who slept by whom tonight. Nobody told her what to
do.

Fully dressed, Sara slept by Deke that night. But she as-
suaged her conscience by telling herself that The Bounty
Hunter had given her little choice. In fact, no choice. She'd
come back from the river with the coffeepot to see him

opening her bedroll and placing it right next to, and almost touching, his. Not able to make a loud scene without alerting Coburn to the tension between them and their suspicions of him, she'd put down the coffeepot and silently yanked her bedroll a good two or three feet away from Deke's. At a gurgling sound from Coburn, the two combatants had looked over at him. His chuckling faded, but his eyes had widened. When they continued to stare silently at him, he immediately yawned loudly, got up awkwardly, scratched, stretched, and made a great show of not being aware of them as he prepared himself for bed.

Sara immediately turned her attention back to Deke Bonner, but not quickly enough. She almost pitched forward onto him when he yanked her bedroll right back where he'd placed it originally. She strangled a yelp of anger and surprise, letting go only to sweep her hair out of her eyes and to right herself. She turned her nastiest and most threatening glare on the loathsome rodent. The rat's narrowed eyes and slightly inclined head dared her to yank the bedroll again.

His fierce look saw hers and raised her one. The fight went out of Sara. And he'd made her worry about Coburn shooting her in her sleep? Ha! More likely, that was Deke Bonner's plan for her. But worse than that, he had her pillow; she couldn't sleep without her pillow. She acknowledged defeat with a thin-lipped glare, which only made him smirk, but she felt she'd gotten in the last word by showing him her back while she sat Indian-style on her bedroll and defiantly brushed her hair with her ornate silver brush.

Far from taming her hair, the brushing she gave it only made it that much more shiny and full; before she was done, it fairly crackled with the same electricity that trilled through Sara, a trill she named anger and refused to accept as anything else. The fact that Mr. High and Mighty Deke Bonner was lying on his bedroll right behind her, close enough for her to feel the heat from his body, had nothing to do with it. In fact, Sara felt triumphant when she heard a low groan come from him. So, he was admitting defeat. She bet it would be a long time before he told her to wear a hat again.

Deke offered up ten years off his life to be able to call back the groan that escaped him while Sara Dalton brushed her hair. Yes, she'd presented her back to him to show her anger, but what a slim, enticing back it was—little round bottom and all. And her little round bottom had jiggled provocatively, almost right under his nose, with every stroke of the brush through her moon-colored hair. He offered another ten years off his life to be able to reach out, grab her around her waist, and jerk her right under him and—

Deke jerked over onto his back, bent the knee closest to Sara, and flung an arm over his eyes. Damn. If he kept this up, he'd have to get up and go dig his own grave right now, lie down in it, and scrape the dirt back over him. One more ten-year allotment and he'd be behind.

And just what the hell was she doing with a pillow, a silver comb and brush set, night clothes, day clothes, ribbons, scented soaps, creams and lotions and such out on the prairie in the middle of No Damn Man's Land anyway? She was proof positive that this was no place for a woman. It was a wonder that her mare hadn't buckled under the load of female gewgaws that she'd brought along. Yeah, she had all the comforts of home, but did she have any extra ammunition in those engorged saddlebags of hers? He doubted it. Deke decided that when he did indeed find her brother and cousins, he'd shoot them for sure, if for no other reason than having such a frustrating female relative.

Just when he believed the blood that had raced to his groin was going to return to other parts of his body, Deke felt Sara shift her position and lie down next to him. It was going to be a long night. Her nearness caused him more concern than anything that Coburn—probably the harmless, lonely old man he appeared to be—might be capable of doing. Deke let out a long breath he hadn't realized he was holding. And sucked it right back in again when he lowered his arm, his hand inadvertently coming to rest on Sara's hip. Realization dawned on him, and his eyes flew open just in time to see her fist heading for his nose.

Chapter Seven

Only Deke's lightning-quick reflexes saved his still swollen nose from further damage. He deflected her blow by stopping her arm in midair with a hand so large, compared to her slim forearm, that his fingers met and closed over each other, even after encircling her arm. He raised himself on his other elbow and leaned over her. Mindful of Coburn's softly snoring presence only a few yards away, Deke kept his voice low. "Uh-uh, Sara, you only get one chance a day to break my nose. You already had yours when you put your shoulder into it this afternoon."

That stopped her, but only for a moment. "Get your damned hands off me, bounty hunter," she hissed.

"I don't have them on you, Miss Dalton. You're the one trying to punch my nose."

"You're the one who grabbed my—"

"Your what?" Deke knew it was wrong to toy with her; hell, she just might shoot him like she kept threatening. Maybe he should have put his bedroll over by Coburn's, but

61

here he was. And toy with her he did.

"My—my bottom. You put your hand on my bottom," she finished in a rush. Reflected firelight and moonlight showed her black eyes to be snapping. "Let go of my arm this instant."

"Or what?"

"What?"

"Let go of your arm or what, Miss Dalton?"

He let her think about that, enjoying the play of emotions over her face as she glanced this way and that, trying to come up with suitable options. Finally lighting on one, she looked him right in the eyes. "Or I'll scream."

Deke pretended to think about that for a moment, but all he could really think about was the way her breast was pressing against his and the way her mouth was opened in an unconscious invitation. "Are you sure you want to do that?"

And now she was looking at him differently. Her expression had softened, turned wondering. It completely unnerved Deke. Especially when she didn't say anything. His gaze locked with hers; he knew what was going to happen, even if she didn't. And he also knew it couldn't happen—not under any circumstances. But tell that to the quart of blood that had settled below his waist.

In an effort to regain control, Deke let go of Sara's arm. To his utter surprise and shock even, since she professed to hate everything about him, she didn't lower her arm or scramble away from him or slap him or any of the other things he'd expected. Instead she put her upraised hand to his cheek, smoothing his flesh and moving her fingers down over his lips. Ignoring every instinct in him that told him to push her away, Deke gently captured one of her fingertips between his front teeth and moved his tongue over the sensitive tip of her finger. He saw her look wonderingly up at him. He let go of her finger; she offered him another.

Every hair on his body seemed to stand on end, as if mimicking his rigid manhood. If he didn't stop himself—them—right now, it would be too late. And he had no idea how

experienced or inexperienced this woman beneath him was.
This woman beneath him was—dammit, she was Sara Dalton. And here she was using her femininity, her experience,
to capture him.

No. He didn't think that was true at all. She'd never be-
haved in any way that would lead him to believe she was
capable of such low-down dealings. In fact, she'd stayed
away from him, practically avoided him, if that was possible
while they rode together. And he had every reason to believe
she was a woman of honor and morals. *So explain this*, his
conscience railed, while he took yet another fingertip between his teeth to nibble it gently.

Then he was out of fingers. He looked at her, her face
framed by the most beautiful and unusual hair he'd ever
seen; her full, soft lips parted slightly, showing white teeth.
Her delicate nostrils flared slightly, and her half-closed eyes
were full of invitation. Deke had never seen a black-eyed
blonde before; her coloring had intrigued him from the first
time he'd laid eyes on her.

He lowered his head and took her mouth; he'd meant only
to taste her, to satisfy his curiosity, and then to pull away.
But the resounding sparks that fled through him told him that
this kiss, the sweetest thing he'd ever tasted, was also the
worst mistake he'd ever made. She must have felt the spark,
too, because at the moment of contact with his lips, she'd
bucked as if shocked. But Deke was not yet ready to let her
go. He took her fully into his arms and melted further into
her when she wrapped her arms around his neck. God, he
needed her sweetness.

Her kiss answered so many questions he had about her.
She was innocent; she knew nothing of kissing. But she was
also a quick learner, a very good student indeed. She only
momentarily resisted his tongue's insistence on entry into the
slick cavern of her mouth. But once she was breached, she
pulled back for only the slightest moment before she caught
on to the dance of their tongues and offered him the same
pleasure he was giving her.

Through the slanting, slashing wetness of their kiss, Deke became aware that she'd moved her hands to his hair and even now had handfuls of it clutched in her small fists. She was holding him to her as much as he was holding her to him. So she was just as hungry for sweetness, for tenderness, as he was. With the thought came sanity and a return to reality. Neither one of them could, or even dared, seek this intimacy with the other. Cursing himself for a fool, both for being the one to start this and for being the one to stop it, Deke pulled away from Sara's warmth.

The cool night air that crept between their separated bodies when Deke moved away from her brought Sara's eyes open wide and her senses back. Seeing Deke Bonner leaning over her, his mouth wet with her kiss, Sara stiffened. She'd kissed The Bounty Hunter! And kissed him as if she meant it! How had that happened? The last thing she remembered was trying to sock him in the nose for putting his hand on her hip. And here her own hands had been on his face, his hair, his shoulders . . .

"Get off me, bounty hunter," she hissed through clenched teeth. Breathing raggedly of his male scent, the night air, and the campfire, Sara attempted to stare him down.

"Gladly, Miss Dalton," he replied after a long moment of holding her gaze, his own unreadable.

Then suddenly he was all smooth compliance, as if the kiss had meant nothing to him. And that stung worse than the realization that she'd been a willing participant. With an abruptness that surprised her, given the warmth of their kiss, he pulled his arms out from around her, leaving her lying on her back with her knees bent, and rolled back onto his own bedroll until his back was to her. And that was that.

Sara lay there, staring up at the stars. Her belly, on which she rested her interlaced fingers, roiled with the aftermath of what had just happened—and what could have happened—between them. For nothing would she acknowledge the hot tears that coursed into her hair at her temples. By forcing her mind to a numbing blank and by lying immobile for what seemed like hours, Sara finally found relief in sleep from her turmoil and confusion.

That next morning saw Sara, Deke, and Coburn on the trail together. Close questioning by Deke at breakfast had established that Coburn was indeed who and what he said he was—an Indian trader. His lack of goods and a pack animal had been satisfactorily explained as having been sold, mule and all, his last time out in the Territory. In a rare show of trust for the denizens of No Man's Land, Coburn had shown Deke a wad of money, explaining that he was on a replenishing mission this trip. He was venturing back in to buy from the Indians to sell to the settlers up north. Such things as fine Indian ponies, blankets, baskets, buckskins, and jewelry went real fast, he assured him.

"And besides," Coburn had added, "I do believe I might be a help to you two when we meet up with the Injuns. I might smooth your way across their lands, seein' as how I trade with the tribes. An' I can tell you, some of 'em's friendly; some of 'em ain't. But all of 'em's right particular about who crosses their land, 'specially if'n you ain't got their say-so. Now, I don't know where you two's headed— and it ain't none of my business, I reckon—but I can tell you this—you head on into the Indian Territory, and you will meet up with the local citizens."

Deke had exchanged a look with Sara at that point; she'd shrugged her assent. A slight inclination of his head had acknowledged her vote. But Deke hadn't been quite finished with Coburn. "What's in it for you?" he'd asked the old man abruptly.

Sara had made a little noise at Deke's abrupt manner of questioning Coburn, who in her estimation had been nothing but forthcoming. But the cheerful Indian trader hadn't seemed the least bit put out, so she'd kept her peace.

"Well, I reckon there ain't much in it for me, except I'd have more'n old Jezebel to talk to. And she's done heard all my stories."

For some reason Sara certainly couldn't fathom, Coburn's answer had assured a cautious, cynical Deke.

And so Coburn had earned his place alongside Sara and Deke. Sara couldn't speak for Deke and what he was thinking, but she for one was glad for the older man's presence. He possessed a wealth of knowledge about the Territory and about life in general; and, like a traveling philosopher, he would share his verbal wealth without even being asked. Sara hoped that the weary miles, fraught with nothing so dangerous as the smoldering, many-layered tension between herself and Deke, would pass all the more pleasantly for Coburn's presence.

And they would, she realized, as long as Coburn didn't ask them too many personal questions. Too much airing out of their situation might rend the already wispy-thin veil of their—what was it? A truce? An understanding? With a delicate snort, Sara realized that what existed between her and Deke Bonner defied labeling.

Her snort brought Deke Bonner's gaze to her face. She meant to return him look for look, but something, perhaps the set of his features, drew a sharp intake of breath from her, much as if he'd reached over and slapped her. His eyes betrayed a dark knowledge, almost as if he were allowing her to read his mind. Then he pulled low the brim of his Stetson, looked away, and set his ebony gaze on the horizon.

But his message was as clear as if he'd shouted it: A third party, in this case Coburn, with them for any length of time would only make things worse between them. Now there could be no talk, no exploration of each other's personalities, no feeling out of each other's resolve in this matter of her kin and his bounty warrant, no testing of each other's mettle and temperament so that, when the showdown came at Robber's Cave, each would know exactly how the other would react. And both of their lives depended on that knowledge.

She couldn't believe this. The one thing she'd feared the

most—being alone with the bounty hunter—was now the thing she needed the most. And not because of his kiss last night. She raised her chin a notch and gained Deke Bonner's eye again. When his gaze settled on her lips, Sara shivered in the sweltering heat.

Chapter Eight

"... And then the next thing I knowed, me an' old Jezebel here found ourselves plumb up against the biggest, the meanest, the smelliest—"

"Shut up!"

Taken aback by Deke's unwarranted rudeness right in the middle of yet another of Coburn's wonderfully vivid stories, Sara turned an appalled expression the way of the heretofore quiet, even disinterested, bounty hunter.

Apparently, Coburn wasn't going to sit still for Deke's behavior, either. "Well, you ain't got to be so—"

Deke grabbed Jezebel's reins, causing the old mare to nearly stumble to her knees. "I said shut up, and I meant it."

"Deke Bonner, what in the world has—"

"Shut up." He now turned his threatening glare on Sara. "While you two have been lost in that ridiculous story, I've been watching our company. And if you'd been paying attention, you'd have seen them, too."

"Company?" she squeaked out, every nerve standing on end. She started to pivot in her saddle, trying to find the "company," but Deke's words froze her in position.

"Dammit, don't let them know we see them. Sit still and keep riding like nothing is wrong."

Them. There was more than one. Sara's sick stomach and pounding temples urged her to jump off her horse and run away as fast as she could. Then, hating the coward who seemed suddenly to rule her passions, she retorted, "Well, if you want us to just keep riding and to act like we haven't noticed them, why'd you grab Coburn's reins and nearly knock Jezebel over? I am just a woman, but to me that doesn't seem like a natural act. At least, I wouldn't think so if I were the Indians watching us."

Deke only stared at her, but Sara saw the muscle working in his jaw. She dropped her hand to her rifle scabbard.

" 'T'ain't Injuns, is it?" Coburn ventured, apparently no longer put out with Deke.

Sara, her mind spoken, pressed her lips together and watched Deke for his response. He ignored her and answered Coburn. "No, it's not Indians."

"I figured as much," Coburn said, nodding his head. He then turned to Sara, acting as if he owed her an explanation or a lesson in survival. "If'n it'd been Injuns, Sara, we wouldn't've seen 'em at all until they was on us."

Sara gave an almost imperceptible nod as if she understood, but she didn't really. Where would Indians have hidden themselves and their horses on this flat prairie? Her next thought, though, belied that; where indeed had their "company" hidden themselves? Her line of vision revealed nothing out of the ordinary. And yet Deke had obviously been tracking strangers long enough for him to know they were being followed by men who didn't want their presence known, meaning they had to be up to no good.

Defeated, knowing she would have been dead twelve times over if she'd been out here by herself, Sara swallowed her dose of resentment and immature anger. Foolishness right now could get her killed.

"Just keep riding, nice and slow. They're behind us and to my left," Deke said in a low and soothing voice. He'd let go of Jezebel's reins by now and had positioned himself just to the rear of Coburn's and Sara's horses as those two rode side-by-side.

Once again, just as in the buffalo stampede of a few days ago, he'd placed himself in a position of danger to protect her, Sara realized. When would she ever learn? Bounty hunter though he might be, he was still chivalrous, if not downright protective. Sara wondered if she could, or would, do the same thing for him. She couldn't imagine any situation in which she might find herself his protector. Well, except one—Robber's Cave and the Dalton Boys.

As always, the thought of that confrontation made her knees go weak and her heart pound. One potentially fatal situation at a time, she chided herself, bringing her attention back to the present danger. If they didn't get out of this, there would be no Robber's Cave to worry about.

"Go on with your story, Coburn. Just like before," Deke advised. "And make for that stand of trees to your right. Nice and slow, now. Keep that old nag at a walk."

"Well, that's one good thing, 'cause old Jezebel can't do much more than walk." With a little chuckle, Coburn turned his bony mount a little toward a skittish Cinnamon, effectively herding her toward the cover of the trees. Almost immobile with fear and tension, Sara allowed herself to be directed. Dear God, she prayed over and over. No other words would come to her. Only, dear God. It would have to be enough.

"Now, me and old Jezebel here, when we seen that big, old, smelly bear . . ." Coburn began, taking up his story as if he'd never been interrupted. With a loud voice and big gestures, he peppered the air with his tangy speech, all the while moving them closer and closer to the trees. As they inched along, he worked his rifle out of its saddle holster and signaled Sara to do the same thing.

Biting her bottom lip to keep from screaming out her fear, Sara forced her nerveless fingers to work the straps loose that held her Spencer repeater in its holster. Thus occupied, she turned her head slightly to ask Deke the question uppermost in her mind. "What do you think they want?"

"Want?" he replied. "They want anything and everything we've got. Including our lives. Except maybe for yours. Most definitely they'd want you alive."

"Me?" Sara was sorry she'd asked. "What are we going to do?"

"We're going to give you to them, Miss Dalton."

Sara's heart froze into a chunk of ice. Surely he didn't mean that. She exchanged a quick look with Coburn and then turned her head to see Deke quirk up one corner of his mouth and wink at her. If they got out of this one, she was going to kill him. That he could tease her at a time like this! Suddenly she had no trouble getting her rifle ready to fire. Suddenly she was murderously angry, no longer afraid. Suddenly the liquid fear in her veins turned to fighting blood. Suddenly she—

Suddenly she knew why Deke Bonner had teased her. And it had worked. She was now ready for "company." Well, it didn't matter; she was still going to kill him. And save her brother and cousins the trouble. "You bastard," she said in a low, level tone.

"I have proof to the contrary, Miss Dalton. Now, do you happen to have extra ammunition for your fancy repeater in those overstuffed reticules of yours?"

They were now at the trees, acting for all the world as if they'd meant all along to stop here. As she dismounted, Sara took the bait, even knowing Deke Bonner's baiting of her was to keep her anger and thus her courage up. "I'll have you know, Mr. Bonner, that I have saddlebags just like you. I did not bring a reticule with me. That would be ridiculous under the circumstances, don't you think?"

"Oh, I do agree. About as ridiculous as a pillow, a silver

brush and comb set, a bed gown—'' As he talked, Deke
helped Coburn position and tie the three horses where they'd
be out of the line of fire.

''I keep all those things in my saddlebags, just like you
do,'' Sara retorted, all the while digging through her overstuffed saddlebags, past her bed gown and pillow, to locate
the buried ammunition.

Deke stopped his surveillance of the surrounding terrain
and turned to her. ''Surely, Miss Dalton, you don't mean to
suggest that I have a pillow, a bed gown, and a sil—''

''You know exactly what I mean, you—''

''If I might interrupt right here.'' It was Coburn. Sara and
Deke turned to him as one. Sure he had their attention, if
only for the moment, he went on, wagging a finger at Sara.
''Let me see if'n I have this straight. Your last name, little
lady, is Dalton. Like the outlaws.'' Sara did nothing to indicate assent. She cut her gaze over to Deke at her side; he
was looking very stony-faced.

Wide-eyed, Coburn turned to Deke. ''And you—you're
Deke Bonner? The bounty hunter?'' Upon getting no response from the two, he took his beat-up, floppy-brimmed
hat off, swiped at the sweat on his brow with his forearm,
and replaced his hat. ''Well, if that don't beat all.'' And then
something else occurred to him, something that made his
voice rise in pitch and volume. ''And you two are riding
together?'' A thought struck him. ''And you two, a Dalton
and a Bonner, were worried about me and what I might do?
Well, if that don't beat all. Yessir, if that don't beat all.''
And then another thought came to him. ''Now, hold on just
a darned minute. I got me a Dalton and a Bonner right here.
Mayhaps I ought to ride out and warn them fellers out there
to go on off while they still can. Now, what you two got to
say to that?''

Deke finally spoke up. ''I'd say you're too late, because
here they come.''

''Dear God,'' Sara prayed out loud.

If they'd expected the riders to arrive in a blaze of gunfire, they'd have been wrong. Gratefully so. Still, the three had their hands full of gunpower when the five scruffy, evil-looking men drew near the stand of trees. Deke called out for them to stop when they were in range.

The riders complied—all too cooperatively. Their grins as they held their mounts in check and the fact that they kept their guns holstered were somehow more frightening to Sara than an out-and-out gun battle would have been. At least that way, they would have known whom they were dealing with. But now the three were vulnerable, she realized, as they waited for the riders to state their business.

Once again, Sara found herself eternally thankful for the bounty hunter's huge, intimidating presence. Sara realized that she had to force herself to stand her ground to one side of Deke, her Spencer sighted square on the heart of one of the riders. She could not give in to her urge to hide behind him, and it did nothing for her confidence in her own survival abilities. How many times must it be brought home to her that she never would have made this trip safely on her own? Needing Deke Bonner was a terrible thing to have to admit to herself.

"State your business," Deke called out. For once, Sara was glad for Deke's direct, gruff way of communicating what was on his mind.

One of the riders was a big man dressed in the remains of a Confederate-gray uniform and wearing a slouched, greasy, wide-brimmed hat. He spat onto the ground and called out, "It seems to me that since there's five of us and three of you, I ought to be the one asking the questions."

"I didn't ask a question," Deke reminded him, keeping his six-shooter on the man speaking. "And I'm the one with the drop on you. Now, state your business."

The man's face hardened, as did that of his companions. Sara blew out a long-held breath. This could turn ugly at any moment. And she hoped that moment wasn't too far off; her arms were nearly shaking with her effort to keep her rifle supported. An instinct warned her that was exactly what these jackals facing them were waiting for—a relaxing of their vigilance. Sara gripped her rifle all the more firmly and tried not to think of how slick and sweaty her palms were.

Wearing a belligerent expression on his face, the big man exchanged a cocky smirk with his men and called out, "This here's our land you're crossing. You got to pay us a toll if you want to pass on through."

"Try again, mister. This land doesn't belong to anyone— that's why it's called No Man's Land."

"Yeah, well, you see, mister, we done changed the name. We now call it This Man's Land." That drew a snide chuckle or two from his friends. "What you got to say to that?"

"This," Deke said, narrowing his gaze to slits under the shade of his black hat. Then, with less warning than a rattlesnake would give, Deke shot the man, blowing him right off his mount.

"Son of a bitch!" yelled one of the dead man's flabbergasted companions as he and the three other robbers fought for control of their startled horses and drew their weapons. But they could not have been more shocked than Sara was at Deke's raw brutality in killing the man.

But one thing was for sure—the moment for things to turn ugly had arrived. Deke, Sara, and Coburn dropped to the ground as one, as if they'd rehearsed, and began firing.

Screaming horses, men, and bullets echoed across the rolling prairie. Dust churned; horses pitched and bucked; birds took noisily to flight; and Coburn's shouts and war whoops of delight sounded every time a robber fell dead to the ground. Sara had no idea if she'd hit anything or anyone, and she didn't even care; sheer panic kept her trigger finger pumping. When only one robber remained alive, he worked furiously to jerk his mount around to make his escape. Sara thought the gun battle was all over when Deke stood up, but she couldn't have been more wrong. With a cool, calculated precision that was absolutely terrifying to her, Deke took aim and shot the man out of his saddle, putting a hole in his chest before he could turn his horse.

Now the gun battle was over. In the ensuing silence, broken only by the grunts of the terrified horses and the calls of wheeling birds overhead, Deke reholstered his Colt. Coburn picked himself up clumsily and brushed himself off, chuckling deeply. Sara put her forehead to the stock of her Spencer and took several dust-filled breaths into her lungs. Coughing violently and fighting tears, she acknowledged to herself that she could not have stood on her own right now if her life depended on it.

When she raised her head, she saw two things. A few feet away, Coburn was bending over one of the dead men and going through his pockets. And Deke's broad back was almost right in front of her. A sweat stain dampened and darkened his shirt between his shoulder blades. The heat and exertion had caused that, she knew, not fear. No, not fear. Never before had she been more afraid for her brother and cousins than she was right now. Deke Bonner was a stone-cold killer. And she would do well to remember that.

Afraid, angry, and shaking, Sara picked herself up and forced her wobbly legs to bear her weight. One or two determined steps brought her right behind Deke; she grabbed his shirt sleeve and jerked on it, meaning to spin him around to face her. Her self-control slipped a little further when the only effect she had on him was to turn his torso about a quarter turn. But he did look down at her, his eyes still stony and narrowed, the bloodlust still shining in their black depths.

Sara's throat closed a little, but she managed to gasp out, "What in God's name were you thinking, killing that man like that?"

Deke stared hard at her, as if trying to remember exactly who she was. "Which one?" he finally asked, his voice as flat as his eyes.

That stopped her for a moment. "That first one!" she practically screamed, pointing in the direction of the carnage but keeping her gaze on Deke.

"It was him or us, Sara."

"But he didn't even have a gun in his hand," she protested, even though she knew he was right.

Deke now turned fully to her and put his large hands to his waist. "And what would you have had me do? Let him arm himself and maybe shoot me? Or you? Or Coburn?"

"We . . . we might have been able to . . . to talk our way out of this. It was worth a try, for God's sake. But now there are five dead men, whose blood is on our hands and our heads."

Deke stared very hard into her eyes; Sara willed herself not to look away. Her chest rose and fell in time with the scared-bird beating of her heart. Angrily she pushed back clinging tendrils of sweat-dampened hair from her face and scrubbed at her nose with a sleeve.

Deke's expression changed, softened. "Better them than us, Sara. Did you think they were out here on church business? Hell, no. You heard them. They meant to rob and kill us, at least me and Coburn. And they meant to have you—everyone of them—until you were dead." He was silent for a moment, as if allowing her to picture that grisly scene. After a moment, he asked, "What would you have done—if you'd been out here by yourself, I mean?"

Sara looked down at her dusty boots. In a low voice she mumbled, "I would have killed as many of them as I could before they killed me."

His rough, callused hand came into her line of vision as he tucked a finger under her chin and raised her head until she was looking into his eyes. "That's exactly what I did, Sara. And I didn't like it, either."

Lowering her eyes, she turned her head sideways to free her chin from his hand. He didn't stop her or say anything else as she walked off, feeling drained and weak. She sat down with her back against one of the sandbar willow trees that made up this stand and watched Coburn picking the bodies clean and gathering up the dead men's horses. When she could watch that no more, and didn't care to see Deke reloading his Colt, she got up and turned into the trees, care-

fully making her way down the shallow bank of the cheerfully oblivious and gurgling stream. Squatting down and
using her cupped hands as a scoop, she splashed handful after
handful of water over her face, neck, and arms. If only the
water could wash the dirt off her soul, she agonized.

"Sara." She turned abruptly at the sound of her name
falling from Deke's lips. Hatless now, he stood at the top of
the slope, leaning against the trunk of a willow. How long
had he been there?

"Go away," she said, turning back to the water.

"And where do you want me to go?"

She didn't bother to answer him, not even when she heard
the soft crunching of loose gravel and saw a tiny avalanche
of it run by her feet, telling her he was descending the slope
to come stand by her side. "It just came to me that it's not
those men up there that have you so shaken."

She looked up at him now, so close to her that she could
touch him if she moved only an inch or so. Her pain only
deepened when she realized that she did indeed want to touch
him; that hadn't changed at all. Despite everything.

"Is it?" he prodded.

"No, it isn't." She stood up now, wiping at her face again,
and looked at him. He was so achingly handsome and virile;
it would have been better for her if he'd been unspeakably
ugly and deformed. But he wasn't. She should hate him, she
kept telling herself. And she couldn't quite forgive herself
for not hating the man who fully intended to kill her kin for
the bounty. For the money.

"You saw those men and thought of your brother and
cousins, didn't you?"

Sara took a deep breath and looked up through the spreading branches of the willows, concentrating on the dappled
sunlight that filtered through and made this small copse seem
almost magical—if you didn't know about the blood and
death just over the slope. She lowered her gaze to Deke.

"Yes," she said. "You're going to kill them, aren't you?
Just like you killed those men up there. And with just as

much warning. And then you'll gather up their bodies and their horses, just like Coburn is doing, and take them in for the money. Because that's what it's all about, isn't it, Deke Bonner? Money.'' When he didn't say anything, she went on. ''Tell me this, bounty hunter—how are you any different from those men up there that we just killed?''

Deke put a hand out to her, but she stepped back sharply, refusing his comfort.

Chapter Nine

Deke withdrew his hand and stuffed it into the pocket of his denims. He could hardly stand to look at Sara's piquant and tearful face. How could he make her understand? Hell, he wasn't even sure he did anymore. Did she have to look so achingly heartbroken, just like a little girl, with all that silvery hair going every which way? He wanted nothing more than to take her in his arms and soothe the hurt away. And this tender feeling of needing to comfort someone— he'd thought that side of him had died with his mother and sister.

His mother and sister. That's what all this was about. Not really the money, although it was important. Hadn't his mother and sister died while the Daltons were robbing a bank? Weren't their deaths because of money? God, what a coil this was. And it didn't help at all that Sara Dalton, guilty by reason of being kin to the Daltons, was so damned . . . everything he ever wanted in a woman.

"How am I different, Sara?" he ventured out loud, fight-

79

ing to control his need to touch her, to press her to him, to shield her from all the hurt he'd caused her. Despite what he'd meant to say to defend himself, he heard himself saying, "I'm not."

Her face changed at his words; he couldn't quite name it, but it seemed he'd just confirmed something in her. She pulled herself up to stand tall, no longer looking like a child in need of comfort, but more like the determined, independent woman she was. "I didn't think so," she said with deadly calm. And then she left him standing there as she made her way up the slope of the streambed.

Deke sucked in a deep breath and ran his fingers through his hair. He heard Coburn calling to her and heard her respond. But he didn't move. Not for long minutes. Then, defeated somehow, he turned to the water, just as Sara had done; he squatted down and scooped handfuls of the purifying liquid up and over his head. The irony of a mock baptism and its implied forgiveness of sins was not lost on him. Had Sara been seeking absolution also? If so, for what? He turned his head to look up the slope. But she was gone.

Coburn had been able to catch four of the horses which the dead men would no longer need. The horses were still saddled and bridled and strung out behind him on a length of rope, which was tied to the pommel of Jezebel's saddle. Coburn rode beside Sara and tried to explain his actions to her. Deke, on the other side of Coburn, could have told him to save his breath, that she was pretty put out with both of them. But he didn't. What Sara thought of Coburn now, after seeing him scavenge the dead men's bodies, was between her and Coburn.

The late afternoon sunlight, just over Deke's right shoulder as they moved in a southeasterly direction, worked to bake the ground right under the horses' feet. The heat rising in waves, as if it were being given off by the tall grass itself, shimmered and danced with the horizon. Watery mirages floated just above the ground, making it seem as if there were a cabin and people just at the end of their vision.

To take his mind off the heat and his own problems with Sara, Deke listened in on Coburn to see how he would fare.

"Coburn, I don't really want to hear—"

"Well, I want you to hear me out, Sara. It means somethin' to me for you not to think any less of me."

Deke looked over at Sara as she turned bleak and wintry eyes on the old man. Ashamed for him, Deke looked down and then straight ahead.

"You see, I wasn't takin' nothin' for myself. There was sign on those men that they'd taken most of their belongin's from some Injuns around here that I happen to know." He jerked his thumb back to his remuda of horses. "Like these here horses. They's Injun ponies. Now, these here Injuns that I know ain't got a lot to start with, except a bunch of young'uns to feed. I reckon this here money I got off them men and these here ponies might make things a little easier. Like mebbe some good can come out of all the bad those varmints have done to innocent folk."

When Coburn fell silent, Deke looked at him and saw a stubborn look on his face. He then risked a glance in Sara's direction, wanting to see her reaction to Coburn's seemingly pure motives for such a base and degrading act. He was surprised to see her looking at him, and not at Coburn. Her expression was no longer the dead one she'd been wearing since the gunfight a couple hours ago. She looked more . . . alive now, he guessed. More like her old self. She probably thought the grin that his resulting relief carried to his face was meant for her, instead of being about her, because she returned it, like a peace offering.

Her old self. He'd known her only a little over a week, just counting their time on the trail and not in Plains, Kansas. And yet, for him, she already had an "old self." Interesting. In fact, with every passing mile, Deke had more and more trouble remembering what his life had been like before Miss Sara Dalton entered it. But that wasn't the question that nagged him. No, the question was what was he going to do when she left it?

Deke watched as Sara turned her attention to Coburn's bruised mood. He gained the impression that he was watching a mother dealing with a child she had wronged somehow.

"Coburn, I'm so sorry. I should have known you weren't . . . like that. Will you forgive me?"

Coburn fussed about a bit in his saddle and made gruff noises, but he came around. "I reckon so. You ain't knowed me but a few days. But still, I seen your eyes when you was watchin' me, and I knowed you got the wrong idee. I just felt I had to speak my mind is all."

"Well, I for one am glad you did. Now we can put the whole incident behind us?"

They fell silent after that. Deke wondered, though, if any of them would ever be able to put the whole incident behind them. As someone who had been paid to kill for most of his adult life, counting his time spent as a spy in the Union Army and now bounty hunting, he knew that every death on your hands left another notch on your heart.

A little bit later, Deke suddenly realized that the mirage of the farm and people had not vanished at all, nor had it moved back with the changing horizon as they approached it. It was still there, and it was no mirage. There was most definitely a farm in the near distance. He hadn't paid much attention to it since they were moving over low, rolling hills that alternately brought into view and then hid the land's features. The farm was still a ways off when Deke reined in his buckskin stallion. Sara and Coburn did likewise and looked at him, waiting expectantly.

"That farm out there, Coburn—do you know who owns it?"

"Well, I reckon I do," Coburn said, wiping at his sweating brow with his sleeve. "That's them Injuns I was telling you about. We won't have no trouble from them—once they know you're with me, that is."

Deke thought about that for a moment. "I don't think

we'll ride in with you, Coburn. It's best we go on."

"We?" Sara interrupted, drawing the attention of the two men. "You know, you two aren't the only ones making decisions here. I for one want to go in with Coburn. You, Mr. Bonner, can ride on if you like."

The men exchanged a glance and then looked wordlessly back at Sara, who pressed on. "I'm tired. The sun's almost down, and we've got to camp somewhere. I'm hungry, I want a bath, and I especially want someone to talk to besides you two."

Deke just looked at her; her frowning face set the punctuation to her words. There was no way in hell he was riding on without her—she'd get herself killed before she got over the next hill. Turning to Coburn, he said, "Then I guess we better let you ride in first. With the likes of those robbers running loose around here, the Indians are probably pretty trigger-happy. I know I would be."

Deke caught the look that Sara sent his way; it plainly said he was already trigger-happy. He decided to ignore her for the moment, but still her superior air irked him and he took it out on Coburn. "Coburn, what in the hell are Indians doing farming out here in No Man's Land?"

"Well, it sure weren't my idee for 'em to, Deke. You act like they squatted on your land. These here ain't all full-bloods no how. These here is a full-blood Arapaho married to a white woman. And this here land we're sittin' on is purty close to the Cherokee Outlet, which the Cherokee was made to give to the Cheyenne and the Arapaho by the U. S. Govamint. Now, does that satisfy you, Mr. Bonner?"

Feeling somewhat sheepish, Deke covered it with a show of gruffness. But still, it didn't help his mood any that the snickering he heard was coming from Sara. One part of his heart, though, was glad she could laugh again. "Just go on in and announce our presence."

"Oh, I expect old Ben Nighthorse already knows we're here."

"How would he know that?" This from Sara.

"I couldn't rightly tell you, Sara," Coburn said, absently scratching at his arm. He lowered his voice conspiratorially, "These Injuns can talk to birds and critters, and I do believe they talk right back."

"That, or he can see us as plainly as I've been seeing his farm for the past three hours," Deke said, throwing the mystery to the wind.

"Well, I suppose that could be, too," Coburn grumped.

Deke exchanged a grin with Sara over Coburn's head.

"Well, I guess me and Jezebel might as well go on in first, like you said. Now, you two keep them nags of yours out of her way when we get close. This here farm is like home to her, and she gets up a mighty head of steam when she gets a whiff of the Nighthorse place. She's liable to run right over you."

"Warning noted," Deke responded seriously, but he doubted that Jezebel could get up enough steam to run over a snail. He kindly kept that observation to himself. And he wasn't the least bit fooled by Sara's clamping of her hand over her mouth.

"Now I suppose you two don't want the Nighthorses to know your last names, now do you?"

Deke looked at Sara, who met his gaze and then looked down. "I don't suppose it makes much difference," Deke answered for them both, believing that Sara could read the message in his eyes: That's why we should have ridden on.

"Not out here it don't," Coburn replied. "These folks ain't got no law to rush to. And they sure as shootin' ain't goin' to inform the outlaws. They mind their own business. A man tends to live a lot longer that way."

With that last comment, Coburn put his heels to Jezebel's bony flanks. As they approached the Nighthorse place—Coburn in the lead with the four horses strung out behind him, Deke and Sara to either side of the remuda—children of all ages, sizes, and complexions, accompanied by as many dogs and cats, poured out of the sod-and-wood house. Their boisterous welcome spooked the horses—all of them except Jezebel, whose gait had not quickened in the least, despite Coburn's warning. While Deke controlled his prancing, side-stepping stallion and Sara did the same with Cinnamon, Coburn added to the confusion by hollering and war whooping right back at the kids.

Deke looked past the children to see two adults, a man and a woman, standing on the wooden porch of the house. The man, a tall Indian with a long braid, held a rifle loosely in his hand. The woman standing next to him was wiping her hands on an apron; she was nearly as tall as her husband. They waded through the swarming Nighthorse children, who now milled around the riders, laughing and talking and cling-ing to their stirrups, pant legs, or skirt. Deke and Sara had their hands full making sure their mounts didn't tromp on a child or a pet or two, but Coburn and Jezebel, no doubt used to this reception, plodded forward as if nothing were out of the ordinary.

Coburn yelled out two names; two older boys, both dark-skinned with long black hair and bare torsos, separated them-selves from the other children. "Sam, John, you two boys get on over here and take these here horses to your pappy."

"They was stoled from us two days ago," a little blond girl, clinging to Deke's boot, informed him.

Deke smiled down at the little girl. She was cute as a button, wearing a worn but clean cotton dress. She was also barefooted, obviously totally oblivious to the rough ground over which she walked. "Yeah, I heard that from Coburn," he answered her.

"How'd you get 'em back?" she asked, looking up at him, blue eyes curious. A smaller girl, sucking on a thumb and carrying a kitten draped over her arm, trailed along behind her sister. She too raised eyes to Deke.

Deke thought about how best to answer her question. "Well, you could say we talked them into giving them back."

The blue-eyed blonde snorted her opinion of such tactics. "You shoulda killed 'em."

Amused but taken aback, Deke nodded his head. "I'll try to remember that next time."

A greeting was called to the riders from the tall Indian on the porch. "Ah, Coburn, you come bringing gifts."

"Well, I reckon I do, if'n you can say bringin' you your own stock back is a gift." Coburn reined a catatonic Jezebel in at the foot of the one step that led up to the porch; then he made a less than graceful dismount.

Deke and Sara remained atop their horses. They hadn't been invited to dismount yet.

"And you honor us by bringing friends."

Coburn turned to Deke and Sara and then back to his friend. "Ben, Etheline Nighthorse, these two here are Miss Sara Dalton and Mr. Deke Bonner."

There was a moment of silence during which the children and their pets drifted away from the riders and arranged themselves all over the front porch, the smaller ones clinging to their mother's skirt. Mrs. Nighthorse remained silent in the deep shadows of the overhanging porch roof; she now held a fair-complected baby in her arms.

From under the shade of his hat brim, Deke watched Ben Nighthorse's face; there was no doubt that the tall Arapaho recognized the names. Deke heard Sara's nervous sniff, but he didn't look at her. He fully expected Mr. Nighthorse to tell them to keep riding. Deke was used to people's reaction to his name and reputation, but he doubted that Sara, having always lived on her own land surrounded by loved ones, had ever been subjected to the scorn associated with the Dalton name. And it didn't do anything to soften his heart toward her brother and cousins that their actions had brought shame to her.

"You are welcome in our home." It was that simple. "Tennie, Caroline, Willy, come take our guests' horses for them." Three children came off the porch to do their father's bidding. Once Sara and Deke had dismounted, Ben told them, "Come. You must meet my wife. Then we will have a meal together."

No questions, no curiosity, no animosity. Just like Coburn said, Ben Nighthorse minded his own business and left others to their own. Deke liked this Arapaho man, perhaps more for what he hadn't said than for what he had. Feeling expansive now that Sara had been spared further hurt and embarrassment over her name, Deke surprised her and himself by taking her elbow as they stepped up onto the porch. For his gentlemanly effort, his reward was a raised eyebrow in a surprised face. But he noted that she did not pull away.

"My wife, Etheline Nighthorse." Ben drew her out of the shadows.

Sara sucked in air sharply through her nose; Deke's grip on Sara's elbow tightened as he made the same noise. Etheline Nighthorse was the ugliest woman Deke had ever seen. Ever. He didn't like to be cruel, but there was the truth of it. Even what he assumed was her smile of greeting came across as frightening. It wasn't that she was deformed in any way, nor monstrous, either—the poor woman was just down-home, everyday, nondescript ugly. Deke chastised himself for his unkind, ungrateful thoughts. Mrs. Nighthorse was their hostess and about to prepare them their first decent meal since they'd left Plains. At least Deke hoped the meal would be decent.

Mrs. Nighthorse, in a surprisingly lilting, almost musical voice, told them that three more mouths to feed was hardly a bother. And she set out to prove it. The men were relegated to the porch, where Deke sat on a rough wooden chair, which he rocked back on two legs; then he swung his booted feet up to rest, crossing one over the other on the split-log rail in front of him. Ben hitched a hip on the same railing and leaned his back against one of the sturdy posts that supported the overhanging porch roof. Coburn took the rocking chair with a proprietary air and caught Ben up on the news from Indian Territory.

When the conversation turned to that day's events, Deke listened with half an ear to Coburn's almost fictional account of how they'd gotten the horses back from the robbers. Of infinitely more interest to him was what was going on inside the house. He told himself that was because he was hungry. He found that by looking over his left shoulder, he could see in through the open door to the interior. To see how the meal was coming, of course.

Mrs. Nighthorse—Etheline as she'd admonished them to call her—was supervising all but the youngest children in what had to be their everyday chores at mealtime, judging by the precision and the ease with which each child carried out his or her specific task. There was no chaos, no sass, and no laziness; if you wanted to eat, you did your part.

Deke finally let his eyes rest on the one person he wanted to see. Sara. He watched as, with a simple, matter-of-fact gesture, as if she'd known Sara all her life and trusted her implicitly, Etheline handed over two babies, just big enough to toddle; to Deke, they looked just alike and of about the same age. Twins, probably. Apparently Sara was to feed the little ones while their mother oversaw the preparations for their meal.

Deke watched, in male awe, Sara's ease and loving ways with the babies and how they instantly responded to her, their bright little eyes dancing and chubby little fists waving. She sat one of them on a chair, which she pulled to her and straddled with her knees, and held the other in her lap with her arm around its back. She then alternated spoon-feeding the little tykes. There was no awkwardness to her movements, no hesitation. She cooed and cajoled them into eating every bite in the big bowl Etheline brought her. Deke was amazed. Sara Dalton was completely at home in a kitchen and with babies.

To Deke's total consternation, he felt his throat begin to close over a lump of tenderness for Sara Dalton. As he turned his head away from the scene, his consternation turned to total embarrassment when he realized that the other two men had fallen silent and were watching him with amused expressions on their faces. Deke could only imagine what sort of silly, sappy look he'd had on his face as he watched Sara.

Bringing his feet and his chair down with an abrupt gesture, he stood up, settling a manly frown on his face. He hitched his denims up at the waist, tugged on his gunbelt, stepped off the porch, and turned to go around back to the corral. "I'd better check on the horses."

The male laughter that followed his retreating back did nothing to assuage his pride.

Upon hearing the male laughter outside, Sara turned her head to see Deke striding purposefully off the porch. He turned to his right and disappeared from her line of vision. It was only when the baby in her lap, a one-year-old named Sally, stiffened in protest that Sara realized she'd been sitting there with the spoon poised in midair, a tempting bite held halfway between Sally and her twin brother, Theodore. Quickly, she made *shh-shh-shh* sounds and gave the bite to Sally. Theodore's brows met over his nose at this error in order; that was to have been his bite. Sara quickly spooned up another bite and poked it in his little bird-mouth before he could protest.

Thinking she had covered her momentary lapse in attentiveness, she looked up to see Etheline staring at her, a half-smile emphasizing her ugliness. A sigh of guilt and a little laugh escaped Sara. Her shrug said "caught."

"Men can be the most vexin' of creatures, can't they?" Etheline offered as an opening.

"There's no limit to their vexatiousness," Sara agreed, but not offering more. She wasn't sure she wanted to talk about Deke Bonner.

"Mr. Bonner is a right handsome man."

Apparently, they were going to talk about Deke Bonner whether she wanted to or not. "Yes. Yes, he is. So's your Ben." It was a cheap ploy—and it didn't work.

"Well, you're real kind to say so. But I don't think I've ever seen a man like Mr. Bonner before. He could certainly turn a girl's head."

Sara thought about that. Yes, she supposed he could. But

not this girl's head. "I imagine he has turned his share of heads in the past." And she'd bet the farm that he hadn't stopped at their heads.

Suddenly irritated by thinking of Deke Bonner with other women, she made a face that startled a squawk out of Theodore and raised Etheline's eyebrows. Quickly, Sara schooled her features into a more pleasing picture and wiped the boy's supper from his face with a wet cloth Etheline handed her. Etheline pulled the chair back and stood Theodore on his feet. He quickly toddled outside, only to be snatched up by his father in a playful gesture. Etheline held her hands out for Sally, who was dozing in Sara's lap, her little head pressed into Sara's bosom. Handing the child over, Sara smiled at Mrs. Nighthorse. She was a kind woman with a romantic soul. Here she had so many mouths to feed already but had not even hesitated to open her house to total strangers and even treated them like family. Etheline returned Sara's smile and turned to take Sally to a homemade crib, one which had obviously been put to frequent use.

With the baby down, Etheline returned to frying chicken. Sara went to stand beside her. "Is there anything I can do to help?" she asked.

Etheline spared her a glance as she worked expertly to keep the chicken turned. "You could just talk to me. It ain't often I have another woman to talk to."

"I have the same problem, riding with Mr. Bonner and Coburn." Sara gave her a look of womanly commiseration.

Etheline's answering smile turned to a shy, assessing look. "If it ain't none of my business, you just say so, Miss Dalton, but—but what are you doing riding with Mr. Bonner? I'd suspect he'd be one to be huntin' your kin."

Sara looked down and then backed up. "He is hunting my brother and cousins. But so am I."

Etheline gave up even pretending to be tending the chicken and gave Sara an assessing but not unkind look. "And I'd wager not for the same reason a-tall."

"You'd win that wager, Mrs. Nighthorse."

Etheline's expression changed, softened. "Like I said earlier, call me Etheline. I believe you're goin' to need a friend as much as I do."

Sara felt a pang in her heart. "Thank you, Etheline. Call me Sara." Both women smiled; Sara wondered if her smile looked as conspiratorial as Etheline's did. Then, to change the subject, she looked around the large room of the rough cabin and commented, "It must be awfully hard out here for you and your family."

Etheline smiled down at the chicken and pulled a string of mousy hair from her face, tucking it behind a large ear. "I suppose it is. But it ain't near as hard as it was living among folks. You see, my folks was missionaries to the Indians, and they took Ben in when his family died. When we growed up, one thing led to another, and . . . well, it was bad enough me bein' so ugly and all, but when I married an Indian . . . well, folks can be cruel." She paused for a moment, then went on with a more cheerful air. "We're happier out here. And we find that the outlaws and Indians leave us alone one heck of a lot more than so-called decent folk did."

Sara felt so terrible for Etheline, and for her own earlier response to this woman's physical appearance, that she had to bite her lip. In a moment, she was able to talk. She put a hand on Etheline's sleeve. "I'm sorry. I've had a taste or two of folks' cruelty myself."

Etheline jerked her head towards Sara. "But you're such a pretty thing, Miss Dalton. And your man ain't—Oh. I see what you mean. It's your name, ain't it? It's your kin and what they done."

Sara removed her hand from the other woman's arm and looked down for a moment, picking at the crispy skin of a chicken leg on a huge platter right in front of her. She decided to let slide Etheline's comment about "her man." This was no moment to correct the poor woman and make her feel worse. "Yes, it is. It's just something I can't help, wasn't responsible for, but have to live with. You see, I wasn't sure, once Coburn told you my name, that you'd welcome me here.''

Etheline turned to her with a start of surprise, laid down the fork she'd been using, and took Sara in her arms for a hug. ''Oh, honey, there weren't never no question about welcoming you here. Don't you fret on that none. Why, when your kin was last through here in July on their way back to Choctaw land, they was the kindest young men you'd ever want to meet—like always. Such manners. Not at all like them other sorry critters they was ridin' with.

''But onct those men rode off to do no-good and left your kin here for a spell, they even helped Ben patch up the old barn out back. Oh, yes, the Dalton Boys, but not them other men with 'em, are always welcome guests here.'' In her eagerness to assure Sara of her welcome, she had another thought that lit up her face. ''Why, wouldn't it be a regular holiday here about if they was to show up whilst you was here and save you a long trip to the Choctaw Nation?''

Chapter Ten

Sara's mind reeled while her knees buckled. Had Etheline Nighthorse not been holding onto her, she would have crumpled into a heap on the floor. Jim, Travis, and Cody had been here? Here? At the Nighthorses'? Obviously more than once. Sara stiffened. And they might show up again at any moment. With Deke Bonner right outside—with his warrant. And her saddlebags. The map. Dear God. Deke had said he was going to check on the horses when he stepped off the porch. He could already have the map of Robber's Cave!

Without a word to explain her actions, Sara tore herself out of Etheline's arms, ignored her anxious "Sara!", flew out the front door past a startled Coburn and Ben Nighthorse, dodged assorted dogs and cats, whipped around the corner of the house and met with—collided with—Deke Bonner coming back toward the front of the house. In his hand were her saddlebags.

"Give me those!" she screamed, tearing and clawing at

his hands, fighting him for all she was worth, not giving him a chance to hand them over.

Deke fended off her blows as best he could with his raised forearm. He turned his hips sideways to her and raised his leg, bent at the knee, to block her kicks to his shins. "Goddammit, Sara, what's wrong?" he bellowed. "What happened?"

Sara, even in her sheer terror and desperation, realized that she had an audience. Openmouthed children came from nowhere to stand and watch, their faces mirroring the stupefaction of Deke's. Then, when Deke turned in a tight circle, trying to talk to her and to get a hold on her, Sara saw Etheline, Ben, and Coburn behind Deke. Their looks ranged from Etheline's fearful face to Ben's stony one to Coburn's concerned one, even though he alone of all the onlookers probably had the best idea of what this was all about.

"Give me those saddlebags, Deke Bonner. And you give them to me right now," Sara snarled, beyond caring what impression she was making on the Nighthorse family.

Deke held them up. "These? You want these? Damn, Sara, all you had to do was ask. Here." He held them out to her. "Take them. I sure as hell don't want them. I thought you might want your brush and things. I was bringing them to you."

"Liar. You were going to steal my map." She jerked the bags away from Deke and dropped to her knees right there in the dirt and grass. She tore open one of the bags and hunted feverishly until she came up with the map, in the exact spot in her bag she'd put it and folded in the exact manner she'd done herself. Her crouching posture slumped in relief as she held the precious map to her bosom.

In the heavy, heated silence that followed her actions, punctuated only by lazy, buzzing insects and an occasional sniff or shift of weight on the part of the onlookers, she heard Ben Nighthorse ask, "What is that a map to? Gold?"

"No, Mr. Nighthorse, it isn't," Sara answered him, all the while keeping her gaze on Deke's hard-as-stone face. "It's something more precious than that to me—and to him."

"There's not a damned thing you or that map have that I want—or need, Sara Dalton." With eyes narrowed to reptilian slits, Deke turned on his heel and stalked around to the front of the house. After a moment or so of awkward shifting of feet and eyes, the onlookers followed him.

Left alone with her humiliation, Sara held to her heart, along with her map, her secret knowledge of the large "X" that marked the cave inhabited by the Daltons. But even that was of small comfort when she was struck by the full knowledge of the consequences of her rash behavior. By her own words—the very act of telling Deke Bonner that there was something of value for him too on the map—she'd given the bounty hunter ample reason to wonder, perhaps for the first time, exactly what other information her map might contain. Now it became of even more dire importance to her to keep it hidden.

Focusing on that, and refusing to think on about the widening but necessary gulf between her and Deke, about how the closer they got to Robber's Cave, the less they could trust each other, Sara bent down to pick up her scattered belongings. The tears that blurred her vision couldn't hide from her the fact that her hands were shaking.

Her task completed, Sara dropped her arms limply to her sides; the heavy saddlebags hung from her fingertips. She couldn't bring herself to move or to face the people in the house. Yes, she was very embarrassed that the Nighthorses and Coburn had witnessed her acting like a crazy woman, but even more than that, she needed to be alone out here to think about what to do next—if she should ride out by herself, maybe just leave in the dark. Whereas only a few minutes ago, she would have been content to spend a few days here—any time out of the saddle was welcome—now she felt an overwhelming need to get away, to find Jim and Cody and Travis, to keep them safe from Deke Bonner. After all, she did have the map. And she didn't need Deke Bonner any more than he needed her.

"Sara."

Hearing her name spoken aloud in the quietly descending dusk, Sara jerked in surprise. She then quickly assumed a resigned air of anger and indifference before she acknowledged Deke's presence, without actually looking at him. Some things were just too difficult right now. "I thought you were hungry," she commented, diffidence uppermost in her tone.

"I am. I thought you were, too." He stopped just out of range of her fists and boots and hitched his thumbs in his gunbelt.

"I am." She looked at him fully now. Without his hat on, he looked almost boyish.

"Well, then are you coming inside to eat?"

"Why? Do you want my chicken if I don't?"

He made a huffing noise and ignored her sarcasm. "You need to come inside."

"Why? Are you afraid I'll ride out of here by myself, leaving you—"

He straightened up, stabbing his pointed finger at her and raising his voice. "That's exactly what I thought you'd be thinking. Let me tell you—don't even try it."

"What's it to you? You said you don't need me or my map. I agree. You don't. You're a pretty sorry bounty hunter if you have to hide behind a woman's skirt."

Sara would not have been surprised to see smoke come billowing out of his ears, so red was his face right now. Afraid she'd gone too far, yet glad she had, she struck a defiant pose with her hands on her hips and didn't give him a chance to speak before she continued. "Look, what I do is none of your concern. You said it yourself—you don't need me. You know the way to the Choctaw Nation. I'm the one who needs the map. I'm sure you can make up a story to get past the lookouts. So why do you care what I do?"

After a moment of silence, he said, "I keep asking myself that same question. Maybe you should, too—maybe you should ask yourself why I care what you do."

Either his words, tantamount to an admission of caring, or his tone of voice, she couldn't have said which, made her look at him, her enemy, in a new light. When she did, the tears that had balanced on the ends of her lashes spilled out onto her cheeks.

"Dammit," Deke swore forcefully. His emotion carried him over to her in two long strides, but still he was careful not to touch her. He pulled his bandanna from around his neck and held it out to her.

Sara looked at it, realizing that his gesture was a peace offering—peace for the moment only, maybe, but peace nonetheless. Before he could withdraw his bandanna and his offer, she took it in a swiping gesture, wiped her eyes, blew her nose loudly, and put the bandanna in her saddlebag. Deke seemed not to notice; at least, he didn't comment.

In the silence that followed, Sara read Deke's fierce expression to be an assessment of her and a weighing of something heavy on his mind. She knew that the pounding weakness in her limbs that flopped her stomach over had nothing to do with the thick twilight heat that alone could make breathing conscious labor. Reluctance to hear his thoughts, so seldom voiced by him—and so upsetting to her on those rare occasions when he did speak his mind—nonetheless kept her still.

Damn him, Sara thought. Nothing had changed between them. At least, nothing that kept them apart had changed. Robber's Cave still loomed like a nightmare. But everything else had changed, was still changing. Even now, damn him, Sara could not lie and say she was immune to him. For the first time she admitted to herself that she wanted to be in his arms—and not just for comfort, either. It was that simple . . . and that devastating. The urge to melt into him, to put her arms around his neck, to wet his mouth again with her kiss—

"I know what you're thinking, Sara Dalton."

"You do not, Deke Bonner," Sara practically yelled, half terrified that he might.

His eyebrows came together over his nose. "I think I do. And you better not try it. It's not something you can do by yourself."

Ignoring for the moment the fact that he was trying to tell her what she could and couldn't do, Sara allowed the absurdity of this disjointed conversation to get the better of her. She bit back a grin and put her hands to her waist, cocking her head to one side. "Maybe you better tell me what it is you think I'm thinking."

His shifting eyes told her that maybe he wasn't quite as sure of himself as he had been a moment ago. Strangely enough, seeing him uncertain of anything softened her heart toward him. "That you still think you can go off by yourself to Robber's Cave?"

Sara almost laughed out loud at his question, said as if he were afraid of giving a wrong answer to a schoolteacher. She shook her head to let him know he was wrong, thinking that the last thing her struggling heart and erratic pulse needed was endearing small-boy antics on the part of this big, strong bounty hunter.

"Well then, what?" he fussed irritably, his hands going to his waist to fiddle with his gunbelt, as if assuring himself of his masculine authority and power.

As if Sara needed a reminder. She believed that he had no idea that his bottom lip was poked out in the tiniest of belligerent gestures. Another small, personal detail she'd just noticed about him. Why was she doing this to herself? It could only lead to heartache. She should just walk away, be done with him, but even that right now was hard to do with him so close to her that she could see the dark fringe of lashes that framed his deeply black eyes. All she had to do to touch him was to reach out. And when she realized that she was doing just that, she snatched her hand back. Deke's eyes reflected that he hadn't missed her involuntary gesture. "This is the biggest damned mess I ever saw."

"Me, too," Sara said, not at all sure they were talking about the same mess. She bent over to pick up her bag.

When she straightened up, she found herself being gathered almost forcefully—as if he'd been overwhelmed with a desire for her which he could no longer deny—into Deke Bonner's arms. Her saddlebag and the all-important map dropped unceremoniously onto the hard ground at their feet. If only their differences could be thrown away as easily. But uppermost in Sara's stunned sensibilities was the tantalizing, even forbidden, question: Could it be that he too was feeling these strange tuggings that kept them knocking heads and locking hearts? She looked up into his handsome face.

"You've got to trust someone, Sara. I know it must hurt like hell for that someone to be me. But for now, I'm all you have. And you're right, you know—I don't need you to get to the Daltons, but you need me to get to them. As crazy as that sounds, there it is. Hell, yes, I could ride on right now, could have back in Plains or at any point on this trip. But I—I couldn't ride off and leave you to fend for yourself out here. People like the Nighthorses are few and far between. And it's tough as hell out here, pretty much like you've already seen it. One minute you're involved in killing, and the next you're feeding babies. But a woman who looks like you do—well, you need me."

Sara was stunned by this speech of his, which contained more words than he'd said to her in days. After a moment of looking up into his face, of allowing her gaze to rove freely over his features and watching him doing the same thing to her face she gave herself up to the moment. His words were by no means a declaration of love, and they were one-sided. She recognized that. But that made them no less true. He was all she had right now, and very likely all she'd want . . . ever. With that admission went her heart. "Oh God, Deke, what are we doing?"

Just before he claimed her mouth, he breathed, "We're making the mess even bigger."

Sara's answering whimper was lost in Deke's mouth. She felt his kiss down to her toes, which curled in her boots. She would have joined her saddlebag in a heap on the ground if she hadn't wrapped her arms so thoroughly, so possessively, around his neck. He held her no less ardently as his mouth possessed hers. His swirling tongue, so eagerly received by her own, his questing lips, so hungrily claiming her own, became all that she knew or felt. When he finally drew back, he couldn't have known it, but Sara did—her heart was in his hands.

And nothing could have made her sadder—or more afraid.

Chapter Eleven

The Nighthorses proved indeed to be folks who minded their own business. When a flushed Sara and an equally bruised-looking Deke finally joined them for supper, not one word was said, by adult or child, about Sara's outburst or about how long it had taken Deke to get Sara to the table. For that, Sara was very grateful; it was bad enough to make a fool of yourself in front of strangers, but even worse to have to hear it discussed.

When Deke entered right behind Sara and caught Etheline's eye, she smiled and jumped up from the table, leaving the meal already in progress, and produced two plates which she'd obviously set aside and had heaped with fried chicken, potatoes, squash, and thick slices of bread. There had to be a dairy cow on the property because there was butter and milk. Never had anything ever tasted better to Sara, so wrung out was she from her emotions and famished from her exertions of this long, exhausting day.

It was only after Sara and Deke, sitting side by side at the table, had eaten their fill of the supper fare that Etheline, with the help of two of her daughters, produced four berry pies. Groaning, but eager-eyed for the treat, Sara looked at the older woman. "How in the world did you have so much food on hand—not to mention four pies—when you didn't know you'd have extra mouths to feed today?"

"Ahh, but I did know. Ben told me." She gave her solemn husband a smile and then turned back to Sara. "I was already cookin' your supper when you rode up."

"Ben told you?" It was Deke, and he sounded skeptical.

"Yes," Etheline explained, nodding and wiping her hands on her apron as she surveyed the pies before her, as if trying to decide which one to cut first. "He always knows things before they happen."

"Did he know about the men who stole your horses?" Deke's tone wasn't exactly confrontational, but he was making Sara squirm.

"Why, yes he did, Mr. Bonner. He had Sam and John set them out to pasture beforehand." She cut a big piece and set it in front of Deke. "Just so's the thieves didn't have to come close to the house and hurt somebody when they took them." Deke looked askance at the woman and then turned to her husband. "Why didn't you just hide the horses or shoot the men when they came?"

Sara could hold out no longer. She kicked Deke under the table just as he took a huge bite of pie, then smiled innocently, her hands folded in her lap, while Deke choked the bite down. The fork he replaced on his plate now had bent tines. It pleased Sara mightily that Etheline Nighthorse pounded his back for him for all she was worth. He deserved no less; and she supposed she deserved the evil glare he sent her way. Only when that furor abated did Ben Nighthorse give Deke his softly spoken, considered answer.

"Because I knew that you, Mr. Bonner, would get them back for me in three days. I will not kill over horses—only if my family is harmed. I have had enough of dying."

"But you'd allow me to do it for you."

Sara's second kick hit only air. Deke had wisely moved his leg this time before speaking. For the life of her, she couldn't understand why Deke was baiting this kind man, whose food had just filled their stomachs.

A sudden stillness settled over the people sitting around the long, rough-wood table. Even the littlest of the Nighthorses didn't seem to know where to look. Ben spoke again, not the least insulted or perturbed—to outward appearances anyway. "I cannot change what will be, Mr. Bonner. I can only see it, and even that is not of my choosing."

"You killed them men?" All heads turned to the other end of the table. It was the little blond, blue-eyed girl who'd questioned Deke about how he'd gotten the horses back. She looked hugely pleased with this revelation.

Deke caught Sara's eye before he answered the child. "Yes, I did." But apparently he wasn't willing to be the only villain—or hero—here. "And so did Coburn and Miss Dalton."

Coburn and Miss Dalton shot him weighted glances.

"How come you didn't bring all five horses back? You only got four."

Before Deke or Sara or Coburn could defend themselves, Ben spoke up again. "That is enough, Jane. The horse will come home on his own. I have seen this thing."

There was no arguing with that. Not from anyone gathered around that table. It was a good thing for Deke Bonner that he also wisely chose silence in the face of Ben's clairvoyant pronouncement. Especially since Sara had slipped her fork into her lap, fully intending to surreptitiously use it as a three-tined sword if the need arose. Teach him to move his leg.

A moment later, when the little thumb-sucking sister nodded off, her dark little face nearly landing in her plate, supper was declared over. Once again, the Nighthorse children went smoothly into motion, each one attending to his or her assigned task that would quickly see everyone abed. Sara offered to help Etheline with the younger children while the

older ones tended to the clearing away of the meal, but Etheline would not hear of it. She directed her brood and sent
Sara scooting out of the way.

Not knowing what to do with herself, she went outside
into the warm, quiet evening. Deke was alone on the porch,
one knee bent, his booted foot up on the low railing. His
arms were crossed and resting against that knee. It was too
dark out for him to really be looking at anything, with the
moon not fully risen, so Sara figured he was just thinking.
She came to stand very close to his side.

When he looked at her and smiled, but didn't say anything,
Sara suddenly felt awkward, thinking of the kiss they'd
shared not thirty minutes ago. Was that what he'd been thinking about? Needing an opener, she asked, "Where are Ben
and Coburn?"

Deke grunted a laugh. "They went to take the fifth horse
back around to the corral. Seems he showed up while we
were eating. Just like Ben said he would."

Well, she was stuck now; she certainly hadn't wanted to
pick that bone of Indian second-sight contention again. She
decided to be neutral. "Strange, isn't it?"

"Not so, really. All creatures know their way home."

"I suppose." Then she risked the first personal question
she'd ever asked him. It occurred to her that he knew quite
a bit about her, while she knew nothing about him—except
that his mother and sister had been killed by Southerners.
Still, she felt their earlier kiss gave her the right to ask,
"Where's your home, Deke?"

He looked at her—at her mouth, at her eyes, at her
bosom—and then straightened up to stand towering over her.
Sara's throat went dry when he put his hands on her upper
arms and brushed a featherlike kiss across her forehead. She
wanted so much to take just one step forward and lay her
head against the expanse of his chest and to wrap her arms
around him—and stay like that forever. But Robber's Cave
kept her standing where she was.

"Do you remember what Coburn said when you asked

him that same question on the first night we met him?''

Sara frowned, trying to remember. She came up empty. "No, I don't. What'd he say?''

"He said he supposed his home was right there with us. So, if I believe like him, then my home is right here with you. Where's your home, Sara?''

Perhaps it was the warm night; perhaps it was her tiredness or the relative security she felt for the first time in days here amongst civilized folk; perhaps it was no more than the full moon just now cresting over the treetops; but whatever it was, it made her say, "My home is where my heart is.''

"And where is your heart, Sara? Is it in Plains, Kansas?'' He bent his head to take nibbling kisses from the corners of her mouth. There was no doubt that he was trying to seduce her—or, God forgive her, that she was letting him.

"It used to be,'' she breathed on a whisper of desire. The sensations of his touch washed over her in tender waves. "But now I'm not so sure.''

"Let me make you sure, Sara Dalton. Let me.''

If her life had depended on it, Sara could not have spoken right then, so caught up was she in the things Deke was doing to her right there on the front porch of the Nighthorse homestead and in full view of anyone who would care to look. And yet she didn't stop him—not when he claimed her mouth again; not when his hand went to her breast and felt for the hardened bud of her nipple; not when his other hand cupped her buttock and pulled her hard against his pelvis.

When he finally released her mouth, she was his. She gasped out a "yes" and, raising herself on her toes, finally planted a kiss just where she'd wanted to all along—at the base of his throat where his pulse beat as erratically as she was breathing.

Her kiss evoked a deep, groaning sound from him, unusually loud in the stillness of the evening, but no one came to investigate. Almost before she knew it, Deke had picked her up in his arms and stepped off the side of the porch, heading around the house, past the corral, and to the barn.

Never in her life had Sara felt so afraid of the unknown—or so safe. How could it be otherwise, when he held her against him so tightly that she could feel his heart beat against her ribs as she wound her arms around his neck.

Only a few steps around the corner, Deke stopped suddenly. Sara stopped her thought-drugged inventory of these new sensations of him against her and her against him, to look up into his face. She'd seen this look before—on the face of a raccoon that had been caught red-handed in her henhouse. Already dreading what she'd see, Sara turned her head in the direction of the horse corral, between the house and the barn, to look where Deke was staring so hard. Uh-oh. Stopped in their tracks and facing them not more than ten feet away were Ben Nighthorse and Coburn, both of whom looked as if they were trying to figure the best way around an enraged bull. Should they stick together or split up?

The standoff lasted only seconds, but Sara knew she'd never forget their faces. Or the fact that it obviously hadn't occurred to Deke to just put her down. Beyond embarrassed, she turned her face into Deke's shirt and squeezed her eyes shut. As if that were a signal, Deke started forward at the same moment she heard the footfalls of the other men, obviously walking toward them.

"Evening." Both men spoke as they drew even with Deke. Their voices contained not the least inflection or acknowledgement that they had seen a thing. Her ears and cheeks burning, Sara pressed further into Deke, willing herself invisible or, at the very least, tiny. Still, she heard the older men's hurrying footfalls, which clearly said neither man was of a mind to stop and chat.

"Evening," Deke answered, his stride also remaining unchanged. His voice, unbelievably formal and maybe a little too loud, rumbled against Sara's ear. "I believe I'll turn in now."

"Yes," Ben Nighthorse agreed, sounding as if he were addressing the king of England. "I believe it is a good time for bed. I trust you have everything you need."

"Why, yes, I do," Deke replied pleasantly. Marveling at her own newfound audacity in committing such an act, Sara nevertheless pinched the bounty hunter for his flippancy. His grunt of pain went unremarked by the men who sounded, to Sara's ear, as if they were tripping over each other or the step to get up on the front porch behind her and Deke.

Since Deke made no comment on their encounter with Ben and Coburn, she didn't either. Alone once again, the mood not completely shattered, Sara opened her eyes and looked around. "Where are you taking me?"

"To a place you've never been before." He was grinning down at her in a raw, sexual, piercing way that caught her breath in her lungs and completely restored the mood.

Sara was titillated all the way to her toes; the promise of naked pleasure, so long only the subject of wonder for her, melted some secret place down below and made her want to rip this man's clothes off him. It was too late for questions of right or wrong. In fact, the consequences of this act never entered her mind. There was only this night, this man. All she could think about was how finally she was going to get to rake her fingers down that abdomen of his—and find out where that thin line of black hair went. Feeling emboldened by his incautious words and wanting to hear more, she asked, "And where would that be?"

"The Nighthorses' barn," he answered, coming as close as Sara had ever heard him to a teasing manner.

Her laughing response, which brought up the heads of the horses in the corral to stare at them with much more benign expressions on their faces than Ben and Coburn had, also brought a shock with it—she was sharing a secret, intimate joke with Deke Bonner. And she liked it. Almost as much as she liked the feel of herself in his arms. Just then, he set her down on her feet inside the barn, but not before he kicked the door closed behind them.

When she looked around curiously, her eyes finally came to rest on a bed big enough for two—clean blankets over

sweet-smelling hay, her pillow lying at one end—which had
been made in an empty stall. She looked around for Deke;
he was latching the double barn doors. They were alone; the
animals were all turned out in the pasture. She was amused
to note that the barn was as neat and orderly as the house.

Just as Sara was beginning to have time to think, Deke
gently caught her from behind, his hands on her arms, and
planted a hot kiss where her neck met her shoulder. Her gasp
was immediately followed by a melting into him, her back
to his front, her eyes closed, her head resting against his
chest. She felt something hard press into her lower back, just
above her bottom. Must be his gun.

"What are you thinking?" he asked in a husky voice, all
the while exploring with his lips the side of her neck and
her ear. She'd never known that area of her body to be so
sensitive to touch that it could send shivers over her entire
body.

"I . . . I was thinking," she managed to rasp out, but just
barely because he'd slowly slid his hands around to her
breasts and was even now cupping their fullness. His fingers
nuzzled the hard buds that were her nipples, while his mouth
kept up its assault on her senses. Waves of knee-buckling
desire coursed over her, making her feel limp, but she tried
again. "I was thinking . . . there's only one bed. And my
pillow."

He chuckled low and deep in his chest. "All my doing
when you were feeding the babies. That's supposed to be
two beds, according to the two girls who brought the blankets
out here." He paused. "Do you mind that it's one?"

What could she say when his hands had moved to smooth
over her sides, accentuate her waist, and glide over her hips,
coming together over the mound of her desire? His ministrations brought a new awakening, a new sense of opening
down there that she'd never suspected was possible. "No,"
she groaned, meaning about the bed.

Deke chuckled again and turned her to him. "I want you
to know," he began, reaching out to smooth a silvery strand

of moonlight hair from her hot face, "that I didn't plan . . . what we're doing right now. I was going to let you have all that soft stuff and take my bedroll outside. It's still not too late to do that."

"No!"

He smiled down at her again and hugged her to him. She quickly returned his embrace, perhaps holding him tighter than he held her. Into her hair, he said, "I mean it, Sara. There'll be no going back from here. Are you sure you understand what's about to happen? Tomorrow will be too late—"

Her hands and her mouth cut his words off when she ripped open the front of his shirt, sending a button or two flying, and found that black, crisply curling hair and those hard, lean muscles she wanted so badly. A sudden fury, driven by her newly awakened desire as much as a need to feel every sense come to life after the death and violence and terrors of the gun battle that afternoon, seized her, and she pulled and tugged on his shirt to get it loose from his pants. She didn't struggle alone for more than a second or two before she heard Deke softly swear "Damn" and begin helping her.

When his shirt was off him, Sara stepped back, but only enough to have all of him in her sight. She couldn't seem to let go of him, though. None too gently, her hands moved up and down his arms, his neck, over the planes and ridges of his chest and abdomen. She was as amazed at the warm, hard feel of him and the sense of leashed power he exuded as she was by his absolute shuddering stillness under her touch. He was allowing her free range of his body. There was no way she couldn't notice the effect her hands and her gaze were having on him. She now knew that hadn't been his gun that had pressed into her back; he wasn't wearing his gun. But he was wearing the very obvious evidence of the length and depth of his desire for her.

She could stand no more. If he didn't touch her soon . . . As if he could read her mind—or the raging fire in her that

her eyes just had to be reflecting—Deke took a step forward
to claim her. But he was more gentle with her than she'd
been with him, for he showed her the power and the beauty
of going slow by undoing each small button that held her
shirt closed; Sara bit at her bottom lip every time his fingers
brushed her flesh or rubbed over her thin camisole. Finally
the shirt was loose and off. He did move a little quicker when
it came to her split skirt, but still he peeled it off her as if it
was skin. No wonder snakes molted if it felt this good.

He then urged her to sit down on the makeshift bed, which
she did obediently. He knelt in front of her; off came her
boots and hose. She had on only her camisole and thin drawers. That was when shyness set in. Some of the heat that had
to be coloring her cheeks now came from innocent maid-
enliness. And Deke seemed to realize that, seemed to know
her need for reassurance at just this point.

He tucked his index finger under her chin to raise her gaze
to his. The most tender smile she'd ever seen him wear rode
on his lips. Ohh, his lips . . .

"Sara, you're the most beautiful woman I have ever seen.
Ever. And I'm not just saying that because I have you here
in a bed. I have thought that from the first moment I saw
you on your own front porch in Plains, Kansas."

"So are you," she said, using her last vestige of a girlish
voice and tugging free of his hold on her chin to look down.
Not knowing what to do next, or indeed what came next, she
picked at a thread in the soft blanket under her.

His soft laugh brought her widened eyes up. What had she
said that was so funny?

"You honestly think I'm the most beautiful woman
you've ever seen?" he said, his wide smile revealing straight,
white teeth.

"What? No! Man! You're the most handsome man I've
ever seen. And I've seen a lot of men—"

"Have you now?"

She stopped her babbling attempt to correct her first mis-
statement. "I mean, just their faces. Not their—"

He put a finger to her lips to shush her. "I get your point."

And then it was funny again, and they shared another laugh, another intimate secret, another kiss, with Deke still kneeling in front of her, and words were unnecessary. Then he sat down by her and removed his boots; Sara would have liked to help him, but her trembling innocence still held her immobile. Watching him undress was no less pleasurable and no less a revelation to her still-girlish sensibilities. Barefooted, he stood up, towering over her, and slowly undid his belt. Leaving the ends of it hanging loosely to either side of the opening, he unbuttoned that, too, all the while keeping his eyes on Sara's face. She prayed she wasn't wearing that look of almost worshipful begging on it that she'd seen on children's faces when they wanted a treat. But then she didn't care if she was; it was how she felt, and she wouldn't apologize.

Then he slid his pants off his hips and down his legs with one athletic gesture; she noticed that his ridged abdomen sucked in with his graceful movement. She also noticed that he was built as powerfully as a wild stallion; every muscle on him showed its clearly defined ridge or line that bespoke its function. And he gleamed with a light of his own, framed as he was by the row of open windows behind him that allowed the moonlight to filter through the barn and somehow make this rough, crude structure seem like a magical place. Sara suspected it always would be just that, too—in her mind, at least.

When Deke straightened up, she caught her breath at the sight of his barely restrained erection under his close-fitting thin drawers. Deke did not give her time to dwell on it, but immediately came to her and pulled her up to him. "Come on. There's a stream that runs out back of the barn. I think it's deep enough to wash in."

Sara let her breath out. "Oh, good. I was so afraid to tell you that I feel grimy from the day. I don't want you to think I smell."

"I don't." He laughed, pulling her along behind him, stopping only to pick up a length of toweling and a piece of soap that he must have gotten from Etheline or one of the kids earlier. "At least not any more than I do."

She hit at his back, evincing a yelp from him as he opened a small door at the back of the barn. And sure enough, once they'd slipped through it, there was a gurgling stream lit perfectly for them by that bright moon which also revealed a small stand of peachleaf willows surrounding the water, making this area a secluded but brightly lit glen.

Picking their way carefully through the scrubby undergrowth, her hand still in his, they melted into the cool water with sighs of welcome. A scene flashed through Sara's mind of the first time she'd been in her drawers and in deep water with Deke Bonner—just after the buffalo stampede at the Cimarron River. But the vision fled when he turned to her, took her other hand in his, and floated backwards, pulling her with him until she was lying on top of him but not weighing him down, thanks to the buoyancy of the water.

Sliding along the length of him like that until her body was lying over his made Sara forget any maidenly misgivings she might have had. Her hardened nipples dragged over his chest as he captured her by her waist and stood them both on their feet. Her senses awake and eager for every new sensation, she even relished the squishy, muddy feel of the stream bottom under her feet. Something about her face must have been funny because Deke stepped back from her, laughed low in his throat, and sluiced a small, quick spray of water with his hand toward her.

It hit her just below her neck. "What?"

"Nothing. You're just enjoying the hell out of this, aren't you?"

"Aren't I supposed to?" she countered.

"Yeah. Yeah, you are. I just suspected you might—I don't know, change your mind."

Feeling ever so slightly evil, Sara teased, "And if I do?"

Deke grinned a heart-lurching smile. "If you think you're

going to at all, please do it now while I'm in this cold water.''

Sara frowned. ''Why?''

Now he threw his head back and laughed out loud. Sara knew she should have shushed him before he brought the entire Nighthorse household down on them, but she just couldn't. The sound of his lightheartedness, so unexpected, so endearing, was too wonderful to interrupt. Even if it was at her expense.

''Sara Dalton, you are priceless,'' Deke complimented her, tears of laughter squeezing out at the corners of his eyes.

''Well . . . good,'' she came back lamely, having no idea what she'd said. But if she made him happy . . .

''Come here,'' he said, reaching out for her and pulling her close to him.

Sara had no idea what to think when he put his other hand under the water and fiddled with something on himself. Her slightly embarrassed, slightly scandalized reaction opened her eyes and her mouth.

''The soap,'' he said, holding it up triumphantly. ''I put it in the waistband of my drawers.'' There was no way in hell Deke Bonner could look innocent after so cheap a trick. But he tried.

''You lowdown—'' It was his turn to get splashed.

He didn't even bother to brush the water out of his face while he laughed at her. ''Come on, Sara, you can tell me. What'd you think I was doing?''

Mortified beyond words, Sara pulled away from him, terrified that she would break out in a naughty giggle. ''Stop it, Deke Bonner! Let go of me!'' she shrieked instead, furiously trying to get out of the water.

''Not on your life, woman—at least not until I scrub you down good, get the trail dust off you. I like my women clean.''

Sara turned back to him and splashed him again. ''I'm not your woman. Quit saying that.''

He leered right into her face. "You're getting ready to be."

With a quick grabbing motion, he had a firm hold on her and began very impersonally and very industriously washing her all over, right through her camisole and drawers. "Kill two birds with one stone," he said. He even dragged her to a shallower part of the water to get at her bottom and her legs. He worked so efficiently that Sara had no time to be embarrassed. But she did wonder . . . Using her most droll tone of voice, she commented, "You seem to be really good at this. Do you do it often?"

Deke stopped long enough to straighten up and wipe at his nose with a soap-flecked forearm. "Every chance I get," he assured her.

"You are not a nice man."

"Never said I was," he agreed. The washing continued. Sara gave up talking to him and allowed him his fun. Through with her body, he ordered her to a floating position in the water; when she had complied, he thoroughly, and a little more lovingly, washed her hair. His strong hands working her scalp nearly put her to sleep right there in the water. But there was apparently no rest for the weary or the contented when Deke Bonner was on the job, for he righted her with military precision and, to her shocked dismay, handed her the soap.

"You want me to—"

"I most certainly do."

"But I can't. I never—"

"This is a night for firsts. Here's your next first."

Before she could protest further, Deke took her hand that held the soap and put it to his chest; he rubbed her hand in small, slow circles, around and around, and Sara picked up the motion on her own, a sense of wonder propelling her movements. He really was the most handsome man she'd ever seen. She looked him all over, following the path of her hands, delighting in every new and unexplored part of him as she came to it.

Feeling bold, but not bold enough to look him in the face yet for fear of breaking her trance and becoming self-conscious, she even returned his favor by bending down to kill his other bird with her one stone—washing the drawers that skinned over his hips and thighs. And then her eyes were caught by—oh . . . that was what he'd meant about cold water. Her cheeks flamed, as much at her own naivete of a few minutes ago as at the part of him she was just now washing. That area only needed a quick, light touch, she determined, striving for industriousness now, which was not lost on the scoundrel who was receiving her ministrations. His grunt of laughter earned him a smack to his rock-hard thigh.

"Ouch," he said. But she didn't believe it. There was no way anything she could do to him could hurt him physically. Then it struck her, and stopped her hands momentarily. Maybe not physically; there was no way her strength could ever be a match for his. But what about emotionally? What about his heart? Couldn't caring for her get him killed at Robber's Cave? Wasn't he leaving himself open to a much more tremendous hurt by their impending intimacy than even she was? Wasn't he the one who was so hopelessly outnumbered?

She looked up the length of him until she could see into his eyes, feeling for the first time the possibility of this tall, strong, beautiful man's death at her kin's hands. He looked very solemnly back at her; he couldn't know what she was thinking, so he just had to be reacting to her serious face. And he just stood there, waiting for her to work out whatever it was she was feeling. His black eyes, now as dark and as liquid as their watery habitat, pierced through to her very soul. Sudden tears pricked her eyes, which Sara tried her best to blink away. But a tiny sniff escaped her; in its wake followed the salty tears.

Then Deke was reaching down to her and pulling her to his chest. That one unspoken but understanding act provoked hysterical sobs from her; she clung to him as tightly as she'd ever clung to anything in her life. She knew, but couldn't help, that her fingers had curled slightly, pressing her nails into the skin of his back. He didn't protest; he merely kissed her forehead and rubbed her hair. When the flood of emotion began to abate, Sara realized that he'd been talking to her in a low, soothing tone, perhaps the entire time she'd been crying.

"I can't," she gasped out. "I can't. Oh God, Deke, I can't let you do this."

"Shh, Sara, shhh," he said into her hair. "I know. And it's going to be all right. I swear to you. Somehow, I promise you, I will make it all right. No matter what it takes."

Chapter Twelve

That night, Deke ended up holding Sara. Just holding her, nothing more. He was beginning to learn that after every storm of tears she endured, she slept for hours. She sure cried a lot for such a self-professed tough woman. Big tough woman; that thought brought a smile to his face. She had intended going across Indian Territory by herself, armed with her pillow, some damned map, a Spencer rifle, and a fragile little mare named Cinnamon, for God's sake—and take on the murdering, thieving bastards, including her kin, at Robber's Cave, providing she made it that far by herself. And she even bested him, Deke Bonner, in some battle she waged in her head almost daily. But look at her now.

He looked over at her, illuminated by the bright moonlight. Like a balled-up kitten, she lay curled against his side on their bed of straw and blankets in the barn, her head resting in the crook of his shoulder and arm, her long hair a soft cloud fanning out around him and her, her arm draped over him. Deke lay on his back, one arm around her, his

117

other hand stroking the soft flesh of her forearm as it rested on his abdomen.

Bonner, you're a walking dead man, he admonished himself, quirking his mouth up to laugh at himself. This girl with her silver hair, and comb and brush set to match, was going to be the death of him. He knew that in his heart. Hadn't she already made him lose his edge? His deep sigh expanded his chest wall, causing Sara to shift and resettle herself in her sleep even more firmly against his side. Deke rolled his eyes when he felt her firm breasts press into his ribs. Squeezing his eyes shut, he put his forearm over them, steeling himself against his rising desire with a few choice but raw phrases he'd learned in the war. Being a gentleman and a savior of young women from their own misguided missions also pretty much meant being a monk, he realized. But tell it to his hard erection which, though restrained by his drawers, still strained upwards toward Sara. Well, hell, that was one part of him that knew what it wanted.

But Deke couldn't let himself off that easily. His other head knew what it wanted, too—and she was lying right next to him. He looked over at her and suddenly wanted out of his skin. For the first time in his life, he wanted to be someone other than Deke Bonner, Union Army spy, bounty hunter and avenger of his family's deaths. Always before, he'd had a clear sense of purpose and of himself. . . .

But that was before Sara Dalton entered his life with her waves of silvery hair, her crazy but considerable bravery, her misdirected loyalty to a brother and cousins who were no more than common desperadoes. Her tantalizing curves were meant for a man's pleasure, like her womanly softness and her motherly tenderness—even her silly bed gowns, one of which she had on now. All of it. All of her—that was what he wanted. Everything about her. Even her tears and her temper. Yes, even that misguided loyalty. After all, loyalty to family was definitely something he could understand; in fact, it was what drove him. How could he fault her for that? Hell, he loved her for it.

He what? His start of shock at his own turn of thought nearly jerked him upright. What the hell was he thinking? He didn't love her. Sara chose right then to mumble and frown in her sleep; she unconsciously gathered him back to her, draping her firm, slim thigh over one of his. Deke looked at her pressed to his side, and laid his head down with a resounding thump. He didn't love her. It was becoming a litany, repeated each time with more and more self-convincing emphasis. He didn't love her.

Then why did he feel the sudden need to jump up, get dressed, saddle his buckskin, and get the hell away from here? If he had a lick of sense, that was exactly what he would do. He toyed with that idea for a moment, mentally seeing himself riding off alone before anyone was awake. But even in his mind, he saw himself keep looking back . . . and then reining in his horse and turning around. Dammit!

He couldn't do it. Numb, Deke lay unmoving, letting the sobering wash of acknowledgement run over his body. He stared unblinkingly up at the rough beams of the barn's crude roof while his thoughts crystalized. Finally, he admitted it to himself—to stay here, to continue on his present course, the one in his heart as much as the one over land, was certain death for him. But after all, he'd made Sara Dalton a promise to make everything all right for her. He'd chosen his destiny. With acceptance came weariness; Deke rubbed a hand over the straight line of his mouth and the angle of his chin, then put his arms firmly around Sara, resting his jaw against the sweet-smelling softness of her clean hair—hair that he'd washed himself—and closed his eyes. His last thought, before sleep claimed him, was "Bonner, you're a dead man."

"I know, Etheline, there's nothing I'd like more, either, than to stay for a few days. But I can't. I have to go. I just want you to know, I will never forget your kindnesses to us. And thanks for this hat."

Etheline reached a hand up to take Sara's as she sat atop Cinnamon; she spoke in a conspiratorial whisper, all the time cutting her eyes over to Deke Bonner, astride his buckskin and looking mighty peevish. "You don't have to thank me; the sun can be mighty cruel. And I reckon you're right, Sara, about movin' on. Now, I don't mean to hold you up none, but I just want to wish you the best of luck in finding your kin. And—and to tell you that I'll be praying that your troubles all work out for the best, the Good Lord willing."

Sara, the incongruous, red-flowered sunbonnet perched on her head, felt a sudden and intense warmth for this very ugly woman with the very beautiful soul and the deep faith. She squeezed her new friend's hand, wondering in her heart if she'd ever see her again. "Thank you, Etheline. For everything. Kiss those babies for me."

Etheline, tears in her eyes, nodded and then stepped back, assuming a brisk, motherly stance. She eyed her happy brood and began giving orders. "Now, all you kids step back. Get out of the way. Ben, get James over here; he'll likely get under the horses' feet."

She then called after Coburn as the three riders started to move off. "Now, Coburn, you get yourself on back by here real soon, so's we can know you're alive. You hear me?"

Coburn turned a bit in his saddle and waved his acknowledgement. Sara looked back, too; the Nighthorses, except Ben, who maintained his calm dignity, were all waving and whooping just as they had yesterday evening when she, Deke, and Coburn had ridden up. Sara smiled and waved back at them one last time. She would miss them; and she was terribly grateful that neither Ben nor Coburn had mentioned meeting her and Deke last night when she'd been in Deke's arms as they'd headed for the barn. God alone, since the men weren't talking, knew what they must think.

When she righted herself in her saddle, she looked over at Deke. He hadn't looked back—only straight ahead at the trail in front of them. She couldn't quite square him today with the tender man who'd held her all night and who had kissed away her tears. He acted as if last night hadn't happened at all. Had he already forgotten his promise to her to make everything right? Not that she would hold him to it; how could she? Sara sighed; this morning he was grim, giving only terse answers to any questions asked him. She had no idea what could be wrong this morning that hadn't been wrong yesterday, so she just attributed his mood to his "trail temper."

Beyond that, though, she didn't suppose she could blame him in the least for his mood; after all, last night certainly hadn't turned out the way he had so obviously hoped it would. Sara's cheeks flamed at the memory of her own wantonness—and then at her flood of tears. No, it hadn't turned out as she'd wanted it to, either. Yes, her virginity was still intact, but now her heart was in danger of being broken, no matter the outcome of their journey. For whether her kin or Deke Bonner were left standing at the end of this journey, she, Sara Dalton, would lose. Not that she was responsible for Deke being here; he had his own mission. But that didn't stop her from worrying, even when she had too much else to worry about already.

She'd given her promise to her dying mother that she'd bring Jim, Travis, and Cody home. And nothing or no one was going to stop her—not even Deke Bonner. To go home without them, to just give up, was not something she would even consider. She'd promised. Still, she wished with all her heart that Deke would just turn his horse around and ride away, that he'd say the bounty meant nothing to him. Sara's stomach quaked at the thought of never seeing Deke again, but at least he'd be safe, and that was quickly becoming of more importance to her than she was willing to admit.

And somehow, Ben Nighthorse had known that, too. His last words to her, spoken as she'd saddled Cinnamon this morning, still rang in her ears: "Many things will come to pass on this long journey of yours. I have seen them. You will need the strength and the great heart of one other than yourself. You must, too, listen to your own heart."

She'd wanted to question Ben, to beg him to tell her what he'd seen. To tell her, just as Deke had promised her, that

everything would be all right. But she knew better. Ben
would keep his visions to himself. Besides, to know the future, to know what lay at the end of her journey, could be
worse than knowing the past and the present. But she was
sure of one thing—''the strength and the great heart of one
other than herself'' had to mean Deke's. For perhaps the
thousandth time, Sara wondered if they'd both be alive when
all this was over.

And so the morning wore on for Sara. Sensing that Deke
and Coburn were both in as thoughtful a mood as she was,
she remained silent and gave herself up to the sheer enjoyment of the warm morning breeze that brushed the sky a
deeper blue. She looked around her, peering out at the world
from the depths of her wide-brimmed sunbonnet, feeling ridiculous but shaded. The ground they were covering was flat
and rocky, but it was softened by tall, undulating buffalo
grass and countless wildflowers of red, yellow, purple, and
blue that waved merrily at them as they plodded past. Sara
felt an uplifting of her spirits, despite herself. Only the hardest heart could remain glum with such natural beauty providing a feast for the senses. She had a sudden urge, one she
didn't give in to, to lift her arms up to the sky and shout her
thanks to the heavens. She did, however, allow herself a carefree smile and a deep breath of dewy morning air.

She looked over at Coburn, who was smiling at her.
''Feels good, don't it? Hang onto that 'cause not more than
two to three days away, we're goin' to run into where the
Beaver River meets the North Canadian. That's Cheyenne
and Arapaho land. If a fella was of a mind to, he could follow
that most of the way before dropping on down to the Choctaw Nation and over to Robber's Cave. Now don't look so
at me. 'Tweren't hard to figure out: You're a Dalton a-
huntin' for yer kin. Ain't no secret—at least in these parts—
that they's a-holed up there. So now, like I was sayin', take
up the South Canadian and you can count on the comfortin'
presence of army forts through Injun lands, mostly contrary
Seminoles and Chickasaw there.''

Sara looked at Deke, who returned her stare, confirming that there was no use denying to Coburn what he already knew. Deke asked him, "Where are you headed from here?"

"Well, I ain't ridin' off from you jist yet—that is, if'n you don't mind the company—but I reckon I got to get on over to a certain Cheyenne settlement up a ways in the Cherokee Outlet. There's a little squaw there that gets a might upset if'n I don't show up regular-like."

Sara smiled a secret smile, envying Coburn his simple vagabond life. She couldn't remember a time, since after the War Between the States began, when her life had not been fraught with worry and tangles of one sort or another. But she supposed Coburn's was, too; something had to have driven him to a life of wandering the lawless Indian Territory. And Deke Bonner's—what drove him? Sara didn't realize she was staring so hard at Deke until he called her on it.

"Did I sprout horns, Sara?"

His voice was not the least bit amused. He was acting as if she and Coburn were an imposition on his time. Well, she supposed they were, but it still made her snappish. "No," she answered in kind, "but if you did, who among us would be surprised?"

"Not this again," Coburn muttered. But Sara couldn't know if he meant her and Deke's baiting of each other or his Jezebel's stopping, for the second time this morning, to relieve herself mightily. That put him a few yards behind them. The three had been riding with Coburn in the middle, but now Deke swung his buckskin over to ride beside Cinnamon and Sara.

"Let me see that map of yours," he said without preamble.

Sara gave up her inventory of his strong, virile features under his black Stetson, a habit so automatic to her now that it was a second or two before she could recover and answer him, giving exact, pointed emphasis to each of her words. "I am not—*not*—going to show you my map."

"Dammit, Sara, I'm thinking of you. The only reason I want to see it is to see the route your brother mapped out for you. It's probably not only the quickest way, but it will also be the safest."

She hadn't thought about that, but still she couldn't believe his gall; did he think she was that naive—that besotted with him—that she would just docilely hand her precious map over? "And that, Deke Bonner, is the exact reason why I will not let you see it."

He rubbed a large, well-formed hand over his mouth and chin, but even that gesture did not quite hide his muttered oaths. Sara waited him out, giving him look for look and even pulling herself up taller in her saddle when he did the same in his.

"Fine," he practically bellowed, startling Cinnamon into a tight little dance. "Then would you, Miss Dalton, be so kind as to look at the damned thing yourself and tell me which route *you'd* take if you were alone?"

Sara calmed Cinnamon with pats and soft words, then shot Deke Bonner a hot look and said, very sweetly, "Of course, Mr. Bonner. But I thought you knew your way through Indian Territory. You've seemed to know, anyway, at least up to this point. You certainly haven't needed any directions from me."

"And I still wouldn't—if I weren't with you. By myself, I would travel much faster and in a more direct line, I assure you."

Glad as she was at his revelation that she was indeed slowing him down in his mission to kill her brother and cousins, Sara couldn't resist baiting him. "Well, who's stopping you? Go ahead."

Deke leaned toward her threateningly. "Don't tempt me, Sara Dalton. Don't tempt me. Now, will you, or will you not, make this misbegotten ride easier on yourself by looking at that damned precious map yourself—since you don't trust me with it—and tell me the route Jim Dalton mapped out for you?"

That was the first time Deke had used her brother's name. Maybe she could dare to hope that Deke was beginning to see her kin as people instead of as rewards. Still, her doubts ran deep. "I will—but only if you'll move away while I do."

Her sweetly sarcastic expression didn't last long as she watched the effect of her words on the bounty hunter. Deke turned red from the neck up, like water in a new well. She fully expected his black Stetson to fly off the top of his head to give vent to the steam that had to be building up for an explosion. Instead, he dug his heels into his buckskin's flanks; the huge stallion responded with an explosive leap that catapulted him into a headlong gallop at a ground-pounding pace that suited his rider's fury. The powerful steed, given his head on a bright, clear, not yet suffocatingly hot morning, announced his pleasure with flying mane and tail. In only a moment he was much farther away than Sara would have believed possible.

As she watched in stunned silence, she heard Coburn, off to her right now, say, "What got into him?"

Sara looked at the Indian trader, eyed his rifle held at the ready, his face red under his floppy-brimmed hat, and said dryly, "You can put the gun away, Coburn." She added, when he continued to stare uncertainly at her, "He asked to see my map."

"Oh." He appeared to think on that for a moment or two, all the while giving his pommel a look as if he'd just now realized he had one. He then looked up to stare straight ahead at Deke and his horse disappearing over a hill. Finally, he looked over at Sara. "For the sake of the argument, I'm just goin' to pertend like I have the slightest idea what you're talking about."

He replaced the rifle in its leather strap on his saddle and spoke to his nodding old nag, patting her thin neck. "Easy there, Jezebel. Easy, girl. There ain't nothing to trouble yourself. Now don't go gettin' all riled. Settle down now, that's right. Careful now or you'll buck me clean off."

Sara looked away to keep from laughing out loud; Jezebel

was asleep, if she was anything. Sara finally had to hold her bottom lip firmly between her teeth to kill her mirth. When she could keep a straight face, she turned back to Coburn to try to explain. "I told him he had to move away while I looked at my map."

Coburn nodded at her, keeping an appropriately serious look on his ruddy, friendly face. Then, as if at a silent command, they both turned their heads to look off into the distance, where Deke and his horse were quickly becoming dots on the horizon.

Coburn took his hat off to scratch his head and then, replacing his hat, he turned to her, all earnestness in his blue eyes, his head tilted back slightly to peer at her from under the low brim of his hat. "You know," he began slowly, "if I was a bettin' man, I'd bet he's about far enough away so's it'd be safe for you to peek at your map. You reckon?"

A gale of laughter wanted very badly out of Sara's lungs and throat, but she forced it back down with a valiant, not completely silent struggle. Reining Cinnamon to a stop and standing in her stirrups, she pretended to judge the distance between them and Deke. "Ohh," she drew out finally, moving her head from side to side as if trying to get a better angle on the view, "I suppose so."

She sat back down on her saddle and looked over at Coburn. They both exploded with loud barks of laughter at the same time and leaned over their mounts' necks, trying to save their cramping stomach muscles. Sara could stay on Cinnamon no longer; weak with laughter, hot from the physical exertion of her hilarity, she slid off Cinnamon to sit in a limp heap on the hard earth. She could barely keep the reins in her hands. All she needed was for Cinnamon to bolt—and for Deke to have to chase her down yet again.

Another seizure of laughter took hold of her with that thought. She could just imagine his face! Wiping at her eyes with the backs of her hands, she looked under Cinnamon's belly and saw, on the other side of Jezebel's sagging middle, Coburn sitting on the ground and holding his sides as he pitched forward in the throes of a fresh laughing spasm.

And then that was too, too funny. Sara pitched backwards, hit her head too hard on the packed ground, yelped, and gave vent with laughter to every bit of anger, fear, and tension she'd felt since 1861. From the sounds coming from two horse bellies to her right, Coburn was having a high old time, too.

Sara lay there, her hands folded over her middle, her knees bent, the storm abating and then erupting in a staccato set of giggles every now and then, only to hear her name being called out in a rough voice. "Sara!"

She looked to her right. "What?"

"I ain't going to be able to git up on my own."

She turned on her side. "You're not?" Even that was incredibly funny for some reason.

To Coburn too, whose problem it was. "I got a bum leg." They both screamed out afresh at this bad news. Sara rolled back over onto her back.

"Sara!"

She looked back over at Coburn.

"You reckon Deke's coming back a-tall?"

"Oh, God," she drawled, trying to regain control of herself. "I don't know." She forced herself to sit up and look around, but mostly ahead. She lay back down and looked over at Coburn, who really was framed beautifully beneath Jezebel's belly. "I don't think so. I don't see him anywhere."

"I see," Coburn said, peering at her with his head lowered almost to his shoulders—Jezebel's belly really did have a bad sag in it. "Well, then, how do you feel about homesteadin'—oh, I don't know, say right about here?" He pointed to the ground directly under his backside.

That did it for Sara. Her bladder could stand no more jokes. She jumped up, let loose of Cinnamon's reins, commanded the startled horse to "stay!" and took off for a stand of scrub oaks mercifully over to her left. Never before had she undressed so quickly, or relieved herself so violently, aided as she was by her contracting muscles as she let loose what she hoped was her last peal of laughter.

And never before had she gotten dressed so quickly as when she heard Deke's voice. He sounded mad. "What in the hell is going on here? Where's Sara? Coburn, are you hurt? No? Then what the hell are you doing sitting on the ground? Sara! Where in the hell are you, dammit? And where's Cinnamon? If I have to chase down that damned mare one more time—Sara!"

Sara stepped out from behind the trees, taking in the scene before her, but especially the dust still settling from where Deke had reined in his sweat-flecked and blowing stallion. She hurriedly put the finishing touches to her toilette and walked briskly toward the towering figure of the angry bounty hunter, whose back was to her. A few feet away from him, she announced her presence with, "How'd you get back here so quickly?" There was genuine respect in her voice for this particular feat of his. "I knew that buckskin was fast, but—"

The look on his face when he whirled around at the sound of her voice stopped Sara as surely as if she'd met with a wall. Was that relief she was seeing, or was he getting ready to go for his gun? Could be both: relief that she was close at hand so he could shoot her and get on with his life. Suddenly unsure of how to proceed, she cut her gaze over to Coburn, still seated on the ground and acting as if he had the best seat in the house for this spectacle. No help from that quarter. Sara looked back at the bounty hunter.

He'd tucked his thumbs in his gunbelt and adopted the forbidding glare that more usually described his features. "How'd I get back so quickly? I cut around through the hills and circled back, right on your flank." He paused, staring accusingly at her. Sara had a sinking feeling in the pit of her stomach. "For only a few minutes at a time were you ever out of my eyesight when a hill or some trees blocked my sight of you. And for all the attention you two were paying, I could have killed you both—if that had been my intention—before you ever knew what hit you. Now, where the hell were you just now?''

Though tremendously relieved to hear that wasn't his intention, Sara knew he was right. Yet another reminder that she needed him. Now how would she explain why Coburn was on the ground and why Cinnamon, the poor little thing, was nowhere to be seen? Their laughter must have seemed to be at Deke's expense, she mused, all the while keeping her eyes on his itchy trigger finger. Right now it didn't seem so funny, what with him being so close. ''Well, I had to go . . .'' She waved her hand vaguely in the direction of the trees from which she'd just emerged. ''You know.''

Deke followed her vague gesture with his hawkish glare, looking intently at the trees as if they held the answer to some big mystery. He looked back at her. Sara wondered if Coburn would come to her aid if Deke decided to choke the life out of her right then and there.

''That doesn't explain Coburn being on the ground.''

Sara was stuck now; she bit at her bottom lip and shifted her weight from foot to foot. She tried to be angry at his treating her like a bad little girl caught by her father in some lie; after all, she was a twenty-four-year-old woman. But her response was, ''Why don't you ask Coburn?''

That one's glare told her what she already knew—she was a traitor. She died the thousand deaths of a coward when Deke narrowed his eyes at her and then walked over to the heavyset older man, who sat with little dignity in the dirt, his legs bent sideways and his hands clasping his boot-covered ankles, and began pulling him upright, an awkward scene at best, despite Deke's considerable strength.

''What happened here, Coburn?'' the bounty hunter persisted mulishly—in Sara's opinion—once he had the old Indian trader vertical again.

Coburn brushed himself off, righted his hat, and squared his dignity. Then he hooked his thumbs into his front pockets and told what Sara figured was the biggest, and probably the most obvious, lie of his life. ''Why, that Jezebel got all riled and bucked me off. She musta seen a rattlesnake . . . or some-thin'.''

"Or something," Deke commented dryly.

Not knowing when to quit, Coburn went on. "That snake musta spooked Cinnamon, most likely."

"Most likely."

She and Coburn were losing badly. And the day wasn't getting any cooler there under Deke's direct, single-minded glare, no less intense than the August sun. Apparently Coburn was as reluctant as she was to tell Deke they'd been laughing at him. At about the point when Sara wished some-body would just shoot somebody else, anything for some relief, the stalemate ended when Cinnamon trotted up, thus giving them all something to be happy about and to remark on. At least Sara and Coburn were as happy and chattery as if Cinnamon were Santa Claus on Christmas morning. But Deke—muttering under his breath something about "in all my born days . . ."—just shook his head and went to tend his horse.

While Coburn drank his fill of water from his canteen, Sara did the same from hers, even sparing her little mare a bit of the wetness. She then stood patting Cinnamon and covertly watching Deke's tending of his stallion, feeling no small dose of pure feminine appreciation for his male form, including the play of his powerful muscles as he uncinched the saddle, hefted it off, and laid it on the ground, following that with the woven saddle blanket. His stretching and bend-ing tautened his denims; his rubbing of the buckskin's coat with literally the shirt off his back left him bare from the waist up. His motions dried Sara's mouth. She reached for her canteen again, never taking her eyes off the pleasing spectacle that was Deke, and very absentmindedly took a long swig of the tepid water.

She knew firsthand how strong and yet how tender those hands were. Desire, seemingly never more deep than just under the skin of her consciousness since she'd met this hard, handsome man, coiled in her belly. Her knees weakened; she held tightly to a handful of Cinnamon's mane for support. She even forgot to be angry with the bounty hunter for acting as if he were a scolding father, and she and Coburn recalcitrant children. Or even for asking to see her map.

The map.

As if she'd communicated those two words to Deke's brain, his hands stilled and he turned to face her. Sara's mouth was really dry now.

"Sara," he called out, sounding one heck of a lot more benevolent than he would sound in a second or two. "What route should we take from here, according to your map?"

Chapter Thirteen

Deke couldn't believe it: She hadn't even looked at the map yet. She didn't have to tell him that; it was evident on her face. If he had an ounce of sense, he'd get the damned thing out of her saddlebags himself, despite her protests. But he just wasn't capable of taking from her anything she held sacred. Having to admit that to himself did nothing to improve his mood as he stood there staring at her. He was as weak as a newborn puppy when it came to Sara Dalton. He ought to be flat mad at her, ought to just . . .

Finished with staring a hole through the most exasperating female he'd ever met—or had ever wanted so completely— he turned back around and continued rubbing down his horse. It was only when the stallion stamped a foot and tossed his head in protest that Deke realized how much abrupt vigor he'd brought to the task. With a whispered ''Whoa there, big fella; easy,'' which was as close to actually talking to, much less apologizing to, his mount as he had ever come, Deke rubbed more gently and with longer strokes.

One day he'd just have to name the damned buckskin—especially if he was going to continue this new habit of talking to it. That damned woman was driving him to befriend his horse. Just like Coburn and Jezebel. He could see his future now; he'd be out in some godforsaken hellhole of the West and babbling to his horse, wondering what had gone wrong with his life.

All of a sudden, he felt a tapping on his bare, sun-warmed shoulder. Turning around, his shirt still in his hand, he looked down into the bonnet-covered head of Sara Dalton. As near as he could tell, what with her face being hidden by that damned red, ridiculous bonnet Etheline Nighthorse had given her, she was looking at his chest. The bonnet had to go. He liked to see his quarry's eyes.

"What, Sara?" He'd intended the exasperation that he heard in his voice. He needed to hang on to that hard emotion toward her, because his heart wanted desperately to feel something akin to tenderness for her effort to please him. She'd tried to cover her hair under the bonnet, but long silvery-blond strands of it hung from every part of the bonnet that it possibly could. There was just too much hair.

"Here." She held out a folded square of paper.

Deke's heart lurched. That could not be the holy map.

"You look at it. I can't make heads or tails of it."

He knew better; she'd consulted it a hundred times that he'd seen, and probably countless times that he hadn't seen. She knew that map as well as she knew the contours of his chest. Clearing his throat and his thoughts, Deke surprised them both by saying, "No. Have Coburn look at it. He knows this area better than I do."

Now she looked up at him, her sweet face all but lost in the bonnet and the veil her escaping hair provided. Her bottom lip was poked out slightly. "I want you to look at it."

Deke looked away, took a deep breath, and returned to the fray. Looking into her black eyes, so dark even in her tanned face, he argued, "Why me? Why now?"

She dropped her arm and looked at her boots. "Last night

you said I had to trust somebody. You also said there was no one but you."

Deke's heart went out to her; all she had to do was grab it. He also put a hand out to her, touching her arm.

She didn't offer the map again; instead, she looked up at him, a pinched, sorrowful look on her little-girl face. "Please, Deke. My mother is dying. Help me."

Deke squared his jaw and clamped down on his back teeth. He felt his cheek twitch, his eyes narrow. In the usual course of events, this meant he was angry or readying for a gun battle. But not this time. This time he was trying to unclog the emotion that wrenched at his gut . . . and his heart. She hardly ever mentioned her mother, so sometimes he forgot the tragedy in her life that made this dangerous trip of life-and-death importance to her.

"Give me your map, Sara," he said softly, at last accepting her offer of trust. For now.

Slowly she brought her hand back up and held out the map. Deke took it with just as much reverence as it was presented, fully aware of the ramifications of this act. In some indefinable way, once he read her map, he was on her side. After tossing his shirt over one shoulder, he unfolded the map and held it down for her to be able to see it too. She stepped around to stand at his side and peer over his arm as he read it. The moment was so very fragile, but still Deke wanted to grab her to him and protect her from all of life's hurts. But he couldn't, so he didn't.

"Well," he finally said after a close read of the map, which to his eyes contained no deep, dark secret information that he could ascertain, "the South Canadian River it is."

"Where?" Sara asked, looking first up at him, nearly hitting Deke's chin with the elongated brim of her bonnet, then down again at the map.

"Right there," he answered, pointing to a squiggly east-west line that ran across the map. "That's the South Canadian. See? Here's the army camps Coburn mentioned. I figure we can still follow the North Canadian for a ways, at least until we get to Chisholm's. And there we can drop down to the South Canadian River.''

Sara nodded her agreement, then looked back up at Deke, as if waiting for him to comment on something.

"What?'' He really had no idea.

She quirked as if she was disgusted. "Do you see now why I didn't want you to see my map?''

He looked at it again, closely. He looked up, stalling, found Coburn, who was no help, dozing under a willow. Finally, he was forced to look down at Sara and admit his ignorance. "Sara, I don't see a thing unusual or precious on this map. Certainly nothing that should have gotten me attacked last night just for holding your saddlebags. All I see are some lines, some instructions to you, and an X that marks the Robber's Cave area.'' He shrugged his shoulders helplessly.

She really huffed out her disgust this time. "That's it, Deke Bonner—it's as plain as the nose on your face. The X! Look at it. That's not just the cave area, that's the exact cave where Jim and Travis and Cody are. Now do you see why I couldn't let you see it?''

"Yeah,'' he answered her, giving a solemn nod of his head. "I guess I do.'' He kept his eyes on the map, but especially on the X that marked his enemies. He now understood her actions in protecting that vital piece of information from him, but what he didn't see or understand was why she was now pointing out something to him that he had so obviously missed. He could only surmise that when she trusted, she trusted completely. Which only made his life harder.

Deke found himself hoping against hope that the Daltons would be nowhere near Robber's Cave when they arrived. It was more than a remote possibility that they'd moved on by now. After all, Sara's map had to be over a year old, because his own investigating had revealed that the Daltons hadn't been to Plains for well over a year. So there was no guarantee that the gang was still using the cave as a hideout. They could be anywhere. And talk at the Nighthorses' had revealed that the Daltons had been there not too long ago. He had never heard which direction they'd been headed from there, but Deke figured that as misbegotten as this trip was, the Daltons were probably headed right now for Kansas and home. And here he was trying to catch up with them by going in the opposite direction. Well, hell; he was beginning to hope he never caught up with them. Not if it meant betraying the woman standing next to him.

Unbidden came the faces of his mother and sister as he'd last seen them, alive and smiling. What about his betrayal of them and their memory if he didn't confront the Daltons? Confront them? He'd sworn to do more than confront them. And he'd also sworn to make everything all right for Sara. As if the gesture would help him think, Deke ran a hand through his hair; this predicament he was in had more coils that a twenty-foot rattler. And was probably just as deadly. He didn't see how things could get any worse.

Until Coburn called out. "Deke. Sara."

Deke needed no more than that urgent quality he heard in the older man's voice to tell him something was wrong.

Instantly alert, Deke put a hand on Sara's elbow to stop whatever she'd been about to say. "What is it?" he called back.

Coburn turned from staring off into the distance to his left to look at Sara and Deke. His face sober, his voice flat, Coburn said, "I think you'd better come have a look."

Deke's gut knotted. He could only imagine what Sara must be feeling. As if in answer to that thought, she clutched at his bare arm, her long, slim fingers warm and strong on his biceps. But her wide-eyed expression required reassurance. Deke covered her much smaller hand with his and squeezed gently. Forcing himself past his own trepidation to smile down at her, he said, "Don't worry, Sara. It will be all right. Didn't I promise you that?"

When she gave him a wavery smile, he winked at her and, with a hand to the small of her back, propelled her toward her horse to get her Spencer repeater. As he walked just behind her, he wished for someone who could reassure *him* that everything would be all right.

"What is it?" he repeated to Coburn when he stopped next to him. Sara was behind them, pulling her rifle out.

"Well, it's looks to me like some kind of greetin' party. A Cheyenne greetin' party."

"Friendly?" Deke asked, drawing the shirt off his shoulder and letting it drop to the ground. He resettled his gunbelt and almost automatically ran his fingers over the butt of his Colt. He felt, rather than saw, Sara's presence next to him. Every instinct in him urged him to move in front of her, to protect her. But he stayed where he was.

"Well, let's just say I wish they was Arapaho. I can't rightly tell their intent from this distance. But the fact that they let us see 'em bodes well."

"Are we on their land?" This was Sara.

Deke looked over at Coburn with her. He appeared to be mulling this over, as if calculating the direction and the distance they'd ridden today from the Nighthorses' homestead. "I reckon we could be. We've come far enough, I suppose."

"What do you think they want?" Sara asked, her voice high and quavery.

Deke knew she was thinking of the robbers they'd killed only yesterday—and what he himself had told her they wanted with her. He wished now that he hadn't been so blunt. She needed to be calm and cool now, not panicky and trigger-happy.

"What do they want? Can't rightly say," Coburn replied, continuing to be maddeningly noncommittal. "They may just be curious."

"But you doubt it," Deke finished for him, all the while with his eyes on the slowly approaching Cheyennes. Seven. There were seven of them. Armed with bows and arrows. Not usually a match for guns, but in the skilled hands of seasoned Cheyenne warriors . . . ?

"Yep. I doubt it most seriously. They ain't none too

friendly with the whites." Coburn said that as if he wasn't one of "the whites." He went on, as if the sound of his own voice reassured him. "They hadn't had none too friendly a treatment from the govamint, no sirree. They's a mighty mistrustful lot. Mighty mistrustful."

"You ever had dealings with this group before?"

"Well," Coburn announced, removing his hat to rub his forearm across his sweating head, "these here specific ones don't look none too familiar, but I reckon I probably been in their camp a time or two. Leastwise, I hope I have."

By now the seven Cheyenne warriors were ranged in front of the three white trespassers, but at a cautious distance. After a moment or two of silence all around, one of the warriors, a handsome, powerfully built man, raised a hand and uttered something that to Deke's ear was guttural and abrupt. But apparently to Coburn, the warrior's words were music to his ears, for his weathered and lined face broke out into a huge smile.

"What'd he say?" Deke asked, keeping his voice low and his eyes on the warriors. He felt Sara press against him.

"Just keep smiling," Coburn said, also staring at the warriors as he spoke to Deke and Sara. "They want us to come with them."

"They what?" Sara whispered urgently. "Then why are you smiling?"

"Wouldn't want to insult them, now would we, and mayhap get ourselves killed right here?" Coburn kept up reassuring gestures and smiles for the benefit of the unsmiling, patient Cheyenne.

"Better here, with seven to three odds, than in their village," Deke remarked evenly under his breath.

"Odds don't matter none to these old boys. If'n they was goin' to kill us, we'd already be dead, skinned, and trussed up neater'n a Thanksgivin' turkey. But I think we'll be keepin' our hair, since they don't usually invite the evenin's entertainment to just follow 'em home—they take 'em along, if'n you get my drift."

"Those are mighty reassuring words, Coburn," Deke commented dryly.

"Best I can do, seein' the lay of things," Coburn said out of the side of his smiling mouth.

The same Cheyenne warrior gestured at them and spoke what gave every impression of being a command.

Coburn answered him shortly, then turned to Deke and Sara, looking them each straight in the face, keeping his face carefully blank. "Mount up. And do it nice and easy-like. Sara, I'd advise you to keep that there bonnet on; that there hair of yours is raisin' a mighty curious interest in our hosts."

Coburn's cautionary words to Sara, and her small gasp of reaction, stopped Deke in the act of scooping his shirt up off the ground; horse sweat or no, he wasn't going along shirtless. He straightened up slowly, looked out the corner of his eye at the curious warriors, then at Sara. Her eyes were as wide as an owl's right now. Deke winked at her, trying to reassure her in any small way possible. Then he drew his filthy shirt on, buttoned it, tucked it in his denims, and came to stand beside her, taking a proprietary hold on her arm. He then stared boldly back at the young braves, all of whom straightened up on their ponies and glared back.

"Deke, what are you doing?" Sara whispered urgently.

"Just letting those young bucks know you're mine." He looked down at her with a soft smile but hard, glittering eyes. He intentionally tightened his hold on her arm to keep her from jerking away.

"I'm *yours*? Have you lost your mind?" Her whispering voice was low, incredulous.

"Would you rather be theirs?" he asked pointedly, nodding his head towards the Cheyenne.

Her eyes widened even more; then the resistance went out of her. She grabbed his shirt and quickly shook her head.

"That's better. Now get your horse and do everything Coburn tells you." Then, as an afterthought when she turned away to walk towards her mare, Deke added, "And tighten the strings on that bonnet. I don't think I can fight an entire tribe of Cheyenne over you.''

His words stopped her in her tracks. With her back to him—and the interested Cheyenne—she quickly stuffed as much silver hair under her inadequate bonnet as she could and retied it tightly. Without a word or a glance backward, she mounted her mare and presented a straight, brave face to the men, Indian and white. Deke felt better about her frame of mind now; all he'd had to do was get her Dalton up.

He then went to his buckskin, saddled the tired animal, and mounted up. There would be no more delays—they were on their way to a Cheyenne camp. Deke urged his stallion forward, purposely putting himself right by Sara. Coburn took up his protective place on the other side of her, effectively blocking out the warriors, who nonetheless formed a loose circle around their captive guests. Deke's intent was to give the warriors no chance to see up close the scared, beautiful face that bonnet was hiding.

The ride was long and hard, not because of the pace, no more than a canter, set by the warriors or because of the sun's pounding heat, but more because of the very fact of the Cheyenne's presence all around them. To Sara, they felt like two hundred instead of the seven they actually were. Especially when some of the younger braves would suddenly, without a signal or warning that Sara could discern, break away from the group, whooping loudly, their bows raised in the air, their long black hair flying, and race their bareback mounts at breakneck speeds across the uneven ground. The older warriors just grunted their opinion of such youthful antics. But despite herself, Sara was dazzled by their expert horsemanship and high, youthful spirits.

As she openly watched them, her inital fear at their sudden outbursts subsiding, she even smiled at Coburn.

He chuckled and shook his head. ''I hope you're enjoying this display, Miss Dalton.''

"Why?" She felt her smile begin to slip.

"Why, because it's all for your benefit. Them young braves is showin' off their skills. I wouldn't show no partiality for any one of 'em, if'n I was you. You might have to pick one of 'em later on, if'n you was so impressed."

Sara swallowed her smile and very nearly her tongue as she choked at Coburn's laughing words. She glanced over at Deke.

He was staring a hole through her again. "You're just trying your damnedest to get me killed, aren't you?"

"I didn't know," she whispered urgently.

Deke set his mouth angrily. "Well, now you do. Try to look unimpressed, please; I'd like to keep my hair. And you don't have to whisper, Sara. They don't understand us, whether we're speaking low or loud English."

Sometimes that damned bounty hunter could act and sound as peevish as an old-maid schoolteacher, Sara fumed.

The blazing afternoon wore on with no stops for rest, food, or water, and no incidents worth noting, thankfully. The small party kept pace with the traveling sun. Judging by its position over her shoulder, Sara determined that they were going northeast—right into the heart of Cheyenne country in the Cherokee Outlet and in exactly the opposite direction from Robber's Cave. Well, there was no helping it. This wasn't the first time the thought occurred to her that she could face only one deadly calamity at a time.

Along about sunset, they approached the Cheyenne's encampment, a small village of circular tepees nestled against an outcropping of high hills and among a dense copse of willows, black walnut, and elm trees. Sara's darting gaze was caught by the lowering sun's glint off the surface of a creek that ran behind the east-facing tepees. The setting was actually very picturesque and unthreatening, even to Sara's wary eye, but only their heretofore silent escort appeared happy and at home when the villagers came out in force to greet the arriving party, their numbers swollen now by three. The people, copper-skinned and clad in buckskins, formed two lines for the riders to advance along; they appeared curious, wary, shy—just how Sara herself felt.

She chanced a quick glance at Coburn and Deke as they walked their horses through this unlikely gauntlet, the seven warriors still with them, riding fore and aft of their white guests. Just like her, the two men were busily taking in the scene before them. It cost her nothing to admit that their eyes had to be more practiced at gauging moods and dangers than hers were. So she asked, her voice now at a normal speaking pitch, "What do you think?"

Coburn answered first. "Well, Sara, there ain't no war party preparations goin' on, that's for sure. The whole village would be in a uproar if'n that was so. No, looks peaceable enough to me. See all them hides stretched out over to the right? Them's buffalo; must have had a recent hunting party. That's meat drying on them high racks in front of the tepees—keeps the dogs and the younguns away."

When Sara had no more than wondered why Coburn was telling her all this about buffalo, Deke cut into her thoughts and answered her unasked question. "Which doesn't explain, when a recent buffalo kill just yielded all that fresh meat and our esteemed escorts should have been here in camp sharing in the feast, just what the hell they were doing out on the prairie. What or who were they scouting?"

"Couldn't have said it better myself," Coburn chirped, echoing Deke's unease. And heightening Sara's.

Right then the warriors in front of them reined in their mounts in front of one of the tepees that to Sara looked no different from the others surrounding it. But the Cheyenne all quieted and waited expectantly, telling Sara as effectively as any words that something important was about to happen. She tried to ignore her heart's pounding and the drizzle of fearful sweat that trickled slowly down her spine.

Without ceremony, the central flap on the tepee parted and out stepped an older Cheyenne man and two women. The man, of average height for the Cheyenne and with a heavily jowled, intelligent face, spoke briefly with the same warrior who'd talked with Coburn earlier that day.

Coburn turned to Sara and Deke, keeping his voice low and respectful. "This here is Chief Walking Stick, and them women he's counseling with is his wives. Cheyenne women run the camps as much as the men. Lucky for us, I ran into him at his winter camp a year or two ago. Traded mighty successfully with his folk. He's a pretty good old boy if'n you don't rile him none. He's askin' that brave about us— like where'd he come across us, what were we doin'."

"And what's he saying?" Deke asked pointedly, obviously not feeling any more reassured by Coburn's words.

Coburn actually chuckled after listening to the conversation for a moment more. "He says we wasn't doin' nothin'. Says we're lazy, and we looked lost to him. These Cheyenne ain't got much use for whites as a whole."

"So I gathered," Deke commented. "Then what the hell are we doing here? Can you get any of that from their talk?"

"I'll try," Coburn allowed. "But knowin' Cheyenne ways, we won't be told nothin' until they're good and ready."

And that proved to be true, for Coburn's attempts to speak to the chief were cut off by abrupt gestures from one of the braves. So, still ignorant of the reason for their "visit" to Walking Stick's camp, the three, after being told through Coburn to dismount, were taken to a tepee close to the river, which was Wolf Creek, Coburn told them.

"These Injuns is acting mighty peculiar-like," Coburn allowed when they were alone inside the tepee.

Sara turned from surveying the neat, orderly contents of the tepee to ask, "How so?" She curiously picked up a beautifully woven basket and looked it over.

"Well, for one thing, Deke still has his Colt strapped on; and for another, there ain't nobody guardin' us." He was peeking out the flap and looking around as best he could through the narrow opening he'd allowed himself. "I can tell you our horses is tethered about five yards off. We could be on 'em and gone before anybody knowed any different."

Sara seriously doubted that, especially in Coburn and Jezebel's case, but she very kindly kept that observation to herself. She turned to share a smile with Deke, but he was occupied with grimly checking his Colt revolver. Obviously, he was no believer in Cheyenne hospitality, or at least of its lasting.

"Uh-oh! Here comes some boys with our saddles. Well, look at that—rifles and all. Now if this ain't the dangedest behavior for a bunch of—" With that, Coburn moved away from the opening more quickly than Sara would have thought possible. His sideways, crablike motion was almost comical.

Sara looked to Deke to see what he made of this and saw him very grimly watching the tepee flap. At least he'd holstered his revolver. Then Sara remembered that she was holding the basket—someone else's property. She guiltily dropped it as the boys—three dark-skinned, very serious youths of twelve or thirteen—brought the saddles in, laid them down, spared the white people a deprecating glance, then stalked out single-file.

Sara moved to her saddlebags immediately and sorted through them. "I hope everything is in here."

"Oh, it will be. One thing the Cheyenne don't tolerate is a thief amongst themselves," Coburn said cheerfully enough as he worked to stoke to life a banked fire in a shallow pit in the middle of the tepee.

Suddenly ashamed of her automatic assumption that because they were Indians they would be thieves, Sara's hands stilled. She looked down for a moment, thinking, wasn't she the one who'd just been going through another person's belongings? When she looked up, she caught Deke's gaze on her. He smiled at her as if he understood, which only made her feel worse. Getting to her feet, she looked around. "I wonder whose . . . home we've taken."

Deke, his arms crossed over his chest, looked slowly around and then up at the opening at the top of the tepee which allowed smoke out and air in. He finally looked back at her. "Some high-up warrior, I'd guess. What do you think, Coburn?"

Coburn, having gotten the fire up and going, providing their only light in the otherwise dark interior, was now occupied with unrolling a sleeping mat. He was obviously at home in a tepee and with things that were Cheyenne, and he corroborated Deke's estimation. "Oh, I do agree. I do believe this to be the home, given the signs and pictures of battle on the outside, of the big whoop-te-doo what brought us into the village."

Intrigued, but with no idea how Coburn could tell all that, Sara followed his example by pulling out another mat and unrolling it. The Cheyenne bed, woven mats, colorful robes, and a buffalo hide were clean, even fragrant. In fact, she marveled, she would have expected the tepee to be close-smelling and airless. But it was none of those things, especially since the three boys had left the flap open. Since no threats had been made against them, and they had their belongings, Sara began to let her guard down and was actually beginning to look on this interlude as a real adventure. Last night she'd slept in a barn with Deke, and tonight she would sleep in a tepee with him. All the other nights, they'd slept in the open on the ground. She wondered if they'd ever sleep together in a bed.

Surprising herself with the turn of her thoughts, so unbidden, she forced her mind to other, more appropriate thoughts. Letting her hair down from the confines of the bonnet seemed safe enough now; besides, she was sick of looking out at the world from the deep tunnel provided by its elongated bill. Before Deke or Coburn might realize what she was about and lodge a protest, she quickly untied the long ribbons under her chin and whipped the offending bonnet off her head. For once in her life, she thought the cascading sweep of abundant, silvery curls felt good and right.

Just after she tossed the bonnet aside and as she was running her hands through her hair to massage her scalp, into the tepee stepped the owner, the same warrior who'd brought them into the village. Whatever he'd been about to say died on his lips as he stood there with his mouth open. Since Deke and Coburn were standing closer to the opening than Sara, they had to turn around to see what had rendered the tall warrior speechless.

And there was Sara Jane Dalton in all her radiant and silver glory. Sara wished she could kick herself. Hadn't Coburn told her to keep her hair covered and what could happen if it was seen? She knew how she looked; no one, least of all the awestruck brave or the frowning Deke or the wide-eyed Coburn, had to tell her. Hadn't her brothers and cousins teased her all her life about her white hair, as they called it? And hadn't her mother always marveled at her daughter's beauty, given the combination of silvery blonde hair, lightly tanned skin, black eyes, and dark brows and eyelashes? Well, her mother may have thought all that was beautiful, but right now the combination could be deadly—for them all.

With obvious effort, the brave tore his gaze away from the vision that was Sara and turned his attention to Coburn and the matter at hand. Whatever that was. He exchanged a rather lengthy, almost heated conversation with Coburn, with far too much pointing at her, Sara felt, and which finally resulted in all three of them following him, Sara without her bonnet, she and Deke without a translated explanation, through the village. At every turn, her hair caused a stir among the villagers. She even felt a few hands reach out as she passed to touch her hair—not roughly, but admiringly. She tried to be brave and smile, but Deke's forbidding scowl and his hand clamped on her elbow made it hard to be congenial, especially with him practically dragging her along with his lengthy stride. At this clip, he could walk her to Robber's Cave in two or three days.

Once again, the trio was stopped in front of the chief's tepee. Chief Walking Stick and his somber wives stepped outside into the same air of expectancy that had permeated their earlier appearance. Once again, the heavy-jowled chief spoke soberly with the warrior. And once again, the gathered people listened in respectful silence.

But for the first time, the chief also acknowledged Coburn—with what appeared to be respect. Right now Sara was extremely grateful for Coburn's obviously good reputation with these honorable people. She tried to imagine their reception if they'd ridden in with a liar and a cheat, but her mind cringed from that scene. She forced herself to focus on where they were again being escorted, this time by the entire village. She looked up at Deke, who spared her an intense glance, and was grateful for his tall, powerful, comforting presence—for perhaps the thousandth time since she'd left Plains, Kansas.

At about the middle of the village, by Sara's judgment, they were stopped again in front of a huge fire, ringed with smooth, round whitish stones, that had all the earmarks of a ceremonial or ritual place, given the quiet reverence with which the Cheyenne attended the area. Just as Deke had missed the X on her map, Sara realized that she must have missed the significance of their being brought here, when the evidence was probably right under her nose.

"Deke, what—?"

"Look, Sara," he said quietly, pointing to the other side of the fire. "Over there, sitting between the two old women."

Sara, confused, first tried to look through the leaping flames, but could see nothing. Deke, his hand still on her arm, pulled her a little to her left. "There," he repeated, whispering urgently.

Sara peered intently around the flames. And then her breath caught in her chest, held there by the pounding dread in her heart. She had to hold on to Deke for support. For there, seated on the ground between two old Cheyenne women, were two terrified children. Two terrified white children.

Chapter Fourteen

Sara's first crazy thought was, what were those children doing in this Cheyenne village? And where were their parents? Afraid she knew, she looked at the seemingly docile Cheyenne. Her next thought, not so crazy, was what were she, Deke, and Coburn doing in this Cheyenne village—alive? Were the two events related? Did the children's presence explain theirs? She turned to Coburn; his face was wiped clean of expression as he too stared at the children, a boy of about twelve and girl of seven or eight years, who were huddled together in fear, but appeared unhurt.

"My God, Coburn, what's going on here?" Sara whispered urgently. She felt Deke's large hand clamp over hers as she clutched his sleeve, offering her a modicum of reassurance.

Coburn ran his large-knuckled hand over his mouth and chin, a gesture she'd seen Deke perform countless times when he was upset. "I can't rightly say. This is gettin' more and more peculiar by the minute. Let me see what I can learn."

With that he turned to Chief Walking Stick and his wives. Anything he might have been going to ask was forestalled by the chief's abruptly raising his hand and signaling, with one or two phrases, for them to follow him. As Deke muttered a choice phrase or two of his own under his breath about how someone better start giving him some damned answers, the chief turned to head back the way he'd come, confident that the whites would follow him. And they did— right back to the chief's tepee. Sara kept looking back at the children for as long as she could, until they rounded a tepee that took the central fire out of her line of vision. She could see the mute pleading in the children's eyes; the crippling fear in her heart matched their expressions. Dear God, what could all this mean?

As if he'd read her thoughts, Deke, his arm around her shoulders now, said, "Just remember, Sara: We're alive, and they're alive. There've been no threats, no torture. The children looked fine, just scared."

"My God, Deke, we have to get them out of here. The stories I've heard about what these people do to white captives—"

"None of which they've done to us. Or the boy and girl," Deke interrupted her, using an emphatic tone with her. "Just hang on to that, Sara. And don't do anything foolish."

Like what, she wanted to ask him? Make a run for her horse, stop at the tepee (as if she could distinguish it from any of the others) for her saddle and her rifle, find Cinnamon, saddle her, mount up and ride like the wind through the village, snatch up the children, and take off at night across the prairie? Oh, certainly that would go uncontested by the Cheyenne warriors.

Sometimes Deke made her so angry. How could he think her so foolish as to—Well, he'd done it again, the thought dawned on her: helped her overcome her crippling fear by making her angry and more determined to prove him wrong. She gave him a look meant to tell him she understood. He managed to smile down at her, even wink. Sara marveled that just one look, one gesture from Deke could leave her feeling so tremendously safe with him by her side. Yes, even here, surrounded by an entire village of Cheyenne. With Deke by her side, everything would be all right. Hadn't he promised?

Even though she'd told herself she wasn't going to hold him to that promise, more and more she found that she was indeed depending on it. And so far, he had made everything they'd faced all right. Maybe he was becoming her good-luck charm.

And she was probably going to need one right about now as the chief entered his tepee, followed by his wives and several warriors, one of whom was their warrior, as Sara was beginning to think of him. He motioned her, Deke, and Coburn to also enter. Once inside, he gestured at them to sit across the central campfire from the Cheyenne. While everyone was settling, there were prolonged moments of silence during which Sara couldn't keep her gaze still. She felt a need to take in everything that she could, from her hosts' faces to the cookfire smells that set off a rumbling in her belly to the rough feel of the buffalo hide under her to the faces of the men who sat to her left and right. Deke and Coburn. She had the sudden insight that it must be hard for Deke, a man of blunt words and direct action, to be patient and assume this secondary role to Coburn, the only one of them who spoke Cheyenne.

Sara's attention was brought abruptly back into focus by the soft-spoken words of the chief. He allowed Coburn to translate for Sara and Deke, which he did. With each translation, a story more and more fascinating—and foreboding—began to unfold.

Chief Walking Stick told first of the successful buffalo hunt from which his village had just returned.

Coburn allowed as how he'd seen the meat and hides.

The chief nodded and thanked the buffalo spirits for giving up their lives that the Cheyenne might fill their bellies. He then said how he welcomed his honored guests to his village.

Coburn thanked him for his kind hospitality. He then turned to Sara and Deke, and with an ironic smile on his face, said, "We're their honored guests, which explains why we have our guns—and our scalps, I s'pose. Never mind that we didn't have no choice in the matter. That's as far as we've got so far—just the pleasantries, as it were."

Deke shifted impatiently next to Sara. She reached over, placing a calming hand on his sleeve.

Next, the chief told Coburn how the Cheyenne of his village were returning to their camp, laden with many buffalo, when they came across a scene of many killings. Much death. Coburn nodded soberly and translated for Sara and Deke. They exchanged glances all around. Whose deaths? Did he mean of people or of buffalo? Surely, they weren't here to hear a grievance over a buffalo kill by whites.

The Cheyenne people were greatly astonished, the chief went on, and very much upset over this tragedy on their lands. There before them, he finally said, were many dead people. Many dead white people. Their wagons were there, but no horses. The whites had been killed with guns, guns the Cheyenne did not have. He paused there for translation— and for effect.

Coburn duly repeated what the chief was telling him. Sara noticed that at this point the Cheyenne chief, even though sitting in a very dignified manner, gave the distinct impression of leaning toward her and Deke, as if to see better their reaction to this news.

"Whites killed with guns? No horses anywhere?" Deke leaned over Sara to question Coburn. "What's his point?"

"He ain't come to it yet. These Cheyenne is great storytellers. You just have to outwait 'em, if'n you want to learn anything."

"Well, hell," was Deke's stated opinion, thankfully uttered without an expression to match.

Coburn turned his face back to the chief and nodded, indicating that he was through translating.

Chief Walking Stick nodded in return and continued, finally coming to the gist of the story—and the answer to why Sara, Coburn, and Deke were here. He told Coburn that the only ones left alive were the boy and the girl. He said the people, meaning the Cheyenne, had searched the site for what might be left behind for their use. Nothing was—except the two children. And here the chief made an important, though chilling, point to Coburn. He said that at first the braves wished to kill the children too. That way, the people could walk away with no witnesses that they'd ever been on the scene. For who in the white man's army that patrolled their lands would take the word of the Cheyenne that they weren't responsible over the evidence of the kill on their lands? Coburn translated all this and paused to look into Deke's and Sara's faces. "It's gettin' a might sticky right here," he added for them. Sara and Deke nodded their agreement.

Deke counseled, "Point out to the chief that he says he has no guns. And the whites were killed with guns. Wouldn't that show they hadn't massacred the settlers?"

Coburn nodded and put the query to the chief. He then listened to his answer and turned back to Deke. "He says they wouldn't be believed. That the soldiers would just think they was hidin' their guns."

"True," Deke conceded. "And how do we—us three— know they're *not* just hiding their guns, that they *didn't* really kill those kids' folks?"

Coburn looked at Deke for a long minute. Sara could tell he hadn't thought of that; neither had she. "Well, I'll be danged. I don't guess we do. Let me put that to him . . .'course, we'll be calling him a liar." He turned back to the chief and asked him Deke's question before good sense could prevail. The chief answered in a terse, clipped tone that almost didn't need translation. The chief's companions shifted and muttered threateningly. Black, glittering eyes bore in on Deke, but it took only the powerful chief's raised hand to control the offended warriors.

Still, Sara clutched instinctively at Deke's arm as his hand went to his Colt. Coburn, a ghost of a smile on his lips, said, "Chief Walking Stick says you're alive, ain't you?"

"What the hell does that mean?" Deke asked, keeping his own black eyes squarely on the warriors who sat across from him.

"I'll ask him," Coburn assured Deke.

"And this time," Sara hissed, "use a little tact, Coburn. I'd like to keep my hair, if you don't mind."

Coburn just chuckled and turned back to the chief, resuming their conversation with Deke's question. He listened, with several nods, to the old chief's response and then turned back to Sara and Deke. "He says he kept the boy and girl alive for the same reason he didn't kill us—even if we wasn't the ones he sent that party out for. They was supposed to be scoutin' around lookin' for who might-a done that deed, but instead they come back with us."

"Well, how then do they know we didn't kill them?" Sara put in.

Coburn and Deke just looked at her, as if waiting for her to come to her senses. Then Deke said, very patiently, "Sara, do you really think we—an old man, a woman, and a bounty hunter—look like we would have killed all those people?"

Sara cocked her head to one side. "Well, for one thing, you don't know how many people were killed, so we might have been able to. And we did kill those five men yesterday who had Ben's horses."

"Well, let's try to refrain from telling these Cheyenne about that, shall we?" Deke came right back.

Another thought occurred to Sara. "Deke, maybe those same five men robbed and killed those poor people. After all, that's what they were going to do to us. And they did have a lot of money on them."

Deke and Coburn looked at her again, as if she were some sort of puzzle they weren't capable of figuring out. Finally, Deke spoke. "You might be right. It could have been them— or any other band of thieving, murdering bastards who commit these deeds on Indian land and then run for the safety of Robber's Cave—''

Deke stopped abruptly and looked at Sara as if he wished he could call back his words. But they still hit Sara with the force of a blow, for they implied that her brother and cousins were no better in his mind than the five men they'd killed yesterday. Coburn hissed at them to quit their arguing. Deke and Sara looked at him and then over at the Cheyenne. The last thing they needed right now was to look divided or guilty in any way. Though angry tears stung her eyes and clogged her throat, Sara squared her jaw and presented a calm face to the Cheyenne.

Seeing that he had their attention again, the old chief went on, speaking slowly and using many gestures. Coburn listened intently; Sara tried to, even though she didn't understand a word he said, because the effort kept her mind off Deke's harsh words, which told her plainly that as much as they'd been through together already, nothing had changed. Deke Bonner, bounty hunter, still intended to serve his warrant. Sara felt like such a naive fool; she also felt Deke's eyes boring into her, as if willing her to look at him. But she just couldn't . . . not right now anyway.

Finally, Coburn turned to Sara and Deke again. "Chief says the boy and the girl can tell the soldiers the truth, that it wasn't the Cheyenne—or any other tribe—that killed all those white folks, and we—''

"How do they know it wasn't another tribe or village who killed them, Coburn?'' Deke asked pointedly, leaning over Sara again. In her anger, she jerked back as far from his touch as she could without falling over backwards. "Did they see anything that told them that? We know the Cheyenne didn't question the boy or the girl, because they don't speak our language.''

"Yep, they did see something, Deke. They saw full heads of hair left on the dead folks. And their wagons wasn't burned. And the hoofprints showed the horses was shod— Injuns don't shoe their ponies. And the bodies was faceup.''

Now even Sara was intrigued, despite her anger and hurt. Obviously, Coburn's words meant something to Deke, who was nodding affirmatively and rubbing his hand over his mouth and chin. But they didn't mean anything to Sara. "Why is that important—about the bodies being faceup? I understand about scalping and burning and horses being shod," she added, not giving the two men another chance to look at her as if she were addle-brained.

"Indians leave dead enemies facedown; their religion says his spirit can't get out if'n he's like that. Can't rise to the happy huntin' grounds in the sky. Dooms him to stay here on earth forever, a lost spirit," Coburn explained.

Sara nodded, and then looked over at the men and women seated opposite her. She hadn't thought of Indians as having a religion. By the time she digested that thought, she had another question. "Why did they bring us back here? What are we supposed to do?"

Coburn looked first at the chief and then back at his companions. "Well, Sara, Deke, it seems the chief, onct he got over bein' sore at his warriors for bringin' even more whites here when he had two too many already, liked the braves' notion that we—the three of us—could take the boy and girl with us to tell their story at that new army supply camp. He don't think it would set none too good for a band of Cheyenne to just ride onto a military post with white children."

"What supply camp?" Sara asked.

Deke spoke first, forcing her to look at him. He looked as if he had a bad headache. "One that's even farther north then here. Where Beaver River mets Wolf Creek—which runs right by this village. There's not much there; no more than a few men looking over the site for a camp that's supposed to go up next year." He then turned to Coburn. "How do we even know if anyone's still at the site?"

"Oh, we can take the chief's word for it. If he says they's there, they's there. These Cheyenne keep a close eye on the soldiers' comin's and goin's in their territory.

"Now I want you to know somethin' else. I offered to

take the kids on up to the camp myself, leavin' you two free to go on about your business, seein' as how I'm headin' up that way myself. But the old chief believes mighty strongly that mayhap it would be best to have you two along. Like maybe you'll have more say-so with the soldiers than an old Indian trader like myself would. An' don't go thinkin' that insults me none, 'cause it don't. I don't hold much with the soldiers, and they return the compliment. They think on me as no better than these here Cheyenne. Wouldn't take my word for the sun bein' up at noon. An' I suppose you get the old chief's meanin'—he's puttin' an awful lot of store in you." Here he was looking directly at Sara. "Allowin' as how he believes you will be honest as a preacher with the soldiers and stand up for his people."

"How does he know we will?" Deke asked, drawing Coburn's and Sara's gazes to him. Sara had thought the same thing. Once again, it hadn't occurred to her until now that the Cheyenne stood to lose much more than she did.

"Well, Deke, you done accepted their hospitality—sampled their sincerity, as it were—and—now don't go gettin' riled on me—you're Sara's man, in their eyes, leastwise. An' it's her they want to speak for 'em."

So unprepared was she for Coburn's words that she nearly jumped up. She turned to Deke; he was looking somewhat sourly at Coburn, showing his displeasure, no doubt, with the notion that the only reason his honesty was assumed and his hair was still attached to his skull was because he was with Sara. So, not only was he second to Coburn in this village, he was third to her. Let him sulk.

"Seems Sara's hair makes her special in their sight for some reason. And, too, these Cheyenne set a powerful store by their womenfolk's counsel, as you've seen for yourself. Cheyenne women are the most high and mighty morally. They feel the same on Sara. So, the way they see it, accordin' to the chief, is that if a woman like Sara would have you, you must be a good man. So they'll tolerate you as long as you're hers."

At Deke's darkening brood, Coburn warned him, "Now don't go disavowin' our hosts here of any of their high and mighty opinions."

With visible effort, Deke calmed himself. With nothing else to discuss, the three looked at each other and then at their patiently waiting hosts. Finally, Sara broke the silence, gaining not only Deke's and Coburn's attention, but that of the Cheyenne as well. "It's not like we can refuse to do this—if for no other reason than for the children's sake. The question is, what do we do with them, since they're orphans now, once they've told their story to the soldiers?"

Deke looked at her in a way that proved he hadn't gotten beyond the point in his thinking of getting the boy and girl to the safety of the soldiers. "We sure as hell can't take them with us. They're in better shape here than they would be at Robber's Cave."

"That's so, an' my life ain't much a-one for raisin' little varmints. And the old chief here, he ain't goin' to want 'em. He's almost a-boilin' to get them and us outa here. Last thing he needs is pesky whites in his village."

Sara was beginning to get angry. "Well, we can't just leave them here—or with the soldiers. Or take them with us. Or leave them with you, Coburn. What does that leave? The poor little things are going to need a family and love and—"

"The Nighthorses!" they all three said at the same time, with enough emotion to startle a response out of their silent, stoic hosts.

"Well, skin me and Jezebel alive and hang us out to dry on a nail by the barn door," Coburn crowed. "They'll take them little varmints in gladly. That's exactly how they got two or three of them kids they got now—from desperadoes who mighta kilt their folks but didn't sink lower'n a snake's belly in a ditch by killin' kids, and just rode in with 'em like they was droppin' off taters."

Sara was stunned by Coburn's revelation that not all the Nighthorses' children were their own natural offspring. She

certainly hadn't seen any partiality on their part for any of
the children over any others. A smile came to Sara's
thoughts—this did, though, explain why the children had
every imaginable color of hair. But perhaps even more stun-
ning to Sara was this example of a sort of law and honor in
such a lawless and brutal territory. Apparently Ben and Etheline's goodness was their very protection from most of the
evil that pervaded this godless land. Now she understood
why they were pretty much left alone, except maybe for the
occasional horse thief.

She refocused her attention in time to hear Coburn say,
"Let me parlay all this to the old chief." She nodded along
with Deke and watched the Cheyenne for their reaction as
Coburn spoke to them at length. And the longer he spoke,
the more their tense faces relaxed. One or two of them even
chanced to look Sara's way, with something akin to respect
in their gazes. She managed to sit a little straighter, even
when Deke's huff next to her told her plainly enough what
he thought of these proceedings. Let him sulk.

When Coburn was through speaking, it was apparent that
this solution—never really in doubt on the part of the Cheyenne, Sara supposed—met with everyone's approval. When
Chief Walking Stick stood, so did the other occupants of his
tepee. He spoke again to Coburn and waited for him to translate. Coburn turned to Deke and Sara. "The chief says
there's to be a big celebration. And we're invited."

Sara looked up at Deke. He looked levelly right back at
her and said, "You're the respected ambassador here. You
thank him."

Biting back her pique, Sara turned to Coburn, gave him
and the Cheyenne her most dazzling smile, very dramatically
fluffed her hair around her head, and said, "Tell the chief
we would be most honored to attend. Tell him I'll even bring
my man."

Chapter Fifteen

The celebration that starry evening in the Cheyenne village on the banks of Wolf Creek was the most primitive and dazzling spectacle Sara had ever witnessed. Whirling dancers in frightening, beautiful costumes moved past her in kaleidoscopic frenzy. Exotic but delicious foods filled her empty belly; throbbing drumbeats set a rhythm in her heart and an almost involuntary movement of her feet to the time; smiling women tentatively touched Sara, her hair, and her clothes; small children placed their hands trustingly in hers, as if touching her would somehow transfer her magic to them. Their innocent behavior, though, edged a perturbed Deke away from her side.

Afraid his huge frown would send the wrong message to their hosts, Sara patted the children and sent them on their way with a smile. Two steps saw her at Deke's side. "Deke, you look like you're afraid you're going to be the main course," she hissed under her breath, never letting her smile slip as the Cheyenne milled around them.

"And you look like you think you belong here," he hissed right back, his frown as ominous as the Colt revolver holstered so low on his hip.

Sara gave him a look meant to convey that she couldn't believe he was acting like this. Was he jealous of the attention she was receiving? She'd thought he was many things over the past few weeks, but petty wasn't one of them.

"I'm sorry, Sara," he said, but not really sounding it. "I've just heard these drums too many times in my life for them to be entertaining for me. These celebrations are usually followed by a raid and by white people dying."

"But you know that's not their purpose this time, Deke. For once these people are placing their trust in someone white to help them. And you're acting like a puffed-up toad because you're not the one they trust."

"A puffed-up—" he strangled out, then grabbed her arm to pull her to him. He leaned right into her face. "Is that what you think? That my pride's wounded? What kind of a vain greenhorn do you take me for? Pride has nothing to do with it. You're a fool if you think we can just sashay into an army camp, let those kids tell their story, and waltz right out. The army's going to have a lot of questions—a lot, Sara. And hearings—that we'll be expected to attend. God only knows how long the army will delay us. And who's to say they'll believe us—excuse me—you and two scared kids who, by the way, may say anything. The Cheyenne may place great store in the wisdom of their women, but you and I know things are different among the whites."

Sara felt her Dalton temper rising; hot with fury, she rose slightly on her toes. "It's hard for you, isn't it, Mr. Deke Bonner, bounty hunter and lone wolf, to put yourself in the hands of a woman?"

"Nothing pleases me more than to put myself in the hands of a woman, Miss Dalton." He paused—long enough for Sara to get his double meaning and to register her blinking response. "But nothing worries me more than thinking about the hundred things that could go wrong between right now and getting to that army camp with those kids.''

"Like what, for instance?" She knew well enough what kinds of things could happen, but her bulldog mood forced her to continue the fight. "What could possibly happen that hasn't already, Deke? We've faced a buffalo stampede, outlaws bent on robbing and killing us, and now this with the Cheyenne. And we've come out alive.''

"So far." Apparently that was all he was going to concede.

"And good things have happened, too. You have to admit that.''

"Like what?" He sounded less angry, more willing to listen. Indeed, his frown was now only a slight crease in his forehead.

Encouraged, Sara went on, softening her tone, even smiling up into his black eyes. "Well, there's Coburn, who's definitely been a godsend with the Cheyenne. And there's the Cheyenne themselves; they're pretty civilized, you have to admit. And don't forget the Nighthorses, Deke. You couldn't ask for better people.''

She'd won. He softened his grip on her arm, and even went so far as to smooth her hair from her heated face. "And don't forget you, Sara. You're something good in all this.''

Her gaze locked with Deke's for a timeless moment as a thrill raced through her. She'd never expected to hear words like that from Deke Bonner, and now that she had, her pounding heart had nothing to do with the deep cadence of the Cheyenne drums. Heartened and warmed by his words, and relieved that they were no longer arguing, she leaned into Deke, putting her head against his chest, her hands flat on his massive chest. His arms stole around her; Sara felt his rapid heartbeat pulsing in her ear. The passing Cheyenne curiously returned her smile, obviously thinking it was for them.

"Well now, ain't you two a picture to warm an old man's soul.''

Coburn's voice, though soft and sincere, still broke the

moment. Deke set Sara away from him, but only as far as his side, where he tucked her against him, his muscled arm protectively around her waist.

"Didn't mean to startle you none. Just came to say I'm goin' to be stayin' in the old chief's tepee this night. Seems me an' him got some catchin' up to do. Maybe even some tradin'. He says to tell you that the kids is sleepin' in his tepee, too, and they'll be ready to go at first light."

"So will we," Deke answered for himself and Sara.

"I wondered where the children were," Sara commented. "We haven't even got to talk to them yet."

"Oh, I 'spect there'll be plenty of time for that on the way up to Beaver River. I seen 'em and spoke with 'em; they're fine. Don't you worry none. And the old chief tells me he's sendin' some of his braves with us, as a pertective escort, mind you. There ain't nothin' we can do about it, so's we might as well get happy about it. I do believe, though, that they're attendin' us to make sure everythin' goes well at the camp, if'n you get my drift."

"Damn. Just what we need." Deke put his hands to his waist and shook his head. After a moment of silent reflection, he conceded, "Apparently our hosts don't trust us as much as they say. Hell, can't say as I blame them. But like you said, there's not much we can do about it if they want to ride with us."

"That's how I see it," Coburn agreed. With that, he turned, his arm around an older Cheyenne man, and wandered back into the milling, celebrating crowd.

Sara immediately turned a stubborn face up to Deke. "I'm not wearing that damned bonnet, braves or no."

Deke ran his gaze over her face and the length of her silvery tresses. "I don't think that will be necessary anymore. Besides, I hate that bonnet, too."

Having won that round, Sara turned a smiling face up to Deke. "I wonder what Coburn'll trade with. All he has are the clothes on his back. And Jezebel. I can't imagine the Cheyenne wanting that old horse."

Deke returned her smile. With a shake of his head, he reminded her, "He has that wad of money he showed us. But still, I believe we'll both sleep better if we don't know what he has to trade with."

With their arms around each other's waists and their shared intimate laughter ringing between them, they turned away from the celebration as if at some invisible signal that it was time to go to bed. Given their feelings of easy camaraderie, it didn't hit Sara, or apparently Deke either, until they were at the raised flap of the tepee that they were now alone—together—for the entire night.

When it did hit, it was with considerable force. Sara gaped at the black hole of the tepee opening and then back up at Deke. His eyes were as deep and unfathomable in the moonlight as was the dark, beckoning hole behind her. Deke's face told her that this was definitely the time for her to make a decision. He aided her by reminding her, in what she suspected was a calculatedly husky, seductive voice, "Remember, the Cheyenne think I'm your man. And you said the same thing, Sara Dalton. So, what's it going to be?"

Every fiber of her being—heart, soul, and body—yearned for Deke's strong, gentle touch and the racing fire of his passion. She tore her gaze from his questioning one, looked back only once at the open flap, and again at Deke. Taking his hand in hers, she wordlessly pulled him with her through the opening.

Once through, her boldness left her. She let go of his hand and stepped back a pace or two. But Deke, feeling no such shyness, wasted no time. He lowered the flap and secured it with its bone and rawhide latch. He then straightened up to his considerable height, skewered Sara in place with his hot gaze, and slowly undid his gunbelt. Sara licked her suddenly dry lips, knowing and yet not knowing what was going to happen between them. It didn't matter; she wanted it. She just didn't know how to go about it.

"Come here, Sara," he whispered, lowering his holster to the hide-covered ground.

Sara feared her feet had grown roots into the earth, so heavy, even leaden, did her limbs feel. She couldn't move. She could only stand there, staring with naked wanting at Deke, unable to name what she desired. He gave her the barest ghost of a smile and held his hand out to her. "It's a step you're going to have to take yourself, Sara. I can't help you."

If someone had told her that the first time she gave herself to a man it would be to be to a bounty hunter in a Cheyenne tepee somewhere in Indian Territory, she would have called that crazy loon just that. But here she was. She took the step—and Deke's hand. And she knew her decision was the right one from the moment his hand gripped hers. She knew then and there that she would have stepped with him off a cliff, trusting him to keep them aloft. When her heart told her it and she were safe with Deke Bonner, she listened. And surrendered.

She surrendered to Deke's punishing, promising kiss as he pulled her into the circle of his embrace. His mouth was on hers, his tongue invading, jousting, thrusting, trying to warn Sara that this mimicked the ultimate act they would commit. But she was oblivious, giving herself up to the moment's pleasure, wondering how anything else could ever feel any better. But this was not a night for kisses alone.

As Deke's burning mouth sought her face, learning every contour of her cheeks, forehead, chin, and her neck, his hands sought the fastenings of her clothes. Sara reveled in the erotic feel of Deke's hands on her increasingly bare skin. Jubilant in the reactions she could elicit from this hard, beautiful man, she took the free rein he gave her to explore and learn his body. Hard muscle revealed itself under her wandering fingers as she undid his shirt and pushed it off his shoulders. When Deke let go of her long enough to shrug his shirt off, throwing it distractedly to the ground, she wondered if her face looked as eager, as intense as Deke's did; she hoped so. Oh, she hoped so.

Before she could think to toss her blouse aside, Deke did

it for her; her chemise quickly followed. Sara had the fleeting thought that she should have some maidenly shame at being naked from the waist up in front of a strange man. Oh, no, Deke Bonner was many things to her, but not strange. Never strange. And so it was with passion-drugged lethargy that she watched, as if from afar, as he dropped to one knee, bent her slightly to hold her to him with his hands on her slim back, and captured her breast in his mouth. The cry that escaped her, as the electric sensation of this most intimate kiss arced from her hardened nipple to the hardened bud of desire between her legs, brought her hands to the back of his head and an answering growl from Deke.

She sucked in a ragged breath and gripped his black, curling hair with her fingers. His response was to capture her other breast, sending swirling sensations and spasmodic ripples through her secret woman's place. When her knees began to buckle, when she began to melt into him, her cheek to the top of his head, his name hot on her lips, Deke stood, picked her up in his arms, and carried her to the bed robes that she and Coburn had laid out earlier.

"You're mine, Sara Dalton," he said, the sound coming from low in his throat. "And I'll kill the son of a bitch who ever says otherwise."

His absolute possessiveness, this almost animalistic, instinctual taking of a mate, thrilled her like nothing else he could have said or done. He laid her gently on the robes, knelt beside her, and ran his gaze over her body. From the depths of his black eyes shone all the leashed power, all the forced slowness, all the necessary gentleness, all the violent passion that corded every bare muscle that lurked just beneath the surface of his powerful frame. She knew in a heartbeat that he could, in his towering lust, tear her apart. But she also knew that he wouldn't. For such was her power over this male.

That sudden insight, that age-old womanly knowledge, made her bold. Not content to just follow his lead, Sara sat up and put her hands to the fastening of his pants. This act rendered Deke motionless under her touch. With his rigid abdominal muscles convulsively sucking in and out with every labored breath he took, with his heavy-lidded eyes watching her, with his hands white-knuckled fists at his sides, he wordlessly urged her on.

And Sara was cruel; she knew from her own reaction to his touch that slowness was tantalizing torture. As the closure to his pants became an opening, inch by terrible inch, Sara made sure her fingers brushed the stiff rod that throbbed with its own life right under her fingers. She kept her gaze pinned on Deke's, triumphant when he closed his eyes and threw his head back, sending her breathed name up and out into the night through the opening at the top of the tepee.

Her hands splayed on either side of his hips, her fingers wide open, not wanting to miss one masculine inch of his flesh, Sara tried to tug his pants, underdrawers and all, off his hips. But Deke wouldn't allow it; he stilled her hands and rolled over to lie next to her on the blankets. Sara turned to him, sending her questing fingers off on an exploratory mission over his chest and back. But it was her turn to be mesmerized into stillness when Deke rolled on top of her, parted her knees with his, and fitted himself into the saddle of her hips. The unaccustomed hardness of his shaft against her throbbing womanhood took Sara's breath away. Deke gave her back her breath with his kiss. And then took it again, his mouth still on hers, when he began the age-old rhythmic thrusting of his hips against hers, despite their clothing. No one had to tell Sara to bend her knees and bring her legs up to lock them around Deke's powerful buttocks. Her body, if not her innocent soul, knew exactly what to do to heighten its own pleasure.

And then he was sliding down her, kissing the line between her breasts, down her abdomen, leaving a moist trail of desire in his wake. And then his hands were at the fastening of her skirt. When she stiffened slightly, he calmed and soothed her with his hands and his kisses and his whispered words of promise. Almost before she knew it, her skirt and thin drawers, no protection against the onslaught of his passion, were gone, along with her boots. He'd stripped her naked, left her vulnerable; her gaze locked with his as he squatted on his knees at her feet.

The girl that was Sara turned on her side away from him, drawing her knees up, shyly modest under his blazing gaze. Thick silvery tresses masked her burning face from Deke. She heard him chuckle, felt him move; this was followed by a moment's flurried activity, followed by two muffled thumps. His boots, no doubt.

Then silence, until she heard Deke calling her name. "Sara, look at me."

Slowly she rolled onto her back, grateful for her long hair, which partially draped her naked, flushed body. Deke now stood at her feet, proudly, boldly, inviting her exploration. She let her eyes travel up the length that was Deke Bonner, all the while marveling at the pure beauty of the masculine form before her. He was so different from her ... and yet they fit together so wonderfully. And the way his ...

Conscious thought was suspended when Deke shrugged out of his pants. The thin skin that was his underdrawers was peeled down next, leaving Deke as bare as Adam to her sight. Sara swallowed hard. Not only was he huge and well-formed, but he was ... huge. Surely, that didn't go ...

Giving her no more time to reflect on what went where, Deke squatted back down again until he was on all fours. With slow, deliberate motions, he stalked his way back up her with lionlike precision and determination, his arms and legs outside hers, his black eyes as predatory as those of any big cat that Africa harbored. And he didn't have to chuckle to let her know he knew she was terrified and that it showed. When his face was above hers, he lowered himself onto her, separating her knees and again fitting his hips to hers. He spared her his considerable weight by propping himself up with his elbows.

"Deke, I don't know what—"

"Shhh, it's okay. I do. I'll teach you."

"But what if I don't—"

"You will."

And then there were no more words between them. Deke took her mouth in a tender, tender kiss, for which Sara was grateful, for her earlier boldness was abandoning her, leaving in its wake all the virginal trepidation that should have come earlier. Now, all of a sudden, everything was so different, even foreign, but especially the sensation of Deke, naked, against her. How could she have thought she could do this? Was she really the one who had taken his hand and led him in here? Where was that wild wanton?

And then she knew. For the wanton in her arched and bucked, bringing her lust-fuzzy mind back to shocked awareness when she felt Deke kiss her. Not there. But there. "No!" she cried involuntarily, not able to comprehend that burning pleasure. Her hands clutched his hair as her knees spasmodically jerked upwards.

Deke used his tongue to stroke her fire once, twice more before Sara could do anything but make low, guttural sounds at the back of her throat. He then lowered her hips from his mouth and pulled himself, full length, up over her. His kiss, this time on her mouth tasted musky, salty, altogether pleasant. Sara had never known she had a taste.

Or this many nerve endings. Or that they all centered down there. For Deke was now poised over her, his body arced over the length of her, probing for entry. Sara brought her knees up again and twined her arms around his neck. He bent again to kiss her—and began the slow, torturously slow, entry into her body that would make them one. One body. One spirit. One soul.

He stopped at the virginal obstruction inside her. "Sara, this will hurt some," he warned her, tenderly brushing her hair out of her face.

"Not as much as it would if you stopped now," she breathed, the wanton in her having won over the modest little miss.

Deke chuckled low in his throat. "Kiss me," he demanded. "Let me take your pain into me. I promise you it will never hurt again."

Sara raised her mouth to his and, her arms around his neck, pulled Deke to her. When their lips sealed, Deke gave a mighty thrust, tearing away Sara's veil of innocence. Her small cry, which otherwise would have sounded in the night, echoed in Deke's mouth and throat. She clutched at his back, raking his skin with her nails; her knees gripped his sides firmly.

Breaking their kiss, Deke assured her, "It's over, Sara. It won't hurt again."

Seeing his gaze travel her face, knowing he was assessing her reaction, Sara fought back the two tears that threatened to escape the outer corners of her eyes. It really had hurt, but she didn't want him to stop. "Please, Deke," she whispered. "Please love me."

"I do, Sara; I do," he assured her, gathering her to him more closely, if that were possible, so intimate was their embrace already.

Sara had no moment to think about his response because Deke began the rhythmic thrusting of his hips against hers, his body in hers, his heart against hers, that carried Sara beyond herself and forced her eyes closed and brought a feminine, wanton smile to her face. She was aware of the rough feel of the blanket beneath her, of his arms around her, of the sounds of distant revelry in the night, of the passion-sheened moistness of their bodies. Deke's face flickered in the dying firelight. They locked together perfectly, the throbbing thrusts of Deke's body curling her toes and locking her legs around his back. Each thrust moved her closer and closer to the spiraling center of her langorous, clutching being.

She knew that her very existence depended on Deke's continuing thrusts. Then, without warning, the sensations he was wreaking on her, the havoc his body was causing hers, the white-hot pulsing heat of her moistness exploded into rippling spasms that moved in hot waves over her, so devastating, so primal, so delicious that Sara was pitched into a world of purely physical, instinctual response. For many a day would Deke bear on his back the marks of her fingernails; for many a night would he remember her animal cries of intense pleasure.

For her entire life she would see the sight that greeted her when she opened her eyes: Deke poised over her, braced on his stiffened arms, the muscles corded in his neck, eyes closed as he gave his last mighty thrust, sending his seed into her womb. And then he stayed like that, not wanting or unable to move; she didn't know which. She only hoped she gave him as much pleasure as he gave her.

And then he collapsed on top of her, his weight supported by his bent elbows to either side of her, his forehead resting on her shoulder. For the next few moments, the only sound in the tepee was that of their ragged attempts to restore normalcy to their breathing. Deke made no move to extricate himself from her; Sara made no move to extricate him, being content to lie within his embrace, the world held at bay by their shared lovemaking. Lovemaking. No wonder they called it that, Sara mused, smiling.

"What are you smiling about?"

Had she been so lost in her thoughts that she hadn't noticed that he'd raised his head to look at her? Sara focused her gaze on her lover. Her breath caught—she had a lover! "I'm smiling about lovemaking."

Deke pulled back a little bit more, a mirthful laugh just hovering on his lips. "Oh? And what about lovemaking has you looking like the cat that ate the canary?"

Embarrassed and stalling for time, Sara purposely sent her gaze roving, anywhere but at him. Which was no easy task with his face only inches from hers. In fact, her entire visible world was his face. Especially when he lowered it, forcing her to look into his eyes.

"I like it," she blurted, feeling very sinful. She scrunched her head down, pressing her lips together to stifle a sudden fit of giggling.

Deke's eyes widened in response to her admission, and

then he gave himself up to the laughter that bubbled out of him. Sara joined him, having no idea, until Deke jerked reflexively, that her laughter would affect other parts of her—and of him.

"Whoa! Damn, girl, stop that!" he begged, practically squirming on top of her.

Which only made Sara giggle more. Which only made other parts clutch and grab more at each other. In only an instant, intimate laughter became serious intimacy. This time, though, there was no need for instruction. Each knew what the other was about. This second time was already a renewal of the beloved ritual of loving response that they'd forged as uniquely their own.

The next morning found the Cheyenne village on Wolf Creek in chaos. A happy chaos, to be sure, but chaos nonetheless. Which also defined Sara's emotions. She'd found upon awakening this morning, wrapped in Deke's strong, protective embrace, that she didn't know how to act toward him. The whole world should have been different, she felt, but it wasn't. Still, she'd been grateful for Deke's continuing warmth and tenderness with her, even though his nearness only heightened her awkward embarrassment.

Perhaps sensing that, he'd dressed quickly in his denims and shirt from yesterday, kissed her lightly, and left their tepee, presumably to find Coburn and the children. But Sara suspected that his purpose had also been to leave her alone to settle her thoughts and to allow her to dress in privacy. She'd dressed hurriedly once he'd left. Now that all her belongings were packed, leaving only the saddles lying to one side, there was nothing left to do but to lift the flap opening and face the world. Would they all know what she and Deke had done last night? Was it written on her face? Would she see knowing smiles and winks, or maybe even censure from the quiet, respectful Cheyenne? She doubted it. Besides, she told herself, squaring her shoulders and taking the one or two steps to the flap, everyone made love. Or should.

Once outside in the bright sunlight, Sara was surprised to find that the world was different. The trees were greener, the water bluer, the sky more brilliant, the people more friendly. And they were all looking at her and smiling. Awash with a guilty flush, Sara found she wanted the nearness of the one person she'd thought to avoid—Deke Bonner. Spying his tall form amongst a knot of Cheyenne over by the trees near the water, Sara walked purposefully toward them, her head held high. She'd done nothing wrong—if you didn't count making love to your enemy, without benefit of marriage. But the Cheyenne didn't know that, she kept reassuring herself.

When Sara approached the group, she saw that Coburn was also with them. She made her presence known with nods and smiles to the Cheyenne and Coburn—and one quick glance up at Deke, who'd never looked more handsome, more virile to her than he did right now, damn him—especially dressed in fringed and beaded buckskins. This was not what he'd been wearing when he left the tepee. Sara paused. What was going on here? Why was Deke, after sparing her a pert nod, glaring at Coburn, who was very suspiciously grinning from ear to ear?

"Coburn?" Sara questioned. Her hands went automatically to her waist.

But it was Deke who answered her, even though he kept the old Indian trader pinned in place with his black glare. "Remember last night when you wondered what Coburn had to trade, and I reminded you about the money?"

"Yes, I do, but—"

"It seems Coburn gave his money to the Nighthorses."

"Oh, Coburn, how sweet. But then, how did you trade—? What did you trade—?" And then she knew. She turned to Coburn. "Oh, Coburn, how could you? You traded Deke's clothes!"

"And yours," Deke assured her. Now his hands were at his waist. "And your comb, brush, and pillow."

"*He what*!" Sara all but screeched. She dumbly looked down at her own riding outfit, as if to assure herself that it hadn't magically changed into buckskins to match Deke's. Then she leveled a look on the old man, who was still grinning and nodding as much as were the curious Cheyenne with him. "But how could you? I mean, I just packed my saddlebags and everything was there. I—"

"Oh, it don't rightly matter none to these good folks. They was willin' to take my word for the value of your property."

Sara took a threatening step toward Coburn; the Cheyenne tensed, losing their smiles; Deke put a restraining hand on Sara's arm. Appalled, she looked up at the ceremoniously clad bounty hunter, ready to plead her case. "Deke, he can't do that! Tell him, he can't do that. Our belongings are not his to barter. I—I can't sleep without my pillow."

Deke managed a grim smile down at her. "I know that, and you know that. Even that old horse trader there knows that. But tell it to the Cheyenne, for if there's one thing they hate more than a thief or a liar, it's someone who goes back on a trade."

Sara kept her eyes on Deke while she absorbed that. Then, barely able to keep her face from showing the ugly emotions she was feeling right then, she turned on Coburn. "You had no right, Coburn. How could you?"

He had the decency to squirm just a fraction. "Well, now, Sara, a man has to make a livin'. And seein' as how these here folk think everything about you is a good luck talisman, I guess I just got caught up in the good feelin's and the revelry—"

"—And sold all my things."

"And mine," Deke cut in. "The only things we have left are our boots, guns, and horses."

At Sara's outraged gasp, Coburn began talking rapidly. "Well now, I 'spect that's rightly so. But of course, I'm more than willin' to share my good fortune with you—"

"Oh, that goes without saying," Sara assured him.

Coburn stumbled over his words just a bit. "Yessir, ma'am, it surely does. Then that's all settled. Now, uh, Sara,

you need to go change out of them hot, confinin' clothes
you're wearin, and—''

Sara wasn't capable of more than an angry whisper. "You
mean to say you sold the very clothes off my back?''

Coburn looked to his left at a young Cheyenne girl and
then at Sara. "It would seem so. What you're wearin' is now
the property of this fine young lady—the chief's daughter.''

Without the obvious pleading in Coburn's eyes, begging
Sara to let him keep his hair on his skull, there was no telling
what Sara's response would have been. Beyond speech,
shaking her head, she looked up at Deke.

He was looking awfully grim around the mouth and eyes,
but he did offer, "I do believe you will look most lovely in
a buckskin dress and boots, Miss Dalton.''

Chapter Sixteen

Miss Dalton, atop her painted and befeathered little mare, was well on her way to the army camp at the confluence of Wolf Creek and the Beaver River. She looked a picture of Cheyenne loveliness in her new beaded and fringed buckskin dress. But she could not summon a smile to wear with it. Her mood was not improved any by the knowledge that she and Deke had the distinct honor of wearing what had been originally sewn as the matching wedding costume for a brave and a maiden of two very prominent families in the camp.

Coburn had assured them that their new clothes were in fact new, never having been worn. So they was gettin' a better deal than the Cheyenne, who got used, worn clothing. And didn't the lucky Cheyenne who'd bartered successfully last night look right smart in their new duds, too, marchin' around the village all self-important in Sara's and Deke's clothes?

With snake-slit eyes, Sara glared over her shoulder at Coburn. He'd better just keep his distance for a while yet. She

tossed her heavy braid, something some giggling young
women had insisted on plaiting for her and fixing in place
with buffalo grease, back over her shoulder to hang down
her back past her waist.

"You have to admit, Sara, this is kind of funny, when you
think about it," Deke offered from her right, where he rode
his equally painted and outraged buckskin-colored stallion.
Coburn, on a somnolent Jezebel, devoid of any decoration,
as if she were beneath Cheyenne notice, was a few paces
behind them. He lead his new packhorse, ladened with his
many purchases from the Cheyenne, and was telling wild
tales to the two delighted children, who rode tandem on one
horse. Bringing up the rear of this strange entourage were
four Cheyenne braves, looking for all the world like martyrs.

"Well, let me assure you, Deke, I'm trying not to think
about it. Especially this damned braid. God, it smells."

"Yes, it does," Deke agreed, maybe a little too vehemently. "But I believe I like it a lot better than that damned
red bonnet Etheline Nighthorse gave you."

Sara nearly bit a hole in her bottom lip to keep from laughing. She wasn't yet ready to give up her black mood; she
could barely acknowledge to herself that she wasn't really
as angry at Coburn as she let on. She was even, on one level,
grateful for his meddling; by hanging on to her anger at
Coburn, she didn't have to deal with last night with Deke.
But the remembered sight of a plump Cheyenne matron parading for all to see through the village in that damned bonnet, long tying-ribbons trailing, as if she were the Queen of
England in the crown jewels, was too much. Despite herself,
Sara chuckled—once, and then again.

Deke caught her mood, a rare smile of pure fun changing
his handsome, roguish features to those of a carefree boy.
"She was as proud as Lucifer, wasn't she?"

Sara grinned and nodded, looking back over her shoulder
at Coburn. She then turned to Deke, a self-deprecating quirk
to her mouth. "You know, one of my many faults is I can't

stay mad at anyone for very long—even when I want to. Even when I should.''

Deke sobered some. ''I'd call that a virtue, Miss Dalton. The quality of forgiveness doesn't reside in every heart. And I think we're all going to need some before this summer is through. I hope you have enough to go around.''

Sara stared at him for a moment and then looked down at the reins in her hands. She didn't want to talk about Robber's Cave today. Not after last night. Deliberately changing the subject, she turned to him again. ''What do you make of Callie Mitchell and Tyler Mack?''

Deke looked back at the boy and the girl with Coburn, and then at Sara. ''I think they'll be all right. A few days of Coburn's wild tales—especially that one about him and Jezebel and that bear he told us a few days back—ought to go a long ways to ease their pain and bad memories.''

''I hope you're right, Deke. They are just precious. But so young to have suffered so much. I didn't think I was going to get them to let go of my hands this morning when we went to fetch them. They need so much love right now.''

Deke was silent for a moment, as if digesting that. When he looked over at Sara, she was startled to see in his black eyes stark acknowledgement that the children weren't the only ones who needed love in their lives. Before she could do anything beyond registering that fleeting impression, it was gone. His face carefully blank, Deke said, ''Well, yeah, I believe the Nighthorses and their brood will bring them around.''

''Me, too,'' Sara said, leaving more unsaid between them than she feared would ever be said.

After that conversation, the day passed uneventfully for the little troop as they kept heading north under the unforgiving heat of the August sun. They drank water from their canteens without stopping. A midday meal was also eaten in the saddle, and Sara was pleasantly surprised to find that dried buffalo meat was leaner and sweeter than beef jerky. She also enjoyed the dried fruits and nuts the Cheyenne had stocked them with before they left the village and its waving, hopeful occupants. After all, if Sara—and Deke and the children and Coburn, of course—weren't successful in convincing the soldiers that the Cheyenne weren't responsible, although the children had already corroborated it, then that village stood every chance of being wiped out in a sudden, sweeping military raid.

Her mind baking in the heat, heavy with such thoughts and weighted down even more with vivid visions of last night, Sara more than once wished for her ugly red bonnet to shade her face—and for soap and water to wash out the increasingly rank, sun-warmed buffalo grease from her hair. How did the Cheyenne women stand it? However, she was beginning to delight in her new buckskin dress, even if she was scandalized to have on no underclothing of any sort— nothing had been sacred in Coburn's trading. Slit up the sides for ease in riding, it was much less binding and more airy than her old clothes. But it also left a lot of bare thigh exposed to the sun—and to Deke's wandering gaze. As if he hadn't seen her bare thighs before, Sara snorted—and then stiffened. What was she thinking?

She looked over at Deke. He was looking at her bare thigh. "Stop that," she admonished; for nothing would she admit that his frank stare of appreciation pleased her.

"Stop what?" he teased.

Sara, her lips pressed together in a straight line, huffed out a breath through her nostrils. "Looking at me."

Deke pushed his Stetson—quickly traded back to Coburn by a shocked youth for Deke's pocket watch after one thunderous bellow of rage from its original owner—up with his thumb. "Stop looking at you? Why?"

"Because . . . it's indecent."

"Well, I'd like to know how it is," he kept on.

Trapped now, Sara could do nothing but forge on. "You're looking at me like I'm . . . it's that vulture thing again."

Completely stymied by that reference, if his face could be

believed, Deke questioned, "Vulture?"

Men. They couldn't remember a thing that was important. "Yes. Vulture," Sara fussed. "Don't you remember—that first night outside of Plains? I remarked that you were looking at me like I was food. And you said, did I think you were a vulture, and I said—"

"—No. You said no you didn't."

Realizing her mistake now, when she remembered how she'd softened towards him even then, she finished lamely, "That's right. It took you long enough to remember."

Deke's out-and-out laugh at her expense did nothing to smooth her ruffled feathers. "You, Sara Dalton, are a true prize," he announced.

Sara wisely chose to leave it at that.

Camp that night was, mercifully, along the banks of Wolf Creek. No sooner had they all eaten than Sara informed the others that she was going to bathe. Coburn surprised her by pulling out soap and a length of toweling. He then went on to endear himself to her forever by handling over her own silver brush and comb set. At her look of wonderment, Coburn told her, "I got 'em back for you, Sara. I seen what it meant to you. I don't want there to be no hard feelin's."

She should have been mad at him; she should have shouted at him. She had every right. But instead, she gave him probably the biggest hug of his life and a smacking kiss on his balding, ruddy forehead. "Coburn, I love you," she crowed.

Coburn reddened; the Cheyenne grunted their opinion of this affectionate display; Tyler and Callie sat wide-eyed by the campfire; and Deke looked as if he wished he'd been the one to hand over her precious items. She turned to Callie. "Come on, sweetheart, you can go with me." When the little girl, a thin, sober, black-haired child of seven years with immense brown eyes, scrambled to her feet and took Sara's offered hand, Sara turned to the bemused gentlemen and announced, "Ladies only." Callie adopted Sara's attitude immediately; so, noses in the air, toweling over Sara's arm, a piece of soap between them, the ladies sauntered off to the privacy of a stand of scrubby but thick bushes along the banks of Wolf Creek.

"Come along, Princess Matilda," Sara continued her play-acting, holding Callie's hand and walking in a very mincing fashion right down to the water. She hoped that a bit of silliness might alleviate any remaining fears Callie might have about being amongst strangers. "I fear we are a might soiled, my darling. It simply won't do for one to have buffalo grease in one's hair for any length of time. Do you agree?"

Callie eyed Sara, giggled, fingered her own braid, and took up the game. "Oh, rather, Queen Gertrude. I find it most awful."

"Quite," Sara intoned, using her best British-snob accent, but intensely relieved that there remained in the girl a spirit of levity untouched by the horrors she'd endured. Sara eyed the water, then her buckskin outfit and Callie's dirty, ragged dress, her only possession. "Oh, dear, I fear we must disrobe before bathing. Otherwise, we'll get our best party frocks wet."

Callie nearly crossed her eyes, so excited was she by this purely feminine silliness. "Oh, you're so correct, my queen."

"I say, my little partridge, I do believe that the last one in the water must either eat a rotten egg—or was the rule that one must lay a rotten egg? I fear I've quite forgotten which. Would you happen to know, Matilda? May I call you simply Matilda? I find titles so boring."

Callie let loose a storm of giggles and crossed her legs, apparently to keep from wetting herself.

"I say, Simply Matilda, your behavior is quite unbecoming for a lady of the court. Do please try to restrain yourself. Now, about that egg business . . . ?"

Tears of laughter streaming down her face, Callie managed to garble out, "Lay it. One must lay a rotten egg."

Sara managed to look duly shocked; she even put a fluttering hand to her breast. "I say, Simply, old girl, are you quite sure? That would seem to be rather a nasty business. I mean, how does one tell if one's egg is rotten before one actually . . . lays it? Have you any idea?"

Bent over, hands on her knees, Callie told her feet, "I don't know, Queen Gertrude. I just always try to be the first one in the water."

"Oh, splendid idea, Simply. Shall we have a go at it, then?"

Callie straightened up. "On three."

"Quite. One . . ." Sara kicked off her boots. Callie sat struggling to unbutton her high-top shoes.

"Two . . ." Sara grabbed the bottom hem of her buckskin dress and began slowly pulling it up over her legs. Callie still sat struggling to unbutton her high-top shoes.

"Three!" Sara whipped the dress off over her head, threw it on the ground, and waded into the sun-warmed water, lowering herself until her breasts were covered. Callie continued struggling to unbutton her high-top shoes. No contest. Princess Matilda, Simply Matilda to her friends, would indeed have to lay a rotten egg.

Not licked yet, even though only one partially unbuttoned shoe marked her progress, the royal princess stood up and pointed at the queen. "No fair! You didn't have any underclothes on!"

"Oh yeah?" Sara questioned in her own voice, wondering if the men in the camp had heard Callie's last remark. "Well, you're the one who said to count to three. Maybe you should have said three hundred seeing as how slow you are."

"Oh yeah? Well, I got the soap, and you don't." Callie scrambled over to the towel and picked it up, holding it up triumphantly.

"Oh yeah? Well, if you got the soap, then I have the water!" With that, Sara sluiced a veritable wave at Callie, drenching the front of her ragged little dress.

The girl's shrieks of dismayed delight brought the men on the run, crashing through the underbrush. Deke arrived first, his Colt revolver in his hand; Coburn was an awkwardly loping second, his long, ancient rifle held at the ready; behind him was a wide-eyed Tyler, a thick, broken branch in his hands; at a more stately pace, no weapons out, and obviously only vaguely curious about the white women's screaming, came the four Cheyenne braves.

Sara, cognizant of her nudity, quickly waded farther out into the water and the darkness, stopping when her head was shrouded by overhanging bushes. From there, she could see and hear the chaotic scene on shore.

"What in the hell is going on here?" were Deke's first words, once he'd assured himself that no one was threatening the ladies; he holstered his Colt and put his hands to his waist. Coburn and Tyler relaxed, too; the Cheyenne already were.

Callie, her thin hands knotting up her wet dress, her brown eyes widened, said, "We were just playing."

Obviously an unknown concept to Deke Bonner. "Playing?"

"Yessir."

He just stared down from his great height at the terrified little girl. Softening some, he went down on one knee in front of her. "It's okay, Callie. I'm glad you feel like playing. Now, where's Miss Sara?"

Since the guns were holstered, and there'd be no danger of the men firing indiscriminately at the least noise, Sara started to call out her location, but didn't get the chance.

"You mean Queen Gertrude? She's right over there—in the water." But there was no one to be seen in the water. Callie's pointing hand came down slowly; she turned huge, liquid brown eyes on a thoroughly confused Deke.

"Queen Gertrude's gone! She's dead! Those bad men came back and killed her!" she wailed, bursting into tears and throwing her thin arms around the surprised bounty hunter's neck. Still, he reflexively hugged her to him.

Had Deke not jumped up, child and all, yelling orders and walking the shore, he would have heard Sara calling out that she was right there. Everytime Sara yelled out, so did Deke. And Callie shrieked louder. And Coburn and Tyler beat the bushes. Frustrated, she just let them rant on. No way was she wading out of this water naked, what with all this company.

Finally, one of the braves put a hand on Coburn's sleeve. Apparently, Coburn was telling them the situation. One of the braves nodded, approached the shoreline, scanned it, and pointed right at Sara. All eyes went to the spot. She waved. Only Callie, Deke, Coburn, and Tyler looked astounded. As for the Cheyenne, they exchanged looks that didn't speak well for the tracking abilities of whites and turned to walk back to the campsite, shaking their heads.

"Sara, what in the hell are you doing? You scared the life out of this child! Come out of there."

"Is Queen Gertrude okay?"

Deke looked at the child perched on his arm. "Who is Queen Gertrude?"

"Miss Sara. I'm Princess Matilda, but she—the queen— calls me Simply. You can, too. Is she okay?"

"She is for now," Deke promised, the threat in his voice obvious only to Sara as she waded closer in, but still stayed modestly covered. Callie slumped in relief in Deke's arms, her head resting on his broad shoulder.

"You know, bounty hunter, you look mighty natural with a child in your arms," Sara teased, treading the water.

Deke gave a start at her words and looked at Callie as if he were just now aware that he was holding her. "Sara, what in the hell is going on?"

He finally put Callie down, who sat on the damp shore and began again to unlace her shoes. Without a word, Tyler went to help with her other shoe as if he'd done it all his life. Coburn stood over them supervising.

Chagrin for scaring them all stole over Sara upon seeing the children together. Feeling a little ashamed, she turned her gaze to Deke. And immediately felt inclined to tease the huge man a little. Served him right for being so damned desirable in those skin-tight buckskins. "Like Callie said, we were playing. Ever heard of it, bounty hunter?"

His hands went to his waist. He looked from a bobbing Sara to where Callie was slowly undressing with Coburn's and Tyler's help, and then back to Sara. "Yeah, I heard of it, Queen Gertrude. And you know exactly the game I like to play. It's an old Indian game, played in a tepee on a buffalo skin. You see, the way you play it is, you have a man and a woman—"

"I know the game!" Sara shrieked, trying to shush him. Her gaze flitted to the two children and Coburn, all of whom looked curiously back at them. Sara turned her hot gaze on an unrepentant Deke. "In front of the children, Deke Bonner. Have you no shame?"

"No," he assured her calmly.

"You are not a nice man."

"Never said I was. But at least I'm not the one carrying on a conversation in the nude. Seems like we've done this before, Sara, and I believe I ended up with a bloodied nose."

Sara had a fleeting image of the Cimarron River just after the buffalo stampede. "That's how I recall it. Now, if you will go, and take Coburn and Tyler with you, Simply and I will finish our baths. I'm as wrinkled as a prune now as it is."

"I'll have to take your word for it," Deke countered, tipping his black Stetson at her in a gentlemanly gesture.

But she wasn't fooled. This was no gentleman. He turned to walk off. Sara, her eyes narrowed and feline, allowed herself full feminine appreciation for his backside as he left, taking Coburn and Tyler with him. When he was out of view, she turned to Callie and smiled. "Come on, honey, let's get cleaned up—and bring the soap, you little ninny."

That next morning saw the travelers up with the sun to break camp and ready themselves for the grueling day ahead. Not that the ride itself would be so long and hard, but this afternoon would see them at the military campsite. At least they'd all gotten a good night's sleep—even without her pillow, Sara fussed. Well, everyone slept but Deke, who'd kept sending her hot looks all evening, then had sat up as the watch through most of the night. No, Sara supposed, having seen her naked in the water hadn't done much to settle his fiery blood. Not that she hadn't been affected by his nearness, especially now that she knew the full implications of his closeness. But what could she do about it, as fully chaperoned as they were?

Her maidenly conscience, so recently violated, troubled her with the more daunting question: Why was she thinking she should do anything about the undeniable, but so very wrong, physical attraction between them? Wasn't Deke Bonner still the enemy? Or had something changed that? No, nothing had changed that. Her head knew the problems, but could not convince her heart of them. If only what she felt was simple physical attraction, then it would be easy enough to control. But it was so much more than that: Deke Bonner was dangerously close to her heart, closer than she was yet willing to admit.

Sara closed her eyes, resting her forehead against the saddle she was putting on Cinnamon. Mistake. Immediately played out for her in her traitorous mind was the scene in the tepee on the buffalo hides. Not one detail was left out by her cruelly sharp memory. Enough! She roused herself, telling her shameful heart that this—whatever it was—with Deke just could not be.

A young voice calling out caught her attention. It was Tyler, running to help Deke. Sara watched the darkly blond boy as he self-importantly grasped the bridle of Deke's restive buckskin stallion while Deke saddled the huge horse. Sara was sure Deke needed no assistance with his mount, but still he asked for the boy's help. Further warming towards the bounty hunter's better qualities was the last thing Sara needed. But still she couldn't deny the evidence of Deke's inherent goodness. Which only made it harder to accept that he was the almost legendary and reportedly the most ruthless bounty hunter in Indian Territory.

Not able to square the good man with his terrifying reputation, Sara settled her attention on young Tyler. The twelve-year-old boy hadn't strayed very far from Deke's side since they'd left the Cheyenne village yesterday—in fact, only to see about Callie. And to the bounty hunter's credit, he'd been sincere and friendly, but not overly so, with the boy. Much as if he knew the serious youngster needed a cool hand now, rather than silly emotionalism; much as if what Tyler'd been through had made him a man, deserving of the respect he was being shown.

Such young shoulders to have to carry the weight of not only his own future, but also that of an entire Indian tribe, Sara sighed. But from the little she knew of him, Sara could already see the strong and loving man Tyler would become.

Now, where was Callie? Sara stayed her hands from saddling Cinnamon and looked around until she spied her jabbering her head off to Coburn as he checked his pack animal over. Last night's silliness had done her a world of good. Sara was pretty sure that Callie's spirit was such that nothing would get the best of her for long. Not as long as she had Tyler nearby.

Just a glance to Coburn and Callie's left brought the Cheyenne to her attention; typically, they sat apart, ready and alert, their handsome brown faces not revealing their thoughts—which might include, Sara theorized, how to deal with all of them if this afternoon didn't go well. That's what they needed, the threat of a massacre to add to the tension.

Well, at least she'd die clean, Sara thought, resorting to grim humor to take her mind off the coming ordeal. She put a hand to her abundant hair, securely tied back with a buckskin fringe she'd broken off the hem of her dress this morning. Rested and clean, Sara felt ready for anything. Last night, she and Callie had washed the girl's dress, too; it might be torn in places, but it was now clean. She looked at Callie again and smiled; the child's black hair gleamed blue in the morning sun. Such a beautiful girl. Sara couldn't help but wonder what would become of Callie and Tyler, even in the warm and loving hands of the Nighthorses. For she knew only too well the deep scars left by losing loved ones to senseless violence. But at least they would have each other.

And that thought brought another concern to the forefront. How in the world was she going to say good-bye to the two children today when they parted at the army camp and left with Coburn to go to the Nighthorses'? The sudden lurching in the center of her chest told her that Tyler and Callie had already earned a place in her heart. To her surprise, she realized that there were tears standing in her eyes and blurring her vision. She quickly swiped at them when Tyler startled her. When had he walked over here?

"Miss Sara," he began, "I've got to say something to somebody before we get to the soldiers, and I can't bring myself to say it to Mr. Bonner or Coburn."

Sara turned to the obviously upset, broad-shouldered boy, who was as tall as she was, and gave him her full attention. That he had singled her out for his confidences only placed a tighter stricture on her heart. "You can tell me, Tyler. I'll listen."

"And you won't think no worse of me . . . when I tell you what I've got to say? You have to promise."

Sudden dread coursed through Sara, but she carefully kept it off her face. Her heart pounding, her palms suddenly sweaty, she readied herself to hear her worst fear fall from the boy's lips. He was going to tell her that the Cheyenne had indeed killed his and Callie's families.

Chapter Seventeen

"I promise I won't think worse of you, Tyler," Sara all but whispered, feeling her insides go icy numb.

"It's about . . . it's about . . . what happened. At the wagons, I mean. Our families . . . and all the others."

"I know," Sara prompted gently, wishing there was something she could do to help him, and wishing she were a thousand miles from here. She reached out her hand, putting it on his shoulder. "Go on."

Instead of making him feel stronger, apparently her tender gesture only made things worse for his tightly held self-control, for a huge tear slid from each of his eyes and coursed slowly, sadly, down his cheeks. "Oh, Miss Sara, it was so awful."

"I know, Tyler. I know it was. But you have to be strong now. Just remember, it's over, and you're safe."

"I don't know that I'll ever feel safe again." His brave facade slipped to a crumpled mask.

God, take this burden from this child, Sara prayed silently. Out loud, she said, "You will be, Tyler. You will be. I just know it. Now tell me what's wrong, son, so I can help you. Was it really the Cheyenne who killed your folks? Is that what you're trying to tell me? Because even if it was, we'll—"

"Oh, no, ma'am, it wasn't the Cheyenne. I didn't lie about that. It wasn't them at all. It was five white men, just like me and Callie said."

So relieved that her knees nearly buckled, Sara reflexively gripped Tyler's shoulder harder. Thank you, God. Now she felt that she could face whatever it was he had to tell her. Until he told her.

"It's something else that's troubling me. Something . . . real bad, Miss Sara. About me."

Sara looked at him for a moment. "About you, Tyler? Honey, what is it?" Afraid for this young man, Sara hugged him to her, even though she fully expected him to protest. Instead, he clung to her, putting his head on her shoulder.

Great wracking sobs were her immediate answer. "I couldn't do nothing to stop them, Miss Sara. I couldn't! I didn't have no gun or nothing . . . I ran. I hid me and Callie behind some rocks and trees. It was all I could do! I swear it! There wasn't nothing more I could do to save my ma and pa. I heard my ma screaming; I still do. Oh, God, Sara, there wasn't nothing I could do." After a series of heaving sobs, he blurted out his deep, dark secret. "I'm a coward! I'm a no-good coward. I should've died trying to help my family, but I didn't, Sara. I didn't. I hid like a dog!"

Now Sara was crying as hard as Tyler. She became aware of other presences near them. Through her tears, she saw Deke, a hard, knowing look on his face. To his side was Callie, clinging to Coburn and sobbing her heart out. Sara's look to Deke questioned if he had heard; he nodded to her and pulled Tyler from her, taking him into his strong, male embrace. Sara hugged her folded hands to her chest and watched the bounty hunter with the emotionally torn boy. Poor Tyler could barely stand from the force of his emotion, but Deke was a solid wall of strong comfort.

After a moment, Deke raised his head and looked over at her and Coburn, his eyes shaded by the brim of his black hat. "Stay here. Tyler and I have to talk." With that, he pulled Tyler away from him and turned him around, putting his hand on the boy's shoulder. Like that, the two walked away; Sara could hear Deke's voice, low and soothing, yet strong and masculine.

Sara looked at Coburn, who was awkwardly patting Callie's black hair as he held her to him. He turned the only serious expression she'd ever seen on his face to Sara and said, "That's goin' to be the most important talk that young man ever has in his life. I just wisht I'da had someone like that there bounty hunter to talk to me at young Tyler's age. Mighta made all the difference in the world as to how I turned out."

Sara smiled at him. "Coburn, you turned out just fine."

He looked down, then back up at her, his mouth working. "It's right kind of you to say so, Sara. Right kind, indeed."

Sara had no idea what Deke had said to Tyler that morning. And Deke and Tyler weren't telling. But whatever the words, they had done the trick. Tyler certainly couldn't be called happy or carefree that afternoon, but he was certainly more light-hearted, less intense and withdrawn. His darting gaze that kept Deke in sight told a story of its own. Sara found a new and warmer respect in her heart for Deke Bonner. She'd never forget the sight of him standing up and cold-bloodedly killing that robber on the day they met the Nighthorses, but neither would she forget this morning when that same man, with a few quiet words, had perhaps saved a young boy's soul. Deke Bonner was a good man, like it or not.

And, like it or not, they were nearing the army camp. To keep the children's minds, and perhaps their own, off the impending confrontation, Sara, Coburn, and even Deke regaled Tyler and Callie with stories of the Nighthorses and their brood of children. The two youngsters had accepted with little argument, once they had been convinced that they really could not tag along with Sara and Deke, that they would go with Coburn to Ben and Etheline's to live, seeing as how neither one of them had any other kin they could go to.

And, disappointed though they were, they laughed readily enough at the antics and descriptions of the large family. But under it all, Sara saw the fear of the unknown in their eyes— and of course their obvious reluctance to leave the security of her and Deke's company. This wasn't surprising to Sara, seeing as how she and Deke and Coburn had in a sense become their family.

A family, Sara mused. If only things could be different, she dreamed, seeing herself and Deke on her farm, raising Callie and Tyler. And Coburn dropping by for visits. Then, angry at herself for the tearing she felt in her heart over these idealized pictures, Sara shook her head and resettled herself in her saddle. No sense making things worse—there was still Robber's Cave, a bounty warrant, and her dying mother to contend with once they fulfilled their obligation to the Cheyenne. And beyond all that, there was Deke Bonner.

Who was just now considering her with intense scrutiny. "What are you putting yourself through over there, Miss Dalton? You've changed expression about four times. You're not sorry about the buffalo hides, are you?"

"Buffalo hides" was quickly becoming a code for their lovemaking. "No," she admitted, perhaps too readily before thinking. Feeling her face coloring, she primly pulled herself up straighter and unnecessarily fussed with Cinnamon's reins. "My thoughts had nothing to do with you," she lied. "You flatter yourself, bounty hunter."

"Do I now? My mistake, ma'am." Grinning in that absolutely devastating way of his, which told her plainly enough that he knew she was lying, he tipped his hat very politely to her and nudged his buckskin stallion into a canter, joining Coburn up ahead.

Hateful man, Sara fumed, all the while greedily drinking

in the sight of his broad shoulders and his easy way in the saddle.

The army campsite, when they finally reached it about mid-afternoon, was really nothing more than that. And, just as Chief Walking Stick had known, it was abuzz with soldiers, all of whom stilled and paid close, watchful attention to the approaching riders. Armed men in blue uniforms came out of tents; conversations ceased; work was forgotten.

"You oughta be a touch careful right here," Coburn advised, reining in and turning to his companions. "No offense, but ya'll look like a bunch of Injuns to them, bein' in them buckskins and in the company of them braves." He turned to Sara. "Why don't you let your hair down some, show 'em you're white? Ain't no young squaws with silver hair that I ever saw. That might do the trick an' let us get close enough to state our business afore they shoot us all."

Good lord, how many times was her hair, by the very nature of its color, going to either get them killed or save their lives? Sara fussed while undoing the rawhide thong that secured it. And indeed, when she fluffed it out around her shoulders, the sight of so much silvery blond hair did indeed cause a stir amongst the soldiers. Both mouths and guns dropped. The riders definitely had the camp's attention now.

"Remind me to use your hair instead of a gun the next time we get involved in a set-to, Miss Dalton," Deke said out the corner of his mouth as he nudged his mount forward.

Sara narrowed her black eyes and just barely stopped herself from poking her tongue out at him. There would be time enough later for sarcastic sparring, she promised herself. Right now, she needed her presence of mind to deal with the soldiers and the children—and the Cheyenne, who were not advancing any closer than the outer perimeter of the army tents. Even though they sat in a close knot on their bareback mounts, Sara felt their hawk-eyed gazes squarely on her back. Better that than their arrows. Taking in and then releasing a huge breath from her tension-tightened lungs, Sara rode into the camp with Deke, Coburn, and the children. She kept reminding herself that these soldiers were not the enemy.

"You're not going to cry again, are you, Sara? You know every time you do, you have to take a nap."

Just who did he think he was? For two cents, she'd box his head and knock that damned black Stetson off. Fortunately for Deke, or perhaps for Sara, no one was with them to read her thoughts and give her the two cents. "No, I'm not going to cry, bounty hunter," she retorted, a curl to her lips that had nothing to do with a smile.

"Good. Then maybe we can make some time now. Or at least start heading in the right direction for a change." Without reining in his horse, he scanned the prairie horizon to his left and right as if picking out their course.

"Don't you miss them at all?" Sara asked, her words pulling his black eyes back to her. Had she really once thought his eyes were like those of a snake?

Deke pressed his wide mouth into a straight line. "Hell, yes, I do. All except the Cheyenne braves. But it doesn't do any good to dwell on the kids. They'll be fine with the Nighthorses. Coburn will see to it."

Sara looked down at her pommel and then back up at Deke. The slanting early-evening sun behind him provided a reddish-yellow backdrop for his large frame, as if that were the sun's sole purpose for existing. "I know. But I just wish that. . . . Never mind."

Deke pulled his hat's brim, resettling it on his head. "Wishing doesn't make it so. You know that."

They rode along in silence for a few more minutes. Then Deke surprised her by being the one to break the silence, and by being the one, for once, who appeared hesitant. "Sara, I . . . Well, I just want to say that you did one damn fine job back there with those soldiers. The Cheyenne were right to place their trust in you."

Sara was stunned, and warmed, by his words. Was this actual respect for her abilities he was voicing? Confidence in her intelligence and discretion? Well, even if he did sound grudging and had as much as admitted that he was surprised at her gaining the ready acceptance of the U.S. Army, Sara accepted his intended compliments. But not without demurring slightly. "Thank you," she said quietly, but surprising herself by the note of shyness in her voice. "I didn't really do anything, except have long silver hair that got us into the camp without being shot. Tyler and Callie were the ones who carried the day."

"They did their part, all right, but don't take your own part lightly. Your hair got their attention, but your words got their cooperation. I believe this is the first instance of the soldiers taking the Indians' side that I've ever come across."

That didn't bode well. "Do you think they'll keep their word—that they won't retaliate against the Cheyenne?"

Deke thought about that for a moment; Sara used the time to study his strong, handsome profile. There wasn't one tiny feature of him that she would change, even if she could. Just looking at his male perfection set her blood racing. She wondered what he thought when he looked at her face; was there anything he would change? Before Sara could begin an uncomplimentary catalogue of her perceived facial flaws, Deke spoke up.

"Yes, I believe they will. They'll have to for now. There are too many people to say otherwise if they were to try to make trouble, at least for Chief Walking Stick's particular village. But I know the army well enough to know they'll find another reason, real or imagined, to attack the Cheyenne. And the Cheyenne are just as liable to give them a damned good reason to, Sara. Make no mistake about that."

Sara's blood ran cold; she knew Deke was right. But she was thinking of Tyler, Callie, and the Nighthorses. They were so vulnerable—and so isolated on their homestead. She wasn't sure she would be able to sleep that night for worrying about them all. She was a real one for taking on the troubles of the whole world, always had been. It got her hurt a lot, but she'd rather be like that than to be cold and uncaring. The way Deke Bonner pretended he was.

Sleep that night proved not to be the problem Sara thought it would be. She was exhausted. Drained. The tensions of the past few days had wreaked havoc on her nerves. She wanted only to sleep, pillow or no. Being alone with Deke felt like being home after company left. At their camp that night, after another filling supper from the provisions given them by the Cheyenne yesterday, Sara opened her bedroll against Deke's, lay down on it, buckskin dress and all, and settled herself against him, her back to his chest—even going so far as to drag his arm around her and use his hand as her missing pillow. Within seconds, she was fast asleep. Exhausted. Drained.

Well, goddamn, Deke thought, lying there providing a bed for a softly snoring Sara. Are you comfortable, Miss Dalton? he fumed in his head. He hoped he didn't have to go for his gun at some point in the night, because his right hand was now a pillow for her cheek. His left arm was now numb from being wedged under her waist, and his left hand from being held by both of hers between her breasts. Despite the admittedly intimate posture of their embrace, Deke found his masculine sensibilities to be outraged by her casual, even callous, treatment of him as if he were no more than a comfortable old bearskin rug she wrapped up in on cold nights. But perhaps even more disconcerting to him was to realize that he did indeed have such a weak-kneed thing as sensibilities. He preferred to think of himself as a hard-bitten bounty hunter. Not a flea-bitten bearskin rug.

Deke huffed air out of his mouth and made small spitting noises, trying without benefit of hands to dislodge a strand of her hair from his lips. That accomplished, he now realized that his nose itched. Great. But God forbid he should try to scratch it and risk waking up her royal highness—what was it Callie had called her? Oh yeah, right—Queen Gertrude. And so, his nose itching, his arm numb, her hair in his mouth, and suffering terribly by his own estimation, Deke finally gave up the argument with himself—one he was losing anyway—and drifted off to sleep. The final insult came with his erotic dreams of the delectable woman sleeping safely and innocently in his arms.

Chapter Eighteen

It was the buffalo stampede all over again. There were no buffalo and no stampede, but the emotions were the same. The sense of fearsome awe was the same. The words were the same.

"Son of a bitch," Deke whispered, his black eyes taking in the scene before him, his large hands fighting to control his stamping stallion. "It's bigger than I thought when we first saw it two hours ago."

Her hands similarly full with Cinnamon's desperate tugs to turn away from the sight and smell before them, Sara jerkily turned her head towards Deke to call out over the booming voice of the summer thunder, "What are we going to do?"

Before Deke could answer, the bruised and roiling sky over their heads, forsaking its soothing rains in favor of showers of lightning, sparked another silvery bolt to the parched ground in the too-close distance, sending the panicked horses into a wheeling dance under their riders. Cin-

namon grunted and screamed her terror at the raging wall of
fire that ate the ground beneath it and swept it ever closer to
the lone riders on the hilly ridge. They were just a week past
their ordeal with the Cheyenne, just a week further southeast
into Indian Territory.

"We're going to run like hell!" Deke yelled back, as his
mount reared in fear and defiance. Cursing and struggling
against the buckskin's superior strength, Deke finally brought
the horse under his tight-reined control. Once more he
quickly, desperately surveyed the burning horizon, at once
black with storm, gray with smoke, and red with spiky fingers of flame that beckoned to the riders.

"Where to?" Sara could barely keep the quaver out of
her voice and her mount from bucking. She tried to see the
prairie through Deke's trained eyes. What did he see that she
didn't? Surely there was no haven of safety for them on these
burning plains. After everything they'd been through, were
they to die ignominiously out here, bested by a late-summer
prairie fire? No! She just couldn't allow it, or accept it. There
had to be some way out, some one thing they could—

"This way!" Deke suddenly yelled, cutting into Sara's
fear. When she looked over at him, he pointed off to their
right. "Make for that soddy, Sara, and don't stop for anything. Ride like the wind; it may be our only chance."

He spurred his mount and was gone, trusting her to follow.
She did, but her heart pounded at a pace faster than the one
set by Deke. Riding across the path of the firestorm seemed
as foolhardy to her as riding across the path of the stampeding buffalo would have been. As Cinnamon wanted to do,
Sara wanted to run from the fire, not in front of it. But apparently Deke knew something she didn't. And she'd been
trusting her survival to his considerable skills for too long
now to question him at this dangerous point. And so she did
as she was told. She rode like the wind and tried not to feel
her insignificance in the face of the inferno to her left. Was
this indeed hell?

Before she could look for the demons that surely must be

after them, Sara arrived right behind Deke at the apparently abandoned soddy house. Reining in a panting Cinnamon and jumping down off her back, Sara tugged on Cinnamon's reins, determined to get her little mare safely through the tiny doorway. But Deke, with only a yelled "No!" grabbed her arm with one hand, tore the reins from her grasp with the other, and practically flung her inside the musty bare interior of the tiny house.

Beyond terror and panic, Sara jerked back around to protest. But she was too late as she clung to the turf blocks of the rough doorway. Deke hit his buckskin and Cinnamon each on the rump with his hat and sent them racing away from the fire, their tails flying as high as flags, attesting to their strong will to flee.

It was Sara's turn to protest. "No!" she screamed at Deke, coming out of the protection of the soddy. "They'll die!" she wailed, fighting and clawing at Deke as he grabbed her by the waist when she tried to get past him.

"No, they won't, Sara. They have more sense and better instincts than we do. They'll be all right!" He was carrying her, kicking and protesting all the way, back into the farthest reach of the damp, thick walls of the soddy, away from the bare entryway. "Now stop it and sit down, before you get us both killed." He scrunched her down on the bare earth floor and crouched beside her, keeping a steel-banded arm firmly around her.

"You left them out there to die," Sara accused him, her voice low and husky. Already the acrid odor of smoke assailed her nostrils and filled her lungs as it poured through the paneless windows and the doorless entryway.

"You ought to be more concerned about your own hide, Sara. They'll be fine; they'll run faster and farther without our added weight to slow them down. If we stayed on them, we just might all die. This is the only way. Trust me." He let go of her and stopped talking to cough and to rub the stinging tears from his eyes.

With terror-widened eyes, Sara watched Deke, even more

frightened by this sign of his human frailty. With a start that only increased her fear, she realized that she thought of him as above such human responses as tears and coughing, even when caused by such a plague as a prairie fire. Suddenly the fire seemed louder, hotter, closer. Sara jumped up, her hands balled into tight fists at her side. "We're going to die," she intoned flatly.

Deke dragged her down beside him again, batting ineffectually at the gathering smoke in the dim interior. "Someday, maybe. But not today."

"How can you be so sure?" she berated him, suddenly angry at him for being human, the very thing she'd once accused him of not being. How dare he have reddened, burning eyes! How dare he be so human, so vulnerable as to jump at the peal of thunder that rumbled across the sky, much as if it were an angry god calling out to them, seeking them in the storm.

"Because the fire will go around us. There's nothing here for it to burn. The sod is too thick, too damp. It can't get through," he said, poking his finger at the wall as if to prove his point. "And the floor"—he stamped his booted foot on its rock-hard surface—"is all earth; no grass or mats or rug or anything to burn. As long as we don't lose our heads, we won't lose our lives."

The fire would go around them? Sara had quit listening after that statement. Around them? As in "around" them? She hadn't thought about that. They were just going to sit here in this tiny, dim hovel while the forces of nature burned all around them? And they weren't going to die today? Deke Bonner was not only human—he was crazy, loco. If he thought for one minute that she was going to just sit here and wait for the fire—

Before her panic could close in around her and cause her to do something stupid, the fire closed in around them. But not completely. Whoever had built and eventually left this soddy had lived here long enough to render its outside walls not much more than hard-packed dirt, just like the floor.

Thank God. So, with only dry soil around the perimeter of the soddy, the fire, though terrifying, quickly passed around their little island of safety. Deke pushed her down to lie on her side next to him when the fire raged closest, explaining to her that it would be easier to breath close to the ground, that the smoke would be worse up by the windows.

Right then and there, Sara vowed never to use an oven again, if this was how it felt inside one. It wasn't until the fire raced past them, seeking more tender, more vulnerable victims than the unyielding prairie sod home and its occupants, that Sara realized she was locked tightly in Deke's grasp; indeed, she was sitting on his lap, her arms flung around his neck, her face tight against his shoulder, her fisted hands full of his buckskin tunic. When had he sat up and pulled her onto his lap? Or had she crawled there? It didn't matter. She was there, and that was enough. Well, it would have been if he'd happened to have a canteen full of water.

She raised her head and looked up into Deke's black eyes. "Is it over yet?" Her voice wasn't much more than a hoarse rasp. The acrid, burned odor of the outside world made her stomach queasy; that, or relief did.

Deke looked down at her, smoothing her smoky hair down her back. "For us, yes."

His strong, handsome face looked tired; he leaned his head back against the lifesaving sod of the wall and closed his eyes, thick black lashes sweeping against his high cheekbones. Sara watched him, intent on his every move. Every now and then he jarred her perch on him with a deep cough. The soddy's air was that of the underbelly of a campfire, but it smelled wonderful to her. They were alive, once more thanks to Deke's survival skills. Once more, she knew she would be dead without him.

Then, suddenly, unexpectedly, a deathly quiet, a chilling calm stole over her, numbing her mind until each word that followed occupied its own paragraph in her mind. Her heart and soul told her that even without the fire, the threat of outlaws, Indians, or stampeding buffalo, she would be dead without him. It was that simple when you loved somebody. The tears came; she would have sworn there was no moisture in her, that the fire had sucked every bit of water out of her body. But apparently not. For here they were—wet, hot, salty tears of triumph and defeat. Sara Dalton was in love with Deke Bonner. Damn him.

Her head went back to his shoulder as wrenching sobs tore from her. She clutched at him convulsively, pulling herself into an even tighter little ball on his lap. She felt his strong arms come around her to hold her soothingly. She heard his words, meant to comfort her.

"Shhh, now; we're okay. We're alive. It's all over."

If only he knew how true that was, Sara wailed inside. For no matter the outcome of this godforsaken journey, it was all over for her. Love thy enemy was now her life. When the smoke at Robber's Cave settled, no matter who was left standing, she would be the loser. The tears dried of their own accord; her sobs lessened to jerky breaths; her eyes opened to stare unseeingly before her. Numb from the terror without and the even greater torment within, her overwrought mind would not allow her to form a picture of who it might be, Deke or her kin, who would be left standing with a smoking gun. No matter who it was, she would never forgive him, or them. If that was the future, then all she had was now, today, and all the days before she and Deke arrived at the cave. "Deke," she said into the smouldering quiet. "Love me. Now."

He moved his head to look down at her and brought his hand up to tuck under her chin, lifting her face to his. "What did you say?"

Sara sat up on his lap, pushing herself away from his chest. She wanted to see his eyes, so black like hers, yet so fearfully different, unreadable. "I want you to make love to me— right now, right here."

Deke looked at her wordlessly, then opened his mouth several times as if to speak, but didn't. He looked around the soddy, down at her in his lap, out the window, then down at her again. "Are you sure?" he finally managed.

"Yes. More sure than I've ever been of anything in my life."

"Why, Sara? Why now?" He pulled a strand of her hair around his finger and rubbed its silkiness. He seemed reluctant to meet her gaze.

"Because I love you," she said without hesitation, without dissembling, without joy.

Her words hung between them in the air, making a palpable presence in the hazy room. Sara felt she could, if she wanted to, reach out and pick each letter of each word, like a ripe fruit off a tree and hold it out to Deke like a coveted prize. Just as she was doing with her heart. The longer the passing seconds stretched out, the longer he sat there immobile, just staring at her, the more her poor heart thudded crazily. Would he refuse the offer of her body? More important, would he refuse the bounty of her love?

When he put his head back against the sod wall and closed his eyes, shaking his head slowly back and forth, Sara died. She watched his Adam's apple go up and down once, saw the erratic pulse at the base of his throat. When he opened his eyes and looked into her soul, a thrill of goosebumps chased each other over her skin. Her throat closed, and her fingertips tingled.

"You can't love me, Sara. I won't let you."

"It's too late, Deke. I already do."

"Goddamn!" he bellowed, striking the earth floor with his huge fist, much as if he were trying to beat the demons of hell back down where they belonged. Sara cringed into herself, covering her face with her hands. Then he set her off him and stood up in one lithe move. "No!" he yelled at her, accusing her and pointing his finger down at her where she sat in a crumpled heap on the packed earth. "You can't! Goddammit, you can't!"

One long, agitated stride brought him to her; he clutched at her arms and pulled her to her feet. A terrified cry escaped her; she knew without a doubt that he could kill her with one crushing blow. But the crushing blow he dealt her was not a physical one. Would that it had been, for Sara knew a thousand deaths when she saw the terrible pain on his face—when she saw the tears standing in his eyes.

"You're wrong, Sara. You don't love me. You can't. You're just scared and glad to be alive. You can't love me, because to love me is to know pain and death and all that's ugly in this life. I won't let you do that to yourself, Sara. Because when this is over, we'll go our separate ways, and you'll hate me—if I'm alive. So don't you ever say that you love me. Don't ever say it," he warned her in a hissing voice.

His ebony eyes searched her face, looking for her understanding of his terrible words. Whatever he saw wrung a cry of pure agony from him, for he rasped out in a hoarse, quiet voice, "Goddamn you, Sara Dalton, for making me love you. And that's enough pain for both of us."

Giving her no time or opportunity to respond, he crushed her to him, one hand on her back, one against her head where it rested on his chest. Sara knew she should be elated because he returned her love. But instead, she felt the despair of the truly brokenhearted. She clutched at him, feeling there was no way she could ever be close enough to him, knowing there was no way she could ever keep him this close to her. Loving someone, the wrong someone, was a terrible agony. There could be no wedding, no happy gathering of friends and family, no years of loving, no children. There would always only be a terrible sadness for what was never meant to be.

"Deke?" she said into the quiet.

He kissed the top of her head. "Yes?"

"Love me. For now. Can we have now? Just now?"

She felt him slump against her, and at the same time pull her more tightly against him. "Oh, God, Sara. All right. Just for now."

And Deke gave her now; he gave her that moment in time, that smoke-filled room on the prairie, that aftermath of near-death, that beautiful moment that was their lovemaking. He was as gentle with her as he was the first time, from the moment he helped her off with her buckskin dress and he shed his tunic and breeches, from the moment their young bodies came together in the giving, loving embrace that re-affirms life and solidifies love. But not once did any word of love pass between them. Not that it mattered in the least, for love resided in their hearts. And that would have to be enough. For now.

If the storm in their souls was still brewing, at least the one overhead had fled the skies. Sara and Deke came out of the soddy to a world turned black and crisp, but blue and clear overhead. Only the ground on which they stood, silently and awestruck, was not burned. Not a tree, not a blade of grass had been spared. Only them.

"I think we died and went to hell," Deke said, more as a voicing of his thoughts than as a start to a conversation. "Come on, let's go see if we can find our horses."

Sara looked all around, not seeing another living thing other than herself and Deke. "Where do you suggest we start?"

Deke pointed off to the southeast. "Over there."

Sara looked but saw nothing. "How do you know?"

"Water's in that direction. The fire would burn out over the water. Not much wind to drive it across."

"Then why didn't we just ride to the water, Deke?"

He looked at her a moment. "I didn't say it was close, Sara. We never would have made it."

"I just hope Cinnamon and your horse made it."

"Yeah, me too," Deke said matter-of-factly, putting his hand out to Sara. "Come on."

Sara took his hand, and they started off walking in a south-easterly direction, much as if they were on a leisurely stroll down a rose-bedecked promenade rather than a charred prairie. After a few paces, Sara turned to Deke. "You know, you really ought to name that horse of yours. I can't just keep calling him 'horse.' He deserves his own name."

Deke looked down at her, smiled, and wiped away an apparent smudge on her cheek. "I'll think about it."

Sara scrubbed harder at the same cheek, embarrassed to realize how dirty she must look to him, even if he did look the same right now. They really were a strange pair out here on the lone prairie dressed in sooty buckskins, with no horses, food, or water. They walked on silently. After a few moments, she said aloud, "Do you like Warrior?"

"Warrior?"

"Yes, for your horse. The name."

"Why does he have to have a name?" There was a bemused grin on his face that didn't set well with Sara.

"Why shouldn't he have a name?" she countered.

Deke stopped, let go of her hand, and put his hands to his waist. "Because he's a horse, not a person. Hell, you don't name a horse for the same reason you wouldn't name a . . . a cow." He took her hand again and began walking.

"Daisy."

"What?" He stopped walking.

"Daisy. My cow, at home in Plains."

Deke stared, withdrew his hand from hers and put his hands to his waist. His dark eyebrows met over his nose. "Your cow has a name?"

Sara nodded affirmatively. "So do my dog and my cat."

Deke apparently gave up the fight. He took her hand again and set them off on their southeasterly course—again. "With all we've got to worry about right now, you want to worry about a name for my horse?"

"Yes, I do."

"Why?"

Sara drew him to a stop, her hand still in his. She fought to blink back the sudden tears in her eyes. "Because it's the only thing in my life right now that I can change, Deke."

Deke stared at her solemnly, let out a deep breath, and ran his other hand through his hair. He then contemplated his boots as if they held the answer to some question of cosmic importance. Almost shyly he looked up at her. "What was that name—Warrior?"

Sara brightened. "Yes! Do you like it?"

They began walking again. "No. It doesn't fit him. Sounds like an Indian pony name." Then, looking as if he felt the least bit silly, he offered, "How about Buck?"

"No," Sara came back after giving it due thought. "Sounds like a deer. He needs something dignified."

"Dignified . . . hmmm." He ran a hand over his mouth and chin. "How about Mr. President?"

Sara laughed aloud. "A little too dignified, I'd say. How about General?"

"Or Sergeant?"

"Or Private?"

Arguing good-naturedly, they walked on through the burned heat of the afternoon, seeking water, food, shelter, and their horses, both named and unnamed.

"Well, there it is—the trading post that calls itself a city," Deke said, reining his as-yet-unnamed buckskin to a stop on a small rise that overlooked a conglomeration of soddies and rough wooden buildings. "It's not much to look at, is it?"

"No," Sara agreed, patting Cinnamon's shoulder as the little mare stamped impatiently. "But it looks a sight better than sleeping on the ground again."

Deke looked at her and grinned. "I thought you liked sleeping on the ground with me."

Sara returned his grin, but added a snort. "Sleep is the last thing you have on your mind when we're on the ground, Mr. Bonner."

"I thought that was the part you liked, Miss Dalton. Or am I wrong?"

Sara very primly raised her chin and perched her head at a coquettish angle. "It is." At the sound of his laughter, she abandoned her pose, feeling the rising heat in her cheeks, and warned, "Don't you laugh, Deke Bonner, or I'll—"

"You'll what?"

She couldn't think of anything. "I'll—just you never mind. I'll think of something. Right now, though, I'd like a bath and a room, and a decent meal, and a bed—my own bed, if you please." Then it struck her. "We can get those things here, can't we?"

"Yeah, we can; at least, what they have to offer at Chisholm's is a damned sight better than we're used to out on the plains. But how do you intend to pay for all this? Plus clothes. I assume you want out of that buckskin dress for good by now."

Sara nodded, looking down at the rather grimy dress. The fire hadn't done it any good, that was for sure; and neither had the two-day search on foot for the horses, which they'd found safely by the shore of the Canadian River, just as Deke had predicted. Cinnamon's reins had become hopelessly entangled in a bush at some point, but Deke's buckskin, Horse for now, had stayed with her. Apparently, unnamed though he was, he possessed the quality of loyalty to a friend.

"I have my own money—what I brought with me from home and what Coburn gave me for my belongings he bartered away. He had the nerve to call the money my share of the deal. How about you?"

"I'm fine," Deke nodded, his jaw squared.

"Well, let's go," she offered, forcing the brightness.

"By all means," he replied, sounding as if he was going to his own hanging.

Men. What was wrong with him now? He was acting like they were riding into a den of thieves and cutthroats.

Chapter Nineteen

The small, unnamed, lawless community that had grown up around Chisholm's Trading House, only one of many owned by the mixed-breed Cherokee trader Jesse Chisholm in this part of the territory, was indeed a den of thieves and cut-throats, any of whom, Deke knew, would think nothing of killing him to get to Sara. Damn her, didn't she realize what a sensation she was causing here amongst these men? The dirt and grime of the trail, even her Cheyenne dress, could not hope to detract from her more-than-ample feminine charms.

And it sure as hell didn't help his cause any that she was just now behind the locked door to the bathhouse—in front of which he was sitting on a chair tipped back on two legs, all their guns hanging very visibly off him. Inside, Sara was sitting in a smooth wooden tub full of suds, cleaning her naked body and singing away at the top of her lungs in a voice both husky and melodic—a sound that grabbed a man's soul and wrenched it.

Deke hit the door behind him with his elbow and bellowed, "Will you hurry it up? And hold it down in there? You're going to have cats caterwauling out here any minute now."

The splashing and the singing ceased after he called out. Deke relaxed—that had been easy. Then the splashing and singing began again with renewed vigor. But this time the song was a decidedly bawdy one that startled Deke into an upright position and stopped traffic, pedestrian and horseback, on the dusty street in front of the bathhouse.

"That does it," Deke promised himself through gritted teeth. After glaring the rough men in the street back into minding their own business, he jumped up, kicked the chair out of his way, grabbed his new clothes, and made for the door. He'd trusted no one, not even the ugly old crone who ran this place and had charged extra for clean water, to stand guard while Sara bathed, so now he was going to have to enforce his own brand of law. Jerking open the door, he practically catapulted himself inside, angry and intent on a scene.

The scene in front of him made him forget he was angry, made him even forget he had a name. Sara was standing in the low tub, all clean and pink in places, brown in others, streaming water and suds down every exposed female curve, her hair forming a wet if ineffectual cloak around her upper torso. And she was holding a bar of soap—which hit Deke square in the chest as he came through the door.

"That does it," he repeated, slamming the door closed behind him and bolting it. He laid down her rifle and his clothes, then undid his gunbelt, setting it aside.

"Get out! I told you I wanted my own bath! You'll just have to wait, Mr. Bonner."

"I'm through waiting, Sara. You've been in here long enough, stirring up trouble." He was undoing the laces on his buckskin shirt.

Sara's eyes widened. "Stirring up trouble? I'm just getting

ready to wash my hair. Why, I haven't even left this room—and well you know it.''

"No need." He pulled the shirt over his head and threw it to one side. "Thanks to your singing, every mother's son out there knows there's a gorgeous white woman in here—naked." He ran his hand through his hair, suddenly damp in the moist air of the bathhouse. He began undoing his pants.

She smiled. "You think I'm gorgeous?"

Deke shot her a glance. "As if that's the point."

She quirked her head to concede the point, and then, waving her hand in his general direction, Sara asked, "What are you doing?"

His hands stopped. "I'm making damned certain every lowlife son-of-a-bitch in this godforsaken hellhole knows that you're my woman; that's what I'm doing."

"It appears to me more like you're undressing," she accused, crossing her arms over her bare breasts.

"You know a better way for me to make my point?" He sat down on the one chair in the small, dim room to tug his boots off. That done, he stood and shrugged out of the tight-fitting buckskin breeches. Naked, aroused, dirty, and determined, Deke bent to pick up the soap she'd thrown at him and then went to join his woman in the tub.

But she had other ideas. She pushed against his chest when he approached the old round, wooden tub, but her wet hands slid off the sheen of his skin, rocking her back on her heels and nearly sending her, bottom-first, back into the water. "Now, you stop right there," she warned. "You paid for clean water for each of us. You have to—have to wait until Mrs. Myers has her boys replace the water."

Deke couldn't stop the twitching of his lips. Sara's gaze kept slipping from his face to the hard evidence of his intent in joining her in the soapy water. "What's wrong, Sara?"

Her face aflame, she flicked water at him with her wet fingertips. "You know damn good and well what's wrong, Deke Bonner. Now stop it and get out."

Deke looked down at himself and then back up at her,

pinning her with a slanted look, the effect of which he knew only too well. "And what do you suggest I do with this?" He indicated his erection.

Sara gasped and took a step back in the water, one hand to her mouth. "Deke Bonner," she breathed. "You horrible wretch. How would I know what men do when there's no women around and they have a—a—"

"Ahh, but there is a woman around, Sara, my sweet. The only woman I want." He hoped his grin was as demonic as he'd been told in the past that it was. Taking advantage of her stunned, if momentary, inaction, Deke smoothly stepped into the tub and pulled her to him. "Here, he said, putting himself into her hand, "let me show you what men do when there're no women around and they have a—"

"Stop it!" she cried, trying to pull her hand away.

Deke let go of her hand and quit teasing her. With a wink from hell, he plopped down in the water and began happily soaping himself, whistling the same bawdy tune that he'd only moments before chastised Sara for singing.

"I hate you, Deke Bonner," she spat out between gritted teeth. Stomping her foot only splashed the water over them both.

Cheerful now that he was naked in the same tub with Sara, Deke conceded, "It would be a lot easier if you did, now wouldn't it?"

"I do. I really do," she swore.

"All right, you do. Now, here"—he held the soap out to her—"will you get my back?" He plopped the soap into her hand and innocently turned his back to her. He cut his eyes this way and that, straining to hear in the ominous silence what exactly her reaction would be. She might say she hated him, but she hadn't gotten out of the tub.

Still, no soap made contact with his back. He turned back around when a splash and rippling of the water around him told him she'd sat down. She was washing her hair, rubbing the soap cake vigorously through the long tresses, a stubborn, defiant expression on her face that made her point: She wasn't going to stand for his ordering her around.

So, while her hands were busy with her hair, Deke filled his empty ones with her breasts. She gasped out her outrage and pummeled the water, trying to smack at his quick moving, roving hands. "Stop it!" she cried out, but a bit-back grin gave her away.

Deke pulled back in the water. "Do you really want me to stop it, Sara? And to get out and leave you alone? I will, if you say so."

She looked at him, the powerful grin wanting to break free. "No," was all she said. Her hands were over her head and full of soap and hopelessly tangled silver hair.

"Come here, silly, and let me get that for you," Deke said softly, warmed to his core. She wanted him as much as he did her. It felt good to be wanted. He took her arm and smoothly slid her through the water to sit, her back to his chest, her legs bent into the curve of his, while he washed her hair. She sat upright demurely, even childlike in her trust of him, and surrendered to the massage of his strong hands.

Deke had never known such quiet but sensual joy. To have a woman like Sara Dalton trust him, love him, was more than he'd ever hoped for in his ravaged life. But they both knew it was just for now. That was the deal—just for now. Lost in his thoughts, Deke didn't realized that his hands had strayed until Sara told him.

"That's not my hair you're washing, Deke Bonner."

Deke looked down. Sure enough, his hands were on her breasts. He had no idea where the soap was. "Whoops," he confessed.

But before he could remove his hands, Sara put hers over his and held them in place on her firm, soft breasts. Deke may have been able to restrain himself up to that point, but not when Sara melted back against him and spread her legs to wrap them around his. "Love me, Deke," she breathed, rubbing her shoulders seductively against his chest. "Mmmm, I love the feel of your chest hair, so rough against my skin."

"Damn, Sara, you drive me crazy," Deke groaned. He quickly turned her to face him in the water and sat her on his lap. But he wasn't ready for the force of her desire.

She immediately took control of their lovemaking, bending forward slightly to capture one of his nipples. The rough sounds coming out of him surprised Deke, but he could no more stop them than he could stop breathing. Apparently happy with that reaction of his, she quickly turned her single-minded erotic attention to his other nipple. Then the little demon took hold of his member, stroking it up and down under the water until Deke cursed again.

"Damn," he breathed, returning the favor by finding and stroking the bud of her desire. He knew when he'd found it because she nearly jumped off his lap, so electric was her response. Flinging her arms around his neck, she kissed his mouth with all the vigor of the swirling action of his fingertips inside her moistness under the water.

When she broke the kiss, she looked at him with all the desire, all the sheer physical eroticism, all the intense love any man could ever hope to see on any woman's face. Her breathing raw and gasping, she demanded roughly, "Take me."

Always one to do what he was told, Deke obliged her. He held her by her waist, lifted her slightly, probed for entry, found it, and slid her down on him, his shuddering reaction matching hers, until he was fully sheathed. Sara wrapped her legs fully and tightly around his waist. She moved to wrap her arms around his neck, but Deke stopped her. "No, not like that. Like this."

He slid forward in the water, still joined with her, using his powerful legs to propel them through the sloshing, cooling bath water, until Sara's back was to the rim of the round tub. He stretched her arms out to either side of her and had her grip the rough wood.

"Like that," he whispered, intently focused on the coming pleasure of the loving task she'd demanded of him. Then, cupping her breasts, using his thumbs to flick at her bud-hardened nipples, he finally began the rocking, thrusting motion that would drive their pleasure and empty the tub of water.

When Sara flung her head back, her mouth opened slightly, her eyes closed, and began moaning his name, Deke captured her waist with his hands, spanning it and thus holding her hips tightly to his. Then he increased the power of his thrusts to the rhythmic, cataclysmic tempo he knew would take them both to the peak of pleasure. The sloshing of the water could not hope to compete with Sara's shortened, gasping breaths that told Deke she was close, just as he was, to that peak, so he moved his hands up from her waist to her shoulder blades and pulled her to him.

Her arms went instinctively around his neck, and she instantly picked up the rocking rhythm driving them now, sliding herself up and down on him with increased intensity, increased ferocity, until the world exploded around them with kaleidoscopic clarity, changing, ever spiraling outward in rippling waves until there was only their need for each other and the feel of their bodies locked together.

After several moments of trying to catch their breath, still joined with their arms locked around each other, Deke was finally able to utter, "Is there anything else you want me to do for you, ma'am?"

Her answer was a playful smack to his head. "Shut up."

"I can do that," he said, grinning, pulling at her earlobe with his teeth.

"I have a better idea. Love me again."

Deke pulled her back to look into her grinning face. "I don't think I can right now. I—"

Sara rocked her hips against his, slowly, and traced the shape of his ear with her tongue, all the while purring softly in her throat.

"—think I can right now," Deke changed his mind.

The water in the tub that had been spared the first time was, in the next few moments, sent overboard.

* * *

"Do you think every lowlife son-of-a-bitch in town knows I'm your woman now?" Sara asked sweetly, her fork poised in her hand. Her words gained the glaring attention of the men at the tables closest to them.

Deke nearly choked on the bite of steak he'd just put in his mouth. When he recovered, he leaned forward over the rough table in what served as the dining room of the natty hotel next to the trading post, to stare hard at Sara. "Would you please try not to insult our dinner companions, Sara? It ruins my appetite to have to kill a man during a meal."

Sara caught Deke's look and his meaning. A quick glance around the crowded dining room revealed several pairs of male eyes boring right back into hers. She looked again at Deke, who nodded and went back to his food. A chill on her skin, despite the close heat of the airless room on this hot night, she quickly looked back at the plain and greasy food in front of her. Still, it tasted like heaven because it was on a plate and she was sitting at a table, all clean and dressed in civilized clothes. And she was, after a fashion, in civilization. Steak, potatoes, beans, and biscuits; green gingham skirt with matching bodice, chemise, drawers, cotton stockings and buttoned-up shoes. Never had she appreciated any of them more.

And didn't Deke look handsome in his new soft-blue chambray shirt, dun-colored denims, and black suede vest? His black Stetson rested on the table. The remainder of their many purchases, including two bedrolls, assorted clothes, provisions, dishes, and coffeepot, were safely locked in their one room—there was no way in hell, Deke had said, that he was letting her out of his sight in this so-called town. Cinnamon and The Buckskin Horse, themselves all curried, were resting easy in the local blacksmith's stable, feasting on oats and hay instead of plain old prairie grass. At least, Sara knew she would prefer oats and hay to prairie grass, if she were a horse.

"What are you thinking about over there?"

Sara looked up at Deke. Why did he always catch her

thinking the silliest things? "About the horses."

He sat back in his chair, his fork clattering to a rest in his plate. "Not that again; not a name for my horse."

Sara laughed, obviously a musical, tinkling sound these men had never heard before, if their quiet attention was any gauge. Deke glared around the room; the men resumed eating. Sara leaned toward him. "No, not that. I was just thinking about how glad I am they're getting a chance to rest. They've had a rough time of it."

"Unlike us," Deke reminded her, his elbows resting on the red-checkered tablecloth.

"I know. I keep wondering what in the world can happen next. We—"

"Ain't you that low-down, snake-belly bounty hunter by the name of Deke Bonner?"

Sara froze, her gaze on Deke. The room was suddenly as quiet as a whorehouse invaded by a Sunday school. Whoever had challenged Deke was behind her. She was very careful not to move, not to distract a grim, narrow-eyed Deke as he focused on the speaker.

"And if I am?" Deke said quietly, all the while lowering his right hand to a point under the table.

Sara's mouth went dry; she forgot to blink. Why was he challenging the man when she was in the direct line of fire? Why didn't he just deny who he was and perhaps save their hides? She didn't know a soul in this town, but she did know that not one of these men, most likely in some sort of trouble with the law themselves, would raise his hand to help Deke Bonner, bounty hunter.

"I thought you was, you yellow-belly scum. You took my brother in to hang."

Chairs scraped back as men, sensing the coming battle, stood and got out of the way. Sara watched Deke's eyes narrow to slits as he sized up his opponent.

Despite her paralyzing fear, she did find the courage to ever so slowly put her hand in her skirt pocket. When her fingers curved around the cool metal of the derringer Deke had insisted she buy earlier today for her own protection, she felt better—but only a tiny bit better.

"Well, I'm sure that if I did, he deserved it. Now, why don't you step out from behind the lady and face me like a man, you stinking bastard."

Sara was sure her insides were shriveling up. The expression on Deke's face was one she hadn't seen since the early days of their journey together. Having gotten to know him so intimately, she'd forgotten just how fearsome, how ruthless he could look—and be. A sudden image of him firing cold-bloodedly at that robber flashed through her mind. Someone was going to die tonight.

After a moment's hesitation, the man moved from behind Sara and came into her view as he stopped between her and Deke at the side of their table. Sara's heart lurched. The man was a mountain in clothes. Bigger than Deke Bonner and four or five other big men put together. Oh, lordy.

One vicious swipe of the man's huge paw sent their table—dinner plates, coffee mugs, Stetson, and all—crashing butt over teakettle across the room. Sara screeched. Men cursed; some fled. Most stayed to see the entertainment. Only Deke hadn't moved a muscle. With the table gone, it was clear to all that his hand rested squarely on the butt of his Colt. "Now, I wish you hadn't done that, mister. You see, not only was that my favorite hat you just sent across the room, but the lady wasn't finished with her meal. I believe you owe her an apology," Deke drawled out, nodding toward Sara.

Sara shook her head no, almost imperceptibly. She knew her fear rode her features like a flea on a dog.

The man looked at Sara. And scared her. "I apologize about your dinner, ma'am. Soon's I kill this here cow dung, I'll buy you another."

Sara tried to shake her head no again, but found she could only bobble it weakly. Had all her muscles locked?

"I don't think the lady wants you to buy her another dinner, friend," Deke said levelly. "I guess I'll just have to.

Now, we can do this the easy way, or we can do this the hard way. You can walk off and let us finish our meal. Or you can continue to stand here; in which case, I intend to kill you.''

''Why, you son-of-a—'' The man slapped leather and drew his gun.

But he was already dead, because Deke drew and shot the enraged gunman square in the chest without so much as standing up. And Sara shot him in the back of the head, also without standing up. Lucky shot; purely lucky. She'd never shot a man before. But now she had. And she felt numb. She couldn't seem to lower her hand. It still pointed at where the huge man's head had been before he pitched back from Deke's bullet and then forward from Sara's to land in a crashing heap over the table next to theirs.

All was still for a few seconds. And then all was noise as most of the men merely resumed their meals, now having something new to talk about. A few men dragged the dead man's body outside to dump it unceremoniously in the street; the hotel's owner fussed around Deke and Sara as they sat silently staring at each other. Sara finally found the strength to lower her gun hand. Deke hadn't even changed expression when he'd killed the stranger, but now his mouth was opened in astonishment as he slowly reholstered his deadly Colt.

Much as if she weren't a part of them, Sara's mind registered the events transpiring around her and Deke. A waiter worked furiously to right their table; then, retrieving Deke's Stetson, he brushed it off, reshaped it as best he could, and brought it over, holding it out to him. When Deke didn't appear to notice, the man, a small, brown-skinned Indian, quickly put it on the table and left. An Indian kitchenmaid cleaned up the remains of their dinner, even sopping up the spilled blood as if it were gravy.

''You shot him,'' Deke finally said, stating the obvious. But his voice held none of the revulsion Sara was feeling for herself at that moment. In fact, if anything, Deke looked slightly amused, even impressed.

"Yes, I did. So did you." Then, "Who was he?"

"I haven't the slightest idea. We didn't get around to polite introductions, you'll remember."

He sounded so matter of fact about the killing that Sara began to feel ill. "I think I'm going to be sick."

Deke sobered. "I wondered when that was going to happen." He stood up abruptly. All eyes returned to them just as the waiter returned with two steaming mugs of coffee. Deke held up a hand and shook his head. The men went back to eating; the show was over. Deke grabbed his Stetson, squared it on his head, threw down some money on the otherwise bare table, and stepped over to Sara, taking her arm and hustling her outside before she disgraced herself in public.

The first sight she saw was the bleeding, hulking body of the man she'd helped to kill lying in the dark, dusty street. A great wrenching heave spasmed her in two. Deke grabbed her up in his arms, at great risk to his new clothes, and carried her swiftly to the nearest alley. Just as he put her down, Sara bent over and lost her supper and her dignity. She had time only to hold her new skirt out of her own way. Once the spasms passed, the tears began.

Deke had been holding her arm and ineffectually patting her back. Now he wiped at her mouth with his bandanna, even going so far as to step over to a water trough to wet it and wipe her face off. "Better now?" he asked, holding her to him.

"Deke, I—I killed a man!" she sobbed, her words muffled by his bandanna which she now held to her mouth.

"No, you didn't. I killed him. You just put a nail in his coffin, sweetheart."

"And—and—and a bullet in his head." She wailed even louder.

"Shhh," he soothed. "The first time's always the toughest."

"The first—first time? I'm not ever going to fire a gun again. I swear it!" She clutched at his new chambray shirt, wading it up in her fist and salting it with her tears. ''I don't want to kill another man ever again.''

''Well, I for one am glad to hear that. That evens the odds a little bit on down the road.''

''Wha-what?'' she sniffed, looking up at him.

''Nothing,'' Deke said, smiling down into her face. ''Come on. You've had a big day. I think you need a drink.'' With his arm around her shoulder, he turned her back toward the hotel. Then he muttered, ''I know I sure as hell do.''

Sleep came easy that night for Sara. With her stomach newly emptied and with the wine Deke plied her with before undressing her and putting her to bed as if she were a child, she slipped into a drugged and dreamless state. Her last wakeful but fuzzy memory was of Deke sliding under the covers with her and taking her in his arms. She remembered snuggling up against him and thinking that at last she had her dream—she was in a bed with Deke Bonner. But it was an innocent, chaste bed, for its occupants were too drained to be anything else.

A man posted outside their door, paid handsomely by Deke, assured them that they would rest undisturbed by any other citizen foolhardy enough or just plain drunk enough to want to test his mettle against the name, reputation, and presence of Deke Bonner, bounty hunter.

The next morning, Sara awoke to feel content, grouchy, and disturbed. It was frightening, this feeling of such complete security lying there in Deke Bonner's arms. She simply could not allow herself to get used to it. Completely awake now, she watched him sleep, cataloguing each and every beloved feature of his face against the day when he would no longer be in her life. He didn't look so formidable, she mused, when he was relaxed, for only in repose were the lines of care gone from his face. Sara reached her hand out to trace her fingertips across the early-morning stubble of his beard as it covered his jaw; Deke's mouth twitched in response to her touch. Sara smiled. This was a face she could look at every morning for the rest of her life.

For the rest of her life. She wondered how long that would be—for her and for Deke. Would a bullet end one or both of their lives in a few weeks at Robber's Cave? And if death came then in an instant of hateful passion, wouldn't that be kinder than a lonely lifetime of bittersweet memories?

Forgetting the promise to herself to never fire a gun again, Sara wondered now how she would die. Defending her brother and cousins? Or Deke Bonner?

Chapter Twenty

As long as he lived, Deke swore, he would never understand women in general, but especially one in particular. Namely, one Miss Sara Dalton. His angry, bewildered mood propelled his long legs across the street from the rough clapboard hotel where he and Sara had spent the night. He'd thought everything was all right when he went to sleep last night.

Deke interrupted his thoughts to look around him in the street. Good; the body was gone. Probably carried off by vultures rather than taken away to a Christian burial. His was a cynical view, yes, but one borne out by years of experience with the type of men and women who populated this tiny outpost of civilization. No, civilization was what the Cheyenne had—not these lawless beggars here. At any rate, the body was gone; Sara wouldn't have to see it again in the clear light of day.

Yes, that's what he'd been thinking about: Sara in the clear light of day. Deke focused his gaze on the livery stable, where he was headed to check on the horses, but his thoughts were back with Sara. He'd expected her to be quiet, maybe withdrawn this morning. But no. She'd been an absolute terror one minute and then a crying little wretch the next. She'd said she wasn't hungry, but then she'd eaten all of her breakfast and half of his when he had it sent up to the room. Then she'd griped at him for making her eat so much and had taken to the bed holding a pillow to her stomach and balling up like a kitten. Then she'd raised her head long enough to say they couldn't leave today, not even tomorrow, and maybe not even the day after that, for she sure as hell—her words— wasn't going to leave a bloody trail across the plains. Not that he had any clue what she meant by that, seeing as how she'd said she didn't intend to shoot a gun anymore. And then she'd jumped up and thrown him out of the room, startling him but not half as much as she did the posted guard when she jerked the door open and threw Deke's pants and boots out into the hallway, along with their owner.

Deke swore, shaking his head and muttering at the memory of the puzzled look on the man's face. Never one to be proud or cocky about taking a life, Deke was nevertheless glad everyone in town knew about last night's shooting so that his reputation remained intact; for once they heard about this morning from the hired guard . . . Deke drew up short and looked around surreptitiously. No one on the surprisingly busy street was staring at him walking along talking to himself. Good. They probably didn't dare after last night's dinner theater.

He resumed his forced march to the livery. And that was another thing. He sure as hell didn't have to worry about staying at Sara's side every minute they were here, however the hell long that was going to be. Last night she'd proved she could take care of herself; in fact, she was dead-eye accurate and as fast as hell, nearly outdrawing him with that derringer of hers. Damn, he hoped she didn't turn that pissant pistol on him one day. One day? Hell, today. All he knew was that he'd been sent posthaste to the laundress in town for clean rags and a lot of them. And once they'd been delivered, he'd been ordered to clear out; she'd even suggested several ways, none of which he could repeat in Sunday school, that he might find to occupy his time for the next several hours or even days, for all she cared.

What in hell she needed all those rags for, he had no clue. She wasn't wounded anywhere; he'd asked her, just before she threw him and his clothes out into the hall, and innocently enough, he thought, if she was bleeding from somewhere. She'd nearly bitten his head off.

Oh, hell. Now he understood. Goddamn. This was just what they needed—Eve's curse, as his mother and sister had called it. Getting slow in your old age, Deke admonished himself. Well, hell, he'd hardly been around women at all—decent women, anyway—for the past several years. He couldn't be blamed for not thinking of something like this. Men, left on their own, as sure as shooting didn't spend one second a month thinking about something as purely female as the "curse."

Arriving at the livery, Deke swore to himself that he would never again wonder, aloud or otherwise, what could go wrong next. Because every time he thought it, something went wrong, sure enough. At the livery stables, he took in a deep breath, catching the mingling scents of leather, horses, and dung; listening, he heard the sound of ringing steel as the smithy's hammer forged out a new shoe on the anvil. It was a purely masculine domain. No damned females and their curses in here to cause trouble.

"Anybody around?" Deke called out at the double-wide doors. All the noise seemed to be coming from the back of the huge barn. The horses all seemed pretty restive, too. Deke's hand went instinctively to his gun.

The proprietor—a large, ruddy man with a long-handled moustache, wearing a leather apron over his clothes—came hurrying forward. His face looked like a thundercloud. "I'm the smithy. Own the place. You own that little roan mare that came in last night, mister?"

Thinking of Cinnamon and hoping that nothing was wrong with her, he admitted, "Yeah, if you mean the one stalled next to the buckskin. Those are my horses. We brought them in last night. Your boy stalled them."

"Wal, gol-dang it, man, why didn't you tell anyone she was in season? I'm lucky to have a barn this morning, what with all them damned studs in there tryin' to git at 'er. And that buckskin of yours? He's the worst of 'em all. I had to git up in the middle of the night and come lead that roan off by herself. And she didn't want to go, either, prime as she is now. An' you hear all that noise back there? That's them studs a-callin' out; they done got the scent now. Now, I ain't never a one to turn away good money, but you got to bed that mare somewhere's else, mister."

Embarrassed, Deke instantly thought of the perfect place for the mare—in the room with Sara, who was suffering from a similar malady. Right now, sharing a stall with his buckskin—he really needed to name that horse—sounded pretty good. "Mister, I'm sorry. I had no idea. Women, huh? They don't tell you a thing. Where is she now?"

Deke's words seemed to mollify the blacksmith's ruffled feathers somewhat. He pointed over his shoulder and turned to go that way. "I'll show you. I 'spect she's safe enough where I got her, if'n you still want to leave her here. I gotta tell you though—when I got here, your buckskin was in her stall. And it was all over, if'n you get my drift."

Damn, Deke fumed. Sara wasn't pregnant—a silent prayer of thanks went up for avoidance of that potential complication—but her horse probably was. And his horse was responsible. It seemed he and his buckskin had the same problem—couldn't keep it to themselves around the Dalton women. Well, it was too late to do anything about it now. But he had to admire his stud's taste in women. That roan of Sara's was a mighty fine-looking little filly. Just like her owner.

After assuring himself that Cinnamon was corraled safely away from the studs in the other stalls, and after checking on his smug-looking buckskin, Deke paid the smithy extra for their board, apologized again for the trouble, and headed for the saloon. Son of a bitch, he needed a drink. And if he ever saw another woman again, it'd be too soon.

He then surprised himself with the thought that he was actually looking forward to arriving at Robber's Cave. Not for anything to do with confronting the Daltons, but more for the fellowship of a bunch of men hidden away from pesky females. Maybe all of them together could pitch in to help him handle Sara Dalton. Deke was certain in his heart that, probably to a man out there at Robber's Cave, there was a woman somewhere in each of their pasts who had driven them individually to their lives of crime. In fact, he was contemplating that life right now. It seemed safer, more carefree somehow.

Pushing open the swinging doors to the saloon called Aces High, according to the hand-painted sign outside, Deke stalked in, looking around alertly out of long habit. After everyone noted his initial entry with no more than curt nods of their heads, he drew no more attention. Good. Ordering a whiskey, he remained standing at the bar, a thick length of wood supported by two whiskey barrels, but turned his back to it; he preferred to face the room. He saw nothing out of the ordinary at first glance. Some men at a card table. A few sharing the bar with him. No piano; no women. Good. He didn't particularly care to hear either one in his present mood. Feeling suddenly expansive, even kindly toward his fellow man, Deke decided that this saloon looked to be the right place for a nice, quiet morning; he might even deal himself into the card game a little later on, he thought, fingering the money in his vest pocket. After all, what could go wrong?

As if by way of an answer, the swinging doors pushed open and in poured some rough-looking desperadoes with long rifles and lean, trail-weary faces. Deke, along with the saloon's other occupants, tensed; the men sharing the bar with Deke opted for seats at an empty table, leaving him alone with the intruders. But Deke gave the appearance of not noticing them as he casually took another sip of the rotgut whiskey and turned to the bar, resting his elbows on it. No one at his back warranted more attention than did the men to his right.

The men, four in all but filling the small room as if they were twenty, placed their rifles on the bar and belligerently ordered a bottle of the best panther-piss, dust-cutting whiskey the house had. The bartender, a man used to bad men, looked particularly pale as he filled their order, Deke noted; not a good sign. He cursed himself for breaking his minutes-old sworn oath never to think what could go wrong next. The consequences were just now crowding him out of bar space. Rather than protesting, he moved down obligingly, losing nothing in the process. A quiet, respectful distance, he knew, was a better vantage point for learning more about men and their intentions than the kind of loud, show-off cockiness that only served to get a less experienced man shot.

And so Deke nursed his drink, leaned on the bar, and listened, doing nothing to draw attention to himself. Indeed, the longer he listened to the increasingly loud rantings of the four men as they drank more and more, the worse he felt about the outcome, not only of this morning in this saloon, but also of Robber's Cave. For these men rode with the Daltons.

It wasn't something he guessed or even knew beforehand. Nothing that subtle. In fact, these men were making sure everyone within hearing distance knew that they rode with the Daltons. Why they were being so loud about their business in a territory full of people who hoarded their privacy, Deke couldn't begin to guess. Either they were just plain braggarts, or they were making a point of having witnesses to say they'd been here at a time when something deadly was happening at another location. An alibi.

That was possible, but it didn't make much sense. There was no law out here to chase them down, no matter what they did. And the Lighthorse, the Indian police, had no jurisdiction over crimes committed on their lands by white men. So that left only men like himself, bounty hunters by trade, to venture into this territory to weed out the worst of the lot. But of even more interest, even vital concern, to Deke was the question of these men's identities. Was one of them Sara's brother? Her cousin? And if not, where were they? Were they here in town somewhere, perhaps over at the hotel with Sara this very minute, or still at Robber's Cave?

His first instinct when the riders came in had been to clear out when he finished his drink, thinking that what these men intended on doing was none of his concern, as long as they left him and his alone. But not now, not now that he knew they rode with the Daltons, or could even be the Daltons.

Was his time with Sara going to be over so soon? Was the gun battle he'd been alternately dreading and yearning for going to take place right here, right now? Was this his chance for revenge for his murdered family? In a way he hoped so, because this way Sara wasn't involved. Well, at least she wouldn't be present. Trapped, stuck, cursing inside, Deke held his shot glass up to indicate a refill to the bartender.

That small movement brought the four men's narrowed gazes to rest on Deke when the bartender quit paying attention to their needs in order to attend this other customer. Deke narrowed his eyes right back at them and stood up to his full height. A tiny sense of relief passed over him when he realized that they didn't recognize him by sight. If they got around to introductions, however—well, he'd face that if it happened. Another wash of relief went through him when he saw that none of these men particularly resembled Sara. But then, who was to say they looked anything alike? Deke's own sister had been a blonde.

"I ain't never seen you here before, mister," challenged the man closest to Deke at the bar, a youngish, brown-headed kid with a long, ugly scar across his cheek. His three companions watched, an evil glee lighting up their faces at this potential fun.

"That's because I've never been here before—leastwise not anytime in the past few months since you've been old enough to drink," Deke replied evenly.

The man closest to the kid cuffed his shoulder as much as to say he got you with that one, kid. The kid was not amused. "You know who we are, mister? You know who you're messin' with?"

Deke wanted to kick himself for rising to the bait and to throttle the kid for dangling it. The last thing he needed, if his hunt wasn't over right here, since he'd like to ride in to Robber's Cave with his anonymity intact, was a prolonged and memorable conversation with these four. And so he backed down. "I didn't know I was messin' with anyone, mister. I apologize if I've insulted you." He even tipped his Stetson at the boy, hoping to mollify his wounded sense of toughness and to restore his standing with his rough compadres.

It worked—after a tense moment of scrutiny, during which the kid sized him up, clearly trying to gauge if Deke was still somehow not taking him seriously. Deke kept his expression carefully blank.

His mind finally made up, the kid reached up, Deke being a good six inches taller than him, to put his hand on Deke's shoulder, a deadly gesture under most other circumstances. "That's more like it, mister. Now why don't you take your drink and go on over to the tables, so's me and my pardners here can have us a good time? Better yet, why don't you just go on and leave; your face is beginning to bother me."

Simply nodding, putting down his full shot glass, throwing a coin on the rough planking of the bar, and walking out of the saloon to the loud hoots of laughter that marked his retreat was one of the hardest things Deke Bonner had ever done. And one of the smartest. That little son-of-a-bitch would pay someday, Deke vowed as he pushed through the swinging doors and felt the hot, dry air of midday hit him square on his hot, strained face. But not today. There was too much else at stake right now. And he'd been outnumbered four to one.

Deke even managed a grim smile. The other patrons in the saloon, who most likely knew who he was after last night, were probably stunned at his show of meekness. Still, he felt relatively sure that they wouldn't enlighten the four about his identity. He had the distinct impression that there wasn't anyone in the saloon who hankered for a conversation with those belligerent bastards. And since he'd ended their confrontation so quickly and cleanly, the odds were in his favor that the four wouldn't remember it on down the line. They probably had three or four incidents like this one every day, given the type of bullies they were.

Then his mood turned as dark as his black Stetson when his traitorous mind tortured him with ugly pictures of that smart-ass punk maybe being the one who'd had his hands on his sister before he murdered her. If that kid was a Dalton, and the other two were anything like him, then Deke knew that, his love for Sara not withstanding, he would have no trouble killing them.

Damn, what a morning, he fumed, heading back to the hotel, trying to decide whether or not to tell Sara about these men. He sure as hell wasn't going to let her go talk to them. So what purpose would it serve to even tell her they were in town? At this point, Deke had no idea what he himself was going to do about them, if anything. They could be liars and braggarts, for all he knew, since it wasn't uncommon for a man or a kid who fancied himself good with a gun to enhance his reputation by claiming he rode with real outlaws.

And too, he and Sara were still at crossed purposes over this issue of his bounty warrant. It still hung between them with all the force of a hanging noose from a gallows. So he really didn't want to bring the subject up unless he had to. Fighting a forming headache—whether from the rotgut whiskey so early in the day or from his rotgut thoughts, he couldn't say. Deke ran his hand across his forehead, rubbing hard with his fingers. What else could possibly go—?

He stopped himself in time from issuing the deadly challenge to the unkind fates. At least he'd thought it was in time, until he saw Sara, silver hair forming a billowing cloud around her, just as did her flowered gingham skirt, come storming out of the hotel, pushing through the door so hard that it slammed back against the wall of the building and rattled the glass windowpane in its casement. Two old men dozing on the front porch of the hotel jerked to wakeful alertness and marked her progress out into the street, as did ten or fifteen other citizens.

Deke stopped in the middle of the street, remembering her quicksilver mood swings of this morning, and warily allowed riders and wagons to flow around him, feeling for all the world that the simplest solution would be to just slap leather and shoot her. Then life would be simple again—if he were willing to cut out his own heart and bury it with her, of course. Too late. She was too close now. Couldn't get a clean shot off. For the first time that morning, he smiled a smile that was honest and purely in fun. He hoped that whatever had Sara so hopped up didn't serve to wipe the smile clean off his face for him, just as surely as if she used one of his own bandannas on him. He remembered just then that she was forever keeping them whenever he let her use one. He meant to take her to task about that one day. After all, his biggest expense on this trip thus far had been for bandannas.

"Deke Bonner, there you are! Where did you get yourself off to this morning? I swear I've been looking all over for you."

"You've been out on these streets alone?" Deke asked levelly, his stomach twisting around the whiskey in it when he thought of her at the unlikely mercy of some of the characters hanging out here at the trading post. What if she'd run into those men even now in the saloon drinking themselves into a really mean state? His sudden gut feeling was that they weren't the Daltons themselves, and that they would have hurt her—or worse.

"I have my derringer," she replied confidently, pulling it out of her pocket to show him.

"A little one-shot pistol, and you feel safe?"

"Yes, Deke. No one has bothered me." She put the loaded derringer back into her pocket to freely knock and bump against everything she came into contact with.

"That derringer probably poses a bigger threat to you than it does to anyone else, you know."

She put her hands to the back of her head to hold her hair off her neck in an unconsciously seductive pose and looked up at him with those big, doelike black eyes of hers that made his insides melt. Then she pursed her pink, shapely lips at him and said, "Can we get out of the middle of the street, Deke, please? It's hot out here, and I have to talk to you—but not about my derringer."

Totally lost in her beauty, all Deke could do was motion her to precede him. Smitten as he was, he was still not one to miss an opportunity to watch a woman's hips sashaying in front of him. But beyond that, neither was he about to cross her today—not with her armed and under the influence of the curse. He intended to be fully cooperative, no matter what she had to say.

Until he heard what she had to say. No sooner were they out of the street, stopping in the shade of the overhanging porch roof in front of the hotel and within earshot of at least ten people, when Sara said, plain enough, "Deke, tell me something—What would you do if I told you I was pregnant?"

Deke nearly choked on his tongue; apparently, from the sounds coming from them, so did three or four other people close by. Completely hornswoggled, he grabbed her arm at the elbow and escorted her handily into the excuse for a lobby inside the hotel. Looking around that threadbare, airless room, he saw no one but the desk clerk, who caught sight of the look on Deke's face and quickly went into the room behind the desk, closing the door after him.

"What in the hell brought that on?" he questioned Sara,

his voice low and hard. As if he didn't know, he conceded to himself; he'd had the same thought earlier today.

The explosion of red onto Sara's face told him plainly enough what had brought that on, and that the lobby was still too public a place for this conversation. "Come on," he said flatly, escorting her up the stairs, not giving her a chance to protest. Once they were safely behind the door to their room, which all of a sudden looked too private for this conversation what with their shared bed dominating the landscape, Deke turned back to Sara. She stood across the room, looking out the one window and wringing her hands together. She looked so damned soul-wrenchingly beautiful in her new clothes and with her hair down—yet so vulnerable that Deke had trouble keeping his heart in his chest.

He already knew what he would have liked to do if she'd been pregnant—marry her and run off somewhere with her, the rest be damned. But he couldn't say that. For one thing, he didn't know how she felt about marrying him. And for another, what about what awaited them at Robber's Cave? There was really no way in hell a compromise could be reached on that score. It was all or nothing for each one of them. And one of them would have to lose everything.

So, once again, the awful truth of their separate lives and separate missions kept Deke quiet. Sara, too. He said nothing, waiting for her, until he finally remembered that she was waiting for his answer to her question: What would he do if she told him she was pregnant?

"Sara," he began, as if no time had elapsed from her asking to his answering. "I would do whatever you wanted."

She turned to him, pain forming a ridge over her nose between her eyebrows. "That's no answer."

He knew that, too. "Look, you're not pregnant. We both know that. So why do we have to have this conversation?"

Her face went red again; she looked down at her hands. He wanted nothing more than to go to her and gather her in his arms, but there was much more than physical distance separating them just now. "I suppose my . . . predicament was hard to keep from you, wasn't it?'' she managed with a weak smile.

"Yeah," he conceded, taking his Stetson off and running a hand through his hair. He sailed his black hat onto the bed, wanting nothing more than to follow it and take her with him, just to hold her. "And I guess we do need to talk about this. Because it probably will come up again."

When Sara's eyes widened and she quirked a grin at him, he thought about what he'd just said. "I didn't mean it like that."

"I know, but it's funny."

"Well, good. We can still find something to laugh about." Even when we're up to our asses in outlaws, Indians, and relatives, dead or otherwise, he thought. Out loud, he asked, "What would you have wanted me to do, Sara?"

She sobered and looked at him, her heart in her eyes. Damn, he could never get past her eyes; if she only knew what a quivering little puppy he was in her hands. Sara drew back the thin, ragged curtain that almost didn't hang from the window and looked outside. "I would have wanted you to go down on your knees, beg me to marry you, declare your undying love, and sweep me up into your arms to carry me off, away from everything and everyone who's come between us."

Damn. Exactly what he'd been thinking. But she also said it with the same wistfulness for the unattainable that he'd felt. "Then, that's exactly what I would have done," he confessed, meaning it, knowing that somehow he would have made it work between them.

She let go of the curtain panel and turned to him. "Don't tease me, Deke. This is serious."

"I'm not teasing. I would have done that."

She looked at him, the question as evident in her eyes as he knew it must be in his own: If they had gotten married, despite all their problems, if she were pregnant, why couldn't they work out their differences even though she wasn't? What was stopping them?

The moment stretched out, became still, heightened some-how, even to the point that Deke was completely cognizant of his own heartbeat, of the trickle of sweat running down his spine, of his eyes blinking, his throat swallowing. He became aware, as if these sensations were somehow separate from him, of the voices and footsteps outside their door, the sound of a wagon out on the street, a horse whinnying some-where in the distance, a dog barking.

It was time to tell her. She needed to know what was driving him. And it wasn't money. "Sara, answer this for me: Were you home when the Coopers killed your father and your brother?"

She clutched at her skirt spasmodically, her face crum-pling. "No," she rasped out past what had to be incredible pain over that memory. A pain of the sort that also laced every waking moment of Deke's life.

"And how do you feel about not having been there?"

"Deke, don't do this. Don't ask me this."

"I have to, Sara. Believe me; I have to. The last thing I want to do is cause you more pain. But you have to know."

"Know what?" she cried out, her face contorting.

"Just answer me. Please. How have you felt every day of your life since then?"

Sara hung her head. "I wish it had been me who was killed. It would have been easier to be dead than to live with the knowledge that I wasn't there to help them."

"I know; I have the same feelings in my life. But if you had been there, what would you have done?"

She advanced on the bed and took hold, with both hands, of the post on her side. Her expression was almost feral in its intensity; her voice was not much more than a whisper. "I would have killed them. Without mercy."

"Which is exactly what your brothers did when they found them. And don't you feel better knowing the Coopers no longer walk this earth, that they paid with their lives?"

"Yes. God forgive me, but yes." Her look changed from stricken to defiant, as if she expected Deke to tell her she was wrong to be glad. But nothing could have been further from the truth; he'd have done the exact same thing. Still intended to.

He nodded his acceptance of her answer. She narrowed her eyes slightly and cocked her head to one side, clearly now at a loss as to where he was going with this. But Deke knew, and he went on—perhaps ruthlessly, but there was no other way. "Now, answer this: If you hadn't had any other brothers to avenge their deaths, if there was only you, would you have hunted them down until the day you died or until you killed them, and let nothing or no one stand in your way?"

"Yes," she answered simply, honestly. But still with a trace of confusion . . . and caution.

Deke took in a deep breath. "That's what I'm doing, Sara. This isn't about a bounty warrant—even one for ten thousand dollars. Remember on that first day out of Plains when I told you my mother and sister had been killed, just like your brother and father?"

She let go of the post and put her hands out in front of her in a supplicating manner, palms up. "Yes, but I still don't understand what that has to do with—"

"I knew you couldn't have known," Deke said sadly, her words confirming for him that she hadn't known of her kin's treachery. He could barely go on; his throat was closing up, and his eyes burned with dryness. He ran his hand over his mouth and chin and looked at her, knowing that his next words would kill for them both their one chance at happiness together. His heart beat dully, thuddingly in his chest. Better to get it over with here than at Robber's Cave.

"I don't think you know it, Sara, but the Dalton boys robbed a bank in my hometown—Independence, Missouri— a few years back. It was before I got home from the war. Three men and two women were killed when the gang botched the job."

"No," Sara cut in, her voice a whimper of dawning, terrible realization. She grabbed for the post again and stared at him with eyes bleak with pain, devoid of hope.

But Deke had committed himself to this course and couldn't stop now. ''I didn't know the men who died that day, Sara, but the women killed by the Daltons were my mother, Adeline Bonner, and my kid sister, Helene Bonner.''

Sara gave a tiny whimper, much like a small animal dying. Deke himself died a thousand times as he watched the color drain from her face. When he took a step toward her, she jerkily held out her hand for him to stop. He did. Looking at him as if he'd just sprung up from hell, she gasped out ''No!'' and slowly fainted dead away.

Chapter Twenty-one

If Sara hadn't awakened from her faint already in Deke's arms, she knew she might never have been able to let him touch her again. Not because she hated him and would shrink from his touch, but—how could he want to touch her? And apparently he still did. How could she be anything but repugnant to him? How had he ever looked at her, touched her, loved her, and not thought about her brother and cousins killing his mother and sister?

She tried to think, cradled in Deke's arms as he stretched out on the bed with her, how she would feel if anyone even remotely related to the Coopers, her father and brother's killers, wanted to touch her in any intimate way. A paroxysm of revulsion swept through her, shuddering her; Deke held her more closely, not allowing her to pull away from him. But he said nothing, obviously giving her time to work toward some tolerable conclusions.

Sara didn't for a moment doubt the truth of what Deke had told her. She knew that if he said that was what had happened, then that was what had happened. Deke Bonner might be a bounty hunter, but he was no liar. But not since that first day on the trail together had she felt such a keen sense of her kin's deaths. Indeed, for one fleeting moment, she allowed as how they might deserve a vengeful death, if they'd sunk so low as to kill women and children for money. No! her heart cried out. This was too awful. She knew Jim, Cody, and Travis better than that. There had to be some other explanation. Dear God, she prayed, let there be some other explanation.

It was then that Sara knew they had to make all haste, allowing for no more delays, to Robber's Cave. Somehow, she had to convince Deke not to kill Jim, Cody, and Travis right off, but to talk to them first. She just knew they could clear this up. It couldn't have been them; for if it were, she was afraid she would lose her sanity.

But if it was the truth, she wouldn't stop Deke. She wouldn't—couldn't—help him to kill them, but neither would she raise a hand or a gun to stop him. But she did need to hear their guilt or innocence from their own lips; she had to know for herself if they were still the boys she had loved, or if they were now cold-blooded killers. She'd rather go home without them, tell her dying mother and her Aunt Jean that their sons were already dead, than escort them home knowing there was the blood of innocents on their hands. And then she would plod out the remainder of her miserable existence, alone there in Plains, devoid of her entire family—but worst of all, devoid of Deke Bonner's love. Oh, God, how could he love her?

Having arrived full circle in her tortured thoughts, Sara opened her mouth to tell Deke, while still in his arms and not able to see his face, what was on her mind. But he spoke first. Apparently she wasn't the only one who had been doing some thinking.

"Sara, do you know a skinny kid, real cocky, with brown hair and a long scar on his cheek?"

With everything between them that needed to be said, Sara

could not fathom where this question had come from. She raised herself, bracing her hand against Deke's broad chest, to look into his eyes. They were as bleak as a January night. She knew her look was one of frank questioning.

He repeated, "Do you know such a boy? Or I guess you could call him a man. He carries a gun like one."

Sara thought for a moment, wondering too why Deke's heart was suddenly pounding under her hand. "No. No, I don't."

"Are you sure?"

His heart fairly skipped a beat then, she noticed. "Yes, I'm sure. Why do you ask?"

For the first time since she'd known him, Sara watched him turn his head away from her direct gaze and lie. "It's nothing. Never mind."

Sara sat up now on her knees, making the creaking bed jiggle under their weight. "Why did you ask me about that boy? Did you see somebody like that? Here?"

Deke turned back to her; the wariness and lack of trust on his face startled her. So they were back to guarding their secrets and to distrusting each other. Then she thought that her own face must look just the same.

"What difference does it make since you don't know him?" Deke countered.

"Well, did he say he knew me, then? You have to tell me, Deke. You have to."

Deke looked at her long and hard. Then, with one lithe move, he rolled off the bed, leaving Sara to stare after him. He walked to the window, pulled the curtain back, and looked out, moving his head as he looked to both sides of the street. "No. He didn't say he knew you. But he did say he rode with the Daltons."

"He what?" Sara breathed. "No one rides with the Daltons! They ride alone. My brother told me that himself."

Deke let the thin, worn, lacy panel fall back into place. He turned a hopeful if wary face to Sara. "When did he tell you that?"

"Why, on his last visit home—over a year ago."

Deke slumped and let out his breath. "Well, apparently things change. Because this kid with the scar is at the saloon here with three other men—"

"Three?" Sara cut him off. Could it be that Jim, Cody, and Travis were right here?

Deke apparently caught the significance of the number three. "What do the other Daltons look like, Sara? Do they look like you?"

If she refused to tell him, she would declare herself to be taking her kin's side. Or she could answer him, and thus make his job easier once he knew them by sight. On the horns of a dilemma, Sara closed her eyes and felt the heaviness in her chest. When she spoke, it was softly. "They don't look like me. They look like you, only not so big. Not so—" She'd been going to say handsome, but stopped herself in time.

"Then it's not them at the saloon. It's not your brother and cousins." His voice was much closer now.

Sara opened her eyes to have her sight filled with Deke Bonner standing by the bed; he was just lowering his hand. Had he been going to touch her?

Just the simple knowledge that he still wanted to touch her, even believing that her family had a hand in his family's deaths, chilled Sara unbelievably. What kind of a cold bastard was he? Then her heart beat in time with the passing seconds; heavy, dull, thudding. Had he used her, pretended to love her, ravaged her for some ulterior purpose of his? But Sara's swirling thoughts could come up with no plausible reason how making her love him would help him any. He certainly didn't need her help beyond using her as a judas goat, as she herself had called it, to get close to the Daltons. No, he'd always been truthful about that.

Then it stuck her. He had more reason to suspect her of trickery, to suspect her of using her body to trap him, than she did him. The look of horror she hadn't been able to keep off her face as she thought these things served to turn Deke abruptly away from her.

Fearful that his own interpretation of her look would be much worse than the real reason for it, Sara jumped off the bed and flung herself into Deke's arms. "No!" she cried with all the love, all the hurt, all the turmoil in her heart.

But Deke's arms did not come around her as they had so many times in the past few weeks. Instead, he gripped her arms and held her away from him. "I expect you'll want your own room now." His voice and his manner were as cold and as distant as February nights.

"No, Deke, I don't want this or any other room. I want to leave this place. I want to ride straight to Robber's Cave. I can't stand this anymore. I have to know—despite what you say. I have to hear Jim say he killed your family before I'll believe it. There has to be some other explanation!"

Deke let go of her and went to the door. With a hardness he'd never turned on her but that she'd seen only last night right before he killed that man at supper, he said, "There is no other explanation. I talked to people who saw it happen, people who were there, Sara. There's no mistake: The Daltons killed two men who worked in the bank. And they killed my mother and fifteen-year-old sister just because they were inside and could identify them. That's your truth." He jerked open the door when he was finished.

Sara stopped him by calling out his name. "Deke!"

He turned to her, his eyes questioning but unyielding.

"Then how can you love me?" Her voice was a terrible whisper of damnation.

His mouth worked; his hand spasmed around the doorknob. Then he looked at her, black eyes narrowed. "How can you love me, Sara Dalton?" he threw back at her. Turning now, he stepped out of the room and closed the door behind him.

It wasn't even noon yet, Sara thought, looking over her shoulder at the sun not yet at its zenith in the dark blue sky overhead. And already so much had happened today. She forced her mind away from the scene in the hotel room; could it have been only an hour ago that Deke had walked out? It seemed more like a lifetime. Sweat beaded her brow and Sara wiped at it with her sleeve; the day held the promise of crushing heat. All the more reason to have her hair twisted and tied up off her sweating neck. A new gray hat, a smaller version of a man's Stetson, sat securely on her head, the chin strap seeing to that. She kept tugging at it, though, its unaccustomed feel under her chin annoying her.

Forgetting her own physical discomforts, she turned her eyes and her thoughts to the worn trail and the task ahead of her. She had to get to Robber's Cave. Deke's revelations only made her more determined. And more scared. She had figured out that if she rode hard, with few stops—and didn't lose her way—she could get to Robber's Cave ahead of Deke. Reining in Cinnamon, she reached behind her to open one of her saddle bags and sorted through it until she came up with Jim's map. Cinnamon, irritable since she'd left the livery barn and Deke's buckskin stallion knickering in his stall after her, tossed her head just then, catching Sara unawares and sending the map to the ground.

"Dammit, Cinnamon," Sara fussed as she dismounted. "Just because you're in season, like that smithy said, and I'm having my—oh, never mind."

Cinnamon laid her ears flat against her head and bared her teeth in a rare show of bad temper. Sara's eyes widened as she stared at her mare. "Oh, go ahead, act like that. You can't have him, so you may as well get used to the idea. Besides, he's nothing but trouble."

Not completely convinced that she was admonishing only her horse, Sara gave up talking to her mare, mumbling about sounding like Coburn talking to Jezebel. She bent over to retrieve the precious map, her only guide now that she was alone on the trail and didn't have Deke's knowledge of the way to guide her. At the same moment, a slight gust tossed and twirled the map just out of her grasp. Thinking several more choice epithets, Sara dropped Cinnamon's reins, told her to "stay!" and chased after the map. She was nearly in tears when she finally made a successful grab for the teasing scrap of precious paper, losing her hat in the process but ending up with the map in her hand—and herself on the hard, dusty ground.

She lay there, her face in the dirt and grass, tempted to scream and kick and cry until she was drained, but fearing that if she did, she might not be able to stop. Pushing herself up to a sitting position, she first brushed the dust and grime off her new split skirt and fancy shirt; then, daubing at her misting eyes, she glanced up, looking behind her for Cinnamon. Her grainy vision revealed that either the mare had grown four more legs, or they were no longer alone. Taking one of Deke's bandannas from around her neck, she scrubbed at her eyes.

Fighting the rising fear in her throat, she was grateful for the weight of the derringer in her pocket. She'd been out here in this territory long enough to know what sorts of desperadoes populated it. Sunday school teachers and preachers were few and far between. No, most likely she was now sitting in the company of a killer, a robber, a hostile Indian, a not-so-honorable soldier, or even—she rubbed at her eyes again and cleared her vision—a damned bounty hunter who didn't know when he wasn't wanted.

She jumped up, folding and stuffing her map into the same pocket that held her derringer. Anger at seeing Deke again made her heart beat faster and her knees go weak—or so she told herself. "Go away, Deke Bonner! You're not riding with me!"

"That's fine with me. But *you* are riding with me. That's the deal."

"Deal? We had no deal! Now, get your damned stud away from my mare! Look at him! The smithy told me what happened. He's no better than you are, seducing innocent women."

Deke blinked once under the shaded brim of his black

Stetson. But he didn't move his nuzzling stallion away from her receptive mare. Did the man have to look so in control, so intimidating, so damned male—all lean and muscled, sitting there tall in his saddle? He ought to be shot just for that, she fumed, her fingers closing around the derringer in her pocket. What he was doing to her heart, and other regions of her body, ought to be illegal, especially when he was The Enemy. And especially when he'd come upon her doing something so ridiculous.

"Innocent women?" he finally said. "Cinnamon's a horse, Sara. Just like—my horse is. They just did what comes naturally under the circumstances."

"And what's your excuse?" she challenged, plodding over to Cinnamon, smartly taking the reins from his grasp, and mounting again. She nearly had to whip Cinnamon with the trailing reins to get her to step away from the buckskin.

"My excuse? What's yours? I certainly never forced you to do anything you didn't—"

"I meant," she said very pointedly, "what's your excuse for being out here, for thinking you can join me?—Again?"

He fell silent; Sara swore his face was red under that wide brim. His hat! Where was hers? Her hands went to her hair, which was coming out of its twisted bun, and her gaze went this way and that, sweeping the ground around them.

"Over there," Deke said, catching her attention. He pointed to a stand of scrubby bushes.

Mouthing words her mother would be shocked to know her only daughter knew, much less used, Sara dismounted, kept a hold on Cinnamon's reins, and practically dragged the stiff-legged mare with her over to the bush that had snagged her gray hat. Jerking it up off the ground, she hit it against her thigh to dislodge the dust, and stuffed it on her head, causing further disarray to her hair. She glared at Deke, daring him to do anything.

His only reaction was to sniff noncommittally. He said not a word, just placing his hand on his stallion's shoulder and patting soothingly when the animal stamped impatiently and fought at the bit in its mouth, wanting very much to be close to the little roan mare. Sara watched as Deke, almost without a perceptible movement, controlled the large, agitated stud with his knees and hands.

He should control himself so well, she fumed. Mounting Cinnamon again, Sara set off down the trail. She hadn't even looked at her map yet and wouldn't give Deke Bonner the satisfaction of letting him see her do it now, but surely she couldn't already be lost, only one hour out of that town, whatever it was called.

"Do you know where you're headed?" Deke asked a few silent moments later.

"Robber's Cave. Same as you." She wouldn't look over at him if it killed her. She was determined to pretend he simply was not with her. Too many things had been said in that hotel room to just go back to the way things had been. No, that was over. For good. Better to concentrate on things she could do something about.

"Hell, I know that. What I mean is, are you sure you're going the right way now, this minute?"

"Are you asking me if I'm lost?" Sara challenged, denying the prickly feeling that maybe she was.

"You're not lost yet, but you will be if you stay on this dirt path. It takes you right back around to the trading post. You need to veer off it about two hundred yards up and start heading more south than east—if you still intend to follow the south fork of the Canadian River, that is."

Why there was a road leading out of town and then right back around into it, Sara could not fathom. Neither could she fathom letting on to this man that she hadn't realized that. "I know that," she lied, also knowing he'd seen her chasing that damned map all over creation.

They rode on in silence for a few more minutes.

"I heard you tried to find those four men."

Sara looked over at him. How did he know everything about her business? "Yes, I did."

"Have any luck?"

"You're the one who knows everything about my business. Why don't you tell me?"

"You didn't find them because they rode out right after I left the saloon. And they went this way. They're probably headed back to their hideout at Robber's Cave. Which means we're on their trail, and had better be pretty careful not to ride up on them."

The last thing she wanted was help from this man who was acting as if this morning hadn't even happened. But she couldn't stop her tongue, not with that dangling bit of bait he'd put out. "Oh, I'm sure there's no danger of your riding upon them, hampered as you are with a woman to be seen to and coddled."

He looked at her angrily. "Meaning that if I rode alone, went on ahead, left you here to find your own way, I could get there before them—lowering the odds and the number of guns against me—and kill the Daltons before you showed up?"

Sara squared her jaw and clamped down firmly on her back teeth; she returned his angry glare, but then said, "That's exactly what I mean."

"Then, sweetheart, have it your way." He tipped his Stetson at her, put his heels to his stallion's belly, and galloped away, leaving only a cloud of dust in his wake—a cloud of dust that clogged Sara's nostrils and brought tears to her eyes.

Chapter Twenty-two

"Dammit!" Deke swore as he reined his stud to a bone-jarring halt and then turned the massive animal around. Peering back the way he'd come, he could see Sara. She was a dot in the distance, but he could see her. This was it, the vision he'd had that night in the Nighthorses' barn, the one where he saw himself getting free of her and just riding off—and then turning around and riding right back. No way was he going to give in to that romantic notion. No way.

"I am *not* going back to her, do you hear me?" he yelled to the heavens, practically standing in his stirrups in his agitation. Her calm dismissal of him and her smug assertion that she could find her way alone angered him. As if that weren't enough insurrection for one day, his normally well-trained, cool-under-fire buckskin let him know what he thought of his master's outburst by parading in an arcing, high-stepping, head-lowering dance that threatened to erupt into a bucking contest. Deke roused himself enough to take a firmer grip on the reins and raise the stallion's lowered head, then began turning him back in a tight circle until he again faced Sara Dalton.

He squinted to see her better. She was still coming, still advancing, albeit slowly. His mouth turned down in displeasure as he tried to think this thing through. Before he knew it, he was talking out loud again; actually, he was yelling out loud again. "I will *not* help that woman anymore! I will not! She's on her own from this moment forward. Let her see if she can find her way to Robber's Cave! Just let her try! I couldn't care less what happens to her!"

At this outburst, the stallion fought his bit and equally startled birds left their tree roosts in a great flapping and whooshing of rapidly beating wings. Deke glared at them as they wheeled off over his head, as if he thought they were somehow mocking him. But the feathered commotion only served to further frighten his horse and keep Deke busy for several minutes trying to control and calm him. When he finally gained the upper hand, both with his mount and his emotions, he looked back to where he'd last seen Sara.

Son of a bitch! She wasn't there. She'd apparently already veered off in the wrong direction. This was too much. The woman had reduced him to gritting his teeth together in sheer temper. Feeling the cords stand out in his neck, Deke knew he was close to losing control. In fact, he had to clamp a hand over his mouth to stifle a yell of pure frustration that threatened to erupt from his belly. Making a valiant effort to get a grip on himself, Deke kept the buckskin tightly reined while he forced himself to breathe more slowly and waited for the sweating heat of his temper to dry up. He removed his Stetson to wipe at his brow, then replaced the black hat and shook his head in defeat.

But more upsetting to him than his near loss of control was the realization that now, since he wasn't in a high temper, he was very close to whimpering. And it was all her fault. Wherever the hell she was. Deke took a deep breath in through his nose and pressed his lips together in concentration, moving his keen gaze from one side to the other of the trail, like a hawk looking for supper. Well, she couldn't have gone too far astray. If he started back now, he could—

Realizing the direction of his thoughts, Deke's shoulders sagged in defeat. He was going back to Sara. In a low mumble, he cursed himself for a fool as he turned his mount and urged him into a gallop, a short run that would see him back by Sara's side in no time at all. He ignored the sudden thrilling of his heart at that thought and quickly squelched the happy grin that replaced his frown as he retraced his steps back to the most frustrating and tantalizing woman he'd ever run across.

That evening, Sara lay on her side at their campsite, her head resting on her bent arm; she was facing Deke, watching him as he sat on his bedroll with his back propped up against his saddle. He was slowly sipping his coffee. She took in every detail of him. He had one long, muscular leg stretched out before him; his other leg was bent at the knee. Since he wasn't watching her, she allowed her gaze to rove over his tall, powerful frame, secretly smiling at the way the skin crinkled at the corners of his eyes when he gingerly took a sip of the strong brew. She decided that she liked the way his mouth worked around the rim of the cup.

"Deke?" she said quietly into the soft night, surprising herself more than him that she'd said his name out loud. After all, she'd barely deigned to speak to him since he'd ridden off from her that afternoon and then had ridden back, only to find her already lost after only a very short time on her own. Never mind the scene that followed.

He looked over at her. "Yeah?"

Sara had no idea what she wanted to ask him, so she blurted out the first thing that came to her mind. "Before the war, what did you do?"

Looking at her as if trying to assess her reason for asking, he settled his features into a hard line and then turned his head to look back out on the black night. "Cattle. My family was in the cattle business. But that was in another life.''

Sara heard the regret, the longing in his voice. "Would you like to do it again? Herd cattle, I mean."

He cut his gaze over to her sharply and then set his tin mug down on the ground beside him. After another moment's hesitation, he crossed his arms over his bent knee, raised one hand to rub at his nose, and admitted, ''More than anything else. But wanting something doesn't make it happen—money does. A whole lot of money.''

Sara thought of the huge bounty on the Dalton Boys. Ten thousand dollars would buy a sizable spread and a whole herd of cattle. She stayed quiet for a moment, figuring he was probably thinking the same thing. That damned bounty warrant. The past two years had provided her with ample opportunity to learn the dirty trade. She knew that some U.S. marshal or deputy—most likely one out of Fort Smith, the starting point for more than one of Deke's predecessors who'd eventually shown up in Plains—had issued a piece of paper with her kin's names on it, a simple piece of paper that could be turned in only to him, along with the men or their bodies, for the stated reward. It was just a job, as one especially nasty hunter had felt the cruel need to tell her when he'd come looking.

But look what that paper was costing her. She cut her gaze over to Deke. It was always between them; it always found its way into every conversation they had, into everything they did. Heaving a deep sigh, more from emotion than sleepiness, she tried a different tack. ''Well, say you got the money somehow. Would you quit bounty hunting and maybe buy some cattle, have a family?''

When he didn't answer right away, she looked up to see him grinning down at her. ''Maybe,'' he said finally.

That bone-liquefying grin of his, stretching lazily over even, white teeth, flopped her stomach over. To hide her flutterings, she poked at his rock-hard thigh with her finger. ''You don't tell anybody your business, do you?''

His grin widened. ''That's what makes it my business.''

Sara rose on one elbow. "Are you telling me to mind my own, Deke Bonner?"

He leaned dangerously close to her, so close that his warm breath fanned her cheek. "I'm telling you to get some sleep, Sara Dalton."

Rattled by his nearness, wanting to take him into her arms but not daring, she abruptly turned away from him and onto her side, presenting her back to him. After the briefest of seconds, she heard and felt him move away from her. As she lay there listening to the sounds of him settling down to sleep close to her, Sara was suddenly awash in guilt, as if she, by virtue of being a Dalton, was keeping him from having the life he wanted. The frown that feeling, that knowledge, brought to her face was smoothed out only when she finally fell asleep.

The next morning, Deke was all business, rushing her through her morning routine, finding fault with all she did. When she finally protested, he shot her a look, adopted a no-nonsense stance and said, "Look, Sara, we've already wasted too much time. I'm getting mighty tired of all the delays, not to mention this trail, this damned flat prairie, this heat, and—" He bit off the next item on his list.

"Me, right? You were going to say me, weren't you?"

"No, I wasn't." He wouldn't meet her gaze.

Sara puckered her lips, feeling her early-morning peevishness rising. "I think you were."

"Well, you're wrong."

She shifted her stance and put her hand to her hip, cocking her head to one side. "Oh? Am I? Then what *were* you going to say?"

"I was going to say I'm getting tired of the way men— every damned one of them we meet—keep looking at you."

Sara made a small deprecating sound. "What men? There's no one out here but us."

"I know that! And you're damned lucky, too."

"I'm lucky . . . ? Deke Bonner, you're making no sense."

"See? I told you I was tired. Now mount up."

Shaking her head, Sara did just that, and they rode out. Side by side. But that didn't mean she had to talk to him. Feeling sick at heart, knowing that they'd never resolve their differences, she kept her own counsel. Over the next few hours of the hot morning, no different from any of the others they'd shared, Sara would, whenever she felt Deke's gaze on her, tug on this strap, tighten that buckle, settle that bit of skirt.

"Is this how it's going to be? The closer we get to the caves, the worse you're going to act?"

Sara jerked her head up to look at him. The worse *she* was going to act? What about his little performance earlier that morning? She looked at his handsome face, now marred with the worst frown she'd ever seen; he could look downright fearsome when he really tried. But she wasn't intimidated, not this time. "Could be," was all she said.

But in her heart she knew it could be no other way. The tension alone over what would happen once they arrived there had been dogging their steps, giving them nightmares, wringing them out in every way possible, and chasing them across the prairie as much as any wall of fire or herd of stampeding buffalo. The dangers they'd faced from without were as nothing to the fears from within that they wrestled with every waking moment. At this point, Sara just wanted it over with—the entire journey, the confrontation with her brother and cousins, the long trip back home to her mother. It had gone on long enough.

Apparently Deke felt the same way, for he looked over at her and said, though not unkindly, "Come on, Sara. Let's give our horses their heads. Let's ride like all the demons in hell are chasing us."

Because they are, Sara thought, but nodded her agreement and put her heels to Cinnamon's belly. She loosened the reins and leaned forward over her roan's neck, making the mare's burst of speed all that more effective. Deke's stallion answered his master's "Hee-ya" with an equal leap, and they were off at a punishing pace, one they maintained for days on end, stopping only for those functions necessary to maintain life and to preserve their mounts' strength.

Too exhausted at night, too withdrawn in spirit at the end of a hard day in the saddle, Sara and Deke refrained, as if by tacit agreement, from the intimacy of lovemaking. Just as at the beginning of their journey together, there existed between them an almost palpable barrier. Walls, no less penetrable for being invisible and of the soul, kept them apart, even while they were together.

Even though the changing landscape was everything Deke had promised her, even though the forested mountains, the free-flowing waters, the blankets of rainbow-hued wildflowers covering sweeping meadows, the fleeting sightings of the abundant wildlife should have lifted her spirits, Sara remained single-minded in her determination to have this leg of the journey over with. She allowed herself only passing moments of enjoyment for her new surroundings when they stopped to rest, water, and graze the horses. She checked Cinnamon closely every day for signs of being with foal, monitoring her rest and eating. But so far, with almost a year until she would foal, the roan showed no signs of wear or fatigue. Lucky for that damned buckskin sire.

And so the days passed, with their self-imposed, ground-pounding pace hurrying them through the Chickasaw Nation, but always loosely following the meandering course of the south fork of the Canadian River around any settlements which looked no different in configuration to Sara than any white town. Indeed, any natives they chanced across seemed more than eager for them to be on their way and off their lands. In fact, Sara and Deke didn't stop or allow themselves to encounter any people or entanglements until they reached one of the many army forts along the river that had been established to protect white settlers and trade routes through Indian Territory.

Exhausted, dirty, irritable, ragged in spirit and dress, devoid of humor and supplies, they agreed to rein in at Fort Arbuckle, newly refurbished and reopened by the U.S. Army following its occupation by Confederate troops during the war. Having ridden hard for two weeks, they were now only a week away from Robber's Cave—and in dire need of rest and any recent news the soldiers might have about the lawless region just to the east. It might not be the army's mission to enforce the law out there, but they would sure as hell, Deke told her, know what was going on and who might or might not be in residence in the pock-marked caves of the Sans Bois Mountains.

The well-fortified outpost, as they approached it, looked as welcoming as home to their trail-weary eyes, what with its high wooden walls, a patrolled guard post at each corner, and the ordinary comings and goings of men and women through the flung-open gates. The rag-tag settlement outside the fort, populated by traders, both white and Indian, and civilians who performed menial tasks such as laundry and gardening for the fort's men, for protection against the solid bulwark of the fort, much like baby chicks around their mother hen, ready to flurry under her solid bulk and protective feathers at the first sign of trouble.

"Follow me," Deke said, gigging his buckskin ahead of Cinnamon when they were close enough to draw attention.

It was a sign of Sara's ravaged state of body and mind that she almost said that was exactly what she'd been doing for the past month. A sour turn to her mouth, she shook her head at his imposing back, gently nudging her mare's sides and grudgingly assuming her position of secondary importance behind him. Just once, she fumed, just once she would have liked to have the lead, to be the one in control, the one to set the way. Then it came to her: She'd get her chance in a week at Robber's Cave, when she'd lead him into a den of gunslingers and desperadoes. And they might not come out. Swallowing hard, Sara pushed that scene to the back of her mind and gladly ceded the leadership to Deke's capable hands. As if there'd ever been any doubt.

Besides, not being the leader left Sara free to drink in her surroundings. This fledgling outpost of white civilization appeared to Sara's prairie-sated eyes to be Mecca. The military and commercial hustle and bustle; the children running and dodging around her and Deke's horses; the neat cabins with wash hanging on lines and gardens skirting them; the remote yet curious stares of the men and women; all combined to renew Sara's spirit. Even out here, life went on. And where there was life, there was hope for the future. Her sour frown turned into a warm smile.

They rode leisurely through the bustle of the haphazard settlement, receiving only cursory glances as they passed in front of the guards posted at the open gates of the fort. Looking back at them, Sara realized that these men probably saw so many travelers just like Deke and her that two more didn't warrant any notice. Not too far from the walls of the fort, Deke reined in at a respectable-looking set of log cabins which sported a hand-lettered sign advertising beds, baths, and meals. Rough they might be, but to Sara the cabins looked like heaven. And they were available.

After securing a cabin from the friendly, talkative owner, a rotund woman with graying hair, Deke saw to the horses while Sara bathed and changed into fresh clothing, including a simple cotton skirt and loose blouse. Even the hard chair right outside the cabin, where she now sat in the sunshine letting her hair dry, felt good to her—at least it wasn't a bouncing, sweating horse. A smile lit her face as she enjoyed the cleanliness, the warmth of the afternoon, and the life swirling around her.

Just as Deke emerged from the bathhouse cabin off to Sara's left, drawing her appreciative gaze to his clean-shaven, freshly scrubbed masculine self, and sat down by her, a commotion close to the fort's walls brought them both to their feet. The gathering crowd hid from their view the nature of the trouble, but braying, cursing, and yelling rose above the general din of the disturbance. As several people ran toward the already sizable crowd, Sara made as if to do the same. But Deke's hand on her arm stopped her. When she frowned up at him, he said, "That's not our trouble. Stay here."

"I want to see what's happening," she railed. "I want to see why that donkey's braying; it sounds painful, like it's being hurt, Deke."

"Pain or not, we can't get involved."

Angered by his uncaring response, she jerked her arm from his grip and wagged her finger at him as she spoke. "Maybe *you* can't get involved, but I can." Then, not giving him another chance to restrain her, she took off at a head-long run, not even stopping when she heard Deke call out to her to come back. The next time he called to her, he sounded much closer, so she knew that he was following her. When she came to the crowd of people, she pushed her way through until she could see the animal which had been braying so mournfully only moments ago.

Parting the last of the people in her way, she stopped short, a hand to her throat, a scream clogging her throat. A big, hard-looking man was getting ready to shoot the tiniest, sweetest, most soulful burro that Sara had ever seen. The poor creature, gray and fat, was tied to a post from which it was trying to tug itself free. The man with the rifle trained on its head hadn't shot it yet only because several people were arguing with him, telling him they would take the little jenny if he didn't shoot it. He didn't seem to be particularly swayed by their arguments. It was his animal, his business, he kept repeating.

"Why are you going to kill her?" Sara cried out, beside herself with emotion when he once again raised the rifle. All eyes, including the shooter's, turned to her, an outsider.

"Don't know as it's any of yer business, little lady," the man said snidely.

To Sara's surprise, Deke pushed past her and strode into the small clearing that the crowd had defined around the man and the burro, who now pressed up against the solid wall of the fort, as if she sought its protection. "If the lady asked, then it's her business, pardner. Why don't you answer her?"

The man straightened up, once more lowered his gun, and scowled mightily. "Who says I got to?"

"I do. Deke Bonner." As he spoke, he worked at untying the knotted reins that secured the burro to the post. He didn't appear to be aware of the gasps and then the deep hush that fell over the crowd when he said his name. Only when the terrified jenny was loose and he'd handed its lead rope over to Sara, who quickly bent to hug the burro's neck possessively, did he look up at the man and then the crowd. Quietly, deadly, he said, "I think I might like to buy her from you. What's your asking price?"

"You—you can just have the burro, Mr. Bonner," the wide-eyed, white-faced man stuttered. "I—I don't want no trouble with you."

Deke narrowed his eyes at the man and held him pinned there. "That's good," he finally said. Only then did he turn away, take Sara's elbow, and lead them through the sudden parting in the crowd that opened in front of them. Sara felt the heat rise to her cheeks as the crowd wordlessly watched them pass through their ranks. She wondered what they'd do if they knew *her* last name.

It was only when Deke took the burro's rope from Sara and walked away from her, leading the shaking little creature off to the crude corral where Cinnamon and the buckskin were, that she noticed that Deke was unarmed.

Chapter Twenty-three

That night, standing at the foot of the bed in their private cabin, Sara toyed with the cotton spread with one hand and looked at Deke across the room from her. He was sitting in a damask-covered chair that had seen better days, intent on cleaning his gun. Parts to the deadly Colt were spread on a small table in front of him. That was what she wanted to talk to him about anyway. "Deke," she called out, gaining his attention. "You were unarmed this afternoon."

He grinned as if at a joke that was on him. "Yeah, well, fortunately only you and I seemed to realize that."

Sara grinned back at him. "Thank you for the burro."

He looked at her in a teasing, quizzical manner and stretched back in the chair, lacing his fingers together at the back of his head. "What are you talking about? That's my burro. I do believe the jenny was given to me. However, ma'am, I am a generous man. I'm sure we could work a trade for her."

Sara shot him a daring look, enjoying the fun, enjoying

the sexual play. "A trade? What do I have that you want?"

His answering look was heavy-lidded, plainly telling exactly what it was she had that he wanted. A thrill of anticipation raced through her; that wonderful heaviness in her belly blossomed into sheer longing. It had been too long. "I'm waiting," she said saucily, cocking her hip and putting her hands to her waist in a clear invitation.

She didn't have long to wait. Before she could have said "Fort Arbuckle," Deke was in front of her, grabbing her to him and taking her mouth in a rough and hungry way that spoke volumes, that tore down barriers, that broke her heart.

When Deke pulled his mouth from hers, she saw a wetness on his cheek, and knew it was from her own tears of sweet, sharp love and denial. "I love you, Deke Bonner," she told him, her heart as full as her brimming eyes. "I know you told me not ever to say it again, but I had to . . . this once."

"God, Sara, I can't stand this." He held her head to his chest. "I feel like this is my last night on earth, like tomorrow I'll be executed."

"Don't say that!" she cried, pulling back and putting her fingertips to his lips. "I couldn't live."

He gripped her arms harder, pulling her closer. "Go away with me, Sara. Leave with me. Now."

"There's nothing I want more than that, Deke. But we can't. Please don't hate me."

He looked into her face, his lips an intense straight line, and loosened his hold somewhat. "I could never hate you, Sara."

He closed his eyes, pulling his head back, stretching the skin taut over the ridge of his Adam's apple. Sara stroked his throat with her fingertips. "Deke?"

He looked down at her, pain, love, and defeat in his eyes. "Yes?"

"Don't think . . . don't think. Just love me. Please."

"I do, Sara. God help me, but I do." He once again captured her trembling lips, but this time with a transcendent sweetness that curled Sara's toes.

Then they shed their clothes as they would their worries, one piece at a time until they faced each other as they'd been made—naked, young, strong, beautiful, and meant for each other. With no clothes, no worries, between them now, they made a sweet, innocent inventory with their hands of each other's bodies, allowing their senses to become as inflamed as their emotions. There was no peak or valley unnoticed, untouched. Their explorations charted new pleasures, fired new needs, claimed new territory.

Then, as if they were magnets with opposite fields of attraction, they came together, savoring this first embrace with a heat and an intensity that defied experience. Movements became rushed, fevered in their haste to convey with their bodies what they couldn't with their words, to achieve physically what they feared could not be admitted by their two hearts—a complete union of their lives.

Deke breathed Sara's name and picked her up in his arms, only to lay her on the bed. He stood there a moment, staring at her, but then he came to her. She held her arms out to him, his name on her lips, as he pressed his weight onto her and she welcomed it, a sigh escaping her that was born of the fire in her blood. She prayed to God to give her Deke's child tonight, that she might always have something of him. And then she gave herself up to the enjoyment of the burning quest of Deke's lips down her body. On top of her, he was holding her sides with his hands and easing his way down, kissing, tasting, sampling her sweetness. Sara was mesmerized by the feel of his roughness on her smoothness, by the feel of his hard muscle on her yielding firmness, by the sensation that her nerve endings were actually rising to the surface, each one intent on feeling Deke's kiss as he passed over every inch of her.

She caught his face, his hair in her hands, not able to voice her pleasure, only able to stroke his features lightly and sigh her encouragement. Deke obliged her, nuzzling the full underside of one breast and then the other; then capturing one nipple in a swirling kiss and then the other; kissing, licking the space that separated her breasts, sucking in its sweetness, and moving down. Sara sucked in her breath, reshaping her abdomen into a concave valley that Deke used as his pillow, turning his head to lay his face there. And there he stayed, holding her, breathing deeply. "I love you, Sara."

Sara, her eyes closed, smiled. "I know, Deke. I love you, too. I always will."

Turning his head now back to his loving task, he tasted the sweetness in the tiny cup of her navel, testing it with his tongue, sipping its fragrant nectar, swirling it with his tongue's tip. An aching, ragged sound tore out of Sara. Deke lowered himself even more on her; his hands now held her hips as he still lay between her legs. He raised himself and turned her over.

Sara, lethargic yet questioning, grasping a thick pillow, turned to look back over her shoulder at him. He was lightly peppering the rounded cheeks of her bottom with tender kisses, smoothing the twin mounds with his skilled hands, pausing at the tiny V at the crest of their juncture, kissing it deeply, crouching over her on all fours. Smiling, feeling safe, Sara closed her eyes and turned her head to sink down onto the pillow's softness. She then jerked spasmodically on the bed when he softly blew a warm breath right over the base of her spine at the curve of her waist. Sara moaned; Deke kissed the spot and turned her back over, spreading her knees.

She looked down at him, wishing she could pull him back up to her, wanting for herself this intimate touching and exploration of his body. And that was her last thought before exploding in a burning pitch of desire as Deke raised her hips and brought her to his mouth and to a fevered pitch with his lips and tongue that threatened to tear her apart. Rigid, her hands clutching, pulling, gathering the sheet in her fists, tighter and tighter, she felt her eyes roll back and feared she would faint dead away. But she didn't, even though her eyelids fluttered and her muscles spasmed. The guttural sounds she heard were coming from her; she couldn't stop them, anymore than she wanted Deke to stop what he was doing to her. The rhythmic contractions of her earthquake climax tore through her, curling her toes, arching her back, and sending a hot, burning wave over her. Deke held her tighter, rode the crest of her response, intensified it, prolonged it, until Sara was gasping, awash in a sheen of fine perspiration, calling his name as desperately as if she'd been swirling down, down in a whirlpool and clutching at him for deliverance.

Her eyes closed, her mouth open, her breathing ragged, her face hot, she felt the bed shift and knew he was coming to lean over her, to lie on her, to take her. Knew when he pushed her legs apart, felt when he pressed himself full length to her, knew when he took her in his arms, felt his insistent probing at the entry to her womb, shuddered deliciously when he slipped inside her, sheathing himself fully in her gently pulsing moistness. Felt the budding tightness begin again as he moved over her, silently, as intently as any predator jungle cat after its quarry, thrusting into her until she could do nothing but cling to him in mortal desperation, and answer him with equal thrusts of her own, accept his plunging kiss that took her breath, tasted of her, and mocked their bodies' motion.

This explosion, this climax, was even better for her because it was shared with Deke, because she was giving him pleasure, just as he was her. She could feel her body clutching him, pulsing around him, drawing him deeper and deeper into her, making sure his pleasure was complete, and his seed was accepted.

Deke collapsed on top of her, his arms out to his sides, not even able to hold his weight off her, crushing her into the bed. But she didn't care, wouldn't have wanted it any other way. She still had her legs wrapped around his slim, powerful hips, still had her ankles locked, still had a completely wanton smile on her face; she was still playing with his hair, running her fingers through its jet-black waving thickness, savoring the feel of him on her, him in her.

And they stayed that way, silent, content, eyes closed,

breathing returning slowly to a shuddering normalcy, hearts beating against the other's chest. But they weren't asleep. Far from it. They were waiting. Waiting for the next act of love. Deke stirred, pulled himself up off Sara, supporting his weight with his elbows, wrapping a silvery curl around his finger. He looked into her eyes, his own black and dancing, inky and smoldering. Sara felt the first stirrings of renewed desire pulse between her legs, but it wasn't only her own pulsations she was feeling. She smiled right back at Deke Bonner, every bit as wickedly as he was smiling at her. Only this time, it was her turn.

Sara had heard once that no good deed goes unpunished. If the things Deke had just done to her body could be called good deeds, and she thought they were, then what she proceeded to do to Deke paid him back, punished him in full. He'd taught her well. Wriggling out from under him, forcing him to withdraw from her, she put her hands to his shoulders, told him "No!" in a saucy tone, and rolled him over to lie on his back on the bed.

Laughing at her, but looking slightly unsure, he crossed his legs at his ankles and put his hands behind his head, knitting his fingers to form a support for his head on the piled-up pillows. He really was quite the muscled vision of maleness lying there like that. "And what do you think you're going to do, ma'am?"

Sara grinned evilly, straddling his hips and running her fingers through his chest hair and over his rock-hard planes. She was determined that it was his turn to lie there squirming and helpless, clutching at a pillow and begging. "You're about to find out, sir."

Feeling decadent and playful at the same time, she set out to discover if the big man could take what he dished out. Barely he could, she soon found out, reveling in her newly discovered power over him. Staying on his hips, trapping his erection against herself, she leaned forward and, with her tongue, teased his nipple as unmercifully as he'd done hers, causing him to pitch forward, emit a rough noise from the back of his throat, and capture Sara by her waist. She sat up, pointed a finger at him, and said, "Lie back."

"Damn, Sara, I can't—"

"You should have thought of that earlier, mister." She crossed her arms over her breasts, cocked her head at him, and waited.

Slowly, cautiously, Deke lay back down. But he no longer looked the least bit relaxed or in control. She'd never seen his eyes this wide. Sara took pity on him, telling him, "You'll just have to trust me."

"Okay," he ceded. "But don't bite."

Sara grinned. "Now why would I do that? And what would I bite?"

He looked at her, bereft of any male dignity or superiority. "I've created a monster."

"Yes, you have. Now, shut up." She then firmly shut him up by teasing his nipples again, raking his washboard abdomen with her nails, kissing his navel, and trailing her tongue down the black center line that ran from his navel to his . . . aha, there it was. She was now straddling his ankles and feet, making sure he felt every bit of her desire. She looked up at him. The coward had a pillow over his face and was breathing raggedly. Sara smiled. Big, bad bounty hunter.

With that, she captured his shaft . . . and realized that she didn't quite know what she was supposed to do with it. So she just held it, trying to think, using her imagination. She looked at Deke. Slowly, slowly, the pillow came away; he looked at her as if she'd just grown two more breasts.

"What are you doing?" he asked sharply.

"I'm not really sure."

"Then come up here. There's too much that can wrong down there if you don't know what you're doing." He put a hand out to her.

She smacked it away. "No. I'll figure it out, Deke Bonner." She looked at it; it pulsed in her hand. She looked back up at Deke. "It seems to like this well enough." Then, turning her gaze back to her filled hand, "Don't you, boy?"

"Don't talk to it. The next thing you know, you'll think you have to name it, for crying out loud."

Sara looked at it again. It was sort of cute, once you got used to it. She cocked her head to one side and looked at Deke, content to tease the life out of him. "Warrior?"

"That does it—" He made a snatching grab for her.

She popped it in her mouth. Eyes wide, shocked, he gave up, raised a white flag, lay down, groaned, begged, clutched at the pillow, squirmed, called her names, said things he couldn't possibly mean, promised her things he didn't even own, would never have—if only she'd quit . . . Too late.

When Deke opened his eyes, Sara was looking at him. "What's wrong?" he asked her, a grin tugging at his mouth. "That's a pretty funny look you have on your face."

"You don't taste like I do," she answered, very matter-of-factly.

Deke roared out his laughter at her and grabbed her successfully this time. But only because Sara allowed him to. She lay obediently to his side, an arm on his chest, a leg over his. She turned her eyes up to him. "Aren't we going to do anything?"

"We can't," Deke had the sad duty of informing her.

"Why not?" she asked, not ready to sleep yet.

"Look," he said, pointing down his length. "It's your fault."

She looked down his length to his . . . length. It was no longer angry. Disappointment rode her mouth as she resettled her head on his shoulder. "What's wrong with him?"

"Him?"

"Yes—Warrior."

Deke laughed and gathered Sara to him again. "Give him a minute or two. He'll come around."

"Well, what can we do in the meantime?" Her chin was resting on his chest.

"This," Deke answered, rolling over on top of her and capturing her mouth again.

* * *

The next morning, as they prepared to leave Fort Arbuckle, Deke felt somewhat sheepish about leading the fat little jenny around to the front of the cabin. It certainly wouldn't do his reputation any good to be seen in the company of an animal with the sweetest black eyes and the sleepiest little demeanor that he'd ever seen. He tried to look fierce and act like the preciously cute animal was not with him, but he feared he only succeeded in looking silly.

Which Sara corroborated for him when she stepped out of the cabin, a bundle of their clothes in her hands, spied them, and had not the manners to restrain her teasing laughter. Deke scowled mightily and wouldn't admit to himself in a thousand years that he was tremendously pleased with himself for securing the burro for Sara.

Sara fell immediately in love with this new pet and wouldn't allow the jenny to be weighted down at all. She promptly dubbed her Miss Petunia and packed only a few items, such as her cooking utensils, coffeepot, and dishes onto the tiny animal. The cacophonous result was much like a one-man band everytime Miss Petunia took a step. Deke rolled his eyes and gave up all hope of ever being able to sneak up on anyone from here on out. Miss Petunia would announce their presence well in advance of their arrival.

An hour or so out, they found the going was slower now, for several reasons. For one thing, they were riding over mountainous country that was thickly vegetated, even forested; there were numerous streams and creeks to be forded; and they had little Miss Petunia to drag along. Her stubby little legs were no match for the long-legged strides of Cinnamon and the buckskin. Looking back at the somnambulent burro trailing slowly behind Sara, a lead rope tied to her pommel, Deke was pretty sure the animal was dead and just hadn't fallen over yet. Did it ever open its eyes?

"Isn't she the sweetest little thing?" Sara trilled, seeing Deke eyeing the toddling pack animal.

"Just darling," Deke allowed, feeling stupid just saying the words.

"Thank you for getting her for me, Deke."

"You're welcome." He looked over at Sara as she turned smiling eyes on her new acquisition. Here he wanted to lay the world at her feet, cover her with jewels and beautiful gowns, give her a huge home, spirited horses, travel the world with her. But she was just as happy with a pack animal.

He grinned, but then the smile fled his face. He'd never be able to give her any kind of a life with him; what was he thinking? Dammit, he knew. "Sara, I've been thinking."

"About what?" she asked cheerfully.

"About us," he opened. She looked so damned desirable right now, with her gray hat hanging down her back over her thick silver braid, and in her riding clothes: a plain skirt and loose blouse that was still flattering to her womanly curves. He hated like hell to ruin her easy mood. But maybe he wouldn't; maybe she would welcome what he had to say.

"What about us?" Her smile slipped a notch.

"I—" he said and then stopped, looking away from her and then back. Her smile had slipped another notch. In the leaden quiet, the only sounds were of the horses' hooves and Miss Petunia's clattering. Deke plunged in, hoping to put that smile right back on her face. "I think we need a plan."

No smile now. "A plan?"

Damn, he was bungling this badly. "Yes."

"I'm listening." Her frown turned her mouth down. She fiddled with Miss Petunia's lead rope around her pommel.

Why was this so hard? Deke wanted to yell; why couldn't he just say it? "Sara, about five or six weeks ago, there was nothing I wanted more than to find the Daltons—and you know the real reason why now—and kill them."

She nodded glumly, still looking down. Were those tears standing in her eyes?

"Well, now I'm not so sure."

She jerked her head up, huge tears spilling out onto her cheeks. But her look was one of cautious hope. Barely above a whisper, she asked, "You're not?"

"No, I'm not. Too much has happened. I'm no longer sure

of . . . of what I want. And I mean you and me. Nothing's all one way or the other anymore. I . . . I think we need a plan.''

A huge, tearful smile stole over Sara's face, lighting every precious facet. Deke, moved beyond what he was willing to admit, hid behind his standard severe visage, but he suspected, from all the twitchings he felt around his mouth, eyes, and nose, that he wasn't quite achieving it. "Now," he went on, frowning mightily and striving for that voice of command that was almost second nature to him, "here's what I've been thinking . . .''

Chapter Twenty-four

There it was. Robber's Cave. A beautiful setting with terrifying implications for so many lives. And so it had all come down to this. Sara swallowed, fear tightening her stomach as she took in the high, rocky cliffs and recesses that pocked this Sans Bois mountainside and provided numerous, though shallow, dens for notorious men to hide in. In one of them were her brother and cousins. The horses and the burro were tethered to a tree back down the trail on this sun-dappled afternoon a week away from Fort Arbuckle. She and Deke had hiked up the mountainside, stopping only when the caves were in sight. Peeking out from behind a huge pine trunk, she looked over at Deke, who sat nonchalantly out in the open on a lichen-covered boulder, poking a thin branch into the soft ground, as if they were out here for a picnic.

True, they were still a good distance off, hidden by the thick forestation from the rifle-toting but still unwary sentry perched on a free-standing slice of boulder as high as five men. But still it set her teeth on edge for Deke to look so unconcerned when her bowels were in an absolute uproar.

"Kind of funny, isn't it? Sans Bois means 'without forests,'" Deke said into the quiet, a half-smile quirking his mouth. He must have been talking to the insects on the ground in front of him because he hadn't looked up at her when he spoke.

As if the name of the mountain range were important! But then she realized that he was trying again to distract her from the paralyzing fear he knew, after so many weeks of riding with her, that she felt. Grateful, even if his attempt wasn't working, she was able to quip, "Apparently whoever named this range had never seen it."

Deke nodded, dropping the twig and resting his elbows on his bent knees, fingers knotted together out in front of him. He turned his keen eyes on the faraway figure of the lookout and said, as matter-of-factly as if he'd been seated in a parlor and was just making small talk with the lady of the house, "More likely, some French trapper hoped to make folks think there was no good trapping grounds here."

Beside herself with agitation, Sara came out from behind her tree to stand stiffly, her hands at her waist, her gaze accusatory. "Be that as it may . . ." she said, leaving the rest unsaid.

Deke finally looked at her and raised an eyebrow. "What? Are you in a hurry to rush in there, Sara?"

She backed down some. "Well, we ought to be doing something besides . . . besides just sitting here."

"We are doing something besides just sitting here. Come here." He waved her over to him.

Sne went. "Look," he said, pointing to the ground at his feet. "See that?"

She nodded, squatting on her haunches when he pulled her down beside him, and looked at a pattern of squiggly lines, circles, straight lines, and fixed points marked with Xs. A map. "This is what I've been doing while you were hiding behind that tree like a fraidy cat. Now, this is how I see it," he said, retrieving his stick and running her through the finer points of his dirt atlas.

"Here we are." Two Xs off to a side. "And there's the lookout on up the trail." A big X at the end of a straight line. "Back here are the caves—well, cave, actually; you'll see when you get there. There's only one true cave. The rest are just ledges with overhangs, big enough to shelter a man from the weather. Anyway, once we get in past the lookout, you'll see that the rock the sentry's standing on is a good seventy, eighty yards from the true mountainside."

"How do you know all this? Have you been here before?" She hated to interrupt him, but curiosity had gotten the better of her.

He looked at her, irritation at this break in his train of thought clearly defined on his rugged face. "Yes. Now, pay attention, Sara. Right here—" A sharp jab with the stick into a big circle he'd drawn punctuated his words. "—marks the cave where your brother and cousins are."

Sara's breathing stopped. "When were you here before?"

Again, that irritated look. "A year ago. Nothing to do with the Daltons. Now, will you please pay attention?"

"You never needed my map at all, did you?"

Impatience etching his every movement, he rubbed his large hand over his mouth and chin, then turned to Sara. "Hell, no. I told you that all along," he said, his brows meeting over his nose. Then he softened some, teasing her by saying, "I've also told you all along that it was you I needed. Only now it's in a different way."

Sara poked her bottom lip out at him, her feathers still ruffled; she wasn't sure if she wanted to hit him or hug him. So, much like a disgruntled hen resettling on her nest, she shifted her squatting position, clasped her hands to her knees, and trained her gaze on Deke's earthen map. "Go on," she directed, making it sound as if Deke were the one who was holding them up. She felt his eyes on her, but she refused to look at him, knowing full well the look she'd see.

"Thank you." Then, "Now, providing we don't get our

asses shot off by the lookout and actually make it to the cave, we'll have the undivided attention of every gunman up there. But that means your brother and cousins, too. Talk has it that the Dalton gang are unofficial ringleaders, which is good for us.'' He swished the stick through the dirt, erasing his map. Sara looked at him. "You got the story straight?'' he asked.

Sara huffed. "Yes, I've got the story straight. What else have we done for a week except go through it every waking minute?''

Deke grinned, but it wasn't a particularly cheerful grin. "Call it training. Now tell it to me again.''

Rolling her eyes, Sara parroted in a sing-song voice, "I lead you in, my silver hair loose and waving so as to get the lookout's attention and not his gunfire. Then I call out my name and tell the lookout I'm the sister of Jim Dalton and you're our cousin, John Smith, and that we have a message for them.'' Here Sara added, with a slanted look, "It's a good thing you look like a Dalton. Makes you less likely to get your ass shot off first thing.''

"Thanks. Finally we're on the same side. Go on.''

But Sara had a question first. "Come on, Deke. John Smith? As if that doesn't sound made-up.''

"There're lots of John Smiths out there. Real ones.''

"Okay. But I just think your name should be something a little more—oh, mean-sounding or something.''

Deke shot her a look, as if he'd rather have shot her. "Like Mr. Snakebelly? Or Desperado, maybe?''

"Never mind, if you're going to act like that.''

"Sara, my patience is about as thin as''—He cast around on the ground in front of him, coming up with a leaf, which he held up sideways to her face—"as this leaf. Can we get on with it, please?'' He let the leaf flutter back to the ground and pinned her with a hot stare.

"Oh, all right.'' She resumed her sing-song litany. "Once we get Jim and Travis and Cody alone, providing we can, we tell them the truth.''

"Which is?''

Continuing her catechism, but in a softer voice and looking down, since this was closer to home, literally and figuratively, Sara said, "My mother is dying, and Jim, Travis, and Cody have to come home with me."

Deke put a hand on her arm; his touch was a warm, gentle squeeze. "See, Sara? Now you can say it without crying. That's the beauty of repetition. Now, honey, what else?"

She looked up at him, dry-eyed but wishing her face weren't so contorted with fear and grief. "The rest of the truth—that you're really Deke Bonner, bounty hunter, and you have some questions for them."

There it was—their compromise. No gunfire. No accusations. No jumping to conclusions or giving in to rumors about what had happened in Independence, Missouri, on the day Deke's mother and sister were killed. Only talk, straightforward questions and answers. They'd go from there, depending on the answers given by the Daltons. Iffy, at best. It could still go either way. But it was the best Sara and Deke could do. It was the only thing they could do, what with their hearts entangled as they were. Sara had assured Deke, outside of Fort Arbuckle, when he'd told her they needed a plan, that her kin were reasonable and would cooperate. He'd looked at her as if he wasn't so sure—and indeed she wasn't even sure of that herself anymore, given all the things she'd heard about their exploits of late—but miracle of miracles, he was willing to try, to listen. She couldn't ask any more than that from him, especially since she herself did not know the truth about the events in Independence.

Done now, Sara took a deep breath, her heart in her throat, and looked at Deke, her eyes as wide as an old hoot owl's, she suspected. He smiled and leaned forward, kissing her gently; Sara kissed him back, holding her hand to his lean cheek, putting into her kiss every hope and fear she harbored in her heart. She hoped it wasn't their last kiss.

Deke pulled back from her, reached around behind her to

loosen the ribbon that held her hair, and said, his eyes warm and reassuring, "Mount up, soldier. We're going in."

How many times in the past six weeks had Deke seen the day he was glad for Sara's silver-blond hair? How many times had it saved them, awing other men into inaction just as it did him? Today and this guard were proving to be no exception. But Deke had never thought he'd live long enough to be glad for all the noise that Miss Petunia made when she waddled along, eyes closed, packed down with Sara's banging pots and utensils. That sound had nearly put him over the edge daily for the week since they'd saved her from being killed. But now? Well, he'd kiss the plump little burro when all this was over. If he was alive, of course.

Deke tried to put himself in the position of the lookout atop the sentry boulder, who was just now staring at them as if they'd dropped out of the heavens unannounced. The way Deke figured it, the first notice the man had that the cave denizens had company had been the prolonged and pronounced clinking, tinkling, and bumping sounds of Miss Petunia climbing the steep, heavily wooded trail. The noises, unaccompanied for such an extended period of time as they'd been before the appearance of anyone else, had to have raised the man's curiosity, if not the hair on the back of his neck.

Then, when something had finally come into view, it'd proven to be a beautiful woman with silver hair and a smile as if her face, a woman who was actually crazy enough to be waving and calling out to him as if she were an old friend, as if she always rode up on outlaw strongholds this brazenly. Deke knew in his heart that it was just that brazenness, so well acted out by Sara—brave despite her sheer terror—that had thrown the guard off. And kept his attention off the fact that Deke had Sara's Spencer repeater barely hidden and trained right on the man's heart in case something went wrong.

Like now. "There ain't no one here name of Dalton,

lady,'' the scroungy-looking man called back to Sara's greeting asking for the Daltons.

She turned terror-filled, what-do-we-do-now eyes on Deke. He prodded her with a slight nod of his head, but was essentially unable to help her at this point. They were in this up to their necks now; they wouldn't be allowed to simply turn around and leave. Sara turned back to the man. "Yes, they are here. I should know—I'm Jim Dalton's sister!"

Deke hoped he was the only one who heard the quaver in her voice. His finger itched like crazy over the Spencer's trigger. If that bastard on the rock didn't get more cooperative here in a hurry, he'd find his chest full of lead.

"You say you're Jim Dalton's sister, eh? What's your name?"

"Sara Dalton."

The sentry's eyes narrowed. "Izzat so? Well now, I've heard Jim say he had a sister name of Sara. But who's yer gennulman frien', sister?"

So the Daltons were really here—the man had given himself away, saying Jim had told him he had a sister named Sara. Deke relaxed slightly. They just might live long enough to make it up to the cave.

"My . . . ?" She jerked around to look at Deke, as if in her terror she'd forgotten he was behind her. Deke didn't change expression in the least. She turned back to the sentry, obviously still rattled at being told her kin wasn't here. "He's our cousin—Deke Bon—Deke John Smith. We call him John for short. John Smith! That's what we call him— John Smith."

"John Smith? Sounds made-up to me."

Sara turned around, a terrified I-told-you-so look riding her usually fine features. Right now she looked like a scared doe. Deke decided to step in; enough of this stupid bastard on the rock. He ripped the covering off the rifle. "Like the lady said, John Smith's the name. And I can assure you I'm for real—as real as this Spencer I've got pointed at your heart."

The sentry, who'd set his rifle down on the rock and was on all fours, leaning over the edge, the better to ogle Sara, was caught completely off-guard. He froze in position, not even moving when his wide-brimmed hat tumbled off his head and swooped to the ground, revealing a head only sparsely covered with hair. "Don't shoot, mister. Don't shoot."

"I won't," Deke assured him, barely sparing a glance for Sara, who was now looking at him with sheer relief. "But suppose you just wave us on through, signal the okay to your friends up at the caves. I don't think my cousin, Jim Dalton, will be any too pleased that you've held us up like this. And we won't even mention the way you're looking at his sister, now will we?"

"No, sir, we most surely won't. No harm meant, ma'am." He went to tip his hat to Sara, felt around on his balding head, then saw it on the ground. A sickly grin on his face, he jumped up and waved furiously at the caves behind him; he then turned back to Deke and Sara. "It's all right now. You can bring yer animals on around over there. Hitch 'em up at the rope. Someone'll be down ta meet ya right directly."

Deke merely nodded, not deigning to speak to, much less thank, such a bumbling fool. Were they all like this? Thinking of the four he'd met at Chisholm's, and wondering if they were here, he knew the fool on the rock was the exception. Getting past the hard men here, none of whom had anything to lose by killing one more man, would not be as easy as getting past their sentry. And not getting killed, once they were let in, would be even harder.

As they slowly rode their mounts forward, Deke drew even with Sara, putting himself between her and the rocks to their right. They'd have to go through him to get to her, if that was their intent. The sentry might not have given the all-clear signal. For all Deke knew, his waving could have been a warning to watchful eyes.

"Deke, I was so scared," Sara whispered to him. "I almost forgot what I was supposed to say. I'm sorry."

"You did just fine, Sara. Just fine." He reached over and took her hand to give it a gentle squeeze, sparing her a glance, but keeping the seven-shot Spencer trained on the hard-looking men who looked too much like animals crawling out of their burrows to suit Deke. He and the men on the rocks had one thing in common—they were all looking at Sara. But for vastly different reasons, Deke knew; he was watching her reaction to see if she spotted her kin. The men were just watching her out of a lust so palpable that Deke was sure he could smell it in the air. He found himself hoping the Daltons showed up in a hurry, but for a very different reason than he'd ever had before. Before, it would have been so he could kill them. But now it was so they could help him protect Sara.

But so far, nothing. No squeal of delight, no sudden intake of breath. So far, the man on the rock was right—there was no one here by the name of Dalton. Except Sara. Damn. And here they'd ridden right into this nest of varmints; now who was the fool? Deke chastised himself.

"Deke, they're not here. I don't see them. What are we going to do?" Sara's whisper was a mere hiss of fear and panic. He looked over at her; her knuckles were white around her reins.

"Easy, Sara. They could be here yet. Just nice and easy-like, get off Cinnamon and hitch her and that burro to the rope, like the guard said. Keep your hand in your pocket and on your derringer. And stay beside me." Deke began dismounting as he spoke.

"Don't worry," Sara assured him, bringing Cinnamon to stand next to the buckskin and dismounting. Despite being up to their butts in bad guys, Deke bit back a grin: The only time Sara didn't argue with him was when she was terrified. Then he noticed her fingers fumbling as she tried to tie the reins around the remuda rope. He covered her hands with his; her hands were like ice, her eyes like ink. Hoping to bolster her courage, he winked at her, took the reins from her grip, and tied Cinnamon securely. Miss Petunia resumed her uninterrupted nap, even when Deke untied her lead rope from Sara's pommel, pulled her forward, and tied the fat burro to the rope too. If they had to get away fast, she would be left behind.

Moving away from the horses, taking Sara with him and keeping his hand under her elbow, he rested the upraised Spencer against his hip and turned to face the few men who had ventured down off the rocks to advance on them. Countless others watched from their rocky vantage points.

"That's far enough," he warned the five in front of him when they were about twenty feet away. From that distance, he could train his attention on them, but at the same time not lose sight of the men behind and above the five.

A swarthy, mustachioed man with bowed legs and two huge pistols, holstered one at each hip, took one more step forward. "It don't appear to me, stranger, that you're in a position to be giving orders."

"Neither are you," Deke replied, lowering the Spencer almost casually to shoot at the dirt directly in front of the man's feet. Sara, her elbow still in his grasp, gave a sharp yelp of surprise, as did the swarthy man as he jumped back, knocking into his shocked compadres. Men high up on the rocks put hands to holsters, but no one drew. So, there was no honor among these thieves, Deke mused; not one of them would probably raise a hand to come to another's aid, but would act only if he himself was threatened. That was good.

No one had to tell Deke that the only way to survive here was to draw first blood. And he'd just done that. He hoped. "Now, I have six more shots left in this Spencer. Anyone want to try me again? I promise you, I won't hit dirt the next time."

"No, sir," a freckled kid with red hair peeking out from under a huge sombrero cheerfully assured Deke. "We ain't got no quarrel with you." The other men nodded their agreement with this.

"Smart kid," Deke replied. "Keep talking respectful like

that, and you might live long enough to shave, boy."

"Yes, sir, I hope so, sir." He tipped his sombrero, the biggest thing about him, to Deke.

Another man, a fat, sweating, older man in a black derby, his pants suspendered to give them a fighting chance at staying up, asked, "Who are you, mister?"

Deke opened his mouth to answer. "I'm"—he promptly forgot his alias—"not anyone you need to worry about, friend. You'll live longer if you mind your own business." His mind racing but not coming up with the alias, he went on. "We're kin to the Daltons. She's Jim Dalton's sister. We've come a long way to talk to them—and not you. Now, where are they? Are they here?"

The five men looked at each other and then at the men on the rocks behind them. Then, facing Deke again, the fat man asked, respectfully, of course, "Pardon us, mister, but how do we know you're who you say you are?"

Good point. Dammit. Deke looked at Sara, who looked back at him. Deke faced the men. "Men, would I ride all the way from Plains, Kansas, with my cousin, who looks like this"—here he pointed to Sara and felt her stiffen—"through Indian Territory and bring her with me to an outlaw stronghold with nothing but my own gun to back me up against all of you for the sole purpose of making up a story just to see the Daltons? Would I do that?"

Deke sincerely hoped they didn't try to answer that, because what he'd just told them was the absolute truth; it was exactly what he'd done, what he was still doing, only he hadn't told them the real reason why he himself wanted to see the Daltons. Sometimes, the truth just seemed stranger than a lie. And more appropriate. He certainly wasn't above using it.

For several soul-sweating seconds, the five men looked at Deke and Sara, at each other, the men on the rocks, and then back at Deke. The fat man spoke again. "I suppose you're right. Only the Daltons ain't here; not right now, anyways. They're out on business. But I suppose they wouldn't mind

you usin' their cave until they get back. Then, if you ain't
who you say you are—well, they can deal with you. This
way.'' He signaled for them to follow him and then walked
back to the rocks, seeming, with the other four men, to just
disappear into the mountain.

Grim, sparing a glance for Sara and gripping her elbow
possessively, not sure that even their professed kinship to the
Daltons would protect them from these men and wary of any
trap or sudden knock on the head that might be planned for
him, Deke followed the five outlaws, Sara in front of him,
through the hidden, needle-narrow entrance to the mountain's bowels. Well, he mused, they'd certainly made their
bed in a nest of thieves; now they would have to lie in it.

''Deke, don't leave me here alone, not even for a second,''
Sara pleaded, not even trying to keep the worry in her heart
off her face.

''I didn't plan on it, believe me,'' he assured her, looking
first at her and then at their surroundings.

Sara, seated on the cave floor with Deke, followed his
gaze. The cave was huge, a pie wedge in shape, but resembling more the gaping, opened mouth of a giant at its entrance, then receding to the back wall, so low only a child
could have stood upright back there. Having thoroughly
spooked herself, Sara let the chill ripple through her as she
scooted forward to the safety of the red-tinged light from
their small fire. But even that didn't help because their re-
flections danced off the cave's walls, distorting each movement, making their shadows seem ten times their normal size,
and adding to her sense of primitive man, ancient rituals, and
violent nature.

As scary as it was to her, she was thankful that she and
Deke, in her kin's absence, were alone in this, the main cave,
proof positive to the truth of the rumors that the Daltons
ruled here—or at the very least, were the unchallenged bad-
dest of the bad. That thought, seconded by the mental image
of the sort of men she'd seen here, didn't go very far in

reassuring her that her brother and cousins would still be the essentially good men she had always known them to be. Trying to calm her jittery imagination and overcome her troubling doubts, she concentrated on the cave's immediate environs. There was all sorts of gear, mostly just the usual things—cooking equipment, blankets, extra guns, saddle blankets—stowed around the walls, evidence that the owners did intend to return. Sara recognized Jim's penchant for order and neatness all around her and smiled, feeling a little better, a little bit more secure.

"What did you find to smile about in all this, Sara?"

Deke's question, but more the sound of his voice, so warm and intimate somehow, brought Sara's gaze back to him. She realized that she'd been so deep in thought that she hadn't been aware of his eyes on her. But now she could see the gleam in his eyes that had nothing to do with the fire's reflected light. "What did I find to smile about? Well, we have this cave to ourselves, thank God. And I can feel Jim and Cody and Travis around me, seeing their belongings here," she answered wistfully.

"And that makes you feel at home?" His words were teasing, but not his eyes.

She wasn't sure how to answer. "Well, somewhat, I suppose. And . . . you're here."

Now he smiled that slow grin of his. He captured a lock of her curling hair and slowly twined it around his finger. Looking only at it, he said, "Tell me something, Sara. . . . "

Under the influence of his smile, her heart began a slow, steady thud. "Yes?" she encouraged warmly.

"Just what the hell is the name I'm supposed to use? I flat forgot out there earlier when those bastards asked me."

Blind-sided by his practical question, so unexpected in the warm cocoon she was weaving in her head, Sara laughed. That killed his grin, which was replaced by a straight line and frowning brow. "Smith. John Smith. Well, actually Deke John Smith, if you want to get formal," she quickly informed him.

The grin came back, but this one was self-deprecating. He shook his head slowly, still playing with her hair, almost as if he wasn't aware of doing so. "Smith. John Smith. That should be easy enough to remember. Can't imagine why I couldn't come up with it."

"Maybe you were just scared."

A snort was her only answer to that ridiculous assertion. This time, Sara had the good sense to look down when she grinned at his expense.

Sara and Deke awoke the next morning to the sound of gun triggers being cocked—right against their ears. Instantly awake from such an ominous rooster call, Sara jumped up with Deke from their shared bedroll, under which she'd nearly buried her head, as if hiding from danger. She clutched at Deke's arm, momentarily panicked, not really seeing what—who—was before her. Deke's muttered curses told how he felt about being caught napping, not even able to draw his Colt with three of the same pointed right at his heart.

Sara stared, blinked, opened her mouth, closed it, squealed, and launched herself, laughing and crying at the same time, into her brother's arms. "Jim! It's you! It's really you! I can't believe it—you're really here!"

Holstering his revolver, he grabbed her, holding her tightly and fussing big-brotherly into her hair. "It really is you, Sara Jane Dalton. I didn't believe it when Red and Fats told me just now. That's why we had our guns drawn. What's wrong? Something at home? Dammit, Sara, this is no place for a woman."

But Sara wasn't ready to answer questions just yet. She tore herself away from Jim's embrace to enfold her cousins, Travis and Cody, in turn. Having holstered their guns, too, they swung her around whooping, exclaiming about how good it was to see such a pretty face from back home.

Then they all remembered Deke. The four Daltons—Sara and her brother and cousins—turned to face the stiff, unsmiling bounty hunter. A momentary flash of lucid foreboding reminded Sara that this moment was what her and Deke's six-week-long ride was all about. And look where she was standing.

In the heavy silence as the men sized each other up, Deke knowingly, her kin trustingly since he was with her, Sara made her way to Deke's side, taking his arm and drawing him forward; he went, but with an unmistakable chill in his bearing. She alone knew how hard this was for him—to actually be introduced to the men he believed to be responsible for his mother's and sister's deaths. But he'd promised to give them a chance, to hear their side, to listen. He'd promised her; and he was just now probably finding out how hard that promise was to keep.

"You the one who's supposed to be our cousin?" Jim said, his expression, as much as his voice, revealing his disbelief. Sara licked at her suddenly dry lips.

"That's the story," Deke said truthfully enough.

Jim, who looked so much like Deke that even Sara was surprised, then turned to his cousins, who flanked him. "Cody, Travis, we got any cousin named John Smith?"

The two shook their heads and kept their eyes on Deke.

"I don't believe we have a cousin with the name of Smith, mister." He then turned to his sister. "Sara, what's going on here? Who is he?" He pointed at Deke as if he weren't capable of speaking for himself.

Before Sara could gather her thoughts, Deke turned to her, taking her by her arms. "I'm sorry, Sara. I thought I could do this, but I can't." He squeezed her arms, gave her a regretful look but no opportunity to try to dissuade him before he turned back to the Daltons, adopting a ready stance. "Might as well get this out in the open. You need to know who I am and what I'm doing here. Name's Deke Bonner, and I'm a bounty hunter. I've been looking for you for a long time."

He paused when the Daltons jerked in reaction to his words and made as if to put a hand to their guns. Before

Sara could blink, much less cry out, Deke had his Colt in his hand, aiming it at first one and then the other of her kin. "I wouldn't do that if I were you. You'd best hear me out because my business with you can wait." He paused here, looking each of them in the eye. Apparently seeing what he wanted in their demeanors, he relaxed some. "Good. What you need to do right now is talk to Sara about why it is she's here. I'm going to put my gun back in the holster and turn around to walk out of here while you talk family business."

And then he did just that; he holstered his gun, held his hands up in a neutral position, then walked out of the cave, pushing aside the thick brush at the entrance.

All the Daltons, including Sara, stared at the rustling brush after Deke disappeared. Sara breathed slowly and deeply, forcing air past the constriction in her throat. She then looked down at her boots and finally raised her head until she was looking into three sets of angry Dalton eyes.

As usual, Jim was the one to take control. From the distance that separated them, he asked her, in a voice that said all the emotion was flattened out of him, "What in the hell are you doing here? Something's wrong at home, isn't it?"

Sara looked down and then up at her brother, knowing this was going to hurt. When Momma died, the only immediate family she and Jim would have would be each other. "Yes, something is very wrong. It's Momma, Jim. Doc Turnbull says she has consumption. He gives her about six months to live. I came here to get you to come home. She wants to see you, all three of you, before she dies."

For several moments, no one spoke, each attending to his own grief. Only a sniff or a shuffling of feet broke the heavy silence—until Jim lashed out at Sara. "Dammit, Sara, what you're asking is impossible! You should have stayed with Momma. She needs you, girl. You could have been killed trying to get here. And the worst part is, we can't leave— and believe me, we want to. It would have been better for everyone if you'd never come, if you all just thought of us as dead. Look around you, for God's sake! Do you have any idea what kind of sick, evil men are here and what they could do to you? Do you?'' He squeezed his eyes shut, pinched the bridge of his nose with his thumb and index finger, and spat out, ''What were you thinking?''

Sara covered her face with her hands as if Jim had slapped her; her muffled cries reverberated off the cave walls, but no one came to her to comfort her. She wanted to hold her brother, to tell him she was sorry and not to say such horrible things. But she knew it wasn't over. There was still more she had to account for with Jim, Cody, and Travis. When Jim asked her, she felt as if her heart would lurch out of her chest.

''Why did you help Deke Bonner find us?''

Chapter Twenty-five

Deke couldn't remember a time in his life when he'd been this angry—except after learning his mother and sister were dead and how they'd died. His steps slowed; to his utmost surprise, he realized that his anger was tempered with the stirrings of sympathy, the beginning of understanding for Jim Dalton. His enemy, yes; but also a man who'd just learned his mother was dying, and who'd already lost his wife, brother, and father to murderers.

Deke grimaced, purposely hardening his heart again; knowing how it felt, how could Jim have killed two innocent women? No answer would come. And the worst part of it was, Jim—and his cousins, for that matter—didn't look like, didn't act like the cold-blooded killers of their reputations. They looked more like farmers and husbands—young ones, too. They were practically babies. And, as Sara had told him, they looked just like him, or enough like him to be his brothers. Deke had never had a brother. Unable to sort out his thoughts, he stopped; he had no idea where he was going, hadn't even had a destination in mind when he'd stalked out. Of course, his choices were limited at Robber's Cave.

He honed in on his surroundings, turning his keen gaze this way and that, trying to get his bearings and looking past the men on the various ledges who resembled birds of prey waiting to swoop down on the weak or the unwary. Try as he might, Deke just could not reckon with this place, a rich forest with sundrops dappling the undergrowth, a green place alive with trees, wildflowers, deer, rabbit, chirping birds, but marred with jutting scars of jumbled rocks and ledges. At least it was much cooler here among the mountains and trees than it had ever been on the plains. But how could such an idyllic place hold such evil men? They were like a bunch of snakes ruining Eden.

Forcing his mind to the task at hand, Deke took in his immediate environs. He hadn't seen much of the area yesterday, but had been led directly to the Daltons' cave. He looked around, staring past the few quiet, suspicious men who slithered along on the worn trails that ran ledge-to-ledge, apparently too intent on tasks or misdeeds of their own to worry about who he was or what he was doing. Good. That was the way he liked it.

Deke saw that he was off to the right of the lookout boulder, as he thought of it. He looked up; different man up there today. Probably shot the other one for being stupid. So, if the rock was there, then the horses were over this way. Deke set off with a purposeful stride, thinking that grooming the horses, and maybe even that silly little burro, would expend this energy and calm him down. He'd have to go back to the cave sometime, but not yet. Leave the Daltons to their private grief for now. But he did feel badly about leaving Sara there like that, knowing she was hurting, too. He wondered what she'd tell them, how she'd answer Jim's questions.

"Smith!"

If she'd even answer Jim's questions. And when had he gone to thinking of one of the Dalton men by his first name?

"Hey, John Smith!"

Deke thought of the Daltons, all three of them. He figured Jim and Travis to be near his own age, but Cody couldn't be more than nineteen or twenty. But Sara said they'd all fought in the war. Maybe so, but they still had that fresh-faced-kid look, as if they'd never seen killing in the war or since. But Deke knew better. There was no set age or look for a desperado, and he'd sure seen some young ones lately.

"John Smith! Wait up!"

Irritably, Deke silently cursed whoever that damned John Smith was who wasn't answering that squeaky-voiced lit-tle—John Smith? He was John Smith! Deke whirled around, slamming into the kid with the thick red hair. Plowing into Deke's solid bulk, hitting the tall bounty hunter about chest-high, the kid met the trail butt-first, squashing his oversize sombrero under him.

Looking down at the kid, Deke—his legs spread, his hands at his waist, and not feeling them the least contrite for having knocked the boy flat—snapped, "What in the hell do you want? Why are you following me?"

The kid sat there, staring up the long length of Deke's muscular frame. "It's—it's that little burro of yours, Mr. Smith. Something's wrong with it. I thought you'd want to know, is all."

Sara's burro? Great. Deke wanted to scream out loud. What could go wrong next? Oh, no, there it was—that question again, that challenge to the gods or demons or whoever it was that was currently directing his life. But what he said aloud, as he finally relented and extended his hand to pull the kid to his feet, was "Tell me something, kid—"

"Red, sir. My name is Red," he said, gaining his feet again and brushing himself off enthusiastically.

Deke looked the kid over as he bent to retrieve his floppy Mexican hat from the ground and straighten up, only to stand there grinning hugely. To Deke, Red looked like a boy play-ing bad-man. "Tell me, Red, do you wear that sombrero when you pull a job? You know, don't you, that you leave a definite impression behind you."

Red smiled as he punched his hat back into shape. "Yes, sir, I know. That's why I wear it—so's people will know who robbed 'em. So's I can make me a name. But I ain't never hurt no one—leastwise, not yet. Ain't aimin' to, neither."

Deke rolled his eyes, but his heart ached. Somebody save this kid before it was too late. How in the hell was this momma's baby surviving in this place? What the hell had happened in his young life to put him here, anyway? Pushing his Stetson up to rub at his forehead, Deke looked long and hard at the kid, whose grin was slowly fading under such intense scrutiny, but then said, "Come on, Red, let's go see to that burro. What do you mean, something's wrong with her? What's she doing?"

When they came to the remuda rope, Deke took one look at the sagging burro and groaned. The other horses had sidestepped away, leaving a clearing that plainly showed to all passersby that Miss Petunia was quickly becoming a mother. That certainly explained the appetite and her fat belly; Deke wanted to kick himself for not recognizing the signs. Dammit, this was just what he needed. Still, he jogged to her and worked to free her lead rope from the remuda line. When the little mother awkwardly lowered herself to the ground, lying on her side, Deke called over his shoulder to the kid. "Run and get Miss Dalton, Red. Tell her that her Jenny is foaling and might need some help, seeing as how little she is. Tell her not to come alone and to bring some—"

Realizing that Red hadn't answered, Deke looked around. There was the kid, already running back to the main cave. Deke spared his retreating figure a defeated chuckle. The kid must have taken off as soon as he had opened his mouth.

Easing down to a squat, Deke ran a calming hand over the laboring burro's flank. "Easy, girl," he crooned. "Easy." First he checked her progress and then, looking up, he saw that his tall buckskin had turned his head to stare down at him. Thinking of Sara's mare, Cinnamon, and her coming bout with motherhood, courtesy of the buckskin, and forgetting that he was talking to his still unnamed horse, Deke said, "Well, at least we can't pin this one on you, can we?"

The buckskin snorted loudly and stamped his foot, as if incensed that Deke could think he would stoop so low, as if his taste in women had been questioned. Deke chuckled male-to-male and then turned at the sound of a commotion.

It was Sara. And she was coming at a run, her unbound hair waving a silver flag of alarm out behind her. The Daltons and Red flanked her, protecting her against the hot stares of some of the caves' scalier denizens, who also were noting her hair and bouncing bosom and the distinct outline of her long legs as revealed by her billowing skirt. Deke narrowed his eyes at the men, as if he were able to read their filthy minds. Then, unmindful of the picture she made, Sara skidded to a halt and knelt down beside him.

The remaining Daltons, Red, and a curious one or two other assorted bad fellows formed a semicircle behind Deke and Sara. Deke glanced at the Daltons, seeing in their faces that he could trust them to protect his back this time because Sara was here. It was like an unwritten code: They might all want to kill each other, but this would not be the time or the place. Scant reassurance, to be sure, but it was enough for now.

Within a few minutes, the foal arrived safe and whole. Weak and wet, he lay on his side heaving as his mother struggled to her feet, only to stand proudly over him, licking him clean. As for the humans in attendance, despite their circumstances, the surroundings, their pain and uncertainties, subdued whoops and cheers—so as not to startle mother and son—were heard all around. A new life had come into the world. Deke smiled at Sara, who sat back on her folded legs, a beatific smile on her face as she clasped her hands to her bosom. Right then, he wanted nothing more than to reach out to her and take her in his arms, but he found he just couldn't, not in front of the Daltons.

As the little newborn tried several times to stand on his matchstick legs, but failed miserably with each try, Deke

vatched as Sara's smile slowly turned to fear. Finally, she
urned stricken eyes on him, clutched at his arm, unconsciously digging her nails into his skin, and cried out, "Why
:an't he get up?"

"Well, damn, Sara," Travis answered before Deke could.
'You've seen this happen a hundred times on the farm. Give
him a minute. Hell, he just got here. Back off and give him
a chance. Like as not, he'll find his momma's teat then.
That's what he wants. Leastwise, that's what Robert wanted
when he was born."

Deke looked up in time to see the slight puckering of
Travis's features at his mention of his wife and son and tried
not to think that he might be the one responsible for this
man's never seeing them again. He couldn't afford to care—
it could cost him his own life.

Looking back at Sara, who looked ready to cry, Deke
shoved down his misgivings about caressing Sara in front of
her kin and pulled her up gently by her arm. She immediately
turned her face into his chest, clutching at his shirt front. "I
can't watch!" she cried out, a bubbling catch to her voice.
"If he won't stand up, he'll die."

"Well, then," Deke was happy to report, thinking he
knew why this birth was so important to her, thinking that
she'd seen so much death and killing lately that this one
fuzzy, wet creature just had to make it, "you'd better turn
around now because he's on his feet and kicking."

Sara stiffened in his arms, looked up at him as if to gauge
if he were telling her the truth, then jerked around, staring
at mother and son, both of whom were on their feet. Then
she broke away with a loud squeal of delight, which startled
the baby into falling again. Miss Petunia brayed out her displeasure, and Sara quickly righted the little fellow, helping
him to take the first steps toward enjoying his first meal.

Cody broke into the tender moment by remarking, "Who
wants to bet she'll have it named and a place set at the dinner
table for it before the day's up?"

* * *

Just as Cody predicted, within a few minutes of being born, the foal was dubbed Little Ned by Sara, and the men—except Red, who said he had to go practice his shooting—were given the task of getting mother and child back to the cave, where Sara spent the rest of the morning and into the afternoon giving the men orders, demanding that they bring in grasses for Miss Petunia and water in the biggest container they could find and that they rearrange the provisions in the cave to clear a spot for a suitable manger. The men quickly found out it only made their lives harder to argue with her about animals being brought inside.

Sara herself worked alongside the men to shift, load, tote, and stack crate after crate off to one side until she was satisfied that Miss Petunia and Little Ned would be comfortable. And once they were safely ensconced in their makeshift corral, Sara finally allowed herself and the men a pause in the back-breaking work. Working was easier than thinking, she decided as she leaned into a stack of crates and blew out an exhausted breath. At least if the men were working, they weren't shooting at each other. Or asking her questions she didn't want to answer. Or talking about her mother dying. Sara closed her eyes.

Just then, noises outside the cave, like those of horses and men arriving in a hurry, caught the alert attention of everyone in the cave. Sara pulled away from the crates and looked at Deke, then at her brother and cousins. The three Daltons slowly lowered the crates they were carrying and exchanged glances of fear, plain and simple fear, with each other as they stood up. What or who could put those looks on their faces? Responding to the sudden tension in the cave, Sara went to Deke and put a hand on his arm. He looked at her with a very serious expression, but one with a hint of questioning in it, as he too stood with the Daltons.

The concealing brush at the cave's entrance parted abruptly but casually, as if the six men who pushed their way through had every right to be there. The silence was palpable, the tension smothering as they faced each other.

The six newcomers were dusty, dirty, armed to the teeth, and mean-looking. Their saddles were hefted in front of them, and weighted cloth bags resembling full bank bags were hanging from their shoulders. They cut their eyes from the three Dalton men over to Sara and Deke. Sara cringed inside when Deke stiffened and moved his hand to his gun.

"You're that there coward I threw out of the Aces High at Chisholm's! You followin' us, mister?" Without waiting for an answer from Deke, the speaker, a cocky kid with brown hair and a long scar on his cheek, turned to Jim. "What the hell is he doin' here, Dalton? We done told you that you ain't to take on more partners without our say-so." Almost without a pause, he turned to one of his cronies. "Ain't that him, Phelps?"

"Yeah, he wuz the one at Aces High. Yer right. But look whut we got here! Whoo-wee!" The man—a tall, lanky, hawk-nosed scarecrow of a man, all dressed in black—dropped his saddle, assumed a leering grin, and made a move toward Sara as he spoke. His companions laughed and urged him on with rank suggestions of their own. But he had taken no more than one step before four Daltons and one Bonner had their guns trained on him. Sara's stance and fierce expression made up for the size of her derringer.

"Take one more step, mister, and I'll shoot you where you won't ever have need of a woman again," she told him, drawing the surprised stares of her kin her way, but not Deke's. From the corner of her eye, she could see that he looked straight ahead, knowing she was fully capable of doing exactly what she'd just said. Her promise to never shoot another man flashed into her mind, but died a quick death.

"Well, you ain't no more friendly than a varmint, darlin'. But I got somethin' here that'll warm you right up," Phelps continued, not coming any closer but still leering, looking her up and down and making lewd noises. For his effort, all he got were laughs from his companions and disgusted stares from the Daltons and Deke.

His apparent lack of fear at having all those guns trained

on him caused Sara untold shivering, chilled to the bone as she was by the complete lack of humanity in the specimens before her.

"Knock it off, Phelps." It was Travis.

"Shut up, you chicken-livered little puke. What you goin' ta do about it, coward? What's any of you goin' to do about it, huh? Answer me that," the black-clad man sneered, a hand on his gun, his other clutching his crotch, rubbing it obscenely while puckering his mouth up in kisses at Sara.

Just as she felt the bile rise in her throat and heard several guns cock—and not all on her side of the cave—Deke fired a single shot, hitting the grotesque man square in the forehead. He hung there for a second, as if suspended upright, his lips still puckered, his hand at his crotch, as if waiting for the attendant yelps and curses of shock to subside before doing a slow pirouette to the cave floor. Everyone looked at him dumbly.

"I had to do that once to a rabid dog. It was a kindness, the way I saw it," Deke said calmly, drawing everyone's shocked gaze to him. Pointing his weapon at the remaining five newcomers, he added, "The woman is a lady. But more important for your continued state of good health, gentlemen, she's a Dalton."

"My sister," Jim added, the cords standing out in his neck, his knuckles white around his gun.

Deke nodded grimly at the men facing him and continued. "Now, I don't know what your previous arrangments have been here in this cave, but starting right now, you're going to find sleeping quarters elsewhere until we see fit to leave. Anything in here yours?"

The stunned outlaws nodded affirmatively.

"Too bad. You'll have to leave it for now. But take your dead friend with you. He's messing up the place, and from all the braying you hear, you can tell he's upset Miss Dalton's burro. And you don't want to upset Miss Dalton's burro. Now, go on; get out."

The men got out, dragging the dead man with them and

leaving a smear of blood on the cave floor. As they struggled with their various burdens, saddles and bank bags among them, they didn't forget to call back threats of retaliation—being careful that Deke knew they were against the three Dalton men only—over their shoulders. Calls of ''We'll get you for this,'' ''You ain't seen the last of us, Dalton,'' and ''Sleep with one eye open'' rang through the cave long after they'd departed.

But as soon as they were gone from view, Sara, like the men, uncocked her weapon and put it away. But unlike them, she slumped into Deke's waiting arms. The Daltons were suspiciously still and quiet behind them as Deke soothed her fears, his hands stroking her hair and his lips kissing the top of her head. With him holding her close and with no words spoken, Sara came to some conclusions. This day was probably the most bizarre of a whole six-week string of bizarre days. She'd long ago given up changing to a bed gown on this trip; Deke had convinced her that her finer instincts toward civility and civilization would get her killed out here. She now knew that to be true. Constant vigilance and hardheartedness were what were needed to keep body and soul together. She had the terrifying vision that if they all—she, Deke, Jim, Travis, Cody—stayed here in this godforsaken place much longer, they'd be just like the men here, nothing more than animals, for whom killing was a way of life. And she'd seen for herself that it only got easier and easier. That thought firmed her resolve that she wasn't leaving here without Deke and her brother and cousins. They were in this together, for now they had even greater enemies than themselves.

Chapter Twenty-six

Almost immediately after the five men left, footfalls outside the cave brought them back to instant alertness, their guns in their hands. Sara spun around to face the sound. The just departed outlaws' hurled threats reverberated in the cave's interior. Was trouble to find them again so soon? Her fear roaring in her ears, Sara waited with her men for their unknown visitor to make his presence known.

The thick, concealing brush parted to reveal a cheerfully smiling Red, who instantly sobered upon seeing the guns aimed at him and threw his hands up, knocking his sombrero off. "Don't shoot! I ain't armed." He followed everyone's stare to look down at his two pistols and realized his lie. "I mean, they ain't loaded." Then apparently he thought better of that, too. "No, I mean, I don't mean no harm."

Everyone slumped in relief, cursed, sat down, shook their heads, and sent the kid frowning looks. Only Sara thought to ask him what he was doing there, to which he answered, as he leaned over to pick up his hat, "I came to tell you all what I heard from Dawson and them. It ain't none of it good.''

Suddenly, to Sara, he looked older than his years, wiser than his experiences. For the first time, she noticed lines in the boy's—young man's—forehead and at the corners of his mouth. Her heart went out to him. What horrid side of life had he seen already at his tender age?

"Tell us what you heard, Red," Jim Dalton called out.

Apparently taking that as an invitation, Red stepped over to Jim and the other men and stood in front of them to tell his story. Sara joined them, sitting by Deke, who put a supportive arm around her waist. Her kin glared at her, communicating their obvious disapproval of her easy intimacy with the bounty hunter, but they said nothing. Sara lowered her eyes at their obvious censure, then raised her head, looking at Red, who kept twisting his sombrero in his hands as he spoke.

"Well, after you throwed them out of the cave, and before they all realized that I was so close, Dawson and them said as how they was going to get you back—was going to kill every last one of you. All except Miss Dalton, that is. Beg your pardon, ma'am, but you they want alive. For a while.''

The cold prick of dread that washed over her was as nothing compared to Jim's answer to that.

"We'd all have to be dead for that to happen," he spat out. Cody and Travis nodded their agreement, accepting that possibility.

When Deke's hold on her tightened, she looked up at him only to see him returning her kin's level stares. Dear God, was it going to take a threat to her to put these men on the same side? Jim's oath and their exchanged looks, tantamount to a death pact between them, sent a cold shiver over her skin. She decided right then that the last bullet in her derringer would be for herself—she'd die by her own hand before she'd allow her family or Deke to die trying to protect her from those heartless men. Then, anger that her kin would associate with that sort and thereby put her into danger, that they themselves were outlaws and had made this trip necessary for her, raised her chin a notch, despite her very real fear for them all. If they didn't get all those fears and doubts out in the open soon, they would tear each other apart. And make it easier for those men to kill them all. As they'd threatened.

"What else?" Deke tersely questioned Red, answering the Daltons look-for-look and then turning his gaze on the kid.

"Well, then they said that they was coming for you tonight."

"Maybe we ought to stop right here for a minute." All eyes turned to Deke. Once he had their questioning attention, he turned his gaze to Red. "Where are you in all this?"

Red looked startled, but then he blurted out, "I'm right here with you! That's what I decided right off when I heard what J.T. and Abe and Bart and them was threatening. I'm right here for you, guns and all. I lay my hat with yours. Jim and you all ain't been nothin' but good to me, so I'm on your side. I don't even care if I get killed. Of course, I hope I don't. I hope you don't. I mean, I hope we all—"

"Just so you know the lay of things, kid," Deke interrupted him. "There's a fight coming. No doubt about that. You stick with us, you could very well end up dead." He let the kid absorb that while he turned his gaze to Sara and the other Daltons. "We all need to realize that. We're outnumbered, out-gunned, our backs essentially to a wall in this cave. Trapped like this, there's not much chance in hell that we'll all, if any of us, come out of this alive. Even providing we can all decide to stick together."

Through talking, he looked at the Daltons, who remained as still as granite. Deke had, after all, given them a crawful to absorb. He then turned his gaze to Sara. She squeezed his arm, feeling the powerful play of warm muscle under her touch. She tried to give him a look that communicated her support, that said she would stand by him. He acknowledged it by covering her hand with his own before he turned once again to Jim, a man who was no relation to him, a man who had possibly killed his mother and sister.

Jim's answer was by no means reassuring. "We don't have much choice right now but to stick together, so we will. But there's something you should know. The way we see it, it ain't over yet between us. And the way we, Sara's kin, feel is this—The only reason you're still alive, Bonner, is because of the way Sara obviously feels about you."

"I could say the same thing about you," Deke replied just as coldly and without hesitation.

A brooding silence followed. Sara looked down at her lap, her face getting hotter and hotter by the second. Then she proudly raised her head to look boldly at her brother and cousins. She was proud of her love for Deke, and nothing could change that. And if that love was the glue that held them all together, then so be it. Because she wasn't giving up on any of them.

It has come down to this moment, the moment she'd known would happen, had feared from the first second Deke Bonner, bounty hunter, had simply ridden over beside her outside of Plains, Kansas. And it was just as awful as she'd feared. Despite every prayer and action of hers, there was essentially nothing she could do to resolve this. Tears, pleading, words—they were all she had. But she now knew that they wouldn't be enough to change the way any of them, the men she loved most in the world, felt about each other. This certainly wasn't the first time in her life that she'd felt helpless in the face of overwhelming circumstances. Hadn't she lost most of her family in the war? Wasn't her mother even now dying? But it was the first time she had no hope for a better tomorrow.

Those thoughts crowding her head, she looked around her at the clammy, unsympathetic cave. And then she realized that she couldn't count on any kind of tomorrow. This cave just might be her tomb.

She quickly blinked back scalding tears, abruptly pulling away from Deke, whose eyes she couldn't meet just now. She walked quickly to the back of the cave, hoping the men would assume she was just checking on the burros and wouldn't follow her. She desperately needed these moments alone. After only a few steps, though, Little Ned wobbled up to Sara and sniffed sympathetically at her long split skirt. As she put her hand out to pet him, he whuffed in a snort that netted him a noseful of dust-laden fabric, eliciting a tremendous sneeze that shocked him into a baleful braying that also gained him the attention of the men, turning a bemused Sara toward them when she heard a masculine chuckle or two. Little Ned's mother, though, was not amused, if one could judge by her laid-back long ears and her single bray to her offspring to get back over there and out of the way. When he scampered back to his mother, Sara was able to chuckle, a somewhat watery sound to be sure, but no less cleansing.

She then openly wiped at her eyes and went back to the circle of men, sitting once again by Deke, who surprised her by being the first one to hold out an olive branch—a temporary one, but a peace offering nonetheless. As if there were no bad blood between him and the Daltons, as if they'd always been on the same side, he asked, sounding almost casual, "Who the hell are all those men I threw out of here?"

"They're Lucky Dawson, Jack Bennett, Abe Diamond, Bart Coleman, and J. T. Dedmon," Jim answered grimly.

Sara pulled in a deep breath; those names were almost legendary and were on as many wanted posters as the Daltons'. Deke too was impressed; he ran a hand over his mouth and chin and let out a low whistle. "Damn. You travel in some pretty mean company. That kid with the scar talked about you being partners. So how did you hook up with them? From what I can see of you—no offense, but you're not of their cold-blooded caliber."

Travis took over from here. "None taken. We're mighty well aware of that. We just seemed to fall into their scheme. We came along at the wrong time for us, but the right time for them."

"What the heck does that mean?" It was Red. Everyone

looked at him as if they'd forgotten, given his uncharacteristic silence for the past few moments, that he was still here.

"It means," Cody answered, exchanging glances with his brother and cousin that only they understood, "that they'll come back—and come back strong. It means we're sitting here talking when we should be doing."

"Cody's right. They'll be back—and soon," Deke commented, his gaze traveling slowly around the circle, his black eyes conveying the dire but unspoken message of impending battle.

Apparently seeing what he needed to, he stood up in one athletic movement, bringing everyone else to their feet. Even though no one had said or decided as much, it appeared to be understood that they had put aside their differences for now and were following Deke's orders. "Get your guns and ammo ready. Load everything you've got. Sara, stoke up that fire—it'll light us up after dark, but we've got no choice if we're going to see what we're doing. We need to stow away anything that's in our way here, things we might trip over, or kick and make noise—like the coffeepot, the plates, things like that. Travis, Jim, Cody, we can make barricades at the cave's entrance to give us some protection. Use that gear stacked up along the walls and stagger them."

"You need to know something else, Bonner," Cody said into the quiet that attended Sara's and the men's moving around, setting about performing the various chores assigned them by Deke. When Cody spoke, they all stopped and stared at the youngest Dalton; he shot his male kin a stubborn look and then returned his gaze to Deke. "There's crates of stolen guns at the back. And a hell of a lot of money. They're going to want that."

Sara looked at Deke; he had that hawklike, assessing look on his face as he stared back at Cody. "I'm glad you told me that. Show me where they are, son; we'll get the guns for our own use and hide the money somewhere else in the cave. I don't know about you, but it will give me no end of pleasure to use their own guns against them, the bastards."

The others nodded and murmured that they shared a like sentiment and again set about readying the cave for the fight of their lives. As Sara worked at stoking the fire, she tried not to think that there wasn't much time left before those five men—and whoever else they could enlist to join them— swooped down on them with guns in their hands and death in their hearts. There wasn't much time left to say what needed to be said.

In a sudden panic, she jumped to her feet and called out Deke's name. He'd been talking with Cody, but stopped in mid-sentence and turned to her, his face unreadable. Which only made it harder for her to get out the whispered words. "I love you . . . for everything."

He smiled, just barely. "Yeah, me too." He winked and turned to follow Cody, who was slowly feeling his way along, his hands on the rock walls in the thick blackness of the cave's low ceiling. Then Deke surprised her by calling out to her after she'd already turned back to the campfire. "Sara."

She spun back around, her heart in her eyes. And all the other eyes were on her and Deke. Seeing them staring, Deke looked down, put his hands to his waist, then looked up at her. "I . . . I'll make sure the burros are tied up back here out of the way of stray bullets."

She smiled and nodded, understanding what he couldn't say. As she turned back to her tasks, her gaze caught those of Jim and Travis. The obvious censure in their faces chased away her smile and caused her to look away first.

The next several minutes saw Sara and the men grimly, almost silently, hustling to ready the guns, the cave, and themselves. They all knew that this was to the death, theirs or their enemies'. Their silence, coupled with the solemn tasks they were performing, gave Sara a heightened awareness of every single noise and sound from outside the cave. It seemed to her that she stopped in her tracks, looking to the cave's entrance whenever any noise, no matter how commonplace, drifted into hearing range and forced her tight-rope-taut awareness to the cave's gaping mouth.

She hated it that thick brush hid the outside world from their view; whereas before the brush had seemed protective, now it seemed sinister. She hated it, too, that Cinnamon and Deke's buckskin were tied off some distance from here, as were, she assumed, her kin's horses. They could never get to them, if the need arose. Thinking these things, weighing these problems, she turned to Deke, who was now only a few steps away from her as he helped Cody to load one after the other of the rifles they'd carried forward to place at the different barricades that Red, Jim, and Travis were still erecting.

She called his name, almost in a whisper, but one that seemed to echo off the cave's waiting, palpable stillness. When he paused in his work and looked at her, she said, "The horses. What about them? Shouldn't we get them? And that brush—shouldn't we cut it down so we can see them coming? Do you think there's time?"

Deke nodded and weighed her words, as if trying to figure out how best to go about those tasks. While he thought, he continued loading the contraband rifle in his hands. "Good thinking," he finally said, sounding almost absentminded as he spoke and turned his gaze out into the approaching dusk. Sara knew that quick mind of his was working furiously.

Then, apparently having it figured out, he turned and called out in a hiss to Red, who spun around from his task with Travis of erecting a barrier out of blankets, bedrolls, and crates, only to raise his eyebrows in silent questioning. Deke signaled to him, and the boy came at a trot, like a trained puppy. His eager face reflected his willingness to take on whatever task Deke might have for him.

"Red," Deke began, putting his large hand on the boy's thin shoulder, "they may not know out there that you came in here—or that you're still here, if they did see you come in. Now, listen up. There's something I want you to do. You're the only one of us who can risk sticking his neck outside this cave right now. What I want you to do just might cost you your life, so you have to decide whether or not you want to do this. And no one will think less of you if you say no."

"I'll do it—whatever it is. Just tell me," Red said without hesitation, looking briefly like the man Sara hoped he got every opportunity to become.

Deke nodded briefly, his lips pressed firmly together. "All right. You know which horses belong to me and Sara and the Daltons? Yeah? Good. Is yours close by them? Okay. I want you to be careful, but sneak out, gather the horses, and tie them just to the other side of that stand of cottonwoods to the right of this cave. Think you can do that without getting your sombrero shot off?"

Red answered, a cocky, confident grin on his face, "If I can rob banks and stages—even a train or two—by myself, I reckon I can gather up a few horses and tie 'em up okay."

Deke exchanged a look with Sara, bemused doubt as to the truthfulness of the boy's claims to those illegal activities riding his features. Sara put a hand to her mouth to keep from laughing at the expense of Red's pride. Deke then shook his head, punched at the boy's skinny arm, and said enthusiastically, "All right, desperado, go get 'em. And try to have a look around, see what's going on. And don't get yourself killed."

Sara didn't know if Red heard Deke's last comment because he was already scampering out the brush-covered entrance, his floppy sombrero in his hand, and looking this way and that before sneaking off in a loud clinking of guns and spurs. Sara smiled warmly at the kid's antics, as much as at his unquestioning loyalty and bravery, then turned back to Deke, who was shaking his head and letting out a deep breath. "I hate like hell sending that kid out there. If he's not back in a few minutes, or if I hear any trouble, I'm going after him. Should have gone myself anyway. Damn!"

She put her hand on his arm. "He'll be okay. I'm willing to bet that everyone here knows him and ignores him. They probably look right past him, thinking he's harmless."

"Even leading six horses over to this cave?" Deke asked her.

Sara didn't know how to answer that, so she didn't. She just bit at her lip and frowned, turning her eyes to the cave's entrance and its tangled brush, which still rustled from the boy's passage through its interlocking branches. Something and someone else to worry about, she sighed. Then, feeling Deke leave her side, she turned her head to see him crossing the cave's width to talk softly with Travis and Cody; he was punctuating his words with gestures which indicated to Sara that he was going to have them cut down the brush now that their barricades were ready. And once that was done, there was nothing left for them to do but line up the loaded rifles, hoist their weapons over the tops of the makeshift barriers, try to see through the descending darkness . . . and wait. And wait.

Many ominous minutes later, Red almost got himself killed before the fight began when he created a startlingly loud stir of noise by sliding down the steep slide of upthrust rock that was the cave's outer right wall and landing, as if by a puff of magic, right in front of the men.

Five weapons were cocked, aimed; five shooters sighted, recognized the kid, heaved a collective out-whush of air, uncocked, and went limp. Red stood at the cave's mouth, looking as if he could see his own body lying on the ground at his feet; his hands were raised as high in the sky as he could get them. "Don't shoot!" he whispered loudly. "I got the horses. Everything's ready. Hey, where're the bushes?"

"Red, will you get in here and be quiet, or do I have to shoot you just to shut you up?" Cody hissed at him, his eyes narrowed over his rifle, which pointed at Red's heart.

"You ain't got to shoot me, Cody. I'll come in right quiet-like," he squeaked.

"Then do it!" Cody fairly screeched while still trying to whisper. "And keep your voice down!"

Undaunted, Red scampered inside the cave, weaving his way through the staggered barriers and nodding to each of

the Daltons as he passed them. Like a private to his ser-
geants, he went straight to Deke and Sara, but very impor-
tantly waved his hand at the other men to join them. Given
the circumstances, the Daltons quickly and unquestioningly
hustled over, coming in a crouching run.

"What'd you find out?" Deke asked. "What's going on
out there?"

"Well, more'n one thing, it seems. For one, Jack and
Lucky and them can't get no one to fall in with them. The
other men know what they're like and all and don't want no
part of this here fight."

Sara couldn't believe this. "So what are they going to do?
Sit around and watch and take bets?"

Red looked at her; she looked around the close circle. Jim
and Cody were nodding. Deke and Travis were still watching
Red's face. "No, ma'am, they're not. Fact is, see, they're
lightin' out."

Travis disputed that with a snort. "Who is? I don't see
the likes of Abe Diamond and Bart Coleman and J.T. Dedmon taking to their heels."

"Not them," Red interrupted. "Not any of them men,
Travis. They're still out there. I mean the others—all of 'em.
They're taking to their horses right now and hightailing it
for parts unknown. Said they needed peace and quiet."

This news was greeted with silence and exchanged stares.
Then Deke took hold of Red's arm. "You mean to tell me
that it's going to be us—six of us—against five of them?"

"Yes, I most surely do," Red crowed. "It's starting to
look like a ghost town out there. But there's more. See,
Lucky Dawson—the kid with the scar on his cheek—well,
he figured out who you really are, talk is. Says he's gunnin'
for you special. It weren't me that told him, neither. I want
you to know that, 'cause I want to stay here and—"

"Red, Red. Yeah, you can stay here. That's fine," Deke
cut him off. Sara didn't think he was even aware that he was
stroking her hair down her back as his darting gaze and for-
ward-looking stare told her he was quickly assimilating this

new information, looking for a way to turn it even more to their advantage. Finally an ironic grin lighted his features as much as did the fire's glow in the cave's blackness. But dark was beginning to settle outside as well. Deke took a quick look over his shoulder and then turned back to them. "They'll be here any minute. I don't guess I have to tell you what we're up against. Numbers here aren't as important as guts, cool heads, smarts, and a good aim."

Nodding heads agreed with him. Then Jim said, "We know what and who we're up against. But not you, Sara. You've been through enough. I want you to get to the back of the cave and stay there. Better yet, I think you should slip out now, get to your horse, and—"

An outraged objection poised on her lips, Sara rose to protest vehemently, but never got the chance because a rifle's report sounded in the quiet night, sending a bullet whizzing threateningly close to her head before it pinged off the rock walls inside the cave.

Chapter Twenty-seven

With a gasp of surprise and fear that mingled with the star-tled yelps and curses of the men, Sara reflexively bent double and then went to the ground to put herself fully behind the crude barrier's protection. No one had to tell her that the protective weight instantly on top of her and pressing her into the rock floor was Deke Bonner. Or that the scurrying and shuffling sounds she heard were her brother, cousins, and Red hustling to their posts. Then all was quiet again, but there was no telling when the next shot would sound—and find its mark.

Sara elbowed Deke to get off her, which he did, rolling to his side and then cupping her chin, none too gently in his all-too-evident fear, and said, his voice low and husky, "Are you crazy? Why'd you raise up like that? Are you trying to get yourself shot?"

Sara turned her head to free her chin from his grip. "No, I'm not, but I'm telling you right now, Deke Bonner, that I don't care what Jim says—I'm getting my Spencer and going to my post. And don't you try to stop me, either, because I can carry my own weight . . . what are you grinning at?''

"You're in this to the end, aren't you, Sara?"

She had no idea what he meant by that and so frowned up at him. "Yes, I am. Whatever you mean. This gunfight, this—this thing with my brother and cousins, the law, you. To the end, Deke. I love you all.''

He caressed her cheek, his black eyes soft as he took in her features. Finally, he looked into her eyes. "Get your Spencer, Sara Dalton. I'd be mighty proud to stand alongside you in this fight. And if I'm still standing when it's over, I'll—''

"Don't say 'if'," Sara whimpered, hushing his words by pressing her fingertips to his mouth. She could not sustain her anger in the face of such a terrible possibility as Deke's death.

He put his long, strong fingers over hers and pressed them to his lips in a tender kiss. Then, looking into her eyes again, his black eyes revealing his knowledge of the worst possible fate for himself and yet also promising the declaration of eternal love she knew was coming, he whispered, "If I'm still standing when this is over, I'll . . . I'll name my horse.''

So caught up was she in the romantic spell he was weaving right there on a cave floor, surrounded by outlaws, their lives in dire jeopardy, that she didn't at first absorb what he'd said to her. "I love— What did you say?"

"I said I'll name my horse. I thought that would make you happy.'' He dodged her slapping hands while he spoke, his low chuckle fueling her embarrassment.

"Of all the nerve, Deke Bonner. I could be dead at any minute and all you can think of is your stupid—''

"Don't call my horse names.'' He grabbed her hands, pulled her to his chest, and held her there, straining and struggling though she was in his embrace. "Shhh, listen to me. Listen to me, Sara. Are you listening? Good. I love you more than my own life. Do you hear me? I would die for you—in a thousand ways. In fact, come to think of it, I almost have in the last six weeks.''

Sara stilled in his embrace and looked into his tanned, handsome face, memorizing his features in case she had to take them with her to heaven. She knew what he was doing. He was trying to get her Dalton fighting spirit up. Just when his face changed, when it softened, when his eyelids drooped lazily, when she felt him lowering his head to hers, she raised her head to meet him—and licked his nose. That got her released in an instant. She bounced on her derriere, catching herself with her outstretched hands and stifling a deep giggle at his shocked expression.

Swiping his shirt sleeve across his wet nose, he turned a devilish grin on her. ''You're going to pay for that one, Sara Dalton.''

''Uh, excuse me, you two.''

Sara and Deke sobered and looked around to see Jim crouched behind their barrier with them, a grim expression on his face, a long rifle held in his hands. ''I hate to interrupt your moment and all, but we've got a pack of wolves howling at our door. I just thought we might want to watch out for them.''

Chagrined, feeling the heat of embarrassment on her cheeks and knowing Deke must be feeling something of the same, Sara answered for them, ''Sorry. Deke was just telling me what a good job we did with the barriers, right?''

''Yeah, that's it,'' Deke said flatly. He then got up slowly, being careful not to rise too quickly and thereby expose himself to a well-aimed bullet. He reached over, retrieved Sara's Spencer repeater, handed it and her ammunition to her, and positioned himself right alongside her at the barrier to the farthest right of the cave's mouth.

Thus assured of their vigilance, Jim crouched and hustled back to his post. Seeing her brother safely positioned once again, Sara looked out into the thickening night, thinking the darkness was more of an ally to the men outside than it was to them in the cave. Only Deke's warm, reassuring presence so close to her side kept her courage up. She looked up at his profile as he kept his sharp gaze on the night. She could see his eyes moving left to right, yet he kept his head still. She was sure he had the sight and hearing of a wildcat, so as long as he looked relatively calm, she felt the same. Still, he was looking deadly serious, as was everyone else, but he spared her a glance and a smile from the corner of his mouth when he either saw or felt her eyes on him. Sara could not sustain his gaze; it was too full of the possibility, the probability, of all their deaths. Still, she knew that with his eyes he was trying to tell her of his love for her.

She closed her eyes and squeezed back sudden tears, forcing her mind from their dire dilemma. Opening them after willing the tears away, so dangerous just now when she really needed to see clearly, she looked back over her shoulder into the cave's gray gloom trying to find Miss Petunia and Little Ned. But someone had put the fire out, making it impossible to see the interior. Still, by concentrating and attuning her senses, much like a dog perking up its ears and raising its nose to the wind, she thought she detected soft rustling noises at the back of the cave. In fact, a snuffling snort just then, in conjunction with a muffled thump, told her that mother and son were indeed in the far recesses of the cave and so were relatively safe. Sara smiled to herself. The two burros were very quiet, much as if they knew the need for a hushed silence, much as if they understood this all-too-human predicament. She wondered how they felt about it.

Her answer was immediate. An ear-splitting, screeching bray that was too deep to be Little Ned's filled the cave, reverberated off the walls, sent waves of sound out into the night, and drew everyone's stunned attention to the back of the cave. But as soon as they all turned around in reflexive reaction to the sound, coupled now with the foal's bleating and some heavy thumps and grunts, guns began firing outside. The men, cursing and yelling instructions to each other, turned back around to answer the gunfire. But not Sara. The noises at the back of the cave had to mean something. Something was wrong there. With a certainty born of dread, she knew what that something was—someone was back there with the burros. She didn't know who or how, but she did know someone was back there. And it wasn't a friend.

Crouched down on her haunches and facing the back of the cave still, Deke's legs to her right, she trained her gaze on the darkness, terrified yet half-expecting a shadowy enemy to appear. She looked up at Deke; he was oblivious, concentrating heavily on this engagement that meant all their lives. No stranger to battle, he stood unflinchingly with all the coolness under fire of a bear stealing honey from enraged bees. Sara pushed herself forward to see around Deke's legs; she wanted to assure herself of everyone else's well-being. Quickly she found Jim. There were Cody and Travis, together as always. And yes, there was Red. Everyone was still standing, thank God. And even Red was looking calm and deadly; maybe he really was the outlaw he professed to be.

Thus assured of everyone's health, Sara turned her heightened awareness back to the cave's recesses. The burros hadn't calmed any; they were still braying and bleating. Sara concentrated so deeply on the blackness that her eyes began watering; she blinked rapidly to focus, knowing in her heart that the burros' panicky braying was not simply from the bullet-ridden chaos around them. She bit at her lip as she tried to think what to do. Torn between a pressing warning that screamed in her head to investigate and the fear of what she was walking into, she remained where she was. If indeed someone was back there, he hadn't fired any shots, and Miss Petunia's hooves, tiny but deadly sharp, seemed to be handling the situation. For the next several heart-stopping, lead-filled moments, Sara watched and waited, registering the total chaos which reigned around her as bullet after bullet thudded into the barriers or ricocheted off the cave's walls and roof. She knew she should be helping the men, knew she should be using her Spencer to give them the advantage, but she couldn't ignore the hair standing up on the back of her neck and her arms that told her plainly to watch the back of the cave, that said the danger was back there, despite all the lead flying through the air from without.

Glancing up again at Deke, so deadly grim, his face sweating as he worked to reload one of the contraband rifles, Sara knew what she had to do. She had to go to the back of the cave and deal with whatever—whoever—was back there because no one but her could be spared up here right now. Screwing up her courage, she gripped her rifle tightly and willed her thumping heart back into a steady beat. She stole another glance up at Deke and silently spoke her love to him. There was no way she could tell him her intentions; he would argue with her, and she couldn't allow that. Too much valuable time would be lost, perhaps even lives.

And so she abruptly set off at a low crouch, her primed and loaded Spencer held firmly in both hands. She thought she heard Deke hiss her name, but she couldn't be sure, and she didn't look back. She moved with all the stealth and sharp-sensed cunning of her cat Calico when he was stalking a hapless bird back on the farm in Plains. An image of the farm flitted through her mind. Would she ever see it and her dying mother again? Or would she die here with her men? No, she couldn't allow that; the irony would be too terrible for her mother, Aunt Jean, and Olivia, Travis's wife, to bear.

Thus determined, Sara skirted cautiously along the cave's dank, rough wall, using her left hand to guide her through the palpable blackness of the cave. When she came to the frantic burros, she patted and soothed them, then moved on, thinking that this was what it was like to be blind, a frightening thought that haunted each step she took back into the cave's depths.

A screech of sheer terror ripped out of Sara's lungs when two long, powerful arms snaked out from behind her, much as if they were appendages of a living darkness, and jerked her up against a solid, sweating bulk that had to be a hard chest. The burros brayed fiercely, masking the clatter of her Spencer hitting the rocky ground. Through the red haze of her panic, Sara heard voices at the front of the cave yelling and realized that there was less and less gunfire to be heard.

Then she felt the cold steel of a gun barrel press into her temple and heard a voice, disembodied by the inky dark, say, "Now, hold real still there, missy, if you hope to live to see the sun come up tomorrow."

Her absolute inability to see anything made the man's voice all that more frightening. The bile rose to the back of her throat at the same time her bones turned to liquid. When she began to wilt, her captor grabbed her up closer to him, forcing Sara's breasts into his chest. His arm like a rock log around her back, he growled a warning for her not to try anything funny. Sara blinked her eyes rapidly, trying to dispel the stars at the backs of her eyes; she didn't dare faint. She had to stay alert, had to get herself out of this somehow before her helplessness got the men killed.

She heeded the voice that spoke threateningly into her ear as she was awkwardly walked, after being turned around roughly and gripped tightly from behind just under her breasts, toward the front of the cave. Concentrating on each step, afraid that if she or he fell, his gun might go off since his finger was on the trigger, she was nonetheless able to register sounds peripheral to her consciousness. Sounds like the silence—there was no gunfire at all now. Then she could hear men running; but who and to where, she had no idea. The man behind her spoke again, admonishing her once more not to try anything foolish.

It was then that she recognized her captor's voice and knew, with bone-chilling dread, that he was the young one with the scar—Lucky Dawson, the one who said he was gunning especially for Deke. Dear God, she'd meant to save them all by coming back here to investigate, but now her rash action would probably get them all killed, for now the determined outlaws had a hostage to use as leverage to get close enough to kill them and get back their guns and money. How could she have been so stupid?

For no one had to tell her that this man, who wasn't much bigger or taller than she was, had sneaked in through some secret entrance her kin hadn't known about and was probably supposed to shoot any of them he could until the other four closed in on them in the confusion. He had been foiled, until now, by the frantic braying and kicking of the two burros. But then she'd made it easy for him by giving in to her curiosity and wandering into his range. She wanted desperately to kick herself, or perhaps allow Miss Petunia to do so. Then she realized that she didn't hear the burros anymore; a stubborn poking out of her bottom lip boded ill for her captor if he had harmed the helpless animals in any way.

As she was dragged by her assailant into the dubious red light of the torch-lit front of the cave, Sara's dread was confirmed. There in front of her, but several yards away, were Deke, Red, Jim, Cody, and Travis—all unarmed and with their hands up, facing her with two armed men close upon them and pointing rifles at their backs. Behind them, one to each side, stood two other men with pistols also aimed at Deke and the others; each of these men held a fiery torch in his other hand, thus lending a macabre light to the scene. Sara swallowed hard at their elongated, dancing shadows, so black against the bloodred and sulfur-yellow of the torches as they wavered over the gray cave walls; she felt sure they'd all died and gone to hell for their sins.

Her moment of intense relief when she saw that no one she cared about was wounded was dashed when she realized that neither were any of their adversaries. So the odds were still five to six, but the six were no longer armed and the five were. Fighting against paralyzing despair, she forced her mind to work over the metallic taste of panic at the back of her throat, hoping to grasp any straw, any thread that could free their feet from this bear trap of a situation. But it looked hopeless from where she stood, wrapped as she was in the arms of the enemy.

"Look what I got, Abe! Ain't we lucky? And ain't we the smart ones not tellin' the Daltons about that other way into the cave up at the top? I shinnied down that narrow little hole and then landed right smack-dab on the back of a danged burro. Like to have killed myself, I did, gettin' off,''

Lucky called out, sounding maniacal in his glee.

Sara fought against rising hysteria, forcing herself to think, because the time was here for simple action and, hopefully, dumb luck. But what action; what luck?

The outlaw with his gun on Cody, Jim, and Red laughed triumphantly, obscenely. Sara decided he must be Abe. He then confirmed it by calling back, "That's real good, Lucky; that's real good. This is even better than I ever hoped."

Lucky called back, "Ain't that for sure! And hey, Abe, Bart, this here silver-haired woman feels pretty good. Worth gettin' killed over, I'd say. Whoo-wee, you need to git you a handful of this female."

Sara almost died when Lucky put his hand over her breast, kneading it painfully. Her hands came up to pull at his fingers, but he was too strong for her. His sick laughter at her desperation and helplessness, his lewd noises and encouragement for her to fight him harder was enough to make Sara fear she would be sick.

"Get your filthy hands off her, you lowlife son-of-a-bitch," Deke hurled, taking a step toward her. Jim, Cody, Red, and Travis were right behind him.

"No!" Sara screamed out raggedly. "Don't! They'll shoot you! Don't, please. I couldn't stand it."

Deke stopped at the sound of her cry, but yelled across the distance, "He'll have to shoot me, Sara; he'll have to." He then turned his eyes on Lucky. Sara swore they took on the hooded, hypnotizing, deep-black characteristics of a rattlesnake's; even his voice was a low, slow hiss of sound. "Take your filthy hands off her, Dawson, you coward. Face me like a man. It's me you want, not her."

After the briefest hesitation, during which Sara assumed he was sizing Deke up, Lucky did move his hand away from her breast. But he didn't let her go. "Now, what makes you so sure of that, bounty hunter? Maybe I'll just kill you, and then I'll have her."

Deke started to take another step toward Sara, but several guns behind him clicked into cocked position. "That there's just durn far enough, bounty hunter. All of you just git your hands back up. And one more step outta any-a you, and you all get it," another one of them said.

Travis turned slightly to look over his shoulder. "What's stopping you, J.T.? You're going to kill all of us anyway. You waiting on Lucky to tell you what to do, like always?"

"Shut up, Dalton, before I make you the first one," J.T. threatened, swinging his gun to Travis's back and then back to Deke's quickly when he made a feint in J.T.'s direction.

It was then that Sara caught on to their taunting of these evil men: They were trying to create a diversion, trying to catch their enemies unaware, so they could better their odds of survival. Sara tried frantically to think of a way to help, but couldn't.

But then she caught Deke's eye—or he caught hers. Perhaps their gazes had just sought each other out. What was he doing? His facial grimaces would have been comical under any other circumstances, what with quirks of his mouth and dipping and raising of his eyebrows, and tic-like jerks of his head to one side. Was he wounded somewhere? If not, what was he trying to convey? A quick up-and-down revealed that he looked whole and hale—so what, then? Sara almost unwittingly began using her own facial grimaces and tics to try to let him know she didn't understand, but to no avail.

Then Jim called out, drawing all their gazes. "There's something you boys should know. Once you kill all of us, you'll have the guns, but not the money. We moved it."

One of the men holding a pistol and a torch advanced on Jim, putting the torch dangerously close to his back. "Well, Jim, mayhaps you'd just better tell us right now where it is before I send you to hell—already all burned up."

"No!" Sara screamed. No one seemed to notice.

"That won't do you any good, Bennett," Deke said over his shoulder. "He doesn't know where we moved it."

Bennett took the torch away from Jim's back and walked over to Deke, placing it close to him. "Well then, bounty hunter, why don't you just be the one to tell me?'' he sneered. Deke just looked at the man and turned, almost casually, to face forward, to face Sara. Bennett took a step back, turning to his left and right to share a laugh with his compadres at Deke's expense. They enjoyed a few comments amongst their cocky selves to the effect that Deke was a coward.

But what Deke was doing was using the time to look fully and questioningly at Sara. He then cut his gaze to Lucky, behind Sara, apparently saw that he wasn't looking at him, then mouthed a word or two at her, at the same time nodding his head. She frowned her eyebrows down to her nose and gave an almost imperceptible shake of her head. Deke grimaced and repeated the process—and this time Sara got it. The derringer. Deke was asking her if she had the derringer! Her heart nearly pounded out of her chest; she'd completely forgotten about it. It was in her pocket, and it was loaded. One shot. She had only one shot, providing she could get to it. But how, held as tightly as she was? But then she knew. And Deke himself would kill her when he realized what she was about. But she couldn't help that now. It was up to her to get them out of this. Or die trying.

Suddenly, into the relative quiet, she said to Lucky, but loud enough for all the men to hear, ''I know where the money is.''

''Sara, what are you doing?'' Deke called out, sounding—for the first time since she'd met him—afraid.

''I'm throwing in with the winners. It's that simple. I'm going to buy my life with the money—and with my body,'' she added, too sick at heart to look at Deke or Red or her family.

''Dammit, Sara, you don't know where—''

''Yes, I do, Deke Bonner. You shut up!''

''Sara—''

''Shut up, bounty hunter. Let the lady talk.''

Sara looked at the speaker, who stood with a torch behind Deke and Travis. He hadn't said a word before now, but he looked like the most dangerous of the five.

"That's right, Deke, you shut up." Committed now to her plan, she rushed on, turning as much as possible in Lucky's arms. "I know where the money is, and I'll take you to it at the back of the cave. And then I'll—give you all what you want. But you first."

"No!" rang out in the cave, coming from Sara's men.

Lucky turned his sadistic smirk on the men held under armed guard, then smiled—an oily, evil gesture—down into Sara's face. The tense silence in the cave only deepened while they awaited his answer. But Sara knew exactly what he would say; the dread washing over her only seconded what she already knew. "It's back there in the dark? And you want to take me to it, so's no one can see us? A modest little thing, ain't you?" He then turned to his friends. "What you say, Bart? Should I take me a torch so's I can see her an' make sure she's not trickin' me none—or should I oblige the lady's wishes?"

"You can't hold onto her, a torch, and a gun all at the same time, Lucky. Go on, but don't be all night about it. We got work to do. And save some of her for us," Bart answered, looking at Sara, his expression somewhere between a leer and a threat. But it didn't matter; if her plan didn't work, she was dead anyway.

"Whuu-u-wee! I get me some of the Dalton woman and I get to kill me a bounty hunter, all in one night. This must be my lucky day," Lucky crowed, immensely pleased with his own joke. He let go of Sara, only to grab her arm firmly in his grip. He turned to the assembled men. "Don't you all start the killing until I get back with the money. She might be lyin'." He gave Sara a twisted look. "An' if she is, she won't be back."

"She doesn't know where it is," Cody cried out. "I do! I hid it! Take me instead, Lucky."

Lucky snorted and looked at Cody as if he were something nasty on the bottom of his boot. "You never were too bright,

Cody. Now why would I want you when I can have a woman, stupid?''

But Cody didn't get to answer, because like an enraged bull, Deke charged—only to be hit on the back of the head with a rifle butt. Sara screamed out his name. As Deke passed out cold and fell to the ground, Bart, who had stepped forward to strike him, commented almost casually, ''I was hoping that big son-of-a-bitch would do that.''

Seeing Deke fall, Lucky was instantly, dangerously livid and screaming about how the bounty hunter had better not be dead because he was his to kill later; in his maniacal anger, his grip on Sara's arm went beyond painful when she cried out and tried to lurch away to get to Deke's prostrate form. She could see blood oozing from Deke's head onto the cave floor.

Bart holstered his pistol, held his torch up high, and knelt down over Deke, prodding him, feeling his neck; the others kept their guns trained on their muttering captives, giving them no chance to create a disturbance. ''Nah, Lucky, he ain't dead. He's just plumb knocked out cold. Now, go on—get the money and have your way with the woman. Like I said, we got other things to do tonight.''

Instantly calmed down, Lucky jerked Sara towards the back of the cave, toward the covering darkness of the dank throat of Robber's Cave. Hearing her men's almost strangled calls for her not to do this, pleading with her as she turned her back and went with her captor, Sara's limbs turned to mushy oatmeal. She could barely walk. But she had no choice that she could see. If this didn't work, they were all dead or worse. So she might as well go on her own terms. She was betting six lives on her belief that Lucky Dawson—cocky, smug, evil—would never think that a woman could best him.

When the cave's darkness absorbed her and Lucky into its black wetness that allowed only vague shadows to be seen, the game, the bet, became real. Cursing and kicking at the stamping burros, he pushed them aside and said, ''Get, you dumb animals. Get! Now, little lady, show me that money. And then me and you is goin' ta have us some fun. I'm goin' ta show you some things I bet you ain't never seen before. And I just know you're goin' ta love it.''

Lucky Dawson had no way of knowing how much his words pleased Sara, her eyes narrowing. For one thing, she now knew the burros were all right. For another, even though Lucky didn't seem to know it, his greed, his lust, and the covering darkness were now her allies. If only he weren't holding the arm she'd need to dip into her pocket for her derringer. ''You'll have to let go of me so I can feel my way along. It's too dark back here for me to see the exact crevice where we put the money. I need both hands.''

His grip tightened while he pondered this. Sara mentally ticked off the seconds, knowing that each one that passed might hold an opportunity for the men to create a disturbance and for Deke to wake up. Just when she thought Lucky wasn't going to buy her logic, he let go of her arm, but took hold of her loose shirt collar at the back and then pressed cold steel into her ribs. Sara slowly dipped her hand into her pocket. ''Just remember, woman, I got the gun, so I make the rules. And another thing. It don't matter none to me which way I take you—alive or dead. You got that?''

Her fingers curled around her tiny weapon, even as nausea swept over her at his words, rendering her capable only of a ragged, ''Yes.''

''Good. Then get to it. I got something for you in my pants that's just itchin' to get out.'' With that, he shoved her forward, right into the cave's wall, smacking her shoulder and hip into the unforgiving rock, forcing a ringing cry from her—and jolting her derringer from her hand. The clatter it made when it hit the rocky floor got Sara jerked tightly back against Lucky, his gun's barrel prodding her ribs painfully. ''What the hell was that?''

''I—I don't know,'' Sara stammered, yelping when he sandwiched her between the unyielding cave wall and himself, his knee pressed into her lower spine. Her cheek was bruised against a jutting boulder. Thinking beyond her pain, knowing time was short, and with her blood roaring in her ears, Sara tried to mentally calculate where the gun had landed. It had hit her boot when it fell; which way and how far would it have slid from there? "I think I knocked a rock loose."

"You think I'm stupid, don't you? It ain't no rock that makes a noise like that. Sounded more like metal to me."

Thinking that at least he hadn't shot her yet, Sara hedged, "Then maybe it was the lock on the strongbox. We—we didn't lock it. It was hanging open. I—I could've knocked it off. That's it, I'm sure. The money is right here."

Lucky took a second or two to think about that. Waiting for a bullet in her back at any second, Sara smelled the rank odor of fearful sweat—her own—and heard male voices from outside their covering darkness calling out to them. Time was running short; they would come to investigate soon when they didn't hear any noises of . . . sex. Sara swallowed convulsively and chewed on her bottom lip. And nearly fainted with relief when Lucky relaxed and pulled back, releasing her from the rock wall. "Okay, you got just two minutes to hand over that money. Get to gropin' for it in this danged darkness. Just remember, I got a hold on your shirt and a gun in your ribs. You do anythin' a-tall funny, it'll be the last thing you do."

"I know the rules," Sara said, surprised at how calm and level her voice sounded. She knelt down slowly, with Lucky bending over her, and began running her hands quickly and efficiently over the hard floor under her. Please God, let me come up with that gun, she prayed, knowing full well the irony of a prayer asking for help in committing murder. "It's here somewhere," she boldly said out loud, knowing Lucky would think she meant the money.

"It better be, or you're a dead woman," he jeered. He then twisted his body, without releasing her, to call out over his shoulder, "Hey, Abe, Jack, I got the money! Now I'm goin' to have me some fun."

You sure are, you snake, Sara thought venomously, curling her hand, this time as securely as an eagle's talon around its prey, over the comforting form of her derringer. "Here it is," she said, hearing the finality in her voice.

Lucky whooped in glee and yanked Sara roughly to her feet. Twisting around, despite his hand still on her collar, and absolutely beyond fear, Sara stuck the derringer's barrel against Lucky's forehead, said, "Here's your fun, you bastard," and fired. Lucky Dawson made not a sound as he jerked spasmodically and fell to the ground already dead but taking Sara, a cry wrung from her throat, with him in a macabre heap that mimicked an embrace.

Over the panic roaring in her ears as she frantically tried to free herself, lodged half under his dead weight as she was, Sara could hear someone calling out Lucky's name—and someone else calling out hers. It sounded like Deke. But she couldn't answer because as soon as she did, the men with Lucky would know he was dead and would retaliate against the unarmed men she loved. So, struggling, heaving, twisting, kicking, jerking, making almost involuntary little mewling sounds of honest effort that she knew could also be interpreted as lovemaking, Sara bought herself a little time, even knowing that Deke and her brother and cousins were dying a thousand deaths right now.

And then, with a loud cry, she was free. Groping around just a second more, she found Lucky's six-shooter in the dark. Relief coursing through her, she sat and held the gun to her bosom for a brief second. Then, feeling her expression harden like drying mud, tensing her senses into unfeeling hatred, she slowly, gracefully, rose to her feet, the gun at her side, hidden in the folds of her filthy, torn, and twisted skirt. She was ready to come out of the darkness, like an avenging goddess, ready to take on the evil that waited in the torchlight. Stepping over the dead outlaw, not sparing her fallen enemy even a glance, she narrowed her eyes and set her jaw at a determined angle.

Chapter Twenty-eight

Deke was barely conscious, bleeding from his head, and was on his feet only with Jim's grave support. He could hear Sara's grunting cries after the shot rang out; saw Cody vomiting, Travis white-faced, and Red deadly grim. Deke was barely clear-headed enough to build his own slow rage when he finally understood Sara's soul-wrenching situation. And knew why no one went to investigate the shot when Coleman turned to Dedmon and commented that it seemed the only way Lucky ever got lucky was if he first shot the woman.

Their callous words bent Deke over spasmodically, his hands on his knees. He cried out, calling Sara's name in a helpless agony of the soul, his world a red and purple haze. Then Travis pulled him upright, shook him to break through his grief, and pointed wordlessly to the dark depths of the cave. Still not quite comprehending, oblivious to the sudden quiet around him, Deke turned to look where Travis pointed, to where every man was already staring. His eyes widening, he stared in disbelief as Sara Jane Dalton, alone and grim, stepped out of the darkness. She stared wordlessly back at them for a moment and then adopted a spread-eagled stance, slowly raising from the folds of her skirt a huge six-shooter—which she held, two-handed, out in front of her.

Then, with her clothing all twisted, her silver hair a riotous cloud around her beautiful, righteous, deadly expression, she said loudly but levelly into the shocked quiet, "Deke, Jim, all of you, you better drop right now. Because Lucky Dawson is dead. And now it's their turn."

No one thought she was bluffing; they hit the ground and rolled, kicking out at their armed captors, dislodging their weapons and using the element of surprise that Sara had given them, along with her covering fire—one well-aimed shot after another—to gain the advantage. They'd all get only one chance to grab a loose gun, one chance to live, and they knew it. They had to be armed before Sara was out of ammunition. The torches flew out of Bennett's and Coleman's hands, bringing a crashing darkness to the fight, as those two fought to level and aim their weapons at Sara when she opened fire. Only flashes of light from the grounded torches revealed the action and the enemies to each other.

The carefully erected barriers were now useless, since both friend and foe were behind them, but one thing they did provide for their builders was the loaded, lined-up contraband rifles. In the tremendous confusion and grunting of fists connecting with jaws and bellies, and despite the blazing gunfire that split the night, somehow the Daltons, Red, and Deke all managed to come up with rifles and begin dealing death. Screams of pain were now all masculine, and they meant that shooters were finding their targets, that men were dying. But there was no way to tell in the dark exactly who was doing the dying—it was every man for himself. Thanks to a chance given them by a woman.

When it was all over, when quiet descended into the darkness, when only ragged groans and weak cries could be heard, Deke alone stood slowly, bleeding from his head and from a grazing wound to his left arm. He looked numbly around him at the men lying in their own blood on the ground and yelled out his heart's desire. "Sara!"

Agonizing seconds went by, and then she was in his arms, clutching him to her, sobbing out her love and her fear, crying over his wounds and clinging to him as if her very soul could cling to his. Deke let the rifle fall from his nerveless fingers and scooped his one love up into his arms, her feet completely off the ground, her arms wrapped tightly around his neck. He cried brokenly into her silver hair, kissed her precious sweating neck, her dirty and tear-stained cheeks, and apologized in agony over not being able to help her, to stop what Dawson had done to her. Then he raised his voice thankfully to the heavens when Sara assured him that Lucky never got the chance before she killed him. Slowly, passionately, their mutual fears calmed, they just held each other, two hearts beating in time and stilling to normal rhythms.

Assured of Sara's physical and emotional safety, Deke finally allowed himself to lower her to the ground, even though he kept her close to him, determined to shield her eyes from the sights around them. And while he held her warm, shaking body, he was finally able to dispel the terrible cloud of helplessness he'd labored under for not being able to help Sara when she needed him the most—just as he'd always felt guilty for not being home when his mother and sister were killed. He'd turned that guilt, that helplessness, into hatred, he now saw, and had allowed it to rule his life. And look where it had landed him.

"Deke?" Sara said into his filthy, blood-stained shirt.

"Yes?" he answered, kissing the top of her beloved head and rubbing his hand up and down her slim back.

"Deke, I'm so afraid," she sobbed suddenly, crumpling into him like a broken doll.

"I know, sweetheart," he said tenderly, holding her away from him by her arms so he could look into her grimy little face, one that wrenched his heart sideways whenever he saw her cry.

"Look around. Listen," she sobbed. "No one is standing

but us. I hear men groaning. Jim—"

"Stay here," he admonished, tipping her chin up so he could see her black eyes. "Hear me? I'll go look."

"No! Don't leave me! I—I want to go, too. Please."

Deke assessed her and then gave in. "All right."

She nodded, emitting a ragged sigh that tore at Deke's chest. He took her hand and looked around at the bodies. "Here's Jack Bennett; he's dead. And that's what's left of Abe Diamond. Damn. Don't look, Sara." She immediately hid her face in his shirt sleeve and clung tightly to his hand. "Look! There's Cody. Sara, let me do this."

"No! He's my baby cousin, Deke. I have to know."

Taking a deep breath, but loathe to argue with her even if his intention was to spare her further shock and pain, Deke stepped over the bodies of the two outlaws and let go of Sara's hand to kneel over Cody, who was deathly white and still, a red stain slowly spreading over the front of his shirt. At the sound of ragged sobs from Sara, he looked up at her standing there with her hands over her face, shaking. Firming his jaw against this unpleasant task and using every bit of strength he had left, he put his fingertips to the boy's throat. Nothing. His heart began thudding. He moved his fingers. A pulse! "Sara, he's alive. He's hurt bad, but he's alive."

With a cry that thanked God, Sara dropped to her knees and put a trembling hand to Cody's face. "He's alive, Deke," she repeated needlessly, turning a tear-streaked, smiling face up to him. "He's alive. He's warm and breathing. Please, Deke, see where he's shot. I don't think I can do it."

Deke looked at her, her slender, fragile frame belying the strength and courage he knew firsthand beat in her heart and coursed through her veins. There hadn't been much he could spare her on this six-week journey, but he could spare her this much. "I'll look, Sara, but I don't want you here when I open his shirt."

She opened her mouth to protest, but then apparently changed her mind upon seeing something in his face that begged her to understand his reason. She looked down at her hands, twined in her lap, as she sat with her legs folded under her. When she looked up, there was a renewed strength there. "All right," she said gravely. She got up, stood there a moment, and said, "I'm going to find . . . the others."

Deke nodded, but said, "I wish you'd wait for me."

"I can't, Deke. I have to know."

It was his turn to respect her wishes, his turn to say "All right." He watched her walk off, looking this way and that, until she went around a barrier at the other side of the cave. Thinking he'd better quickly check Cody's wound in case she cried out at what she found and needed him, Deke opened the boy's shirt as carefully as he could, what with Cody rousing and thrashing some now, and found the wound. Heaving a sigh of relief and speaking soothingly to Cody, Deke saw that the entry wound was higher than he'd originally thought; it was more toward Cody's shoulder than his chest. Probing around on Cody's shoulder, but trying not to move him, Deke found the exit wound. Good. A clean shot. Thinking to call out to Sara, to reassure her, he turned his head and opened his mouth, only to be looking at Jim Dalton standing over him, looking a little numb.

"How is he?"

"He's coming around. Got hit in the shoulder."

Jim nodded. Deke looked at him; his face was bruised, his mouth cut, his eye swollen. He hadn't even heard him walk up. Six weeks ago he'd have been standing over this man's body, glad for his death, but now he heard himself asking, "You okay, Jim?"

"Yeah, I believe so," he said, rubbing his head. "The last thing I remember is going at it with Jack Bennett. But then someone knocked me on my head with a gun or a rock or something. When I came to, it was all over. Travis said it was Bennett, and that he shot him, but got hit, too—in the leg, but he'll be okay. He's back there bandaging it up now."

Deke nodded as Jim talked, thankful for their unbelievable luck. Everyone seemed to be okay, except for Cody, and even his wound wasn't life-threatening. So everyone was accounted for. Good. And the five outlaws were all dead. Even better. Approaching footsteps turned both men's heads. It was Sara; she stopped, as if unsure she should approach, as if unsure of what she was seeing.

Jim laughed. "I'm okay, Sara. It's really me; I'm not a ghost. You can hug me."

With a cry of relieved delight, she launched herself into her brother's arms. After checking Jim over to be sure he really was alive, she asked, "Where's Travis?"

"Right here," he said, limping up from behind them, his right thigh roughly bandaged with a strip obviously torn from his shirt. He lowered himself painfully to his younger brother's side after Sara gave him a quick embrace. His own chin working convulsively, he smoothed the hair out of Cody's face. Seeing Cody open his pain-glazed eyes and turn his head towards him, Travis said, "You're going to make it, boy; just you hold on. That damned Abe Diamond shot you, but it's more of a flesh wound than anything. He paid for it, Cody. The kid shot him. Quickest draw I ever saw." Cody nodded, closing his eyes. Travis looked up, a frown etching the deep pain lines to either side of his mouth. "Anybody seen Red?"

"I forgot all about him," Deke said as he got up—too fast. He grabbed for the barrier and held on for a second until the cave quit spinning. Sara came immediately to his side and wrapped his arm around her shoulder, putting her own around his waist. Accepting her support, Deke turned to Jim and Travis, saying, "Stay here with Cody. You got any medical supplies in this cave? Good. Start working on him. Clean yourselves up, too. Sara and I'll go get the horses and look for Red. There's no telling how soon the other men who took off will be back, and I think the last thing we need right now is another fight on our hands—"

Approaching horses cut off Deke's words. Looks were exchanged, but no words were spoken. It was best just to be quiet until they saw who it was. From the sounds of the slow, careful plodding up the path that led to this cave, whoever it was showed no signs of hurry. Guns were grabbed by those able and positions resumed, all eyes fixed on the trail to the cave, bathed now in bright moonlight which shone through a break in the tall pines.

"Hey, inside the cave. Don't shoot! It's me, Red, and I got the horses—lots of 'em, too. Is it okay if I come in?"

Everyone slumped. "I can't make up my mind if I want to kiss him or kill him," Travis commented in his off-handed, dry way. Everyone else laughed. Shaking his head, Travis called out, "Get in here, Red. Where the hell you been?"

"Gettin' the horses, like I said. I tell you, there ain't another soul out here but us. If this don't beat all. So I brought these here dead men's horses, too. We can use 'em to haul their carcasses in to the law, huh, Deke?" Red chirped, coming into view with his huge grin unstoppered and trailing a veritable remuda of horses, all saddled, Deke's and Sara's among them. Admonishing Cody to stay put, the others moved outside to help with the horses.

Preoccupied with the thought that it seemed he hadn't seen his buckskin stallion for days, Deke dismissed the boy's chatter, simply nodding his answer, as glad as he was to see the kid unharmed and apparently unconcerned about having killed his first man. When Deke attempted to run his hands over his mount to check him for problems, he was surprised to realize that the buckskin kept laying his ears back, as if displeased at being included in something as common as a string of horses. Laughing, Deke untied him, but the irate stallion side-stepped and pulled against the reins, his wide nostrils flaring in contempt. Red's running by him, yelling out that he would get the burros, did nothing to improve the buckskin's temper.

Soothing his mount, Deke talked low to him—and then he remembered. He looked down at Sara beside him as she worried over Cinnamon. Only she wasn't worrying over Cinnamon. She was looking up at him. And her face plainly said she hadn't forgotten what he'd said before the fight. Jeez, they'd all nearly been killed only a few minutes ago, but he apparently would be held to his promise to name his horse.

"Okay, okay, I remember," he conceded, making a great show of thinking of a name while he stroked the buckskin's velvet nose. Seeing the confused looks on Jim's and Travis's faces as he kept shifting his weight from one foot to the other and crossing and recrossing his arms, Deke informed them, "I have to name my horse."

As one, as if they'd rehearsed it, they both asked, "Why?"

Laughing, at considerable expense to his head, Deke turned to Sara. "See?"

"I don't care, Deke Bonner. We have two hundred things to do yet tonight—uppermost is seeing about Cody—so you just go right ahead and name him. No matter what they say," she finished, pointing at Jim and Travis, both of whom immediately adopted what-did-I-do looks.

"All right, all right, bossy. Uhmmm . . . Buttercup."

"You can't name your horse Buttercup." It was Jim.

"My horse," Deke contended. Jim nodded, allowing as how that was so.

"He doesn't look like any buttercup I ever saw," Travis threw out, pulling at the bandage around his thigh.

"Deke Bonner, you're not naming that huge stallion Buttercup. He'll never be able to hold his head up—"

"Speaking of holding up a head, Miss Dalton, I believe the name Warrior is taken. Am I right?"

Deke's reward for daring to mention her name for his member was a burst of red on her cheeks and a stammering response to her brother's question, "Who's Warrior?"

Deke relented and rescued her—sort of. "Warrior is the name for another pony Sara likes to ride sometimes, right, Sara?"

Absolutely squawking with embarrassment now, Sara took off at a fast clip into the cave. He made sure his teasing laughter followed her, no matter his headache as he just shook his head and waved off her brother's and cousin's questioning glances. Served little Miss Bossy right, Deke thought, as he hurried in after her to make sure she wasn't mad, but all the while telling himself that he needed to check on Cody, too. Maybe one day he'd tell her that his horse's real name, chosen because the first time they'd made love had been in a tepee, was Cheyenne.

Despite their intentions to ride out after the fight, two days later saw them all still at the cave—even Red, whose loyalty and bravery had earned him the status of family with the Daltons, although he made it obvious that he much preferred tagging around after Deke, to everyone's amusement except Deke's. Too, they'd all had a good laugh at Red's reaction to being told he was the one who killed Abe Diamond. Apparently he hadn't realized it in the thick of the battle, so when Travis told him, he promptly passed out.

The night of the battle, Sara had turned the cave into a hospital of sorts, seeing to her cousins's and Deke's wounds, forcing everyone to rest, feeding them too much, and generally clucking over them until, to the men's utter relief, she finally gave in and collapsed into an exhausted sleep that lasted all the next day. More alive on this, the second day, the men began moving around more, stretching stiff muscles, testing a wounded leg or arm. But they found they still tired quickly, still needed plenty of rest and good food and Sara's mothering. Only once had the matter of the bounty come up, but it was immediately shelved until everyone felt stronger, with Travis drawing a laugh from them all by asking Deke to wait until they were better before he killed them.

And so, relieved of that weighty matter for the moment, they settled in at the cave. Surprisingly, only a few other denizens, all silently professing not to want any part of trouble with the Daltons or Deke Bonner, crept back in to claim their ledges and keep to themselves.

Welcome respite though this was, Sara still felt an itchy need—despite the huge bounty hunter's embarrassing her about Warrior—to be alone with him. Only she couldn't come up with any reason to send everyone out. And she couldn't come up with any reason that didn't look suspect for her and Deke to wander off alone and that wouldn't end up with Red trailing after them. Her few attempts at oblique suggestion had fallen on blank stares from Deke. Men could be so frustrating, she fussed, while going through a medical kit, sorting out what she needed to change Cody's bandage. Preoccupied with that, she jumped when someone touched her shoulder. It was Deke's face she was looking into when she glanced up.

"Why don't you let Travis change Cody's bandage, Sara? I thought maybe you and I could, uh, go for a walk. Or something. Maybe take our horses and the burros to that big meadow a ways from here to graze. Let them kick up their heels some."

She knew exactly what he meant and was thrilled, but two could play at oblique. "Well, goodness, Deke, I don't know. I have so much to do here. Perhaps you ought to get Red to go with you."

Deke's face clouded over. "I don't want Red to go with me. I want you to go with me."

Sara tsk-tsked. "Deke Bonner, you sound like a petulant child. Why on earth—?" It was hard to maintain one's dignity, much less one's tone of voice, when one was being hauled up by one's arm, trailing a long swathe of bandage.

"Dammit, Sara. I want you to go. And I don't feel the least bit like a child right now. I've sent Red off on some made-up errand for me, and Jim and Travis are just sitting over there resting—"

"—As you should be, too. You know your head isn't—"

"My head is fine. So's my arm. Now, will you go with me or not?"

Sara relented, grinning. "Of course I'll go with you. I thought you'd never ask."

"What?"

"Nothing. I'll put some food in that cloth bag over there,

and we can eat while the horses graze; how does that sound?''

''Delicious,'' he said, saying the word as if it were a death sentence. ''Get it together fast, before my shadow returns, and I'll take this stuff here to Travis and Jim.'' With that, he took the partially unrolled bandage from her, grabbed up the remainder of the kit, and strode purposefully over to Jim and Travis.

Sara giggled at his hurrying, but quickly set out to gather together a picnic lunch, poking whatever edible thing she found into the sack, and feeling suddenly very lighthearted, almost giddy, at the prospect of this interlude with Deke. It had been so long.

Chapter Twenty-nine

The meadow was absolutely enchanted. Long, tender grass, sweet clover, and wildflowers in sparkling jewel tones called to the horses and the burros the way a playground calls to children outside a schoolhouse. Once the horses were unsaddled and the burros untied, they all took off in a wild gambol that greatly resembled a child's game of tag. Flying tails and manes were the order of the sun-dappled afternoon. Only Little Ned, still jerky and unsteady, looked to be all elbows and knees as he tried his valiant best to keep up with his mother. Despite their intense desire to be in each other's arms, Sara and Deke spared the little foal an indulgent laugh.

Then Sara bent to the task of opening their blanket and spreading out their food. But Deke's hand stopped her. She looked up questioningly, seeing that hooded, intense look that sent ripples of tightening desire through her.

"No," he said softly. "We'll eat later, Sara. Right now I need you more than I need food, or even air."

With that, he took her in his arms for a searing kiss that

should have set the meadow ablaze—and did set Sara on fire. It was hard to tell who was the aggressor, who was doing what to whom as clothes seemed to melt away, and who was more eager, more fevered to feel the other one's bare skin. Sara closed her eyes, allowed a wanton smile to ride her lips, and gave herself up to the pure enjoyment of Deke's strong hands caressing her from head to toe as she stood gloriously naked before him on the blanket in the warm sunshine. He moved over her, kissing a breast, stroking a thigh, teasing a nibbling bite on her ribs, and probing her woman's place with fingertips moistened first in his own mouth, which drew from Sara a sound at the back of her throat that was as primal as the forest that surrounded them.

She was sure she couldn't stand erect another second, being so weak with desire, but then Deke, himself as naked as Adam, knelt before her and drew her to him, holding her by her buttocks. When he sent his tongue swirling around the cup that was her navel, Sara threw her head back, feeling the sun on her face and her hair a warm cascade of silvery curls that brushed down her back and over Deke's hands. Beyond willing pleasure, she stroked Deke's thick, black hair, ran her hands lightly over the planes of his face, and stroked his broad, sun-warmed shoulders. Then a gasp rippled through her when Deke lowered himself to his haunches to bring his tongue to the level of her feminine mound. With her standing in front of him, held fast to him by his hands cupping her firm buttocks, Deke probed the protective curls, found her flame, then licked and stroked and kissed her until she erupted into shuddering paroxysms of requited desire. Her eyes rolled back, the lids twitching as she clutched at his hair. As her knees buckled, Deke eased her down and pulled her under him, the evidence of his desire fairly dancing with anticipation at the entrance to her womb.

So ready for him that she could not hurry him enough, Sara very nearly pulled him into her before he was positioned above her. His deep chuckle of appreciation of this evidence of her great need for him only netted him a brutal kiss as she pulled his head down to hers, claimed his mouth, wrapped her legs around him, and began the rhythm of romance that would dance them through the ritual of love. So deep was her need for him that she almost wasn't aware of him, if that were possible. So exquisite was her yearning for his body that she very nearly didn't give him a chance to participate; she was greedy, thinking only of herself as she rocked to and fro, up and down, seeking her own pleasure, her own satiety. Probably later she would have to apologize to him for using him so, but now . . . no, not now. He'd just have to understand.

Then the inevitable swept over her again, sending heat to her face, curling her toes, and wringing that deep sound from the back of her throat that pitched Deke up and over her even more, that tensed him in position there, made the cords stand out on his neck, closed his eyes, and put an intense grimace of concentration and surfeited desire on his face. Then he collapsed over her, breathing her name, not even sparing her his weight as his sweat-sheened body slipped on hers. As they lay there for several minutes, gasping, hearts pounding, Sara found that she didn't care at all that his crushing weight covered her, but still she pushed against him to gain his compliance with her wish for him to be on his back. She just couldn't get close enough to him, couldn't taste him enough, couldn't feel his muscled body enough, or run her fingers through the crisp and curling hair on his chest enough.

Happy, sated, but still throbbing with desire, Sara bent over Deke to renew her acquaintance with every inch of him. This time, there was no hesitation on his part for her to do as she wished with his body. In fact, he smiled lazily down at her as she kissed her way down his chest and abdomen, and gave himself up to her caressing ministrations. He must now trust her to know what she doing and how to do it, she mused, even as she reached down to stroke Warrior back into an angry state, back into a warlike stance that would see him invade her willing body. Fascinating as it was to her to watch the power her touch had over such a strong, powerful man, Sara was now ready to advance the game.

She looked up into Deke's black eyes to see them hooded, questioning. What are you going to do now, Sara Dalton? he seemed to ask. Sara accepted the challenge and moved over him to straddle his hips. He gasped out a groan and held Sara around her waist as she leaned forward to reach under herself to position Warrior. Then, slowly, deliciously, with her hands on his shoulders, she pushed and settled herself on the velvet-hard length that sparked tiny shivers along her nerve endings. And then she was impaled. She threw her head forward, sending her hair dancing feather-soft over Deke's chest. It was his turn to make little noises at the back of his throat.

This was so delicious, so mouth-drying, just being one with him, that Sara didn't move. Deke lazily opened his eyes and, in a husky voice, asked, "What now, Sara?"

She could hardly think, what with his fingertips raking gently over her buttocks and then around in front to the dark-silver hair that covered her delicate vee and that now mingled with the black hair that was Warrior's nest. "I . . . uhmmm, that feels good . . . I don't know. You'll have to help me. I can't seem to get . . . ."

Deke's gentle, teasing laugh stopped her words and only increased her squirming and wiggling in an honest effort to get the pleasurable rhythm down. "How do you do this?" she asked, desperation edging her voice. This wasn't working.

Deke laughed aloud and relented, holding her hard to him with his thumbs on her pelvic bones and his fingers clasping her buttocks. "Like this," he offered, using his powerful hips to rock them gently in the correct direction, but never overpowering Sara's first attempts to learn the motion herself. And she proved to be a quick student, almost instantly picking up the eons-old dance of entwined lovers. She then took over from Deke, pressed her palms again to his shoulders, closed her eyes, and rode them to a place where only

they existed, where only their awareness of each other con-
stituted their universe, until the starry bursts of effort re-
warded shook them like rag dolls, pitched them convulsively
against each other, and wrung every drop of pleasurable
emotion from them.

Sara understood now why Deke pitched forward onto her
at the end of their lovemaking. It was because his bones had
melted temporarily, she decided, as she lay on him limply
with her damp head on his glistening chest, her hands to
either side of his ribs. Her legs still straddled him—much
like a frog's, she thought with a giggle.

"Oh, lordy, don't tell me that giggle means 'again,' girl.
You're going to kill me," Deke groaned, shifting position
and brushing Sara's damp, clinging hair off her back to let
the breeze cool her.

She laughed a quick chuckle, causing her muscles to tense
around his shaft again. Deke jerked; Sara, a grin on her face
that he couldn't see, then purposely worked the powerful
muscles that held Deke in her. He jerked again. "Don't make
me laugh, bounty hunter. You can't take it," she said while
stroking his powerful bicep and marveling at the leashed
strength in every muscle and sinew of his perfectly formed
male body.

"Oh, I can't take it, eh, Miss Dalton? Well, we'll just see
about that."

A startled squeal wrung from Sara at that instant stopped
Deke's tickling her; he gripped her arms as she lay on his
chest. "Sara, what's wrong?"

"Shush!" Sara warned him, putting a hand over his mouth
as she concentrated on what she was feeling behind her. She
cut her eyes this way and that, trying to relive what she was
sure she couldn't have just felt. Removing her hand from his
mouth, in a scared little whisper, she said, "Someone—
something just licked my foot."

"What?" His loud voice netted him Sara's hand clamped
back over his mouth. He pulled it down and whispered, "Did
you say someone licked your foot?"

"Yes," Sara whispered, near hysteria, her hands fists, her forehead to his chest. "You look; I can't."

"For the love of—" Deke muttered, but he moved her cautiously to one side and raised his head to look down toward their feet. Sara looked up questioningly, fearfully, only to see him do a double-take and let loose a gut-wrenching, belly-busting laugh that split the air and toppled Sara right off him onto the blanket. He rolled to his side and beat at the blanket while he hollered out his glee.

Well, it wasn't half so funny to Sara. Squawking like a wet hen, she immediately rolled to a sitting position, her arms outstretched behind her to brace herself, her knees bent, only to come face-to-face with her assailant. "Little Ned! Why, you little dickens, you!" she cried out, lobbing an ineffectual handful of grass at the baby burro, whose face reflected his intense dislike for the taste of salty human flesh. His tongue licked in and out disgustedly as he backed away. "And you," Sara railed, turning on Deke and thumping his back with her open palm. "What are you laughing at?"

"Your face—" was all the bounty hunter could squeeze out between gusts of laughter as he rolled onto his back and pointed at her.

"Shut up!" Sara warned, her voice an octave higher. "Quit laughing!" When he didn't, she launched herself on him in a belly flop that whooshed the air out of him and got her pinned under him when he grabbed her and rolled over, straddling her, knees bent, in a position that mimicked hers of only a moment ago. Sara stilled and playfully teased, "All right, Mr. Bonner, don't say I didn't warn you!" She turned her head and called out, "Here, Neddy, Neddy, Neddy! Here, boy! See how you like bounty hunter feet. Here, boy."

But Neddy had already spooked and fled to his mother's side. He now stood across the meadow, as close to a grazing Miss Petunia as he could get, and looked back at them as if half-afraid they'd followed him. Sara and Deke, still locked in their loving and playful embrace, laughed at the foal's antics and then looked into each other's eyes. And the afternoon warmed up considerably once again.

"Sara, I've made a decision about something, and I want you to be the first one to know what it is."

Sara looked up from her supper plate that evening at Deke when he spoke. He looked so serious that she had trouble swallowing the bite of biscuit she'd just taken. Choking it down past the lump in her throat, she slowly lowered her tin plate to the cave floor. "What about?"

"It's about your brothers—the bounty."

Sara's heart froze and then began pounding. But still she found the courage to ask, "Yes?"

"I don't want it. I couldn't accept money on them, so I'm not going to turn them in."

Sara felt the hot tears flood her eyes. Deke, sitting across from her at the campfire, wavered in her watery vision. She couldn't say anything.

Deke looked down briefly and then went on. "I've, uh, been thinking about this—about us—and have made my decision. I'm going to tear up the bounty." He looked as if he was going to say more, but instead he paused, running a hand over his tortured expression.

Sara bit at her bottom lip to keep from sobbing aloud. She'd prayed all along for him to just ride away, just forget the bounty on her brother's head. And now he was. Still, she had to know something else. "What about—what about your mother's and sister's deaths, Deke? Can you live with thinking that my—?"

"Killing your family won't bring mine back. It's time I let go of that, if I ever want any kind of peace in my life. So, I just can't turn them in. It wouldn't solve anything." He fell silent for a moment, then went on. "There's something else you should know. This doesn't mean I'm quitting bounty hunting, because that's my life now. And I sure as hell intend to collect the money on Dawson, Coleman, and the rest, even the stolen money and guns. Red said he'd help me get everything to Fort Smith to a marshal friend of mine there. Those bastards deserved to die—and more. I still think they got off too easily. A quick bullet is—what's wrong, Sara?''

As she covered her face with her hands, no longer able to hold back the flood of emotion that overwhelmed her, Sara gave in to the torrent of salty tears that had been building up as Deke spoke. She heard a scraping on the cave floor that told her he was moving over to her. He gripped her shoulder, but Sara was too overcome to look up just yet. She'd succeeded in changing his mind, something she'd not thought possible six weeks ago. So why did she feel so awful? Because she'd won her family, but had lost Deke. According to his words, they'd go their separate ways now, resume their separate lives.

Then Sara knew the truth: The love she held in her heart for Deke Bonner would have to be enough to last her the rest of her life, even if he weren't in it. He could ride off, but he couldn't make her stop loving him. And that was a victory of sorts. Besides, she had something else to thank him for right now. With a watery smile, she threw her arms around his neck, startling him into reflexively returning her hug. Into his shirt collar, with her head nuzzled into his neck, she murmured, ''Thank you, Deke. Thank you for Jim and Cody and Travis.''

''Hey, don't cry,'' he soothed, rubbing his large hand up and down her back, pulling her more securely into his embrace. ''I thought you'd be happy.''

''I am,'' she said, choking past a hiccupping sigh.

Deke chuckled and kissed the top of her head. ''There's more we need to talk about, then. I don't think I have to tell you, Sara, that my not turning your kin in doesn't end their problems.''

Sara nodded and pulled away from him, pulled the bandanna from his shirt pocket, blew her nose with it, and put it in her skirt pocket. She saw Deke's bemused expression as he watched her, but thought nothing of it as she told him,

"I know they're still wanted men, and I know there will be other bounty hunters, other lawmen who will hunt them. But at least now it isn't you—Deke Bonner, the best of them all—who's after them. To me, that means they can safely come home to see Momma now."

"Yes, they can, but then, they always could," Deke told her, sounding the least bit sour; or was it defeated? Sara frowned when he looked away, huffed out a sigh, and shook his head slightly. What had she said to make him look like this? Then he turned back to her, his eyes black and fathomless, like a snake's, and said, "You probably meant that as a compliment to me, didn't you—about being the best at bounty hunting? Don't expect me to thank you, Sara. Doing what I do is a lousy thing that eats at a man's soul. With every man, dead or alive, I turn in, I die a little right along with him."

Sara's heart pounded, chastising her. She'd never known how he felt about what he did. He'd always seemed to hunt men, even kill them, with a cold calculation that was terrifying to behold. Which made this confession from him all the more poignant. What agonies of the soul he must endure. But now, finally, he was letting her in—he was sharing his soul with her. She doubted he'd ever said to another person what he'd just told her. "I'm sorry, Deke. I didn't know," was all she could offer as she shook her head slowly and blinked back tears of pure compassion, one human to another.

"That's because I never told you." Then he changed the subject back to her brothers, nodding his head in their direction outside the cave. "What about them, Sara? Do they go back to this life, this running, this fear? You heard them—they want to go home. And I don't think they mean just for a visit."

Sara looked past Deke, thinking about that, wondering why she'd never seen beyond their coming home to see Momma one last time. It occurred to her that Deke, more than she did, seemed to have their best interests at heart. She was then forced to accept that this whole trip, beyond her telling them about Momma, had been a selfish act of hers. She turned her head to look outside the cave to the men she loved most in the world—after Deke Bonner. Her chin began to quiver; would this nightmare never end?

She'd thought before that she would just order them to turn themselves in, to face the law and be done with it, to take their chances, do a little time in prison, and then come home to run the farm. It sounded simple, but now that the possibility presented itself, she knew in her heart that she could not bear to see them locked up, maybe forever. Ashamed, she looked down at her hands in her calico-covered lap, her fingers all twined together. How selfish could she be—demanding they give up their freedom because she was tired of trying to run the farm?

When Deke reached out to stroke a silver tress out of her face, Sara turned her gaze back to him. "Don't be too hard on yourself," he said, as if he knew exactly what she was thinking. But didn't he always? "Why don't we get them in here and see what they plan to do? After all, it's their decision—not yours, and not mine."

Sara nodded mutely and rose to her feet, knowing that Deke was right and that she too would have to live with their decision, whether it was to continue to run or to turn themselves in. She swallowed hard, feeling herself age with every step she took toward the cave's mouth. A sense of all their futures being decided by this one conversation closed in on her, much like the walls of the cave, which was both haven and prison.

A few minutes later, when they were all seated around the campfire, Sara found she couldn't put her thoughts into words. She'd asked them to come in to discuss what to do from here, saying there was no reason now to stay here. They were all now rested and strong enough to leave as early as tomorrow morning. At her words, Jim and Travis had stopped their currying of their horses, looked at her, at each other, and then at Cody, his arm in a sling and sitting next to Red on a rock and watching them. Without a word, they'd somberly dropped the curry brushes and entered the cave, nodding to Deke and taking their seats, turning expectant faces to him, much as if he were their elected leader.

"I've just told Sara that I'm not going to turn you three in for the bounty," Deke said, putting a direct, blunt edge on the conversation.

"But we want you to turn us in, Deke. We've talked about it. It's the only way. We're tired of running, of not being able to go home. We're not like those others. We want the running to be over,'' Jim said, startling Deke and Sara.

Sara nearly came to her feet in her agitation. "What are you saying, Jim? You can't! You—''

"Sara!" Jim ordered, grabbing her stunned attention and continuing, almost brutally. "We can, and we will. It's not your decision, Sis. It's ours."

Sara crumpled into herself and couldn't even turn to Deke when he put a consoling arm around her shoulders. To hear Jim say exactly what Deke had said only moments earlier— that this decision was theirs, not hers or his—made her family's fate all that more real, all that more dire. The thought of them behind bars nearly crushed her, but not as much as the image of them maybe hanging for murdering the Coopers, their neighbors in Plains.

"Sara, listen up, girl. We want you to hear this, too." He then turned to Deke. "We've got more to say—about your kin, Mr. Bonner, and about us being with the likes of Abe Diamond and Phelps and Dawson," Travis said.

"I'm listening," Deke told them, his voice carefully controlled, as if he were steeling himself for something awful.

"The truth is," Jim began, "that we didn't kill your mother and sister, Deke. It was Dawson and Phelps."

Sara felt Deke go rigid. "The papers said it was the Daltons."

"I know that," Jim allowed. "And that's because they forced us to go with them on their jobs, to be seen around a town before they robbed a bank so we'd be blamed for their doings, so the law would be on us and not them."

"How could they force you?" Sara interrupted, her knitted brow a clear sign of her incredulity. "You're grown men!"

Cody answered her. "Yeah, but my mother, you and your momma, and Olivia and Robert aren't. They said they'd ride up to Plains and kill all of you, if we didn't front for them. And you met them, so you know they'd do just what they said."

Deke, who had been sitting thoughtfully beside Sara, spoke up now. "You're telling me that when I killed Phelps, I killed one of the men who shot my mother and sister, and Sara killed Dawson—the other one?"

"I guess so," Jim remarked. "If that don't beat all. But Deke, I have to tell you, we were there that day in Independence, but we were outside the bank, just holding the horses. We didn't even know about them being killed until others drifted in here and started talking about it. I suppose that makes us guilty in a way. I—I hope you can forgive us and accept that we're mighty sorry."

All eyes went to Deke. He rubbed his closed eyes with his thumb and index finger, sniffed once, and looked over at Jim. "I suppose I can—if you can forgive your sister for bringing a bounty hunter here. I can assure you that she had no more choice in the matter than you all did with those other men."

The Daltons nodded at Deke and then smiled gamely at Sara. But Cody had more questions. "Yeah, that's another thing—how did you two come to be riding together?"

Deke laughed out loud. "That's a long story, son. Maybe Sara will tell it to you one day." Then he turned serious. "Look, I think I've come up with a plan while we've been sitting here. It might work, but it's up to you because all the risk would be yours. You want me to turn you in, and I have to take those bodies to Fort Smith anyway, which is where the marshal is who issued the bounties on you three. I was thinking we could ride together into Fort Smith, instead of parting ways now and you going on home just yet. And when we get there, I'll speak for you with Judge Parker.''

At the name of Judge Parker, everyone stilled, fear and dread on their faces. He was notoriously tough, the only law for hundreds of miles around. He'd purposely moved his court to Fort Smith in an effort to bring swift justice to the lawless western lands. No one who went before him came away unscathed. Sara looked at Deke; he was watching the Daltons, reading what was obvious in their expressions.

"No one said it would be easy," he offered into the silence, drawing their gazes back to himself. Sara looked down, unable to face the bleak, doomed looks on the faces she loved so. "But there's more," Deke continued. "And not all of it bad; at least, I don't think it is." Seeing their waiting, questioning stares, Deke continued. "The marshal I got your bounty from is a friend of mine. We served together in the Army. I think I can talk him into standing up for you, too.''

With that, Deke was finished talking. There it was—the best he could do, all laid out for them. Sara, feeling sick yet expectant, looked from one to the other of her kin as they exchanged silent glances. As always, it was Jim who spoke for them. "We got no choice. That's the best we can do. We appreciate everything you're doing for us—and for Sara."

She smiled at her brother, who sniffed in a manly way and frowned his face to look fierce.

The next morning, after being held in Deke's arms all that night, a bittersweet interlude in the few days they had left together, Sara turned in her saddle to look at their party as they rode out of the Robber's Cave area and picked up the well-worn trail to Fort Smith, Arkansas, a trip that could be accomplished, with hard riding, in only a few days. But it would take them longer, needing as they did to consider Cody's and Jim's wounds, and of course, Little Ned, who was just a baby who tired easily. Sara figured that the playful foal would end up draped over someone's saddle as soon as he lagged behind, since he tended to just stop and plant his feet when he tired, and then bray out his intention to go no farther.

If the future for all of them was uncertain, at least the present was comforting for Sara, surrounded as she was by loved ones—yes, even Red, more like a kid brother to her now than anything else. And she still marveled at how much Deke and Jim looked alike. She found herself wishing her mother could see those two side by side. Sara felt a pang at the thought of her mother. Please, God, she prayed, let her be alive when we get home. She looked back over her shoulder to see Travis and Cody behind her, then Deke and Jim. Behind them was Red with the horses that carried the dead, trussed-up outlaws and the stolen money and guns that Deke intended to turn in for the bounty. And behind those horses came a sleepy-eyed, waddling Miss Petunia with her foal, the contrary Little Ned, right on her heels. What a sight they made. Once again, Sara felt her love for them all surge into her heart. Now if only Deke's marshal friend and the infamous Judge Parker could feel the same toward them.

Chapter Thirty

"Deke Bonner, you old son-of-a-bitch! Back in Fort Smith already? Hell, I didn't expect to see you so soon. Don't tell me you brought the Daltons in already." U.S. Marshal Jake Coltrane stood up from the chair behind his office desk and put his hand out to his friend.

"Jake," Deke returned the greeting, smiling and heartily clasping the young marshal's hand. "Yeah, I have them with me. They're all alive, too. Found them at Robber's Cave. And a few others into the bargain."

After a stunned silence, the marshal sat down heavily, signaling for Deke to sit in the chair opposite his desk. "A few others, too? What'd you do—just ride in and kill everybody there? Or did you have inside help?" Jake's blue eyes sparked with respect and friendship.

Deke sat, then smiled a twisted grin. "Jake, my friend, you're not going to believe this one."

About two hours later, Jake Coltrane knew the whole story. And couldn't believe it. He raked a large, lean hand through black curling hair and looked askance at the bounty hunter sitting on the other side of his cluttered desk. Sitting back in his chair, he put his booted feet on top of the stacks of paperwork piled atop his desk and finally did something besides shake his head and stare. He said, "You've got to be kidding me."

"I assure you, Jake, I'm not."

"The sister of the Dalton gang, Deke? The sister?"

Deke uncrossed his long legs and sat forward in his chair, taking his Stetson off and setting it atop another stack of papers on the marshal's desk. Deciding to ignore the younger man's questions, Deke remarked casually, "When are you going to clean this desk off? It looked just like this the last time I was through here."

Jake waved the question away with a casual, dismissive gesture of his hand. "I hate this damned paperwork. I didn't train to sit behind a desk. I've put in for field work, something to sharpen my skills again, before I get fat and lazy."

"Like what?" Deke asked, thinking of the years of work and training this sharp, dedicated young man had during the war. A finer officer he'd never served with. The kid, as Deke thought of him, since he was six years younger than Deke's thirty, was an absolutely ruthless warrior when on the scent, though. And a devil with the ladies, but he'd always bragged that he'd never succumb to love. Love made you weak, he always said, left you open, made you slow. Deke wondered what Jake thought of him now that he'd told him about Sara.

"Like what? Well, it seems some gun runners out in No Man's Land have taken to ambushing army supply routes, killing the men, and taking the crates of Colts, which keep turning up in Mexico. That's what we need—another war. I believe I'll be working that undercover. But, hell, how hard can it be to catch a gang of gun runners? Say, did you hear anything about that when you were out that way?"

Deke thought for a moment, but then shook his head. "No, I can't say that I did. But I'll keep my ears open."

"Can't ask for more than that. Now, tell me about Miss

Sara Dalton. What are you going to do about her? You know my theory on love, don't you?''

Deke laughed and sat back. "Yes, I do, Coltrane. But you just wait—it'll happen to you one day. When you least expect it—boom, you'll be struck."

Jake brought his chair legs down hard and leaned over toward Deke, peering at him over the paper stacks, and smiled the smile that Deke had repeatedly seen melt more than one young lady's resolve. "I hardly think so, Bonner. Where I'm going—No Man's Land, out on the Cimarron Crossing—there's not too many young ladies to choose from."

Deke couldn't resist. "Son, it only takes one."

"What did he say?" Sara asked the second she opened the door to their hotel room and dragged Deke inside, closing the door behind him. "Did he say he would help? What did he think?"

"Whoa, Sara! One question at a time," Deke begged, holding a hand up to stop her tirade. He sat in an upholstered chair by the window, took his Stetson off, laid it on the small table to one side of the chair, and rubbed a hand over his forehead.

Sara relented in her pacing, seeing how tired he looked, seeing the lines to either side of his mouth deepen. "I'm sorry, Deke. I'm just so scared about this. Anything could happen with them hidden outside of town; anybody could find them and turn them in before you—oh, Deke! Jim and Cody and Travis could hang!"

"Stop right there!" The hand was up again. "Now settle down. Sit over there on the bed and listen to me." He stopped, obviously waiting for her to comply.

Almost stomping her foot in frustration—he'd been gone for hours!—she flounced over to the narrow bed and flopped on it, sending her new rose-colored gabardine overskirt into a puffing cloud of fabric around her. She'd been so worried while he was talking with the marshal that she'd gone shopping at the mercantile while she waited. She'd wanted to surprise him with how nice she looked and had even managed to twist her hair up in a sort of arrangement—anything to make it harder for him to walk away—but now she found that all she cared about was her kin's fate. New clothes suddenly seemed silly in light of what they were faced with. "Okay, go on," she prodded.

But he didn't say anything; he was too busy looking her up and down, as if he'd never seen her before. "Is that new?"

Sara huffed impatiently and grabbed a handful of skirt. "What? This old thing? Of course it's new, Deke Bonner! Now tell me about my brothers! Is your friend going to help or not?"

Deke shook his head and refocused on her face. "Yes, he's going to help. You look beautiful."

With a squeal, Sara jumped up and threw her arms around Deke's neck, then sat on his lap, squirming around and covering his face with tiny kisses and laughing out loud.

"Remind me to tell you more often how beautiful you look," Deke quipped, looking very charmed indeed to have his arms full of an eager woman. He reached around to cup a firm breast.

Sara jumped up and turned on him, her hands at her nipped-in waist. "Not that, Deke Bonner. I'm excited about your friend—what's his name?—helping us."

"Jake Coltrane," Deke answered, looking at her now with clear amusement.

"What did he say? What can he do? Oh, Deke, speak up!"

Deke just looked at her, as if she might be dangerous. "All right, Miss Bossy. Jake said he will go with us to see Judge Parker tomorrow. I told him we're at this hotel—"

"Did you tell him everything—about how the Coopers killed my father and brother?"

"Yes, I did. Then I—"

"Did you tell him about my mother?"

"Yes, I did. Then I—"

"Did you tell him about how those awful men used my brother and cousins?"

"Yes, I did. Then I—"

"Well? Then you what?"

"I was waiting for you to interrupt me again."

"I did not interrupt you."

"Oh. My mistake."

"Well? Go on!"

"That's it, Sara, for crying out loud. The man said he would help. Now, if you'll excuse me, I'd like to go the bathhouse and then maybe have a drink or two. It's been a long afternoon, and I'm tired. We're going to supper this evening with Jake. He wants to meet you."

"Damn," Jake Coltrane said. Dressed in a black suit, embroidered vest, and white shirt, he smiled down into Sara's radiant face that evening in the hotel lobby.

"That's the marshal's way of saying nice to meet you," Deke, in new finery similar to Jake's, said dryly, his hand protectively on Sara's arm, since he didn't like for a minute the silly grin she was giving the handsome young man.

"Oh, I see," Sara cooed in answer to Deke's explanation. "Then, damn to you, too, Marshal."

Deke drew up, startled at her words, but Jake laughed out loud. With that, he ushered them out of the lobby and led them across the well-lit street to the restaurant. With Jake on one side of Sara and Deke on the other, Jake said, over her head, "This explains a lot, my friend. She's beautiful, just like you said."

"Don't get her started," Deke muttered, remembering that afternoon's conversation.

"You better hurry up and marry this woman, Bonner, before I do," Jake offered, his smile showing white, even teeth.

Deke looked down, saw Sara's widened eyes, and read a whole book into her sudden silence. He then frowned down to his chin; had Jake Coltrane always been this irritating, and had he just not noticed it before?

Still, the handsome trio managed to get through a wonderful dinner of roast beef, buttered potatoes, fresh green beans, hot bread, even a rich cobbler, in the dining room of Folks' Boardinghouse, with no more teasing and squabbling. But Deke felt that Jake's ribbing about getting married seemed to have taken the starch out of Sara. He kept looking at her, but she wouldn't meet his gaze.

"That was delicious," Sara commented, drawing the two men's attention as she wiped at the corners of her mouth and put her napkin down. She turned to Jake. "Thank you for bringing us here, Jake. And thank you for helping us. I do appreciate your kindness."

"No thanks needed, Miss Dalton. It's enough for me that Deke believes in you and your kin. Glad to help." With that, he stood up and threw some coins on the table in payment; Deke followed suit and pulled Sara's chair out for her, taking her arm and leading her out of the noisy, bustling room and into the relative quiet of the night. Once there, Jake took his leave of them, saying, "I'll see you tomorrow morning. Try not to worry."

But before he could move two paces away, the evening quiet was shattered by the sound of someone running and yelling. Deke exchanged a glance with Jake over Sara's head, and they both pulled back their long coats and held a hand poised over the butt of their guns. The running and yelling, which sounded like only one person, was getting closer.

"Mr. Bonner! Miss Dalton!"

Hearing their infamous names being called out in the street—they had used fictitious ones at the hotel—Deke froze, as did Sara, their gazes locking. Then the call came again, close enough for them to see Red running toward them, waving his arms frantically. "Mr. Bonner! Miss Dalton! Over here!"

Jake, to one side of Deke, said, "You know that kid in the sombrero?"

"Oh, yes," Deke said resignedly, moving his hand away from his gun and allowing his coat to fall back over his holster. "That's Red; I told you about him."

"Oh, yes—tall tales, big sombrero."

"The same."

Red reached them then and promptly bent over at the waist, putting his hands on his knees, wheezing, out of breath. "I'm sure glad I found you two," he gasped. "I been lookin' for you all over town. It's about Miss Dalton's cousin, Cody. He—"

Red could say no more because Deke had reached out with one arm and hauled Red up to his side. "If you yell out our names one more time, Red, I'll cut your tongue out, you hear me?" he hissed into the boy's shocked face.

"I plumb forgot myself," he tried to whisper, but failed because of his wheezing. "I am rightfully sorry. See, I was scared because it's about Co—her cousin. He'd doin' poorly." Then Red whispered—loud enough to be heard by anyone passing by—"Jim sent me from the hideout to tell you."

Deke still glared into the boy's face, but felt Sara's desperate tuggings on his vest. He let go of the boy, told him to stay right there, and turned to Sara. "Now, Sara, calm down. He's probably just hurting from all the riding." He turned to Red, showing him a narrow-eyed glare that plainly said the boy had better back him up. "Isn't that so, Red?"

Red gulped and stammered out, "Yessir, I'm sure that's it, Miss—ma'am. Just the ridin' an' all. I'm sure he'll be fine come sun-up."

Sara looked from Red to Deke. "No, he won't, Deke. Don't you see?" she whispered urgently. "Jim wouldn't have sent Red into town if that's all it was. We've got to do something! I have to go to him."

"No!" Deke fairly bellowed, forgetting his own rule about lowered voices.

"What's wrong with him?" Jake asked Red, taking over since Deke was busy allaying Sara's fears.

"He was shot in the shoulder back at Robber's Cave," Red told him, remembering this time to whisper. Then, completely out of the blue, he asked, "Are you a real U.S. Marshal?"

Jake stared down at the star on his chest and then looked at the kid. "That would certainly explain the star, wouldn't it?" He then turned to Deke, saying, "Deke, why don't you take Sara on back to the hotel, and I'll take this one with me to get a doc I know, who'll keep his mouth shut, to go with young Red here and see to Cody. Go on up to bed. You've had a hard day." He started to turn away, but then turned back to Sara, put a warm, strong hand on her arm, and told her, "Try not to worry."

Chapter Thirty-one

That next morning, Sara sat with Deke and Jake in the quiet, otherwise empty courtroom. Jake had used his influence as a marshal attached to Judge Parker's court to arrange a special hearing for them before the day's regular docket was heard. In her head Sara kept hearing Jake's words to her from last night: Try not to worry. She'd been saying those four words over and over until they were a well-worn litany in her brain. Try not to worry, Sara. They'll be all right. Try not to worry. She blew her breath out audibly, drawing Deke's gaze to her face.

He gave her a look she could only call assessing, as if he was gauging whether or not he should tell her something. Concerned, she tugged on his sleeve and mouthed, "What?" But he only shook his head and covered her hand with his. Not knowing what to make of that, she put her hands in her lap and turned her gaze back to the front of the courtroom, allowing her mind to roam where it would. The image it presented to her was of herself sitting here between two such tall, commanding men as Deke Bonner and Jake Coltrane. How could they be so handsome, so fresh, so alert this morning?

She'd slept soundly last night, wrung out with worry, but she knew she didn't look as fresh and crisp as they did. In fact, she felt quite rumpled, as if she'd slept in her clothing. Then, without warning, a picture of her in Deke's arms, spoon-fashion, where she'd slept all night, popped into her head. She recalled his even breathing and the warm cocoon of his arms around her. They hadn't made love, hadn't even talked. It seemed that Deke had known that just to be held was what she needed. She smiled at her own expense, thinking, who would hold her after today?

A door opening to one side of the judge's bench in front of her sent Sara's frantic gaze in that direction and brought her wandering mind sharply into focus. She felt the two men, one to either side of her, sit up even straighter; she did the same, suddenly terrified because the moment was here. She bit at her bottom lip, denying that she could feel her own pulse in her ears. Instinctively, her hand sought Deke's; without even looking at her, he took it and rubbed it as if it felt cold to him. She knew she was digging her nails into his flesh, but she couldn't help it. Deke didn't seem to notice.

This was it. The moment was here. A tall, serious man in a brown uniform with a badge, obviously the bailiff, told them to stay seated, that were was a slight delay while the prisoners were being handcuffed, so the judge would be in shortly. Sara swallowed hard. Prisoners? Handcuffed? What prisoners? Wasn't this a private hearing? And weren't Jim, Travis, and Cody still at the hideout? When Deke squeezed her hand, she looked up at him and struggled to recapture her newfound strength and determination, painfully aware that both those emotions were due in too great a part to Deke's nearness and to his touch, two things she couldn't count on after today.

Again Deke gave her that look that plainly said he knew something he was withholding from her. Her heart skipped a beat, and she was filled with a sense of foreboding. Then, into the room, behind the bailiff, stepped Jim, Travis, and Cody: the Dalton gang. Handcuffed. Stunned beyond words, beyond thought, she sat there, immobile, as if she'd grown roots; but then anger, swift and wretched, caused her to jerk her hand out of Deke's. No wonder he looked guilty! Scared beyond rational thought, Sara jumped up and leaned as far over the rail as she could, her arm outstretched, crying out, "No! No! Jim, how did this happen?"

But she already knew the answer to that question. She turned on Deke just as he stood up to pull her back. But she didn't give him the chance, hitting at his chest with her fists. "You liar! You betrayed them! You lied to me! How could you? Is this why you looked at me like you knew something I didn't?"

Sara heard men yelling, heard her name coming from Jim's lips, felt someone's hands on her. But she fought against Deke as he held her and said words she, in her rage, would not listen to. She was capable only of shaking her head in a sick, sweating state of terrible knowledge.

There was nothing the bounty hunter could say that could calm her or the murderous rage that was building in her heart. Deke Bonner had betrayed her after all. She would kill him; it was that simple. How could she have trusted him— loved him? As she cried out yet again in an agony of the soul, her hair falling madly about her heaving shoulders, some of what Deke was saying to her, still with a hold on her arms, began to break through to her stunned mind.

"Sara, for God's sake, listen to me! Listen, Sara! I did not betray you. Do you hear me? I did not betray you or your family. Sara, listen!"

Through her haze, Sara was able to register the sincere look of troubled pain on his face. Something inside her directed her to hear him out. Stilling into a deadly calm, although her breath still came in rasping gasps, she listened. God help her, she still wanted to believe in Deke Bonner. When he let go of her arm to smooth her hair out of her face, she didn't flinch from his touch. She couldn't; she was too heartsick, too devastated. Yet she turned her face up to the man she loved, feeling that as she did so, she was the traitor.

Out of the corner of her eye she could see her kin and the bailiff watching them; she could see Jake, who at some point in her ravings had moved behind Deke, looking down at his hands as he ran his fingers over his hatband. She knew then that Jake Coltrane had a hand in bringing her brother and cousins in. Why couldn't she just die? It would be easier than this, easier than knowing Deke had allowed Jake to use innocent Red to lead him, a representative of the law, right to her hidden and ailing family and bring them in before they talked to the judge. After all, the three were quite a catch for any lawman, quite a coup. But where was Red? Had they had no qualms about killing the boy? How could she have been so stupid? Then Deke spoke again.

"Just listen, Sara. You were so tired last night that I didn't want to worry you. You didn't even wake up when Jake came to our door, or when I got up and left. The doctor Jake sent out with Red came back into town, found Jake, and told him Cody needed more treatment than he could give him in that dirty shack. Then Jake came to the room to see what I wanted to do. He said they'd be fine in the jail, that there was a dispensary there where Cody could be seen to. And that no one would trouble them because he would take them in himself and stay with them until time to come get us. Which is exactly what he did—he slept here at the jail. There was no trick, Sara, no betrayal. You have to believe me. I would never betray you or your kin."

Sara worked furiously through the details of Deke's speech. "You left last night?"

"Yes."

"You weren't there all night with me?"

"No."

"You helped bring Jim, Cody, and Travis in?"

"No. I just told Jake to—for Cody's sake."

"It's the truth, Sara. We came in on our own. He's not lying. It was our decision. Cody was hurting something awful. We did it for him."

Sara spun around and looked at Jim, a painful thing for her with him being handcuffed, but knowing he'd say anything, as he always had when they were growing up, to ease her pain. But then Cody and Travis, both freshly bandaged, nodded their agreement. She cocked her head at her cousins, tried to absorb that, then looked back up at Deke. "Why didn't you tell me this morning?"

"For the same reason I didn't want to tell you now. Look at you—all wild and not listening to anyone. I had to get you over here in one piece—one calm piece. Now, what would you have been like if I'd told you an hour or so ago that your family had spent the night in jail instead of out at that old abandoned shack with Red?"

"Where is Red?" Sara pointed an accusing finger at Deke.

"He's over at the livery getting the horses."

Sara didn't know what to think. She wanted desperately to believe Deke—she needed to believe him, to believe in him. But the shock of seeing the Daltons here had been too great. Her shoulders slumped. "I don't know. I just don't know. I want to believe you, Deke, I do, but I—"

"Then do, Sara. Do." Deke said almost in a whisper, again gripping her shoulders tightly and bending down to peer into her eyes. "Then do."

Before Sara could decide, Judge Parker chose that moment to enter, black judicial robe flowing behind him as he mounted the two steps to his bench. The bailiff called out for them all to come to order and remain standing. Sara tensed reflexively, automatically grasping at Deke's sleeve as she sized up the man who held her family's fate in his hands. His whole demeanor gave the impression of someone in a hurry and not very happy about it. Forced to take in the man's appearance in one frozen moment, she registered a flash of highly polished black boots and dark pants underneath the robe as the judge, a man in his late forties and of ordinary features, sat down, banged his gavel, and told them to be seated.

Sara trained her gaze on the judge again as they waited for him to confer with his bailiff, the man in the brown uniform, and to shuffle papers. With dark eyes sharper than Sara cared to peer into, he kept looking their way, gesturing and murmuring too low to be heard by them. Then, without warning, he barked out, "Marshal Coltrane, approach the bench and tell me exactly what all the commotion was out here just now."

Jake gave Sara and Deke a look that Sara could only call grim and then got up to do as the judge told him. For her part, Sara had very nearly jumped out of her tan riding skirt when the judge spoke. He sounded so angry. Jim, Cody, and Travis didn't have a chance. She felt her heart and her spirits sink. What would this man care about three men whose reputations and list of murders was greater than anyone else's since the war? Would he believe that they weren't responsible? Why should he? It was then that she realized just how delicate the situation was, just how much it hinged on the word of one marshal, a bounty hunter, three outlaws, and a woman. Sara took in as deep a breath as her constricted chest would allow and slowly let it out.

Even with straining forward, she couldn't hear what Jake and Judge Parker were discussing, but the judge definitely looked perturbed, if his quick, cutting gestures were any sign. This wasn't going well. Then Deke leaned over to whisper in her ear, his voice so close that his breath fanned her skin and sent shivers over her skin. "Don't worry, Sara. Jake told me the judge is always like this. It doesn't mean anything."

Sara looked up at him, saw the love in his face, and surprised herself as much as Deke by slipping her hand into his. This more than anything would have to tell him that she believed him, for words failed her right now. Facing forward again, looking straight at the judge, Sara heard Deke let out a breath.

Just then, Jake stepped back and signaled for her and Deke

to come forward. This was it. Sara was sure she was going to faint; indeed the room started spinning when she stood up. She clutched at Deke's muscled forearm, grabbing a handful of his light denim shirt and turning her panic-widened eyes on him. But he smiled reassuringly down into her face, his black eyes speaking volumes. Then, apparently undaunted by the judge, the courtroom itself, or the others present, he captured her gaze, held it, and said, "It will be all right, Sara. I promise you. Didn't I tell you that I would make it all right, no matter what happened?"

Warmed by his words, heartened by his strength, and knowing now that she could trust him beyond a shadow of a doubt, Sara squeezed his arm in response and pulled herself erect, squaring her shoulders. She indicated with a brief nod of her head that she was ready to face the judge.

And it was all over in less than thirty minutes. Deke Bonner was awarded the Dalton bounty, despite his protest that he didn't want it; Judge Parker said he'd carried out the provisions of the warrant, the money was his, and no arguments to the contrary would be heard. Obviously the judge was feeling especially expansive in light of the nature and the combined reputations of the other dead outlaws whose bodies Deke had presented to the court and which were out back and all trussed up for burial. With those added bounties and the rewards for the stolen bank money and the contraband guns, Deke Bonner had come out a rich man. He had enough money to choose his own destiny now.

Jim, Cody, and Travis Dalton were sentenced to the federal prison at Fort Leavenworth, Kansas. They were just now being processed for their escorted trip there to begin serving their sentence. Poor Judge Parker—the harshest arbiter of justice and the fiercest fighter to clean up the lawless Indian Territory—had been subjected to long, glowing reports by Sara, Deke, and Jake of the Daltons' innocence and of the more sterling qualities of the three men. With his elbow bent, his chin resting in his palm, he'd moved not at all during their oratory, except to gaze from one speaker to the other as they told of the Daltons helping old ladies throughout the territory, their work with the Nighthorse children, and their gifts of money to charity and widows. Finally raising an eyebrow at a particularly outrageous claim, he'd even exchanged glances with the Daltons, who could only grin sheepishly and shrug. The upshot of all that verbiage had been a prison sentence.

But Sara couldn't have been happier! She felt like singing as she, Deke and a smiling, swaggering Jake Coltrane emerged from the dour building out into the warm sunshine of a new world no longer overshadowed by fear and doubts for her family. And she had Jake and Deke to thank for everything. Her dread of Deke's leaving her momentarily suppressed, she turned into his arms, oblivious to the stares of people arriving at the courthouse, and hugged him tightly to her. He returned her embrace, kissing the top of her head. "How can I ever thank you, Deke?"

"Thank me?" he teased. "How could you have ever doubted me, girl?"

Sara pulled away just enough to look into his face. His black eyes danced in the sunshine. She cuffed at his head with her hand, then resettled her head on his cushioning chest. "Well, I can't imagine, bounty hunter," she quipped, placing all the emphasis on his occupation.

"Oh, yes—that," Deke said, trying to sound as if that was a small thing.

A third voice interrupted their moment. "So I guess you're happy enough with the outcome?" Jake Coltrane asked, a grin lighting his handsome face.

For an answer, Sara broke away from Deke and pitched herself at Jake; he caught her in his arms and whirled her around. Sara laughed giddily and was set on her feet in time to see Deke Bonner trying not to scowl. Then, turning back to Jake at the same time that she tucked her white cotton shirt back into her skirt and righted her hair somewhat, she told him, "Jake, I don't know how we—all us Daltons—can ever thank you. I will be grateful to you until the day I die."

"That's not necessary," Jake said, looking embarrassed and down at his toes. Then he looked up at Sara. "Just name your firstborn son after me. That ought to be enough."

Sara knew she was supposed to laugh at that joke, and with Deke at her side, she did manage a slight smile to cover the spear of pain that pierced her heart. Without Deke, there would be no sons—unless she already carried one. Instantly rejecting the strong emotion that particular thought caused her, she said, "I'll certainly do that, Jake. Maybe one day. But still, I want you to know how much it means to me . . . everything you said in there."

Jake sobered right up, nodding at her and Deke as he spoke and revealing for the first time that he'd had doubts about the outcome. "Judge Parker is a tough customer, all right. Make no mistake—the outcome could have been very different. I just wish I could have gotten them off completely, Sara."

"A year in Leavenworth, Jake, and close enough for me to bring Momma in the wagon to see them, probably won't be as rough as what they've lived through for the past two years. And they said as much, too," Sara assured him.

Still by her side, although she expected him at any moment just to mount Buttercup, his incongruously named buckskin stallion, and ride off, Deke said, "I agree with Sara. And it was damned good of you, Jake, to offer to ride them up there. I can't believe the judge would allow that, having only you escort them."

Having only you escort them. The words echoed in Sara's brain. Deke didn't include himself in their journey home. Why was she hurt by that, for when had he ever indicated that they had a future together? He might love her, but apparently that wasn't enough to keep him with her. It hurt incredibly not to be "enough" for him. But she'd known, from the first moment she'd set eyes on him in Plains, that his was a restless spirit, one that would not be tamed. She was the fool for loving him. She tried not to let the emotion choke her as she carefully kept her eyes on the young marshal.

Jake was looking acutely embarrassed at being caught doing a good deed, but played it off with a rough gesture and said, "Oh, hell, it was just convenient for Judge Parker and me. I think he knows the Daltons aren't going to try anything. And I've got to go on over to No Man's Land from there anyway to talk with the army about those stolen Colts. Seemed like the smartest thing to do." He shrugged and grinned, but then went on, "I need to go see to the preparations, Sara, and pack my things. That won't take long, and I think the wagon for Travis and Cody to ride in should be hitched up and ready—including the other horses and the provisions—in about an hour, maybe two. Can you be ready then?"

"Yes," was all Sara could gulp out. She could be ready. She fought her instinct to look at Deke, so quiet just now.

"Well . . . good, then. I'll see you right here in about an hour. I'll have your family ready, and we can go."

Sara nodded and chewed at her bottom lip as she turned away. Deke hadn't said a word and wasn't saying one now as he watched his friend walk away. It was over.

For no reason she could fathom, Ben Nighthorse's prophecy rang through her head. She could even hear his voice saying the words. "Many things will come to pass on this long journey of yours. I have seen them. You will need the strength and the great heart of one other than yourself. You must, too, listen to your heart."

She'd thought then, and she still thought, that the strength and great heart of one other than herself were Deke Bonner's. Ben had been right—she had definitely needed him. And he had been with her every step of the way. But their time to separate was here. She turned back to Deke, who was looking at her with an unreadable expression. Slowly, he reached out to brush a lock of hair out of her face; then he smoothed a knuckle across her cheek. If the look on his face could be trusted, then he was in great pain.

"Sara, I—there's nothing more I want than to—I don't know how to say this. I can't be with—go with you. Not like I am now. God knows I love you, but good-bye, Sara," he said slowly, as if he regretted the words. He stared at her for a dark eternity, but then turned and walked away. Stricken, numb, suddenly hot and then cold, Sara watched him until he rounded a corner, leaving her sight.

"You must, too, listen to your heart." That's what Ben had said. Well, she was listening to it. She could hear it breaking.

Chapter Thirty-two

Sara had always hated folding laundry, especially the big sheets off the beds, but now, back in Plains, Kansas, in early December, sitting by a warm fire in the front room of the small Dalton farmhouse, it was a chore she loved. It was simple, mechanical, mind-numbing, and required no thinking. Thinking was what she now hated. That made her laugh—thinking about not thinking. Out of habit, she turned her head to look down the short hall to the back bedroom, thinking her laughter might have disturbed her mother's sleep. Then she remembered; Momma wasn't back there anymore.

She immediately squeezed her eyes shut so tightly that tears formed on her lashes. Don't think about it, Sara, she warned herself, shying away from the raw wound of her mother's death only a week ago. As she opened her eyes, she fumbled in her skirt pocket until she came up with a bandanna—one of many of Deke's she'd acquired somehow—and dabbed at her tears. Then, looking at the square of red cloth, she squeezed it tight in her hand and brought it up to her nose, almost unconsciously trying to find his scent on the material. But she couldn't, for how many times had she washed it in the past two months? Nothing of him remained on his bandanna, just as nothing of him remained in her life. It was two months already since he'd just turned and walked away from her. As if she meant nothing to him.

Enough, Sara, she chastised herself. Think of something more pleasant. Sitting up straighter in her chair, as if steeling her backbone, she cast about in her mind for something pleasing, finally lighting on what she was going to give her loved ones for Christmas. Setting her hands to work on folding the small pile of clean clothes in front of her, she smiled all the way from her heart at the thought of chubby, toddling Robert, such a little miniature of Travis. The baby would be the delight of the season for her, Aunt Jean, and Olivia. She laughingly shook her head, picturing the little boy's delighted chortling and hand-smacking when he came over with his mother, always insisting on being taken out to the corral to see Little Ned, himself as chubby and full of life and antics as was Robert. Those two were made for each other, Sara decided, thinking maybe she'd just tie a big red bow around Ned's neck and present him to Robert for Christmas. She blocked the image of Deke rescuing Ned's mother and then presenting the burro to her at the same moment that the thought presented itself to her consciousness. Don't think about it, Sara. Think about who *is* in your life.

Focusing again on her family, Sara reminded herself that she needed to make the short trip, less than a mile, to take over to Aunt Jean's house a batch of sugar cookies she'd made for Robert. Picking up a pair of her hose, she sighed; perhaps she ought to consider Aunt Jean's offer to move in with them, since she was now alone on the farm. Well, maybe she would, but not now. Right now, the quiet, the remoteness of her farmhouse was what she needed more than anything else. Certainly, the past summer had been enough excitement and heartache to last a lifetime. Besides, she needed to be here to keep the farm going until Jim came home.

Unbidden, unwanted, came the flow of images in Sara's mind of the bittersweet trip to Leavenworth. Sure in her heart that the trip had sped her mother's death, since she'd succumbed within a few days of their return, Sara remained grateful that her mother had been able to see Jim and her nephews one last time. And Sara was truly comforted now in her sorrow that she was the one who'd made it all possible. She stopped her errant memories right there, refusing to think selfish thoughts, such as what the trip to get Jim, Cody, and Travis had cost her in heartache.

Only the good things, Sara, she admonished herself. She thought of Coburn—bless his sweet heart, and the kids, Callie and Tyler, who filled her thoughts and heart still. She wondered how they were doing with the Nighthorses, thinking she would give anything to be able to see them, to have them with her now that she was alone. Ben and Etheline would agree, she felt sure, that they could spare her those two orphans. Sara perked up some. Maybe she would go get them next spring! She smiled brightly, but then it fled her face at the next image in her head: Deke holding a crying Tyler to his chest to comfort and encourage the stricken boy. No! Sara gritted her teeth, forbidding Deke Bonner a place in her heart.

"Mrowwrr."

Sara glanced up at Calico, her appropriately named calico-colored cat, as he roused himself from his afternoon nap to come purr around Sara's ankles. "What is it, fella? What do you want? Want some milk?" she crooned softly as the cat arched its back in a lazy stretch and then padded over to the window, uncharacteristically jumping up onto a low table under the window and then lighting on the narrow sill to sit staring outside. Sara frowned; usually he didn't like that spot in winter, since the glass was cold and frosty. "What's wrong, boy?"

"Mrowwrr," he repeated, turning his head to stare at her

before he raised a paw, licked it, and again turned his head to look outside.

"What's out there? Did you hear something?" Sara said, pushing aside the laundry basket with her foot and standing. She went to the window, took Calico in her arms, stroked his furry head, and looked outside. Nothing. "Silly thing," she said, putting him on the floor. "Don't you know it's winter and all the mice are in their warm burrows?"

From the floor, Calico narrowed his eyes at her, gave her his best dismissive, arrogant stare, and immediately jumped back up onto the ledge and resumed his staring. Now a frown marred Sara's oval face. The cat obviously heard something that wasn't close enough yet for her to hear. Well, whatever or whoever it was, it couldn't be much of a threat because the dogs hadn't set up a howling cry. When she heard that, then she'd worry.

The dogs set up a howling cry as they tore out from the barn and the warmth of their straw beds. Sara went to the window again, feeling her heart beating heavily. Who would be out on a raw afternoon like this? Peering out, looking this way and that, and again setting Calico on the floor, where he stayed this time, she stood in the narrow opening, trying to see anything, anyone. No one. Afraid to think what—who—it might be, she pulled her heavy shawl from its hook behind the front door, wrapped it around her shoulders, tying a thick knot in front, then pulled her loaded Spencer off its hooks on the cabin wall. Thinking she'd just see who was playing games, she jerked open the front door, aiming for the element of surprise, and leveled the deadly Spencer.

At Deke Bonner's chest. Sara's jaw dropped open, but in her shock she didn't lower the rifle.

"Seems to me we've done this before, Miss Dalton," he said, looking from her rifle to her face and back.

Sara couldn't move, couldn't talk for several seconds. Couldn't even register the fact that he was really here. Maybe it was all her longing for the sound of his voice that had conjured him up. People did go crazy from cabin fever, hearing and seeing things that weren't really there. "Deke," she breathed. "Is it really you? Are you really here?"

Just as Deke, or his apparition, opened his mouth to speak, childish giggling outside and off to the right of the doorway captured Sara's attention. Her eyes widened at the sound; she stared at Deke, whom she just now noticed was trying his best not to let her see him looking to his left and shaking his head. "Deke Bonner, what is going on? What are you doing here?"

"Put that damned Spencer down, and I'll show you." A huge grin lit up his face, even as he put his left hand up in a wait-there motion to someone outside whom Sara still couldn't see. When she didn't move, he cried, "We're freezing, girl. Put the gun down!"

Sara looked at the rifle in her hands as if she'd forgotten she was still holding it. She looked at Deke again, fighting a losing battle with the thawing of her heart, then took a step sideways to stand the rifle to the right of the doorway. As soon as she did, Deke—as big and as darkly handsome as she remembered—smiled hugely, lighting up his black eyes, and signaled to persons unknown on the front porch with him.

Sara still couldn't bring herself to be anything but numb and awestruck and weak and fluttery, all at the same time. What was he doing here? Who was with him?

That second question was answered immediately in the persons of two children—Callie Mitchell and Tyler Mack, who startled the breath out of Sara by jumping right into her line of vision and yelling, "Surprise!"

Sure now that she'd conjured up all of them—hadn't she just been thinking about them?—but not caring anymore if she'd lost her mind, she let out a squeal, opened her arms, and took both children into her embrace. On impact, they nearly knocked her over, sending them all, as one, back a few steps into the cabin. Some corner of her mind registered the closing of the cabin door, but for the moment she was occupied with the two children as they all three danced and hugged and jumped around together, kissing, smiling, crying, and generally raising a ruckus that sent Calico fleeing from the room.

Happy beyond belief, finally believing they were really here since they hadn't disappeared when she'd reached for them, she looked up, still holding the giggling, snuffling children one to each side, and searched out Deke for an explanation. Only to get another happy shock. A grinning Deke was standing with his back against the closed door, his arms crossed over his tan sheepskin coat—talking to Coburn.

"Coburn!" Sara screeched, her hands flying to her hot cheeks. She stared openmouthed at him for several seconds before she could run to him, her arms flung out. Behind her, she heard happy cheering and hand-clapping from Callie and Tyler. Coburn had enough time only to scrape his beat-up old hat off and run a hand over his balding head before Sara had him in a huge hug and was kissing his weathered, stubbly cheek as if he was her long-lost father. Not one for a great show of emotion, he blustered and pulled back, holding her at arm's length so he could look her up and down, saying, "You're looking a might scrawny; can't you take care of yerself on yer own?"

Sara laughed with Deke and the children, but then she had another thought, which brought her up short, stood her up straight, and sent her brushing by the bounty hunter, literally pushing him out of her way so she could jerk open the front door and run out onto the porch. It was empty. But she did see, off to the side of the porch, four horses, Buttercup and Jezebel among them. So that's why she hadn't seen them ride up; they'd sneaked in from the side. But that wasn't why she was out there. She turned all around, looking. Then, seeing Deke on the front porch with her, she asked excitedly, "Where're Ben and Etheline? Are they here too?"

Deke smiled, shook his head, and pulled her back inside the cabin, closing the door again. Sara refused to think about the hot electricity of his touch, but could only look up at his beloved face with her heart in her eyes. It took her a moment to realize that he was talking to her. "No, they're not here. But they're fine, and they send you their love."

There was something about the way he said it, the way he said "send you their love" that stilled Sara, that caused her to begin shaking all over. She couldn't stop, couldn't have said why she was shaking, except that Deke was in front of her, filling her sight, her cabin, her heart. A loud sniffing and nervous coughing behind her reminded her that Callie, Tyler, and Coburn were still there. It came to her then what she had to do. "Coburn, if you're not all too frozen yet, why don't you take the kids out to the barn? There's the cutest little burro out there, named Little Ned, that I would love for them to see. And a whole pack of friendly dogs that need petting. Then later, when you all come back in, we'll have hot chocolate and cookies and talk about how wonderful it is to see you all," she said, her gaze going back to Deke when she said "all."

Sara knew she would remain eternally grateful for Coburn's being able to take a hint. Looking from her to Deke and back, he pronounced what a rarin' fine idee that was and hustled the eager kids out the door.

And then she was alone with him. And scared. What was he doing here? She became weak-kneed when he shrugged out of his heavy coat, revealing a red flannel shirt underneath tucked into his denims. As he casually tossed his fleecy coat onto the chair she'd been sitting in, her mind forced her to note that he was as broad and strong and virile as she remembered, maybe even more so. All she could do was watch him, much as if someone had put a spell on her, damning her for all of eternity to just stand there and watch his every move and not be allowed to touch him.

With an I-don't-know-what-to-say-to-you-either look on his face, he put his hands—strong, gentle hands whose touch she could still feel on her body—to his waist. As the moment stretched out, he shifted his stance, bent one knee, ran his hand through his black hair, and ducked his head, finally looking up at her with dark, shining eyes—eyes she'd once thought looked like a snake's. "I—uh, saw the new grave out on the hill as we rode in."

"She died a week ago," Sara said, hearing the flat tone of her voice.

He put a hand out to her and then withdrew it. "I'm sorry, Sara . . ."

"Thank you."

". . . For everything."

A sniff of emotion escaped her at that admission. There were a million things she wanted to say to him, and a million reasons why she should hate him, but all she could think of right then was, "Why are you here, Deke? Why did you come?"

"I . . . Can we sit down, Sara?"

She nodded, and he went to sit on the wooden footstool by the chair in front of the fire. Sara, feeling wooden herself, went to the chair where Deke had thrown his coat, picked it up, held it in her arms as if it was a baby, and sat down with it in her lap. It felt cold and warm all at the same time. And it smelled of him. Deke immediately scooted the stool over to her, close enough so that his knees now straddled hers as he faced her; he put his hands on her knees as he looked up at her, supplication and something else written in the lines and planes of his darkly handsome face.

Sara, very afraid that his familiarity, his touch, would be her undoing, and not quite able to meet his intense gaze, bit at her bottom lip and looked down, picking at imaginary threads on his coat.

"Sara, look at me."

She did, but looking into his eyes, seeing her face mirrored in their dark depths, she knew she couldn't bear to hear his reason for being there; what if it had nothing to do with loving her? What if this was just a favor—if he'd just brought the kids to see her and then was leaving again? She would die if that were true. It was that simple. So, she stalled the moment, blurting out the first thing she could think of. "Where's Red?"

"Red? Sara, I came here to . . . All right, okay, we'll do this your way. Red went with me back home to Missouri for a while. I had some unfinished business there. But then he joined a cattle drive. He's coming here when it's over."

She wanted to ask him what his business had been, wondering if had something to do with his mother and sister, but then she realized what else he'd said. "Red's coming here? Why?"

"Because that's where I told him I'd be—that is, if you'll have me. But before you answer, you need to know two things. One, I stopped at Fort Leavenworth, saw Jim, and asked for his permission to court you. He sends his love, too, by the way. And two, according to Ben Nighthorse and his vision, he says you will have me. So don't make a liar out of him because I'm beginning to believe in his sight."

Her mind couldn't quite filter and digest his simple words. But apparently her heart could because it was thumping wildly, and she suddenly felt very warm. "You saw Jim? Ben had a vision? Did you say, if I'll have you?"

He grinned—a warm, tender thing—nodded yes, and brushed a tendril of her fly-away silvery hair out of her face. That one gesture, so familiar, so loving, was nearly her undoing. She pulled in a deep breath and forced herself to be still, to be calm.

"Deke," she began, saying his name on her exhalation. "Fort Smith. Why did you leave me there? How could you just walk away—after everything that happened? I've died a hundred times since then."

He pressed his lips together, squeezed her hand, and rose gracefully to his feet. He stood in front of the fireplace, his back to it. Facing her, a serious, brooding expression on his face, he said, "Because I had nothing to offer you then, Sara. Nothing but a death-scarred soul and a craw full of bitterness. Two months ago, I wouldn't have been any good to you; I didn't think I deserved your love, your trust." He shook his head at the memory of the way he'd been. "I—I wanted to give you all the money from the rewards and the bounties—''

Sara froze. "Is that why you're here? To give me money? I don't want it.''

"I know that. I said I wanted to then—but not now. Money has nothing to do with my being here, Sara. You have to believe me.''

She searched her soul—and realized that she did believe him. "I do,'' she said quietly. When he slumped a little upon hearing her quiet words, she realized how rigidly he'd been holding himself. She should have been glad he was hurting, that this was hard for him, seeing as how he'd put her through as much pain but to her surprise she found it broke her heart to think of him hurting. "Deke, what changed you in the past two months? What put you on my doorstep?''

He looked long and hard at her, so long that her heart took off on an erratic pace all its own. "I went back to Missouri, like I said.'' He came once again to sit in front of her on the stool; he once again put his hands on her knees as he spoke. "I used some of the money to put nice markers on my mother and sister's graves. I let them know that it was over, that I'd let go of the hate and the killing . . . and my guilt that I hadn't been there.''

Torn with grief for his losses, losses she knew only too well and too recently, she felt tears prick at her eyes. She put her hand on his; he laid his cheek on it briefly before raising his eyes to her again. She wanted to crush him to her as she watched his throat work convulsively as he struggled for control. But she knew this wasn't the moment. When he took a deep breath to compose himself, she did the same. "Red took off then on the cattle drive, and I—well, I just knocked around at home, finally selling the house and land. Then I just drifted, just rode, me and Cheyenne. I always wanted to come to you, Sara; I never wanted to leave you, not for a minute. But I couldn't. I knew I'd hurt you, that you'd be fighting mad and would probably shoot me, like you almost did, if I just showed up on your doorstep—only me and my ugly face. Then I knew what I had to do. I rode for Ben and Etheline's to get Callie and Tyler. I knew you'd want to see them."

Despite the moment, Sara laughed. "Deke Bonner, you're shameless—hiding behind two kids."

He grinned at that. "I guess you could say that. Anyway, I still wasn't sure what to do—about coming here. But Etheline said she just knew in her heart that you'd love to see me."

"You talked to Etheline about me?" Sara broke in, feeling the heaviness, the pain and loneliness begin to lift from her heart. She couldn't believe it. He'd been afraid to declare himself to her—him, the big, strong, fearless bounty hunter.

Deke grinned up at her and gripped her knees tightly. "Yes, I did. Quit grinning. But I guess Ben really cinched it when he took me outside and told me of a vision he'd had about us the night before. He said he'd seen this thing, that I would need the strength and the great heart of one other than myself, and he felt that was you. He also said I had to listen to my own heart."

Stunned at Deke's words, she opened her mouth incredulously. Those were the same words Ben had said to her over three months ago! Now she wasn't sure she believed in his "visions." Was he the seemingly deep, stoic, quiet, mystical man he appeared to be? Or was he a conniving little matchmaker? But not for anything would Sara disabuse Deke of his newfound belief in Indian second sight. Whichever one Ben Nighthorse was, mystic or matchmaker, she loved him all the more for it.

"Sara, what's wrong? You have a funny look on your face."

She focused on Deke's beloved face, one she'd seen shining in all her dreams, one she'd imagined during the lonely times, one she'd always loved, always held close to her heart—even when she thought she hated him for leaving her. She put her hand on his cheek. "Nothing's wrong, Deke. But you have to tell me—what is it you're trying to say?"

He sat back at that and looked at her as if he thought she hadn't been listening to him. "I'm baring my soul, pouring my heart out, down here on the floor, and you don't know what it is I'm trying to say?"

Sara bit at her lip in an effort to keep her mouth from forming the huge grin it so desperately wanted to wear. "No, I don't."

He put his hands on his knees and sat up straighter. "Yes, you do. You're a cruel woman, Miss Dalton."

"I learned it from you, Mr. Bonner," she teased right back.

He laughed out loud at that, and Sara's heart soared with the sound. Looking back at her, he grinned and said, "Sara Jane Dalton, I would like to marry you, if you'll have me."

She quirked her head at him, pretending to consider. He frowned mightily and jumped up. "I'm not asking again," he warned, pointing a finger at her.

Sara grinned at him, barely able to see him through the happy, shimmering tears in her eyes. That damned pride of his! But still, there was something else she wanted to hear from him. She crossed her arms over her chest, encompassing his coat, and said, "Tell me you love me and need me, that you can't live without me. I think I deserve to hear that much."

"What?" Then he gave up. "Oh, all right. I love you and need you and can't live without you."

Sara made a noncommittal noise at the back of her throat.

"Oh, all right, dammit." He came to her, got down on one knee, took his coat from her, and fumbled around in a pocket until he came up with a small black velvet box, which he opened to reveal a gold ring sporting the biggest diamond in its center that Sara had ever seen. He looked smugly at her as she gasped out her surprise and delight and asked, formally, emotionally, "Sara Jane Dalton, I love you. And I think I have from the first moment I saw you right here on the porch of this same house last August. I can't live without you. I'll dry up and blow away in the next wind if you won't have me. You're as much a part of me as my own soul. Will you marry me?''

Sara, her throat thickened with tears and love, had one more thing she had to know. ''Are you—are you still bounty hunting? Because if you are, I don't think—''

''Sara,'' he cut in, ''the only bounty I ever want to claim again is the one on your heart. I swear.''

Sara smiled. ''You already have, Deke Bonner. You already have.''

''Then say it,'' he urged, his turn to prod and tease.

Sara made a face as if she was disgusted. ''Oh all right, dammit, if you have such a need to hear fancy words.'' Then she turned serious. ''I love you, Deke, and I will marry you.''

He looked at her for one shining moment, took the ring out of its box, slipped it on her finger, then laid his head in her lap, gathered her to him, and said, ''Thank God.''

Sara bent over him, laying her cheek on his black hair. And they were quiet, relishing the simple warmth of his love for her, hers for him, and of the brightly blazing fire of their love's bounty that healed two broken hearts.

In a moment, Deke raised his head and looked at Sara. ''We better go get Coburn and the kids before they freeze to death in that barn.''

Sara gasped. ''I forgot all about them!''

They both jumped up, Deke grabbing for his coat, Sara pulling on her shawl. ''Well, don't tell them that,'' Deke warned, opening the door for her.

She passed through and waited for him to close the door behind him. Looking over at the restive horses, her gaze lighted on Deke's buckskin. ''Earlier, Deke,'' she began, stopping when he put his arm around her waist as they went down the two steps, then taking it up again, ''you said you were drifting, just riding, you and Cheyenne. Who's Cheyenne?''

He stopped dead. She looked up at him. He looked decidedly guilty as he looked anywhere but at her. Then she knew. ''Deke Bonner, it's your horse, isn't it? All this time you let me think you'd named that stallion Buttercup.''

"Guilty," was all he said in his defense, laughing out loud. "I gave him his real name because of our first time together in that Cheyenne tepee."

Moved by his sentimentalism, which she'd never suspected, Sara nonetheless smacked at his arm. "You are awful," she said.

"That's not what you said the last time." He fended off her playful attack, taking her by her arms and drawing her into his embrace, then opening his coat to wrap her in his warmth. Once she was there, held tightly against him, he kissed her with a searing gentleness that took Sara's breath away and froze it in a cloud above their heads. Then, pulling away from her, he looked down into her shining eyes, and said, "Come on, let's take the horses to the barn—since I'm staying."

He was staying. It was so simple, so profound. All Sara could do was nod. Deke untied the horses, giving her the reins of two piebald Indian ponies, obviously Callie's and Tyler's, as he led Cheyenne and Jezebel. The betrothed couple walked side by side, hand in hand, out toward the barn, the horses to either side of them. As they walked, not even feeling the cold, they talked the way lovers do.

"You and Jake have any trouble getting here?"

"None. I really like Jake. He's a good man."

"Yeah, he is. A good friend, too." Then, "How's Cinnamon?"

"Pregnant."

"Whoops. I—uh, guess you're not."

"No."

"Warrior and I'll fix that."

A moment of quiet followed that as they grinned at each other. Then Sara asked, "Are Callie and Tyler staying too?"

"Yep. We gave them their choice—they could stay with Ben and Etheline, or they could come live with us."

"And they chose us."

"Would appear so."

"What about Coburn?"

"Well, he was at the Nighthorses' when I got there, so he just came along for the ride. Wanted to see you, I suppose. Said he'd drop by here occasionally, like he does there."

"That's good."

"Yeah." Then, after a pause, "Sara, two things."

"Okay."

"My bandannas—"

"Too late. I'm making them into a quilt."

"I see. Well then, number two: I know you said you don't want the money, but now that we're going to be married, do you suppose we can keep it?"

A feminine chuckle clouded the cold air. "I suppose it would only be fair to use Dalton bounty money to rebuild the Dalton farm."

"Good. I talked with Jim about it when I went by Leavenworth. He thinks he'd like to get a few head of cattle, maybe get into that business along with farming."

"And you?"

"Yeah, me too."

"Then that's what we'll do, Deke. We'll make this old farm grow and thrive, fill it with a bounty of kids and animals and love."

Right then, the barn doors burst open and out poured squealing, laughing kids, playing and running with a pack of grinning, tongue-lolling dogs and a fat little braying, heel-kicking burro, cheered on by one hat-tossing, whooping old Indian trader.

Sara stopped with Deke and watched in delight as they all come running toward them. Deke let go of her hand and drew her to him, putting his arm around her waist. Watching the cheerful riot for a moment, he then turned his gaze to Sara and said, "I think we already have our bounty, Sara. I think we already have it."

Dear Reader:

Any student or lover of the American Old West knows that the Daltons are actual historical figures who did indeed terrorize Kansas and who occasionally hid from the law at Robber's Cave, near what is now Wilburton, Oklahoma. So you'll also know that they rode into the history books much later in the nineteenth century than I've set *Sara's Bounty*. I claim literary license in sending the Daltons on a time-traveling expedition back in history—and for changing their names, lives, and crimes. Call it fiction!

Also an actual historical figure is Judge Parker, who did indeed hold sway and the iron fist of the law over the riotous Indian Territory from Fort Smith, Arkansas. He didn't actually move his court there until a few years after the 1867 date of *Sara's Bounty*. But I needed a scary judge, and he was so perfect.

Manipulating history to fit my needs is such a heady feeling. But perhaps the headiest of all feelings is hearing from you, my readers. So let me know what you think. Please send

an SASE to me at P.O. Box 755; Brandon, FL 33509-0755.
I'll write back—hey, it's what I do!
Sincerely,
Cheryl Anne Porter